YOUNG
MOBSTERS

YOUNG MOBSTERS

THE MET

BRYANT KEITH

iUniverse

YOUNG MOBSTERS
THE MET

iUniverse books may be ordered through booksellers or by contacting:

iUniverse
1663 Liberty Drive
Bloomington, IN 47403
www.iuniverse.com
1-800-Authors (1-800-288-4677)

ISBN: 978-1-4917-5663-8 (sc)
ISBN: 978-1-4917-5662-1 (e)

Library of Congress Control Number: 2015900819

Print information available on the last page.

iUniverse rev. date: 02/20/2015

TABLE OF CONTENTS

YOUNG MOBSTERS

THE MET

*T*his is a year-to-year memoir of the continuing struggle of Columbus George. The time period spans the early to mid 1980s. The main character is Columbus George aka Colo. Columbus struggles with economics, bad influences and tragedies.

There are a lot of obstacles to keep you from coming up in life. The black experience is a bitch! Three out of four blacks in the inner cities will be incarcerated, shot or killed. The other trap is to sell or use hard drugs before the age of twenty-five. Being black in color is obstacle you can't hide.

Your color was your main obstacle. Being smart was another obstacle. When you are black in America there's no roadmap left from your ancestor's history. There's nothing to aid you and your direction & development in America's Capitalistic system. Growing up on the streets of Chicago is rough. Growing up without leadership or guidance, it's virtually, futile.

There is good and there is bad coming up on any set in the city. The story is about three boys. These boys lived on 169th & Calumet St. They had no long family history, but living on that block, the people were family.

It was like they were all non-blood cousins living together in a four-block radius. The only thing they had was, love in Chicago in this time period. One place it came from was an unexpected source, through the gang organizations.

A lot of society wonders about Blacks. Why do Blacks often have such a negative outlook on life? Why do blacks rob, steal and inflict damage to their own people? Why do they tear down their own neighborhoods? Why don't they pull themselves up by their bootstraps, focus and come up?

The major factor's for the problems of today is a dysfunctional household. There aren't fathers or positive male role models in the household.

This is one of the major reasons why things have gotten out of control. Our kids growing up today don't have any strong male guidance. They are confronted with different evils of life, without a guide.

You have to learn from the guys off the corner or on the block. You learn from people who are in survival mode for your information on life.

Drugs, liquor and music videos are among the other variables. One of the main reasons is stemming from four hundred years of brainwashing. It is complicated to even think how deliberate the plans are to keep us searching.

Most of the things you've been taught in the school, some media, radio, movies, cartoons and the different TV programming. This evil programming is set up to continue programming or brainwashing our kids. There's a signal coming straight into your house. Who controls the information that gets to you? What is they're agenda?

It's a well thought out systematic plan to continue to use slave labor. Slavery has been abolished with the passing of the 13Th Amendment. Due to the fact and that fact alone we came up.

There were a lot of white people who've helped black folks to freedom and equality. All people aren't the same. It's just some of the people in power wants to keep their foot on your neck.

President Lincoln a Republican president was the catalyst that helped push this amendment through. Now the Democrats are Republicans and Republicans are Democrats. Depending on the agenda those elected officials are switching sides. You don't know who's who and where's the loyalty to your people?

White folks are way ahead of the game. We have to take the blindfold off. To continue to close your eyes to the truth is our downfall. We are not questioning what's really going on!

This nation was united with the different battles of the civil war. This is a war that literally tore our country apart. This is a war that preludes the end of slavery, the year 1865.

The truth is black folks were just 3/5^{Ths} of a human being. We were close to being livestock in slave owner's eyes. You'll still hear some whites refer to us as monkeys. Still, there was mix breeding and this caused a breakdown in our color. Our skin tone was being diluted. The lighter you were the more privileges you had. This was, because you had some of Massa's blood, in you.

We were known as subhuman's or savages to some white folks in America. The descendants of those white folks are still in play, powerfully. This land was confiscated from the Indians and not founded by Christopher Columbus. It was people already here in America.

Black folks were sold or stolen from Africa. They had a slave work force that worked the land the conquerors were developing. The white folks families who orchestrated that move will never run out of plans and money. They've probably made trillions of profits off that investment and still growing. Now you have free land and you have free labor. You can't get any better than that! The seeds of slavery are still being planted; it's a diabolical plan. It is a plan to keep blacks and minorities fighting and killing each other over money.

This plan has knocked out and created self-genocide to our black leaders of the future. The descendants of those who enacted the plan still think the same way or things would be changing.

When the season changes yearly in the spring, you plant seeds. The seeds they're planting are seeds to brainwash you. When you are released out the womb your brain is wired for control.

People that are in power rarely want to relinquish it. They have the ups on the latest technology and uses it in that way.

Non-leadership is another reason why our neighborhoods have taken a turn for the worst. Lack of leadership or a concentrated effort to either lock up or kill our leaders. Who wants to be a target? Just in my time Fred Hampton, Dr. King, Malcolm X, John F. Kennedy and Robert Kennedy were all murdered.

These guys were our leaders or fought for black folk's interest. Jessie Jackson Rainbow Collation and Rev Al Sharpton are cool, but we needed more. There's the honorable Louis Farrakann, who orchestrated the million man march. It used to be a lot of leaders, but after those killings. Most of our leaders faded.

You have to be a strong man to put your life on the line for your cause. Barack Obama is an inspiration, he's America's first black president. Somebody got to be pulling his strings. Blacks make up about 15% of the population so black folks can't elect him alone. He had a lot of help and what's their agenda?

I was born in the year of 1968. This was a volatile year for leaders for black people. By the time I was born, our black and white leaders were slain. Fred Hampton was slain killed in his apartment by the Chicago police. He was the leader of the struggle at a young age. He was too powerful to live during those times. Mayor 'Bull' Daly was in charge of the police force that cut him down.

Dr. King and Robert Kennedy were killed right after I was born. Who was I to look up to for strength and guidance? The only person I see, who is black that lived and died naturally, was Ralph Bunche.

I didn't even know about him. I didn't learn about him until I went to college. He was our international spokesperson for the United Nations. He's the guy who helped sew up the middle-east peace process between the Palestinians and the Israelis in the 1960s and 1970s.

After masterfully settling issue after issue in the Middle East. When he got home he couldn't drink water from the same water fountain as whites, in the American South. It didn't even matter what he done to the folks in the South. He still was a boy!

Most black people here in the United States are descendants of slaves. Most of us have no idea of where were from, originally. We don't know who we are or our family history. Fuck shit happens to people who don't know their history. We are susceptible to what comes to us, while trying to figure life out. By then it could be too late.

We have no idea how we all got here, except for a slave ship. We have our master's who enslaved us, last name. That's all we have to go on unless you have money for a search.

During slave time most of us black Americans born here were fucked. Once the air hit our lunges. We were sold shortly afterwards from underneath our parents. Now, you don't know your mother or father anymore. Who is left to teach you your family values and history?

The long-term effect from this separation is when brainwashing takes effect. Blacks are still seeking their history. Most are wondering which way to go for success at this time? They are wondering how do you side-step some of these issues.

One of the reason white folks didn't want us to know how to read. Knowledge is power! Now our kids today don't pursue education, why? There's more than one way to skin a cat. We are left to claim street corners and blocks due to this fact.

We've been brainwashed into believing what the teachers taught us, in books as kids. We believed the media and things we saw on TV. We believed the portrayal of what white people want us to believe, we are, to be. Truth to the matter is we had to be the strongest of the strong. We had to be the pick of the litter in order to survive the ocean voyage.

AUTHOR'S COMMENTS

*A*s a child, I felt so distant and lost. I am Columbus George. My family were scattered and my Mom settled in Chicago. Due to the darkness of my skin I felt rejection. I was a smart or above average kid. This made me kind of an outcast double-time coming up. How can I be black and smart?

I just didn't fit in with my age group as far as excelling. In school I knew the material we worked on in class already. I had to constantly go up a level to learn. Therefore, I was promoted to the upper grades. Once up there the older kids in the class rejected me immediately. It seems as, if the older kids were being attacked by the younger smarter kid's knowledge.

This rejection was not only from older kids: I experienced rejection from white people, friends, family and peers in one-way or another. I should've been proud of the darkness of my skin. That means I hadn't been diluted a great deal. I still have African features.

I was fooled into believing my darkness and my high I Q level was bad. I wished I'd known about the money and scholarships that were available to me, because I was smart. I wish I were aware about that straight out the gate. I would've taken advantage, if I'd known. Knowledge is power and knowing is half the battle.

The other part of the battle is the work. I had no problem working. All I had to do was get good grades and that was a given. I didn't know anything about a full ride in college. My grammar and high schools weren't pressing college unless you were an athlete.

Universities will pay you to go to their school, because you are smart. Had I known at the time that nerds run the world! Nerds pay the jocks. Nerds control companies and have vast amount of wealth. All this time I was trying to fit in with the people who one day will be working for nerds. I will try to answer some of these questions by the end of this book. Why!

THE SETTING

*T*his is a look inside the mind of Columbus George. He struggles to stay righteous, while he tiptoes through evil! He is determined not to be a bum or locked up. This is in an era when most of their friends had no fathers in their household.

After the Vietnam War, the structure of the household changed. You can count on one hand the kids that grew up with their father's in the house.

They are some things that are supposed to be taught to your son. Things he needs to know to build a solid base. Mom can do the best she can at rearing her son. The man is definitely needed to shape his son's foundation.

The environment is shaping the kids without fathers. TV programming plays a major part. These are the variables used in shaping our kids of the future. It was a blessing we came up in a time when people stuck halfway together. People really cared what happened to you.

There was a definite need for a father while tackling the streets of Chicago. In sort of a way the streets became their fathers. That's where they went to learn those things that their fathers didn't teach them.

Enter the term "Street Nigga". This is a guy who goes to the streets to get money and power. There is usually a criminal element to his hustle. The boys mother's prepared them as best they could for the streets. The rest they had to wing it by themselves.

They all have strong mothers and motherly figures. The mother factor was very important. They would've easily succumbed to the streets without them. The same street that did a lot of their friends in, they overcame.

The values and goals that their mothers planted in them as youngsters came through. This helped them with the life in the streets. The fathers were on the other hand, were hi and bye fathers. You can't build a foundation like that!

Now he didn't grow up and accomplished any great feat. Nor have they served society to the fullest. Growing up on 169th St. confronting all those issues and making it out was miraculous. When you still have your mind together, that's a great feat in itself. He had a plan it wasn't drawn out, but he had a plan.

His child hood friends knew as youngsters, they wanted to succeed in life! They didn't want to be strung out on drugs. Nor did they want to be the guy on the corner, asking for change. They didn't want to succumb to the environment that they witness day in and day out.

They had to step over dope feigns while going to hoop or playing baseball. They witness women getting the shit slapped out of them for whatever reason. The watched the pimps, the hustlers, the thieves and the bangers control the environment. They will deal with all these factors as young boys.

Throughout their young lives they'll see people rise fast. They will also, see the same people fall. They used other people experiences and learned from other's mistakes. They did this by sitting one of the main characters name John's porch watching everything go down on 169th St. or Rock Manor School. They were involved or had direct contact with the crime element and persevered. Now the boys have a chance to be part of society as positive role models.

SPIRITUAL BATTLE

We are all born in a world of sin. We have to work and struggle to become righteous. We are born in a world where you have a choice to follow good or evil. I believe everyone has goodness in them.

Goodness just has to have a chance to come out. God put the tiniest fraction of himself somewhere in our body. We all can excess him, if we call upon him and believe. The devil is constantly in your ears trying to get your soul!

Parents must lay the foundation of goodness in the child from the beginning. Make sure the child understand the difference between right and wrong. We have to be taught righteousness. It seems we are all born with a selfish spirit.

We must be taught to give and to love one another. Once challenged, confronted and dabbling in evil, you must be aware. Your soul is at stake! You have to know once out in the world. The plan is to get your soul and smother your righteous spirit. Young and old prepare yourself and take Yahweh with you.

CHAPTER ONE

Losing

I come back through the door sweating and out of breath. It's a guy walking behind me laughing at me. He was laughing, because he beat me in a basketball game. We woke up early and hit the court. The sun was beaming in Austin Texas with no tree cover. John has a sweet court right in the middle of the complex where he lives. Harold came to the house and called Emus and I out. He talked shit and backed it up, all the way to the court and back. I tried to play it, but my competitive spirit snaps.

Emus walked through the door with a look of unconcern. I looked at him and said, "Emus damn dog, you let the nigga score".

Big Emus replies, "You win some, you lose some Colo!"

I reply, "naw fuck that I don't lose to a motherfucka with no shoes on! I'm about to jump in the shower so my body and mental can cool off".

John comes in from the store with groceries before I got in the bathroom. He sees us sweating and Harold smiling

He looked and then asked, "You let Harold beat you Colo? Why is he smiling like that?"

I just looked at John without saying anything and walked in the bathroom and jumped in the shower. I still can't take a loss well.

Andrea knocks on the bathroom door and says. "All that talking last night about how cold you are in basketball. You lost to a guy with no shoes Colo?"

I don't even answer. I turned the water up high to muffle what I was hearing from her. I feel the cool than warm sensation of water streaming on my back from the showerhead. I just stood underneath the water for about five minutes without moving.

The sun had sapped my energy, but the water was feeling great. The water streams over my back, while I kept rehashing the last play in my mind. It was my fault I should have pushed Emus under the rim. I had him one on one, but Emus enthusiasm to stick him on the double, clouded my judgment. The game was on the line.

I am pissed off! I lost two games to dude with no shoes on his feet. We were playing 21. At first I didn't want to step on his toes and before I knew it. He hit a couple of shots. Every time he went to the free throw line. He'd hit all three free shots.

He won the first one before I could blink. He was laughing and talking shit all the way through. The next one he did the same thing. Only this time I came all the way back. He jumped out to fifteen quick, I had eight, Emus had six.

The next game I had the clamps on him. This time I stick him like glue, once he hit eleven! I come all the way back and was going to win. Harold had nineteen too, but he didn't have anything left and I knew it. My defense was suffocating him.

The next shot wins. Emus and I checks him up at the top. I was just about to push Emus back to protect the rim. I knew that was the wrong answer when he came out for the double. Dude was cat quick without shoes.

Emus, was way too slow and I know it. It ran across my head he's going Emus way. As soon I think it, he does it. He goes around Emus easily and scores the winning bucket on a layup, with no contact. I am sick to my stomach.

I must have been in the shower a while. When I came out the bathroom breakfast was on the table. Andrea is perfect for John just seeing that move. We sit down to the table to a five-course breakfast with fruit and juice.

We say grace and afterwards Andrea asked, "Colo you had me captivated and laughing all night. Are you going to finish the story on you guys from the Met? I was thinking about it while shopping in the store?"

I answer her, "Yeah I'll do that!"

She then says, "I couldn't wait to get back to finish cooking. You all tossed that 1738s down last night. I knew you all would need to feed that monster, left in y'all stomachs".

I say, "Andrea you are so sweet! Okay I need something to take my mind off being a loser".

Harold still laughs about winning earlier and says, "don't tell me last night you were talking about you could ball".

He is peacocking around in front of his girl Jackie.

Every time he says, "I beat these niggas with no shoes on baby".

Jackie smiles like he is the shit. Jackie brought Harold around the crew. Emus and John has known Jackie every since they got to Texas. She was plugging with Teddy when Teddy was down here a few years earlier.

Teddy is doing some jail time for popping somebody in Texas. A couple years earlier I was down here. I had to bring some bunk ass weed back. I had two pounds of bunk. I get on the train and bring it back. I couldn't catch the dude who sold it to me. Ted did me a favor by getting it all off in nick bags down here.

They will buy that brown shit in Texas. In Detroit, they'll snap on you for that type of shit. All I wanted was enough to get back to Detroit with what I brought. Ted saved me and things turned out all right. He sold it and I bought some fire, with the proceeds.

I looked at Emus while I stuff some toast in my mouth to keep from talking. After clearing the toast I begins where I left off from the night before and say. Harold and Jackie you weren't here last night. I'll feel y'all in a little from last night. I was telling the story on how we came up in Chicago. It's plan and simple. We were young mobsters in our neighborhood. Before the guns came into play, the niggas with the best hands holds the power.

Like I was saying to Tadpole and Andrea. I had trained myself to a style of boxing nobody had ever seen. I mixed a little of Bruce Lee and Muhammad Ali together. I put it together along with some of me. I came up with a wicked concoction of a fighting style.

I had just joined the Black Disciples, an organization a lot of teens joined in my neighborhood. I am fifteen and full fledged, trained and proven gladiator for the Black Disciples. I was on my knuckles as far as money and got a blessing.

I was stealing before I got another job without that paper route. I worked a paper route for four years, until I went to Darobe high school.

I had a hookup from Lamont old dude, Mr. Paxon. We had to go to work on 55th & Garfield. Mr. Paxon had a hook up with the summer Cedar Program jobs for the youths. The job was to learn how to speed-read. I gave him my information and I was plugged. This was the easiest job you will ever have.

I hadn't been making any legal money in a long time. I think it paid four dollars an hour. The only thing about it was located on 55th & Garfield. It was a Vicelord neighborhood so that could be a problem. I was plugged by then and transition had been made. "Treys for days and BD for always". That's when Lamont and I really got cool. We had to go through the same thing. Lamont saw how I carried it.

I had to get on the L and then wait on a bus. Waiting on the bus in the opposition hood could land you a pumpkin head. I was on everything that moved while waiting on the bus. I peered into the cars going by with niggas who had on all red. I looked at the guys walking, the frowns and the smiles. The crooked smile was an indicator. I looked at the buses going the other way and who is on that bus. I kept my head on a swivel.

Niggas will jump off the bus to move, if they catch you sleeping. All these are indicaters that you have to pick up. You might have to skate out of a situation, before it happens. They never moved though and as a matter of fact they were cool to me. We worked with some Vicelords and they knew I was Folks.

The place we were speed-reading was in a big gym on the side of the church on 55th St. They had this program where they paid us to speed-read. I have no idea what the working part was about. It was a priest who ran the joint with the white collar.

I was so happy to be working again that I didn't care about the danger. The coolest thing about it is, during lunch hour, we would play basketball. I would bust their ass in the gym. They would also play after work. That's something I never did.

It was bad enough we had to go over there, but to stay and kick it invited trouble. I was in and out after signing in and out. The whole summer that's all we did. I was trying to get into speed-reading, but I never caught on like I should've. I could read it fast, but I wouldn't comprehend it.

By the end of the summer my gear was straight. I hit Jew Town and picked me up some sweet gear. I was going to start the new school year with a new wardrobe for the first time.

I had new Devil jeans with the pitchforks on the back pocket. I bought Levi jackets and jeans, a couple of Izodes shirts, some new hats and fresh jumpers. I was going to be fresh for the next coming year and couldn't wait. I am coming out sweet for my second year of high school.

I couldn't wait to kick it with Slept Rock and Dave my sophomore year. I was beginning to be popular, because of my fast hands. At the end of my freshmen year I was making my name in the school.

The girls love tough as niggas so it was my time to shine. My father that passed away left me all type of suits and cashmere coats. He had left me array of things he had accumulated over the years. I was just starting to fit them. They had sentimental value.

I started to feel good about myself. I was respected in the hood from my contemporaries and the opposition. I was starting to groom the niggas under me or around me. I was basically giving boxing classes.

My brother could always hold his own weight in the streets, by this time. That karate class did him some justice. He was feared in the streets. He was still going to the Manor and I never had to come up to the school. They knew I was his brother and I would be coming. You see he had the protection of a big brother.

One day I came out the crib and walked past the alley. I see my brother and Willie Days, fighting. Now they're supposed to be best friends right. This was before Willie turned Black P Stone.

I was a real advocate that best friends don't fight each other. I never fought my best friends ever.

Emus and John looks at each other and adds simultaneously, "Nope we ain't never fought each other."

I then say, "I broke up the fight, and then started throwing blows. I banged my brother a few to the body. Bing bam boom! After doing that, I bang Willie a few times too. Bing bam boom!

I told them after banging them, "stop fighting each other, because friends don't fight friends." I dropped B's on my brother first to let Willie know that both of y'all get it. This is our hood and we don't fight each other.

Willie's brother Brain Days and my cousin John Harris had an epic battle. They got in a disagreement while we were playing football in the alley. I don't know what it was about I think Brain was picking on John.

Oh no I remember we were playing tackle in the snow and John tackled Brain ugly. Brain didn't like the tackle. Emus and I were instigating the fight. Sometimes you got to let them go at it, if it's inevitable.

John tells me, "I am about to beat Brain ass cuz."

Brain says, "I'll fuck you up lil boy."

I told Emus, "fuck that football come on they are about to fight." Emus was the artificial quarterback.

Emus came down and said, "fuck him up John" and then told Brain "he wouldn't take that bullshit he done to you."

John and Brain went at it. It was almost liked that fight Robert and I had when I was their age. These two little guys who wouldn't give up. Brain was getting his ass whooped at first. John was banging him. Bango, bango, bango, blows to the face. John was a couple of years younger than Brain too.

Emus and I was commentating the fight. "John gives him a right then a left. Oh oh he staggered him ahooo ahoo hoo hoooooo. Brain looking like he's looking for the towel".

John has been fighting and wresting Larry, Walley and I for years. John is a beast.

John was going to work, until he got tired. Once he got tired Brain was on his head. Bang boom bang booomm.

Emus still commentating, "Oh looks like John is out of breathe. Brain seizes the moment and attacks ahooo hooo."

Emus and I are going crazy, cause Brain looked like he was out.

The comeback was miraculous. At the end of the fight they wouldn't stop throwing blows. They both got so tired after a while and we broke it up. I never jumped in my brothers or cousins fights. I just made sure shit was fair. John edged him out for the victory though! Larry, John and Walley I trained them all to fight so they didn't have to run to me.

Raging Hormones

*M*y hormones were raging out of control. Ever since the fifth grade I would get a boner out of nowhere. I wouldn't even be thinking about a girl and I'd get a stiffy. I hated those times when called up to the black board, with a boner. I had to walk funny and reposition myself where 'Willie' would be pointing toward my chin and not just sticking straight out.

I was starting to notice all the beautiful girls on our block. It's funny how I didn't notice them at first. My gear was straight and I had a little money in my pocket. I wasn't old enough for them, but I was noticing them.

My nephew Derek was over our house one time I was about eleven.

He saw this girl and he said, "look at her legs Colo."

I looked at her legs and I said, "everybody's got legs Derek."

He looked slyly grinned and said, "man look at her legs and her thighs, ooohh weeee."

It didn't' register at the time. He looked at me with the, you don't have a clue.

He then just said, "you'll see when you get older."

Now I see what he was talking about. I was looking at Collota House one day and said, "look at her legs." I was too young to know about legs and thigh at first. I was into long hair and a pretty face. I was too young to know anything about sex. I started learning going over Emus house watching ON TV.

Mr. and Mrs. House put some beautiful girls on this earth. There was Linda, Trita, Comaceta, Ted, Carlotta and Lorita. They all had their own beauty. You know how some sisters look alike. They all came from the same parents, but they had different beautiful dispositions. Feels like I'm missing one.

I hated when Ted died in a car accident a few years back. I always thought she was the nicest sister. She had long beautiful hair and she was stacked. They all were stacked it was her voice. Her voice sounded heavenly when she talked to you.

The words rolled off her tongue when she talked, "heeeyyyy Colo how are you doing?"

It felt good for her to just to say my name. I loved when she stopped on John's stoop to talk to us. We had beauty and grace in our presence.

Mrs. Bilkins's daughter's, Sherry and Rhoda were on the block too. I'd sit on the porch and watched Sherry go in and out the house. She was so beautiful to me. She had the style of a sophisticated woman on the way up.

She rode in Mercedes and upscale cars and wore furs. She has two sons Denatius and Corry. She has yellow skin with a few freckles. I never saw her in gym shoes. These were the ladies on the block to me.

Corky down the block was Lou's girlfriend. Lou was a Vicelord that got cool with the block. We got cool with Lou through Corky and Lou was a Stone. Regina, Denise, and Alisha Stables, they're family.

It was your sister Evon with her fine Italian ass. The other girls were Denise Little and Lamont sister, Mary Jane, Dee Dee, Alisha, Theresa, Kendle and Kenny sister Toni were the girls our age. We were family so I didn't notice any of them at the time.

The only one I notice was Sherry, when I was little. Sherry was another level. Right now I am at the age to start to notice them all now.

Why

*Y*ou remember when Preston Boe smacked the shit out of Linda House. We were about ten or eleven. Preston Boe was calling it for the BD's. Preston Boe came down the block with about fifteen Folks. Linda was sitting on the porch at first with us. She walked out to talk to him. I don't know what happened, because we were on shortie business.

All I heard was this loud as clapping sound. He smacked her right on the corner of 169th & Calumet, bowww Yowww. I guess Linda and Joe were going together at the time. Maybe she missed a meeting or something. I later found out she was Disciple Queen.

I said to myself, "if that's his girl friend why did he smack her?" My mother taught me, don't hit girls. You give them nice things and be nice to the girls. I didn't even know Linda had a boyfriend. She was a tomboy. Linda was fine and climbed trees and played with the boys.

She was a couple of years older than us. She was the youngest child in her family. Anyway, he reared back and smack the shit out of her. After getting slapped she held her face in her hands. It was nothing we could do we were shorties. I always wonder why did he do it?

After she got slapped she walked home. I thought she was going to get Stag and Lando, but they didn't come back. Linda was pretty why would you hit a pretty girl. My hormones were raging though.

I was ready for a girlfriend this year. I am really starting to take notice of the girls on the block. We had some beautiful girls on Calumet.

"Look at her thighs", I would say. I had my gear straight and my game was tight. I was ready for school. I was going to try out for the basketball team too and was sure I was going to make it. My life is starting to see light on the bright side. I was feeling good about myself and my esteem was spiking.

Amateurs

*M*y brain used to short circuit sometimes. When I didn't have money. I felt shallow and worthless. Just before we got that job, we were doing dumb things.

"Yeah you are right Colo. Remember when we stole that car or tried to steal a car", Emus comments. "It was Robert, Colo and I."

I answered, "yep, it was the shortest joy ride in history."

Emus continues, "Neither of us didn't have a hot nickel in our pocket. We were broker than three peas in a bucket. Robert had come back around to kick it with us for the day. He had moved long before high school. When he did come back around we had to get bubbled.

After grabbing a couple of beers we ran out of money. We talked while were drinking the beers. We came to the conclusion we had to get some money. We just didn't know how at first. Robert said he knew how to peel cars. There you go I grabbed a small screwdriver out the crib.

Now how you peel a car, you bust the ignition up with a screwdriver. Pull the pin and the car will start. No key necessary so you know what that means, for three broke little niggas? After a little discussion we were on our way on foot.

First, we walked all the way around to Robert's crib on 187th & Ashland. We were looking at potential cars. We didn't even know what we wanted. We just were going to steal a car and sell the parts. After we got to Robert crib and we didn't get anything, we were more determined. Robert goes in the house and gets a better screwdriver.

Colo and I were the lookout. Colo was on one side of the street and I was on the other. We were watching for anybody coming out the house or just walking up. We had or signals together for each case. I had a different sound than Colo had.

Robert busted the window out of about three cars along the way. He kept getting in cars that had a no tilt, steering wheel. I knew that and I didn't steal cars. You can tell when it is a tilt. It has two levers one to tilt it up or down. The other is the gearshift. We were amateurs and amateurs get caught.

He should've just looked in the window, first. Robert kept busting the window before seeing, if it was a tilt. That's how brand new he was at stealing cars. That's the only ones Robert could get was the ones with tilt. He still was walking up busting the windows with no tilt.

I interrupt Emus and say, "I was saying to myself they're going to take us to jail for vandalism." Robert was no thief he just knows how to steal. Robert didn't have the foresight to know this is something you don't do. A real thief is going to make sure it's there for the taking. Go head 'E' my fault.

Emus then said, "we finally got to this white I think, Rivera. Robert busted the window and got in the car. I heard him starting the car a few minutes later"

Colo and I took off, ran and jumped in the car. We like, "yeah, yeah you got this bitch Robert."

I jumped in the back and Colo jumped in the front and we took off. He screeched the tires and burnt rubber out of the parking space. We didn't even get off the block good and Colo and Robert were fighting over the radio.

Colo shakes my head no and say, "dude I'm telling you I wasn't fighting with him. He just went down to turn on the radio." He wanted to bang the sounds while driving off. Next thing I know I'm shouting to him, "watch out."

Emus looked at me unconvinced and said, "all I know is Robert was steering us into the back of a van." Once Robert looked up it was too late "*BAM*" we slam into the back of this blue van while it was parked. Robert banged his mouth on the steering wheel and Colo smashed his head on the windshield. I'm in the back shouting, "get out, get out the car."

Colo opens his door and jumps out and starts running. Robert hit his door after shaking off the impact. I jumped out the back and haul ass. It was a two door so Colo had to get out so I could get out to run. I had to shake him out of his daze by shouting, "open the door open the door."

People come out on their porches looking at us like we fools. It was some people who saw the accident. They watched us break out from the car after the accident. Just so happen it was a vacant lot in between these two houses. We hit the lot, busting ass through it.

Now just think three little niggas who just crashed into the back of a van. Gets out and starts running. We didn't even make it a block and a half from where we stole the car. We were running through the lot and I was the last one to take off. I shot past Colo through a yard and was on my way.

Colo starts laughing and says, "hell yeah that's when I knew I was dazed for real."

I saw Emus big ass shoot past me then I started shaking out the cobb webs. I said to myself, "Emus is blazing pass me while we're trying to get away." I was dazed for real. It is no way his big ass is running pass me anywhere. I must have been more dazed than I thought.

Emus starts laughing and say, "Robert was holding his mouth running with a screwdriver in his hand." I told him to get rid of the screwdriver. Colo was holding his head.

We ran a few blocks then collected ourselves.

We were walking and Robert asked, "look at my tooth, is it broken?"

I looked and said, "yep it's cracked." Right then he just broke the rest off that was chip. I'm like, "Dammmn that's fucked up!"

We look up after he spit his tooth out. The police was riding by slowly looking at us. We played it off by laughing like shorties do, while hitting and pushing each other. We didn't fit the M O. We didn't look like car thieves. I know they got the call. They were rolling in the direction where we just left. We weren't running at the time, so they kept going. They drove by going to the call and once they were out of site.

We said in unison, "lets get the fuck out of here." Once they give them the description and the clothes we were wearing. They were going to be on us.

I told Robert, "this is over I'm going home." Robert tooth was cracked so he was ready to go anyway. Robert was close to the crib so he just went home. Colo and I zig zagged hitting alleys and back streets all the way from 187th to 169th.

We ran then walked, then ran all the way home. All that looking and walking to steal a car. All those busted windows he fucked up in the process. We get one and that what happened. Colo and I were walking back to the Met, empty-handed.

Colo look at Andrea and Jackie and say. John knows it wasn't like Emmett and I to do shit like we were doing. Robert came up with that idea when we had absolutely nothing to do. Robert didn't play sports like Emus and I. We could have played basketball, but Robert came up with that idea. We were broke and it was hot ass hell too. It was easy to go along. Idle mind's is terrible for broke teenagers.

Being broke meant you were the same ass a bum. The guys on the Met kept money in their pockets. We off the nine, we can't be no broke niggas off Calumet, Harold.

On the way home Emus and I both said, "that was some dumb shit" to each other. When you are young, everything gets rapped up in that moment. You got the rest of your life to live, if you ward off niggas in your ear. That was the hardest thing to tell your friend you hang with everyday. I am not with the bullshit.

This is the life we live

*E*mus and Coole didn't really have to do this shit. They had a good family structure. They had a bunch of cousins, aunts and uncles. Later on, when we started strong-arming people on 169th. I was thinking to myself, "Emus is game, but this is not Emus."

I was watching him while he was on security. The environment was sucking on Emus slowly. Emus is starting to be game for anything. When we hit the streets hard at first. I used to use Emus as strength, to do the right thing! People would owe me money or something for weed. I am ready to smash and Emus would intervene.

Emus was straight his Mom worked for C.T.A. At first there was Bill so he had a father figure, until he was about twelve. Bill had a car and could get around. Emus's family was the first people who had Spectrum or was it On TV?

Emus answers, "we had them both."

I then say, "This was new and Emus people had it. Sometimes when Bill and mother was gone. We'd go in his mother room and watch the naked flicks.

Emus's grandmother lived on 168th & King Drive. He had plenty of aunties and uncles and cousins that were older than him. Emus always could come up with money. He had an uncle who stayed on Michigan. Emus was his namesake. We used walk to his crib to hit him up for quarters, when we fell off the games.

The reason Coole and Emus didn't have to steal anything. Every school year they got the brand new clothes. Emus and Mike was wearing Calvin Klein's, Sergio Valentine and all the latest styles. Michele stayed fresh and wore the latest styles too.

Emus used to where the new Kangaroos all the time. All they had to do was go to school. Emus maybe had a paper route for three days and he quit after the first check. Emus got up late as hell. I always had to come get Emus out of bed. Coole kept his paper route much longer, because he was a hustler.

When I went to get Emus. I'd hear Mrs. Blue cursing Michele, Coole and Emus about cleaning, cooking or whatever. I would be listening before I knocked. You can hear as soon as you walked in the yard.

Mrs. Blue would be snapping, "Clean this motherfucka up you lazy motherfuckas. Michele get your wall crawling ass up and wash these motherfucking dishes."

I never heard a woman curse like that before in my life. I'd sit by the wall on the steps and she'd snap on Coole and Michele.

I had to wait, until it calmed down then I'd knock on the door.

She'd come to the door open it and say. "Hey Columbus hi you doing?"

I'll reply, "Fine, Mrs. Blue can Emus come out and play."

She then turn in yell, "Emus this boy Columbus is at the door."

She tells me to come in and sit in the front room, until Emus finishes. Sometimes I'd wait in the hallway.

His brother Coole was always on some scheme. One time Mrs. Blue caught Coole up at the L selling transfers. Let Coole tell it cause he would be laughing all the way through. You know his Mom worked for CTA with access to the transfers for the next day. She always brought home a stack.

How Coole would do it was catch you before you got on the L or bus. He'll sell you a transfer for whatever time. That is coming and going for half the price. He'd have his stamper, to stamp what time you needed for later.

When Emus had to catch the bus to school she'd leave transfers on the dresser. Emus always used to hook us with transfers. He was selling them too. He had the tokens for us and everything we were straight. I thought she left them for the hood anyway just being cool. She knows we were using the transfers too. She brought home stacks of them. I would come to Emus house just to get a transfer.

Anyway Coole is up at the L trying to catch everybody before they get on the L on 169th & State. He going person to person quickly, before the L comes.

He said he was like, "mame do you want to buy a transfer for whatever time you need, 50 cents?"

The lady turns around and it was his mother, Mrs. Blue. She caught him in mid sentence. Coole just put his head down and she got all in his ass right there in the train vestibule. She caught Coole in the act.

She frowns up takes the transfer and asked him. "Are you going to ask me do I want a transfer Coole? They find out you my child and I will get fired. Get your ass home."

She snatched the rest of the transfers from him.

Coole would laugh shake his head and say, "Columbus hee haa hee it was my mother."

They were no more transfers for us after that move. The transfer game got shelved.

Naw, Emus didn't have to get it in, in the streets! As a matter fact he rarely would do things with his brother. Emus hung with John and I. Some people in the hood didn't even know they were brothers. Coole hit stains all the time and is known. Emus mother probably didn't want him with Coole in the street. Coole was a true thief and hustler. Coole used to have these sayings after blowing all his money.

He'd steal and basically give the money away to his friends and buy plenty of high. Coole didn't have any reservation about spending money. Coole would give you his last dollar. You would then hear later on that Coole hit a stain after just blowing a couple hundred. I guess it was all a come up to him, it wasn't his money.

I'd ask Coole, "why you set shit out like that Coole?"

His response, "we giants out here Colo, let them have that shit, we're giants."

Coole was into everything, but what him, Reggie, Juice, Jake, Brandon were all on back in the day was, pick pocketing. They were top notched cannons.

One day Todd and I went over Brandon's house. He moved by himself on 195th. Brandon and I got to stepping in his room. I had a bag of rolled up joints. It was about twenty or thirty of them. I had them tucked in my pull over jacket.

Brandon was turning me and tapping me while stepping. He spent me one more time and he came out with my bag of weed. I looked at the bag, because I knew I had a bag just like that!

He said Todd, "I got him he don't even know."

Todd looked and said, "yep cuz, he got you."

I took the surprise look off my face and said, "I knew you had them." I reached for the bag and he gave them back. I then said, "you are sweet though! I didn't see, until the end of the play."

I was high and had no idea he Brandon had my shit. I was all into the turns. The cannon game was serious. They all would be dressed in suits carrying briefcases while busting stains. They were dressed for the occasion. Mostly hitting pappies and ladies purses.

I used to watch them work on the bus. They'd get up early with the school kids and the people traveling to work. They would be up at seven o'clock in the morning to hit those stains. They worked rush hour too. Anytime it was a crowd on public transportation. It would be a crew of pickpocket working. You know pickpockets work together. One will bump you one way, while the other is tapping you off.

Once they get you, they would kiss it off. That was making the kiss sound, "swwwwhhhaaaa." That sound means it's sweet and let's get off the bus. It took a lot of guts to go in somebody pocket. I couldn't do it. I'd practice with my friend just to see if I could get them. I was somewhat good, but whatever I got away with I gave back. I would wire you up though and say you were sleeping. I never set out to pick pocket some body I didn't know.

That's why the cannons worked in teams just in case something broke out. It got so bad when these guys got on the bus.

The bus driver would shout out, "there are pickpockets on the bus. Hold your purses close and watch out for the bump."

I'd look at my guys like, "damn they on to you, without saying a word to them." I just couldn't bring myself to search a women purse or sneak in someone pocket.

Yeah, but Emus started going on stains. I never woke up and said I want to steal something. I really wasn't any thief, but I would steal. William Hawkins invoked the stealing demon in me in the third grade. I would steal, if I had to steal. I didn't include stealing out of a store stealing. Stealing from people was stealing to me.

The Lane Job

I wouldn't have gone on this job, but Emus wanted to go! The second and last stain Emus and I went on together! This is when we were about to break in Mrs. Lane house. Emus was on watch out, while we went in the house. Mrs. Lane stayed next to Mr. Henderson Big's father. She stayed a couple doors down from Emus's grandmother.

Pauly talked us into it again. Pauly, Melissa, that's Fonz sister and Fonz hit the house for thousands. I saw Melissa with a roll of money after she came back from the first stain. Emus seen the roll too, that's why he was ready go.

I'm like damn that could have been my money. Pauly and Fonz had thousands too. They had to hit her for at least ten thousand. Pauly got him a gold bracelet and chain after the stain. I didn't go the first time, because I knew Mrs. Lane. I delivered her the paper.

I saw Melissa had a roll of hundreds in her pocket. Melissa told us she got $3600 out the cookie jar! She got lucky, because she was probably reaching for the cookies. I say that, because she loved to eat. Melissa was a tomboy. She played ball with the guys and everything. She could play too for a girl. When going on stains with Pauly. It wasn't any split up of the take.

It was whatever you found in the house was yours. The only reason they took Melissa is, because I wouldn't go with them the first time.

When Pauly came back after the stain they showed the take.

Pauly then would say. "You should have went Colo, Melissa got a pocket full of money."

I said to myself after looking at Melissa knot, "yeah I should've, but fuck that shit." Melissa went and bought her some clothes and some gold. Melissa didn't have girlie gear. She had eczema on her neck and arms that she had bouts with sometimes. She was just like one of the guys. She dressed and talked like a guy.

Now they came to us a couple of months later on a reroll. Pauly wanted to hit the house again. They saw Emus and I on the court-shooting ball. Here comes Fonz and Pauly telling us they were about to hit Mrs. Lane. They had to plug us, because we were back there on the rim. We would've seen them going in the house.

Here's Pauly, "remember last time Colo you missed out. Everybody had some stacks."

Knowing this I said, "fuck it this time I'll look out."

Pauly was like, "naw Colo last time you left us when the stereo came out, fuck that. You got to go in with us this time."

All I wanted was the stereo and I was out. Pauly told Emus to look out in the back. We couldn't look out in the front of the house.

How was I going to let them know? You couldn't get in-between the houses on King Drive. All the houses were stuck together one next to the other. Emus was game and ready to go and I said fuck it.

We dropped the ball and I said, "let's go Emus, fuck it I need a few dollars in my pocket." The only thing is, it's probably burnt up now. It couldn't be no money left after the first hit. I couldn't take the chance on missing out this time. Fonz and Pauly knew just how to get in the house. They also knew how to manipulate us.

We get in through this low window for the basement. She was still working on the house, because there was no stairs to the upstairs. It had a contemporary look on the inside and out.

They had just built that house, but weren't done with it yet. She was living there while they were working on it. We had to come up a ladder to get up to the ground floor. Pauly and Fonz went in and I'm the last one up. They knew the layout anyway. I was walking up the ladder I see some change on the floor. I picked it up.

Pauly was like, "leave that shit on the floor we looking for bank nigga."

We get in the house and start looking around. Pauly and Fonz went upstairs. I was on the ground floor. I see somebody walking on the porch. I see a lady shadow at the front door. I hear the keys rattling at the door. She had perfect timing we just got in the house.

Mrs. Lane was coming through the front door. I whispered as loud as I could. "Pauly somebody coming" and I break back the way we came. I hit the ladder and almost broke my leg, trying to get down the ladder. I barley touch the slacks and almost fell. I made a bunch of noise and Mrs. Lane screams when she sees, it niggas in the house. She didn't see me I was already down the ladder.

Emus hear the commotion then sees me and asked, "what wrong?"

I am scrambling out the window and frantically told him, "Mrs. Lane coming through the front." Pauly and Fonz were right behind me. I ran back to the court and started shooting ball. I was just going to play it off. Pauly and Fonz burnt rubber down the alley back to their crib. Mrs. Lane didn't come out, but you could see Emus and I shooting on the court from her yard.

Somehow word got back it was me who broke in Mrs. Lane house. I thought to myself, "It was just me who was in the house." Somehow the whole block knew or I thought they knew. After that Emus mother and grandmother didn't want me around Emus. I had to hook with Emus on the low for at least a whole year. Now I am the ringleader of people breaking in houses. I am the youngest one and I am the ringleader.

How did they know it was I in the house? She didn't see me. Pauly and Fonz stayed a few houses away from the woman. They didn't have any mask and she had to see them, if anybody. How was it that I was peeped?

Fonz lived three doors down from the lady and Pauly lived at the end of the block. They set me out with the double cross. We didn't get anything so I guess nothing happened. Someone told and it wasn't me, because I don't tell on myself.

This is when the thief tag was stapled to me. I am known, as a thief, in the hood to the elderly Folks. I didn't want that reputation. I used to deliver Mrs. Lane paper. I didn't know her cordially.

Mrs. Lane never tipped me either. I guess I could say that was the reason, but it wasn't. The reason I went in that house was, because Emus wanted to go. I wouldn't have gone, if Emus didn't go.

Every time I did something with Pauly I was the fall guy. How did the police know to come to my house when I stole the stereo? The time when we hit Half-and-Half crib?

Someone could've seen me, but if they seen me then they seen Pauly and Fonz. I didn't hear anything about Pauly and Fonz in the house. I didn't say anything either.

I started to figure out Pauly and Fonz ain't shit. They don't have any honor so they couldn't talk me into shit anymore. Every time I did something with them I get caught.

Worst of all I never got anything in the end. The stereo, the freight job and now Mrs. Lane I was through with Pauly. Three strikes and you are out. I was out. I got no money from none of those jobs. The only thing I got was the thief tag, but I had nothing to show for it. I didn't steal anything and they got the stereo back I took. I was depressed about that!

I backed off Emus, because I didn't want anything to happen to him. I wouldn't tell him about stains anymore for a while. I couldn't hang at his house anymore and I felt ashamed. His people would look at me with disdain, like they seen me go in the house.

It's like they knew for sure and the only people who knew for sure were Pauly, Emus, Fonz and I. We did it on a whim so it was no planning. Let's see, if she's home, if she's not, we're going in the house. Somehow Pauly had her phone number and she wasn't picking up that meant it was clear. The same day everybody on the block knows I was in her house.

I was really barred off King Drive as far as the grownups. Don't bring that boy over here any more Emus. I know I was the topic at every block club meeting.

Emus stuck up for me and said, "it couldn't have been Colo, cause he was with me."

They just thought Emus was taking up for me. Everybody on King Drive thought it was I, but nobody saw me. I was embarrassed and ashamed and I didn't want to come around Emus people.

Maybe Mrs. Lane saw me going down the ladder. She probably knew my silhouette. She ran out the house to call the police. When Pauly and Fonz came down she was already running down the street. That's why she didn't see them. I had to fade on Emus too.

It seems to me I was along for the fall guy. They knew I wasn't going to tell so if something went wrong. I would be the fall guy. I used to wonder why he'd come get us when he didn't need us? If you're hitting the house and you know what it is! You don't need us little niggas.

Little niggas don't go to jail. Momma can come get you from the police station. They didn't tell Mrs. Lane though! She probably saw my clothes or anything. I know she looked out the back to see where they went. She saw it was just Emus and I in the dungeon, shooting ball. She saw me she had to see Emus.

If I saw her today I would ask her to forgive me. I'm really not cut like that! I knew Mrs. Lane and I don't fuck with people I know. Pauly just had a way of manipulating me into doing evil things. Breaking in people houses is evil.

That was the last time I fucked with Pauly and Fonz on shit like that. For now on, if it wasn't about sports. I didn't want to hear about it, not from those two. That's the way it was before I had got that job that summer. I had got that job from Mr. Paxton hookup and now I didn't have to steal. Now I am straight!

Wiped Out

*T*hree weeks before school started. Something devastating changed the course of my coming out. One night it was lighting and thunder storming heavily. It was about 12.30 in the morning and my family, were asleep and in bed. I was downstairs watching TV. I get up and was about to go to bed. I come up stairs and looked on the back porch and it was covered with smoke.

The upstairs back porch was next to my little brother's and my room. I looked out on the porch thinking I was tripping and it was on fire. I shouted loudly, "mama, mama the house is on fire, the house is on fire." Walley was in the washroom and walked right past me, before I noticed the fire.

My sister Barbara had come to her door and looked and said. "yeah Momma it is a fire."

My mother came to the middle of the hall way looked then shouted, "everybody get out the house. Don't grab nothing, just leave, and go get your brother up Colo."

My brother Samson slept in the basement. I ran downstairs to the top of the basement steps and hollered, "Samson get up the house is on fire." I didn't think about grabbing anything at the time. I was making sure my brother was up. Samson shot up the stairs still half way sleep. I waited at the top of the stairs, until he got up

He looked bewildered, but after getting up the steps he asked. "it's a fire in the house?"

I replied, "yeah we got to get out of here. Everybody from upstairs came down the stairs. My mother put on some clothes quickly and came on down.

As soon as we get outside, people walking by started to notice the fire. We took accountability of everyone outside. We had a white and black Boxer named Boe at the time he made it out too.

As soon as we said that, the fire started coming through the front window of our living room. The firemen was called, but wasn't there yet. The fire department was only two blocks away. It seemed as, if the fire swept through the house like a wave.

I thought the fire department would get there and put it out in time. They had gotten there before when Walley was playing with matches and put it out. He burnt down the back porch once before and they put it out.

Our living room was downstairs in the front. The fire had made it to the living room, within maybe a minute and a half. All was lost in the house. If I'd come up stairs ten minutes later.

My Mom sister and brother probably couldn't have gotten out down the stairs. The only other way out was through the windows. They would've all been burnt up cause they were sleep. It was only one way down stairs because the back porch was on fire.

The fire also went next door and destroyed the neighbor's house too. Alex and Anthony stayed next door, the Felton's. I didn't think the fire was going to do that much damage because it was raining.

The fire department arrives at the house finally. They busted the front and back windows and put the fire out. They came in with the ax and went to work. They tore up more than the fire destroyed. They had to make sure it was out. I guess it was procedure.

Lil Todd & Lace came and aided and assisted in our time of need. They were trying to kick the next-door neighbors door in, to get them out. This was all before the fire department came. She couldn't get out down the steps.

Hazel had to come out the window into a blanket that Todd and Lace had. I still thank Yahweh to this very day that we made it out. We lost everything, but our lives so we salvaged the most important element.

At the time all I could think about was all my shit is burnt up. I go back the next day and I just starred at house for about two hours sitting in the cut. I had to take inventory in my mind of everything that was gone: My clothes, my comic books, my art work, my collection of hats and my money was all burnt up.

I was wondering to myself and said, "out of all the houses in the city of Chicago, lightning struck our house". That was the report that came back from the investigation. It was a lightning bolt that hit our house. I couldn't understand why this would happen. We go to church and my Mom serves God faithfully.

I asked Yahweh, "why did the lightning hit our house?" The way the fire started was from a thunderbolt that hit the house, a natural occurrence.

All my hard work had gone down the drain in the fire. My whole existence was wiped out. All my new clothes that I was going to flex in school were gone. All my father's things that we had were all gone. All we had were the clothes on our back literally.

The Salvation Army gave us some things. They weren't name brand things. The clothes were out dated for the times. I couldn't wear that shit. I was a rock in the middle of a hard spot. I couldn't believe I had to start school starving and on bum status. I sat in the cut and just looked at the house in a daze. Yesterday, this time I felt good now it's a totally different life. I didn't get a answer from God that day.

The Harris's came to the Rescue

During our time of need we called the Harris's. They stayed on 17033 Prairie. They had moved from 314 E 170th St. The Harris's came up and moved in their own house by that time. Mrs. Emma, my mother's long time friend came to the rescue.

We had to live with them until we found another place to live. That was a blessing, because we were in the streets. This time of my life was particularly hard for me. I would look up at the sky and say, "I can't believe this!"

Within one year and a half my whole life is out of my control. My dog was put to sleep. My adopted father, my best friend had died from a heart attack. I had gotten cut from the football and basketball. My house burns down and we have no place to live.

I was just getting a handle on the financial part and developing some self-esteem. Now I know I can't tryout for the football or basketball team I have no clothes. How does a kid comprehend all of that? I am fourteen and fucked in the game.

Mrs. Emma and Mr. Henry are special people to me. We didn't have any family to go to at the time. They immediately took that obstacle out the picture. We had a place to live for the time being.

I had a couple of outfits for school, but far from what I needed. I had no money and the Cedar Program was over. After starting high school my freshmen year Denis had lost the branch, but was still delivering out his car.

Before I quit he would bring the exact number of papers to my house with no extras. I just quit I couldn't get the extras. I had a seven o'clock wood shop class I never made. I wasn't able to do my routes and make class.

The whole community came together and helped us out. People in the hood gave us clothes and shoes to wear. I didn't want to go to school wearing some else's shit again. I didn't want to get called out like Curt did me over the jacket in the fourth grade.

I had to do it I didn't have anything else to wear. I know I'm going to get rode unmercifully just like in grammar school. This killed my drive and I knew it. I was mentally drained and didn't have an idea.

I must admit a lot of people helped my mother during this time. A lot of my friends gave me a few things from the hood. Todd and Lace gave me clothes. Freddie gave me some cleats, because he knew I wanted to play football.

I ask Freddie after he gave me the cleats. "What am I going to do now Freddie? All my money was in the house and all my clothes are burnt up. What am I going to do now?" My burnt up comic book collection really, really hurt me. That was years of money and collecting. I started when I was eight years old. That was going to be my come up to have the vintage comic books that I could sell later. Right now Andrea, those comic books would be priceless.

Well Freddie searched him self and said, "Colo I don't know, just keep your head up Folks."

Emus looked out. This is what I mean the hood could have empathy and show love. I didn't even think about the team after that anymore! I would have given it another shot, but I got problems. I don't even have shorts to play ball

I went to live with my father, until we got another place. Now before I left my Mom had rules at our house, but over the Harris's. They were super rules in place. My mother had rules for rules on top of the new rules. Moms didn't want us to be a burden in anyway to the Harris's.

I couldn't take it. Larry was wearing my clothes. John was stealing my comic books. He didn't even collect comic books. He collected baseball cards. Walls got on my nerves. By this time we started calling my brother Walls. I took care of my things. They dogged my shit out.

It was just too many lil niggas around, to me. The Harris's was still working on the house when we came. My mother slept on the couch in the living room. Of course the Harris's had their own room. My sister stayed with daddy Curtis.

It was five boys in all and three girls. The boys were all piled up in the back room upstairs. I had to sneak in late, because I had to be in at nine o'clock. She was trying to chastise me in front of them. I didn't want to be around them with my feelings of helplessness. I wasn't feeling Mom at all, because we're fucked up and she's really stressed. When Mom is stressed she had very little tolerance.

Everything creative wise I used to do, before the fire, I didn't do anymore. I hung all my sweet pictures I drew on the wall in my room. I had a hat collection that's gone. I even had a cowboy hat. I love to draw and spent time doing it. I don't think I've drawn another thing after that tragic night! I picked up something to show my son recently. Other than that I had no passion to do it. I stopped doing this unconsciously.

My emotions were swirling. I haven't got shit, but the clothes on my back. My comic books are gone, my prize possessions. I just couldn't shake those comic books being gone. Seven years of collecting comic books down the drain. Those were my secret treasures. I kept them in mint condition. I could've had a couple thousand comic books by that time.

I tried to start over, but the hit was too devastating. I finally said to myself, "Fuck some comic books I need clothes on my back that shit is over!" The comic books I buy now are getting stolen or ripped up living with the Harris's.

I'd leave and come back in the house and the covers of the comic books are on the floor. My face would crack open immediately and it was nothing I could do. How could I trip over some books when we have nowhere to go?

I am not feeling this shit. I had gotten up to about thirty comic books. I used to have thousands. I gave up the chase it was too depressing. I didn't want any pity from anybody. My pride has taken a blow and pity was not going to help. I still thank Yahweh we weren't in the streets.

I'm so glad that Mrs. Emma and Mr. Henry for taking us out the streets. These are good people that took in a whole family and we're not blood. Who do that? I love them for that, but I had to go though!

I stayed with the old dude, until we moved down the street from the old house. He'd drop or have Butch to drop me off at school that first week. He had gotten me a few things for school. I didn't want him dropping me off though. I told him just give me bus fare and he didn't have to get up. Who has their parent dropping them off at school?

We found a house a couple of months later. We moved to 16959 S. Calumet. It was about a block and half from where we used to stay. Were in our own house, but it wasn't like the old house. My mother put so much love in that house. It was our house though, but it never felt like 356 E. 169th St.. You must buy renters or home insurance, had we had it. We would have been straight.

Sophomore Year

When school started a lot of the students felt sorry for my situation. That didn't stop the ribbing. Sometimes I wouldn't go to school, because the ribbing was unbearable. You needed at least three weeks of marquee clothes and different outfits for school.

Before the fire I had at least two pair of new gym shoes. I had a couple of pairs of bucks. Now I only had a week's worth of sweet shit. It wasn't enough. I had to wear the clothes that I wore last week, all month.

One day I came to school in some Gloria Vanderbilt's. Somebody gave them to me. I thought they were straight. They were almost brand new and had all the blue color in them. I included this pair with my marquee shit. I worn the pants before to school and no one noticed. I didn't know they were girl jeans.

Sterling and Cassius who were up on the styles. They saw the dove emblem on the little bitty pocket and went crazy.

Dave spotted the dove first and he busted me out immediately. "Slept Rock, Slept Rock", while looking and pointing at the dove and laughing. At first I didn't know what he was laughing about.

He finally gets it out while pointing at the dove. "Slept Rock this nigga got on Gloria Vanderbilt's. Dave was busting me out ugly while laughing, uncontrollably, "ahha he got on Gloria Vanderbilt's, my sister wear those jeans Slept Rock he got ha ha ha."

He said it in front of everybody standing in the hallway and it was crowded. Everybody in the vicinity comes over and looks at the emblem and says, "he do got on Gloria Vanderbilt's."

The girls came over and giggled at me. I was shrinking emotionally and fast, right in the hallway and couldn't escape. That same feeling came back from grammar school. When Curt snatched his jacket off of me. I thought it was mine, but he proved it was his.

I was giving it back to Dave and Slept though by cracking back, but what could you do? I just suck it up, because I got the pants on, right now. Like when Slept Rock had on those plastic shoes. It's not going to stop. After that day! Slept Rock didn't wear those shoes anymore either.

I used to call Dave a lemon head. His skin tone was yellowish with a roundish shelled, peanut head. I used to tell Slept Rock to shut up with that big ass dome helium head. I was a little too much for one on one, so tag teaming is rough! You got to go at both of them at the same time.

When I found out they were girl jeans. I had to break away from these niggas. I just left the school too, too embarrassed. I left after 5th period or something, because they caught me going to the lunchroom. I didn't even eat lunch. I never missed eating lunch! I wasn't hungry anymore.

I broke out the back of the school and started walking home down the back trail. I was trying to avoid any contact while I was talking to myself saying, "I got caught in school with girl jeans, over and over in my head. I got caught in school with girl jeans on! They aren't going to ever let that rest."

This particular issue pushed me over the limit. It wasn't that bad about the girl jeans, but it just broke me mentally. It was the preverbal straw that broke the camels back. I had to get money and fuck the world!

Colo Dog

I had made the transition to full blown Black Disciple. They just didn't know it at school. Around the crib I made my bones. Nobody knew Colo Dog, until they put the face with the graffiti. I didn't let Cassius or Dave know, until later my sophomore year that I was plugged. I had a mob they didn't even know about from the Met. I never used them though!

I didn't want Bonner brining me in his office for writing on the walls. I was gone before he knew I was Colo Dog. I was plugged all the way in my sophomore year. I still was low-key except for the graffiti I was laying all around town. I hit the buses, trains and the school walls.

My name traveled from North, South, East and West. You had to read my name. Colo Dog from 169th St. When the title, dog follows your name in the streets. This means that you are a beast, in a specialized area. It might be sports. It might be fighting or anything separating you from just a regular guy. I was now a dog, because of my hands and sports.

I would lay those heart and wings and treys down all over the city. Everywhere my feet landed in the city I let people know I was here. Instead of drawing at the crib I was the graffiti artist around town.

They would know my name even, if they didn't know me. One thing about my graffiti I never disrespected or cracked the five-point star. I never wrote BPSK or All Is Well Killer. I wasn't trying to go around and kill Stones. I was just representing who and what I was and my organization.

I was wicked with a spray can and I was an artist too. I'd hit up the Ace hardware store on 171st in between Calumet and King drive. I left markers alone after a while and went to the spray cans, because it was more permanent. I did my part with the degradation of the city. I am sorry for that, but when you're young, you do young things. My shit was sweet though!

I used to spray the heart, wings and the crown. I'd have the III treys, right next to my name and where I am from 169th. Sometimes I'd throw the GD's pitchforks symbol in, because we were all is one at one time. I like that symbol better than the symbol we had.

Most of my classes were with Cassius my second year. I had one with Dave and that was PE. One time I went to school and my first class was Physical Education. Emus, you know I couldn't smell for years. During the time while living with the Harris's I was all out of wack, with my routine.

I had a certain way I went at my day when I got up in the morning. I simply started forgetting things either it was the deodorant or brushing my teeth. This is something I could not do. I had a man stank at a young age.

My Mom used to say when she caught me funky. "Boy you smell like a nanny goat." I didn't want to smell like a nanny goat.

I had to double up to make sure I didn't stank. I was slipping with my hygiene on a couple of rush days. It was a lot of people getting ready for school at the Harris's. You had to wait for the bathroom. I had this big ass nose in the center of my face and I couldn't smell a thing. I learned from Sterling you better make sure you come correct reguardles of what.

This day we were shooting ball in the gymnasium early in the morning at PE. Dave could shoot, but he could take it or leave it. I was rushing to school and forgot to put on some deodorant. Like always I had to be the last one off the court. We had to line up to make sure everybody stayed for class. You know students will come just for the sign in, and then break.

When I came off the court I notice everybody face frowning up once I walked by. You know first it's a whisper. Like the joke was on me.

Out the blue the girls was like, "somebody's musty."

I immediately got warm and hoped it wasn't me. Everybody in the class is looking at me. They didn't smell it, until I walked over by the line up area. Sterling seen this opportunity and blast me one. I could see him smiling and that's not good. He always had a crooked smile before he laid into you.

I kind of faded by myself so nobody would smell it, if it were, me that smelled.

Here go Dave into action while he's laughing, "Col Co aha haa Co ah Columbus smells like he wants to be alone. Hey everybody Columbus smells like he wants to be alone."

I am standing away from the line up and Dave busts that on me. After he said that people started moving further away from me. The whole line gave a chuckle then an all out laugh. Dave was laughing like a motherfucker. Like I really wanted to be left alone. It was a trip, because I was, standing alone, haa heee.

I felt so embarrassed, but tried my best to play it off. "Fuck you Sterling I just played hard on the court. Something you don't know about." Andrea begins to giggle and then everybody else starts laughing at em.

I took a shower after P.E. but the damage was done. Sterling rode me for about a half a year with that one. Columbus smells like he wants to be alone. He told everybody he came in contact with that day that I stank. That was about the worst thing that happen to me my sophomore year.

It wasn't until years later my sense of smell came back. Now I can smell like a motherfucka, especially with this big as nose I got. I should smell something.

Other than that I was starting to build a reputation in school. My hands were wicked that's all I had. That whole year I worked on getting faster. Since I wasn't on any team. I took my boxing to another level.

A few times when I didn't have a change of clothes. I used to skip school go down town to the Mcvicktis, the State or the Chicago theater down town. I went in the mornings. I watched Bruce Lee flicks or any karate flicks to pick things out I could work in my routine.

I'd come home and work on every realistic move I could do. I sped my hands up, if there's such a thing. I was naturally fast with good instincts. I had obtained a lot of hand eye coordination playing basketball, baseball, and football. I mean to tell you, at this point I was nothing nice, boy was I fast. I would practice shadow boxing and doing karate moves, I saw at the movies

I practiced the Ali shuffle with the counter attack, while shit talking. All this must be practiced. Ali was my hero. The way Ali talked shit and handled his business was amazing when I was a shortie. The way he rhythms and how smooth he was in and out the ring. Ali bragged, but backed it up. At this time I only knew him as a boxer. I was a fan for life.

All the other stuff he did politically, I wouldn't find out until later. They didn't show or tell or write about his politics when I was a shortie. The politics and the stance he took on the Vietnam War. The quote that rocked the World, "ain't no Viet Cong ever called me nigga." Money and prestige didn't run him or ruin him. I liked that about him even more. It takes a lot of character for a man not to sell his soul.

His career didn't take precedence over morals. What took precedence were his Muslim beliefs in Allah. He stood on his beliefs before the money and the power. It takes a strong man to fight the government. Now he is the top role model to look up to, for me. At this time all I knew about was he was a great shit talker and fighter. I could do that now!

I harden up my hands by working with sand. Hours on end in the summer in my basement, practicing and practicing. This was before the house burnt down. I saw the results from me practicing. I was literally trying to catch up with my shadow.

One time I think I did catch my shadow. I could've sworn my shadow stopped working out with me. He was out of breath huffing and puffing while watching me workout. It was quick pause; I wouldn't have noticed, if I weren't so fast.

I saw my shadow take two quick breathes, "haa uh haa." My shadow peeped me looking and played it off, by jumping back in motion with me. Harold I hate to boast, but this is how cold I got.

Harold replied, tell your story Colo I already know half of them. You're boys put me up on you years ago. It was hard to believe, but you all tell the same exact stories. That shadow story I never heard huh huh huh, you out your mind Colo.

I laugh and say, "it was just an analogy, but I was fast. One time Slept Rock and I had detention in school with Mrs. Effren. Mrs. Effren was mean and tried to make you focus. Slept Rock, Punkin, Shorty Antwoine and Smokey, we were all in detention. When Mrs. Effren went out the room of course that was our break.

Slept Rock devious ass would kick something off. Punkin and Smoke both had butters. Finger waves were made with your fingers. Pencil waves were made with a pencil and ocean waves were made with a comb. Smoke had ocean waves and Punk had finger waves. They used some sort of liquid cement to hold them in place after a fresh perm.

Slept Rock laid the challenge, "I betcha y'all can't fuck with Columbus?"

Punkin said, "I go with him it ain't shit."

Slept said it again harder this time, "I bet y'all can't fuck with him."

First it was Punkin and I that squared up. They didn't know anything about my skills. Slept Rock ain't fair he didn't warn them. All three of them, were GD's.

I could see the way Punkin held his hands he was no competition. He didn't know how to set his feet. A couple of fakes, a little of snake style and he was out. Slap slap, I barely got him, but he said he was straight.

It was Smokey turn. Smokey stuck in there longer, but not much longer. Two three good smacks and he was out. I slapped Smokey around so quick and fast. His butter was all out of wack. I knocked those ocean waves out of place and he was straight. That's what got him off the hook. I told him, "man I'm fucking your butter up, cool out," as I stand in strike position."

Slept Rock was standing on lookout by the door and says, "here comes Mrs. Efferin".

We all ran to our seats and got quiet. Mrs. Efferin was no joke as a detention teacher. You could not talk, move raise your hand or anything on your own in her class. When you got out of pocket you get more time in detention with her. This is the hardest thing to have teenagers in a room and you can't talk. This is murder on a teenager. This was one detention teacher that didn't fuck around.

She wasn't scared of gangbanging ass niggas. She was old school and wore a salt and pepper natural. She could have been a Black Panther back in the day with her demeanor. She could have been religious. Like my mother, she never wore pants. She was a person who stood her ground. Let's be honest these niggas at the Darobe were intimidating.

You have to respect people who don't bullshit. She was not one to be bullied by the students. There were other teachers and you knew they were scared of the students, not her. It was the men teacher too. We sat down like we were sitting down all the time. You didn't get caught, if you had security.

Once we sat down Smoke and Punk gave me my P's, "oh yeah you sweet as hell with those guns."

Once Mrs. Efferin came back she immediately let us go to the bathroom. Now right before Mrs. Efferin came in Shorty Antwoine wanted to go with me. I told him, "Antwoine you cool, we straight." I liked him, because he had swag about himself. Shorty Antwoine was just a little taller than Slept Rock. He wanted to show he was no hoe. You could see it in his face that he thought he would fair better.

He replied, "naw I want to go."

I couldn't get Punkin and Smoke like I wanted, because they were on the defense. Both of them more like stayed way out of range. Smoke and Pumpkin kept their head way back. Really just trying not to get hit. I got smacks on them, but they weren't sticking in there, so I could get a good slap off. Shorty Antwoine GD Folks thought he would fair better. I really didn't show them much going against Smoke and Punkin.

Mrs. Efferin let us go to the bathroom, all of us together. This is a no no, you can't let goons go to the bathroom together.

We get in there and Shorty Antwoine said, "come on we can go in here."

In the bathroom it was tight and it was only so far you could back up. Shorty was ready and anxious. I said "all right!" I had the reach, the quickness and the style. This is when I knew I was really fast. Antwoine had heart he stuck.

Out the gate he was swinging trying to hit me. He stuck in there and didn't back up. Wrong Answer! I went to the counter method, while bobbing and weaving. I hit him three times off the counter so fast it was a shame yak yakK, yakKK.

Everybody in the bathroom said about at the same time, "damn that was fast"

I was slapping Shorty Antwoine so hard, it was echoing off the bathroom walls. It was the faints and the set up that got him. He would think I was coming one way. That was the trap. I was coming the way I wanted him to move, yaak YakK again real swift. Antwoine would not quit though! After blazing him a few times I said, "cool out Shorty that's enough Shorty." He face turned red and he was of dark brown complexion.

Shorty Antwoine, still wanted to box after the first onslaught. Punkin, Smoke and Slept Rock told him to leave it alone.

They all said, "he's too fast Shorty Antwoine, leave it alone."

I had to honor that he wanted his licks back, but he wasn't going to get em though! Come on I said and we square up, I fainted, now I had him flinching. I fainted again he flinched then, Yak, he swings, yak, he swings, yak yak yak. After a couple of more slaps Slept and Smokey jumped in the middle like referees and intervened.

After both of them were shouting, "it's over it's over".

They grabbed Shorty so I couldn't hit him after the last smack. They looked at Shorty while wrenching at the eyes, with empathy.

His face was still stinging and sizzling from the slaps. He grabbed his face and just held it, while bent over at the knees. His face was burning like bacon sizzling on a grill, I could tell. I just stood and was kind of amazed at my own speed and power in action.

Smoke and Punk couldn't even bare to watch the match. I was slapping the shit out of em. I gave it up to Shorty Antwoine though! The rest of the guys quit before I got started. I would've never quit either. He's got heart. Slept was really impressed at my quickness.

He knew after what he saw and said, "Columbus you are the coldest with the guns. A'int nobody fucking with you".

Now he's really start pitting me against everybody. I used to be like, "Cassius you ain't shit! You know these motherfuckas can't fuck with me."

Slept come back was, "but Columbus they act so tough. I just want to see you fuck them up. Now they got to shut that tough shit up. I got a good memory. I also got a hommie who will fuck them up." Slept is saying this while laughing then says. "Remember when we were in detention nigga, I'll go get my boy, Columbus."

Cassius doesn't know how funny it sounds to me. I'm going to get my younger friend, to get you, for fucking with me. I know Harold, Cassius and Slept Rock are the same people. I always did that call you by your nickname sometimes then your real name. My mother always did that and I picked it up. She called you by your whole government name when when she was pissed. Anyway, Cassius instigated City and I into slap boxing. He knew City was good so he wanted to see who was the best.

Cassius promotes the match and says, "Columbus is cold I don't think nobody can fuck with him City."

I didn't want to go with City because he was my hommie. He helped me settle in my freshmen year like a big brother.

City was like, "I can't fuck with Columbus."

He knows I clown, but I don't start shit. I acted different around City, because he was more mature.

I told Slept Rock, "naw we straight." You had to really practice to fuck with me. I don't think a lot of people came close. City was hearing my reputation around school and wanted to try me.

Now City is known for his hands in the school. He was fast as hell, but we never slapped boxed each other. City was on a smooth as level. I learned a lot from how smooth he was when we kicked it.

Anyway he said, "come on Columbus I'll take it easy on you."

I'm like, "easy on me City okay", we square up. I tell him, "I was sparing you City." City knew I could go, but he had no idea how fast I was now. I got to feel you out, if I don't know how you box. I'm going to be aggressive just to see, if you got defense. I fainted with the left hand and came with a right hook. I only hit him once. When it landed across the side of his face. It sounded off like the fourth, of July fire works, aaayaaaacckK yakkk yakkk. The sound of the slap echoed and had to fade away.

Slept was like, "shit City damn he slapped the fuck out of you."

I slapped City so hard both his eyes immediately turn blood shot red. I got all five fingers on the side of his face. City wore a carefree curl too. After slapping him that hard, his hair juice was left on the wall. I slapped the Care Free Curl juice out of his hair.

City frowned up and wrenched, from the pain. I guess I surprised him with the speed and the torque. After gathering his self for three seconds, shaking off the slap. I didn't swing again, because it surprised me how hard I landed the blow

City face got serious and he said, "nigga you going to hit me that hard?"

He went to work. He hit me like six straight times. It was fast, but none of them was hard as mine. I let up, because I didn't mean to hit him that hard. I just jumped on defense.

I slapped him harder or as hard as I ever slapped anybody up, until that point. He didn't go down though! I hit him a couple of more times to get him off me then the bell rung. We had to go to class.

City went to his class and we went the other way to our class.

Slept Rock was like, "Columbus you slapped the shit of City. He got you back, but you got him cause that was like the knock out slap."

Slept Rock's Cloud

*E*verything started to get amped up. I started displaying my skills in fights. Cassius just was no good he started everything. That's why we call him Slept Rock a rain cloud would stop over you, when fuck shit was about to happen.

Wherever it stopped it was going to thunderstorm on whom ever. Right before the storm you'd hear Slept Rock's laugh. It was downhill after you heard the laugh, eehhhhH eehhh ahhha haaaa. When you heard that, somebody was taking an ugly.

We were in class this time, when the cloud came into the classroom. We had sex education and Mrs. Smit was teaching it. She was talking about the man penis and how it stretches like a rubber band. This had the class tripping. She didn't sugar coat it. Mrs. Smit was cool.

I knew sex education already so I thought. My Mom taught me the birds and the bees. She said a man put his penis in a women vagina. They do it to have kids and that's where you came from through my vagina.

When she told me this I was nine and thought it was nasty. I said to my self if I have to do it. I would only do it twice, because I only wanted two kids. That was then now I am fourteen and very inquisitive about sex.

When I was eight, she told me don't put nobody penis in your mouth or in your butt. She said she wasn't raising any homosexuals. That's a man having sex with a man. She wasn't raising any pimps. You don't beat up no women and make them work in the streets for money.

She asked me, "how would you like someone beating up on me?"

I answered, "It ain't going to happen." That's all the sex education I needed.

I didn't know anything about a woman's body or how it worked. My question where does the pee come come out if you don't have a penis. I didn't know it was two different holes. I didn't find that out, until later. I tried to play off the shit I didn't know about sex, because I was with guys older than me. They were active.

Everybody was in the class already and waiting on the Mrs. Smit to arrive. She was late. Slept Rock got wrestles and started spitting spitballs around the class and at Melvin.

Melvin didn't bother anybody he stayed off to himself. He was on the football team his first year, because he was big. His sophomore year he didn't play. He just wore the Darobe football jacket all the time. He sat in the front of the class and didn't bother anybody.

We were sitting right behind Melvin cooling out cracking jokes. Slept Rock began shooting spitballs hitting him dead in the back of the head.

Melvin said calmly without looking around, "whoever it is better stop before they get fucked up."

Now you know Slept Rock is never going to stop now. He knew he was close to seeing a fight. Now every time he would hit him. Melvin would turn around looking to see whom it was, shooting the spitballs.

When he turned around, Slept Rock would duff the pen he used, for the spitballs and point at me. Every time he turned around he looked at me with a frown he thought it was me.

I'm like oh boy he thinks it's me for real so I said. "Melvin that's Slept Rock I ain't shooting shit at you. Look Melvin I don't have anything to shoot you with."

Slept Rock saw Melvin looked his way and said, "I telling you it's him Melvin, you my man, I wouldn't do that to you."

I get up and showed him my hands and he saw nothing. That was disrespectful to me I would never do something like that. That was Rock Manor shit I am in high school now.

After getting hit again, Melvin turned around and said, "okay I got something for you" and pointed at me.

Cassius smiled, because he knew he accomplished his mission.

He then said, "he thinks you're a hoe Melvin."

Melvin was biting I said, "Melvin don't believe this nigga. He's the one spitting spitballs at you Melvin". Cassius was more popular so I think he just wanted to believe it was I.

Melvin was a big black stud and wore glasses, but he was no goon. Nor was he plugged with the mob. He was just big and played junior varsity football freshmen year. Anyway somehow we get out the room with no drama and we have lunch the next period.

We go to lunch, which was my favorite class. I always got in the line twice to eat unless they caught me. I stole the tasty cakes they had to sell while in the line. Sometimes they gave them to us with our lunch.

Those cakes used to be good than a motherfucka. City used to sell me his for a quarter. Melvin must have been hungry or in a hurry. He was in front of Slept Rock and I in the lunch line. I thought he said forget about, because we caught eye contact, but he said nothing. He knew what he was going to do. He wanted to eat first. He got his plate and smashed it.

I didn't think any more of the spitball incident. We were doing way worst shit to people. All three of us somehow were sitting at the same table in the lunchroom. Melvin was at one end and I at the other end of the table. The tables were long and about twenty students can sit at one table and eat. Like I said, I didn't think anything more of the spitball incident.

The table was full of students eating. As soon as he finished his food he came at me.

He shouts from across the table, "What's up with those spit balls you were spitting?"

I looked at him first and then said, "It wasn't me Melvin it's up to you to find out who did it." Melvin gets up and walked over to me. I look at Slept Rock, Slept Rock is looking back like, damn, he's checking you, nigga with a smirk on his face.

I tried to tell Melvin without losing my cool. "Go sit down Melvin it wasn't me spitting spit balls at you."

As he stands over top of me he aggressively asked. "Who was it then?"

I answered quickly, "you know who it was, now go sit down."

It was only one other guy sitting next to me in the classroom. Melvin still standing over the top of me, while I'm trying to finish my food. I still had time to go back and get another plate before the line closes. Melvin was pissing me off shit lunch was my best class. I was trying to concentrate. Everybody attention in the lunchroom is on us now.

After telling him to sit down he asked, "who's going to make me?"

Next, he pointed in my face. I knew this is just what Slept Rock wanted and said, "Melvin please go sit down, it wasn't me." I could tell, by me not wanting to get into it with him, amped him up. It fueled his fire, he thought he was punking me. I was giving him a chance, because this is exactly what Slept Rock wanted. The cloud moved over his head and it was about to be a torrential downpour.

Slept Rock giving him the eye, nodding his head and urging him on! You see Slept Rock knew I didn't start any fights. The only way to get me to fight you had to come at me.

Again I looked at him, but this time I said, "don't let him get you fucked up Melvin." He grimed and looked like, what nigga? He pointed his finger at my head again. This time Melvin pushed me with his finger in the forehead like I was a mark.

All I hear was, "oooowwh." People at the table urging him on, but it's a trap. I was still sitting down. I really didn't think he would do it. By the time my head got back in the position it started.

I'm hearing, "ooh damn" from the whole lunchroom. I'm explaining it long, but this happen within a fraction of a second. Your mind processes things quickly. Up until the point when he gets blazed I was cool. I made no aggressive move verbally or physically. I was trying to talk him out of it.

After Melvin poked me in the head. I get up so quick and fast and blazed him, bam bamMM. I knocked his glasses clear across the lunchroom.

The whole lunchroom jumped up and said in unison, "damn."

Dude grabs my jacket to keep from going down. He somehow pulled it over my head.

I kept my balance while keeping an eye on the target. I started swinging with straight hook shots. Bam bam bam I hit him fast and efficient. I was connecting while the jacket was over my head. I cleared the jacket on one side and let them go. Bam bam bam, then clear on the other side, nothing but hooks and then he let go of my jacket.

Officers Guy ran over and broke it up by pulling us apart. Once he gets us apart we had to go to Bonner's office. Bonner was the Assistant Principle. He drags us out the lunchroom and I looked back at the students. They gave me applause as we walked out the lunchroom.

We went in the office and Melvin tells Bonner about the fight. Bonner tells us to sit down, until he can get to us. We were sitting down waiting in the waiting area in the office. I look over at Melvin while were waiting.

I see his eye and lip is growing bigger and bigger and bigger. I stuck his ass good flawless victory too. He didn't touch me after he poked me in the head. Bonner comes back and we both tell Bonner our spitball story version.

"Who was spitting spitballs at him?" Bonner asked point blank!

I answered, "It wasn't me Bonner."

I told the truth and he told what he thought, was the truth.

Bonner looks over big Melvin all fucked up and said, "you let this little dude beat you up like that?"

I just looked at him and he looked at me. I felt bad, because Slept sucked him in a little bit. I looked over and told him, "Melvin I told you it wasn't me, I don't do shit like that."

You let them talk you into thinking it was me who was spitting the spitballs. I never said who it was to Bonner, wasn't my business, I'm no snitch. It just wasn't me is what I told Bonner. I told Melvin, I ain't got no problem with you Melvin." I asked him while sitting there, "Melvin did you ever see me hit you with a spit ball?"

Melvin replied, "No"

I said, "you see, you had the wrong person. You got a problem with me for some reason?"

He said, "naw I could've been wrong."

Mr. Bonner looked smiled and said, "it's settled y'all go clean the lunchroom up. I just knew we were suspended, no question. I said to myself, "that's it, clean the lunchroom, I just gave this guy a, ugly."

I think Bonner low-key like shit like that! Some say he used to be plugged before he started as the assistant principle. I could've sworn I saw Bonner throwing the treys up in the hallway.

He had all the BD's around him when he did it. He could've been saying three minutes too. I could be wrong, but Mr. Bonner liked me. He seen me handle my business and he also knew I wasn't going to snitch.

Melvin started it and it was he, who got fucked up. It was no use of suspending us both. He already was punished. He got what he supposed to get. I fucked dude up. He walked around school for two months, class to class, with that black eye. My name was written all over it. The whole lunchroom saw me get down on your ass.

Columbus is the little nigga who will get up and blow your shit out. I guess that was punishment enough. It was only four people who saw when Ebert and I fought my freshmen year. A lot of people just heard about it. Everybody saw this fight front and center. My reputation and legend starts growing. I am no joke!

They knew I could slap box, but fighting is different. How you going to poke a dog in the head? This is what I made the last part of my nickname legitimate. Colo Dog will get up and beat your ass. The only time you can put dog on your name. You have to be recognized as a dog or beast in something. That's how you acquire it and now I demonstrated why. It was no question about Colo I was a dog.

Melvin went to the B lockers and I go clean up the lunchroom first. After our fight they had a food fight. It was food all over the place. Whenever there was a food fight I never threw any food.

I always sat there and finished my food and nobody threw food my way. That means I was almost a made man.

After we amped up the lunchroom with the fight. Someone jumped and yell, food fight. The whole lunch room, got up and threw food at each other. I knew food was too hard to come by to just throw it. There are hunger people everywhere and they were wasting it. I didn't do shit like that. I had respect for the teachers up, until I ran into Mrs. Richards old ass. That's the only thing I got in trouble for was fighting.

I get into it one more time that year with a girl. She was a GD queen too her name was Duck. I guess I had a sign I couldn't see, that was on me. A fuck with him, sign on my back. Like I said, I kept my shit low-key. A lot of people didn't even know I was plugged. Anyway we used to have these big ass peppermints. We'd put the peppermint sticks in our pickles and rock it like that. I was walking out of class one day with Cassius.

She looked at me like I was a mark and said, "set that peppermint out."

I knew right away she wasn't playing.

I said, "girl get out of my face." Slept looked at her and covered his mouth and hunched his shoulders like, damn. Out of everybody she's fucking with him.

She say it again, "I'm not bullshitting, set it out."

I smirked and said, "oh you got to take it baby."

Did girlie mush me in my face like I was a hoe? It was rhetorical yes she did.

Harold says, "no Colo."

Yes she really mush me like a pussy and said, "run the peppermint."

My mind couldn't believe what she had done. By the time she was coming back off her mush I was on her. She was no lightweight, but why would she fuck with me? I just grabbed her, pick her up and slammed her to the floor gently. I was just showing her my strength.

I let her up after the slam. She rushed me with her head down. I pushed her head down in between my legs and applied a leg lock. This girl can't fight and I don't fight girls. I started making jesters like I was going to hit her, but I didn't. I said, "girl you fucking with the wrong one and I let her go."

She gave me the evil eye and said, "that's all right you going to get yours."

She starts walking the other way pointing at me saying, "you going to get yours."

I shout back, "shut the fuck up before I slam your dumb ass again." I never heard anything about that later, I was wondering. She probably went to the table and her Folks said, "oh no, he is no hoe." It was the end of the year and I had made a definite mark.

Nobody was fucking with me and I had a mob. I was becoming more popular than Slept. My fights were one on one and I didn't need to jump on people.

The only other time Sack's girlfriend Washeen tried to check me in the A lockers. She knows I kick it with her guy. Why did she grab me like a hoe? I don't know! She was a BD queen too, her and Sterling sister, was strong arming girls and guys. They were fucking niggas up to be some girls. They were plugged though!

I forgot Dave sister's name, but it was a ring of them. I said, "'Sheen' what you doing? Let me go! Why do you got your hands on me", I asked her. She just grimed and started pushing me into the lockers.

I gave her a chance so I said, "all right Sheen, you won't let me go?" I grabbed her like fly paper and banged her against the lockers repeatedly. I was slamming her one side to the other bam bam bam bam. Now let me go Sheen. She finally lets me go this time.

I started laughing like, "Sheen I am the wrong one, why are you trying me?" I couldn't let her get away or talk to her girls like I am a hoe. How are you going to let the girls play you like a mark? I couldn't do it! I didn't hit the girls as long as they didn't hit me. I thought that was a fair trade off.

The girls went hard at you. These weren't any regular girls. You had to let them know you ain't no hoe. Shit the girls would extort you quicker than the guys would. I wasn't letting any girl strong arm or take my shit.

The inK

I had chemistry in the old building that year. The old building was Parker grammar school. It used to be the high school before Darobe was built. Darobe still had classes in the old building. You had to leave out the Robe and walk two blocks to Parker. It was all right in the summer time, but in the wintertime I didn't like that shit at all.

First, you were in a warm building going to class. After sixth period I'd have to put on winter garments and walk to the old building for class. After that class, come back to the Robe to finish your day. I should've paid attention in that class, but it was just too much.

The only thing I remember doing in that class. One day the teacher slept. He left the keys in the lock on the cabinet where he stored things. I tore him off for the ink. I stole the Indian ink out the cabinet he kept locked.

Once I got the ink I came back to the crib and we had a tattoo party. All the Folks were getting tatted with Folks symbols. I had ink for the whole hood. I had Smiley put the Colo on my left arm. Mike GD Folks from Park Way Gardens, put the treys and the ribbon on my chest. Representing BD to the heart and BD, until I die.

I had the forks put on my leg by Grimes. I stayed on the court and back then the shorts, were real shorts. I had the forks placed so you can see them while I was balling. This was before Jordan came out with his revolution of the long shorts. I just loved that symbol since we were all is one. I had to have it.

I wasn't plugged with the BD's at the school. Ronald, Donald, Eddie & Elgin McDonald were calling it at the Robe. Dauk also had a position. Don Poncho was calling it for the GD's. I was rolling with City boy and his crew of Black Gangsters.

I was rolling with who were rolling with me. All my friends at the Robe were BG's or GD's I didn't know the BD's off of Halsted like that. I kept my shit low-key because I was under the radarscope as far as banging. Most people thought I was still a neutron. I was plugged across State Street going east with those BD's.

Dave was a GD at first so of course I was hanging with him too. You heard me say at first. One day Eddie McDonald had his mob of BD's coming toward the lunchroom. I don't think Eddie went to the school at the time. They were about ten deep.

Dave had his mob of GD's and were about, ten deep. Folks were throwing up like always. Shouting out, all is one, but Dave started throwing down the treys, disrespecting the BD's.

He was the only one throwing down the treys. Slept Rock and I was standing right there looking at him about twenty feet away. We look at each other wondering what the fuck was he doing? We slid back out the way. Dave was cool with us, but when it came to mob action. He turned into a different person. He had a switch he could flip instantly.

Slept Rock and I would just get out of his way. Dave threw the III down and flew the forks again while smiling like it was a joke. I thought he was losing his mind.

Eddie frowned and with unbelievable eyes asked him, "what's up Dave?"

Dave said, "you know what's up BDK", then smiled and laughed.

Eddie looked, wound up and slapped all the shit out of Dave, aYaaakk and nobody moved. Dave didn't think he would do it, but he did. I think he was challenging Eddie for the power struggle in the school. He was trying to kick some shit off GD's against the BD's. His GD's didn't move, because we were still riding all as one. It was head against head.

Dave took the slap and didn't swing back or nothing. He just looked stunned and faded back. His mob didn't move and the BD's didn't move. He just took the smack. Slept Rock and I looked at each other with amazement. I know for a fact. Dave flows like water with his hands and he didn't let them go. Why did he try to kick it off? I don't know, but those BD's had rank through the school and the hood.

I don't know, if he knew exactly who he was or maybe he didn't see him. Slept Rock and I was dumb founded first, about what he did. Next it was about what he didn't do. If I knew who he was, Dave knew who he was, because all of them were off 169th & Halsted.

I always will remember him getting slapped and he didn't do a motherfucking thing. This could've never happened to me. He probably would have slapped me, but I couldn't roll with it. I would have ducked anyway.

I wouldn't have done no shit like what Dave did, anyway. It was either he knew he was wrong and didn't want the violation or something. I never saw Dave back down to nobody before or since.

What happen right then though was mind bending. No mans going to slap me and get away with it. I'm going to move just off my reaction.

I might get stomp, but at least I'm not looking like a mark. The killer part is, a couple weeks later when Dave flipped BD. Slept Rock and I thought that was very strange.

Slept Rock caught me in school and gave me the lowdown. "Colo, Dave flipped BD"

I was flabbergasted and said, "you bullshitting after getting smacked he flipped BD, wow." I never brought that up to Dave, because that was just too embarrassing. I wasn't like everybody else, when you down, kick you.

He knew that was not one of his best moments. I could see it in his face. He had a lot of pride, but I saw it when he divulged, he flipped BD. The part I wanted to know about is; why did he flip BD after he got slapped?

Anyway it's the end of my sophomore year. I was getting popular like Dave was in school. I had surpassed Slept Rock. Back then knowing how to fight was the power. When niggas are scared to try you or they see what happened to somebody who did try you. Now you've got the power. I was going to be the man my junior year. I was even grabbing a few numbers from the girls. I had this print shop class and I printed up cards with my number on it. I gave them out to the girls.

CHAPTER TWO

Larry

*I*n the hood it was different. Everybody in the hood still felt bad for me. They all look out for me until I got on my feet. The get high was free for a long while. I felt funny not having any money to get high. The hood would throw me shoes, shirts and jackets. Freddie, Lace, Lil Todd, Sacks, and Big D kept looking out for me. These are my hood hommies along with a few others.

I really was ashamed to come around. My gear wasn't straight. I was wearing other people gear. Smiley gave me some Jordan's the first ones that came out. The only thing the bottoms were blown out. The top part looked good, but I had to put cardboard in the bottoms. When it rained my socks would get wet.

This kind of fucked with my pride, terribly. One thing that came up out of that was the love and respect for the people who helped us. The things they did for me would endear me to my guys, the rest of my life.

You see we were poor, but the George family had pride. We were one of the poorest on the block for a while. Nobody ever knew that! My motto was, "a man suppose to have his own. He's got to stand on his own feet and not look for handouts." That's what my mother used to drill in me. Here I am fourteen going on fifteen years old and "I'm back on my knuckles."

Starting over from scratch no clothes no money. I'll hand it to the Harris's. They helped us when the chips were down. They took us in off the streets, our whole family. That's the neighborhood coming together and I witness it first hand. Who takes in your whole family?

Living with the Harris, I thought was cool until all the rules. Larry and I used to kick it all the time too even before the house burnt down. We used to always get a game in on the court, throw the football around or play some strikeout.

Before my house burnt down Larry and John used to steal my comic books coming up. One thing about the comic book game, if you slept you slept. Larry and his brother John were straight cleptos, but who wasn't.

They used to get me when I wasn't home. Come kick it and leave with about 80 of my comic books. I checked my comic books at least three times a week with updates. If we had company I'd check my books. I made sure I knew who was around when my books came up missing. I counted at least three times a week. I checked and it was a chunk missing.

I asked my mother, "whose been in here, somebody got my comic books?"

She said, "John and Larry was here earlier."

I would take off running to their house to get them. I end up having to tell Mrs. Emma and she'd look for them and find them. She'd give them back to me, but the condition wasn't the same. I thought I was good at getting them from other people. Larry and John were tearing me off stacks. They could get in the house and take thirty or forty of them at a time when we were living on 169th St.

Larry used to look up to me and often did the things that I did. I was only a year and a few months older than Larry. Larry used to be impressed about how much respect I got on the block. We did a lot of things together.

I think I was to him, what Lil Todd was to me. When I was coming to that, coming out stage.

The fact still remained though I was "on my knuckles." Under the pressure of being a teenager trying to finally fit. The obstacles were tremendous.

I had to get off my knuckles first. I had to get my hustle together. Even though I hated it I went to school mostly everyday. Looking like who done it and in what century. Always being talked about when I hit the door that year.

Oh don't get me wrong I talked about their ass too. It wasn't like I sat there being a dickface. I talked about their ass too. My Mom would probably give me about fifteen to twenty dollars to go to school for the week. I used to just put it in the game room, the first day I got it.

Well I started saving my money up, after the fire and stopped playing video games. My Mom would throw me something for clothes periodically. I had saved up a little loot.

Mom was trying to roughhouse me when I didn't obey. This is before I went and stayed with the old dude. It was time for her to stop physically trying to discipline me. When she got to tripping on me. I would just leave and go kick it with one of the Folks for a while. That's before I went to the old dude house.

Larry and I both were on our knuckles. The Harris's didn't have much either. When you give and you don't have much, now that's a friend. Anybody can give when they got a lot of money.

Well, I hadn't been at the crib for a few days. Mom and I had an episode. One day I see Larry on the block. Larry walks up with his Mr. T haircut. He loves some Mr. T. I remember when Mr. T was a bouncer in Chicago.

Emus and John says, I remember that!

I was really rooting for Mr. T in Rocky III. I hated when he lost in the second fight. You see how he lost. He was out of breath and got knocked out in the third round. This means he had no strategy other than to knock him out.

Other than that I think those Rocky movies were the most instrumental in the era. In Rocky one and two I was rooting against Apollo Creed. I loved when Rocky ran up those steps threw his hands up with all the kids running with him.

When I was a little older I identified with a guy from the gutter trying to come up. He was from Chicago too and now he is on the big screen. Rocky had made it and was losing touch. This guy Mr. T can be me, is what every kid in Chicago knew. Mr. T gave us inspiration. I wanted Mr. T to win. There were some divisions ethically about the movie, but race never played a part for me. It was what I identified with that caught me.

In Rocky four it was cleverly plotted. All you had to do was be an American and you'd root for Rocky. It wasn't one American black, white, Italian, Polish or Mexican who didn't root for Rocky to win. I liked the ending when everyone must respect everyone and we'd get a long. This was during the Cold War. What I took immediately from all four movies is how to work out.

I did exactly what they did in the movie. Mr. T and Rocky were showing me. I did the one-arm pushups. I did the pull ups and sit-ups. Lace and I ran the hood. We'd run up to 179th and back 169th. I was so charged after walking out the Chicago Theater and seeing Rocky. I couldn't wait to get home to work out. I couldn't do the, punching the cow scene. I improvised and would punch a big bag of dirty clothes, hanging from the pipes, in the basement.

Larry was gone off Mr. T he wore the T haircut and everything. He wore chains, but they weren't real. He stomach was ripped up like Mr.T. He used to say all Mr. T catch phrases. "I pity the fool." I see him walking up, before he sees me. I know him from a distants, because he looks distinctive. I knew the cut and he walks bowlegged down the street.

When he saw me he smiled then jogged across the street then said, "Colo I was looking for you."

Back then it wasn't any cell phones and I didn't have a pager. When I got ghost you probably wouldn't see me for a couple of days. I could be anywhere when I left home.

I answered, "what's up Larry?"

He reply's, "I'm glad you here. I'm about to meet this faggot motherfucka in about twenty minutes".

He almost blew me off John's porch. "Meet him for what?" I responded with my arm shoulders and eyebrows hunched up in bewilderment.

He answers, "dude gave me thirty dollars in the game room."

He said, "if I wanted more just call him. All he wanted to do was suck my dick." He laughs after sliding it out sheepishly.

I looked astonished and ask, "Are you kidding? You're about to go with a faggot motherfucka so he could suck your dick for some cash?"

He was quick with it, "Hell naw! I was trying to figure out how I was going to stick his ass."

Now Larry is only thirteen so I get mad as hell at stud. I hate a perverted motherfucka and Larry knows it. He was thirteen, but he could've pass for ten or eleven, he was short.

Larry finished telling me the deal, "he thought I was a young little nigga. He wanted me to go to his house and chill."

Now dude ran into the right motherfucka. Larry was more of a thief than I was. He played like he was stupid and naive and he was good at it. That's one thing about perverts they love to feel in control. They feel good when they've tricked you or pulled the wool over your eyes.

Larry said, "I got to get him, because he's going to get some little kid."

Again, Larry is thirteen, but as a thief and manipulator. He was at least twenty-five.

He said, "before I seen you, my plans was just to find out where he lived. When we got to his house I was going to change my mind. Tell him that's all right take me home. If he wouldn't I would just break once I had got out the car. I would know where he live and come back and hit him.

A few years back it was a predator that had Chicago seized up. In grammar school John Gacy was caught killing up young boys. Our mothers put us on alert for guys like that! I think the total had got to about thirty seven boys found in his crawl space of his crib.

When we called you a Gacy, it was the same as a faggot at the time. That's what we said in grammar school, dude you a Gacy. Except he was another level, this was a killing faggot.

Larry kept telling me the plan and says, "That's why I was trying to find you. I need you to peep dude out and get his license plates. Just be in the cut, laying low. Dude is riding in a brand new Caddy with the vogues and rims on it.

He wore a suit and his hat, was a Dobbs. He's got a real smooth delivery. Colo dude has been working on me. He would give me five dollars to play the games. The next week he gave me ten dollars. Now he thinks I am his friend and he is mine cause he watches me play. You would never think he was a pervert."

I looked at Larry strangely and said, "I don't know Larry"

He tries to convince me and says, "It's going to be easy once I find out where he lives. We stake it out for a couple of weeks and go back and hit him."

My retort was, "Larry we should just rob him when he shows up." Just then the pervert rides up, but spot us first talking. He was early we weren't thinking how he think. Motherfuckas like him got to get there early. They got to stake the pick up point out just in case it's a setup.

He told Larry to be alone, but caught him talking to me. Now I'm sitting their thugged the fuck out. I catch eye contact with the pervert not knowing. I looked hard at him just being on security. It looked like the car Larry just described.

Larry looked and said, "that's him" and the pervert read his lips. When Larry went to cross the street to go get in the car. The pervert looked at me again and drove off. Larry was damn near literally chasing after the car for a few paces. Dude got on, he smelled it.

I told Larry, "man I glad you didn't get in that car."

Larry responds, "Shit I was just going to make him pay, hit him real good." We went and got a beer and cooled out. Larry and I never saw the dude again. He wasn't at the game room or anywhere else.

If, I'd' seen him again I would've probably hit him anyway. That's one thing we can't stand, that's a perverted motherfucka. John Wayne Gacy took a lot of children's freedoms away with his perversions and killings of young boys. This is a clown preying and killing young men. I couldn't get in anyone car whether I knew him or not in grammar school.

My mother said, "I don't care who they are tell them you got to walk."

That means I couldn't go to a lot of places. You can be a homosexual, but when you take a young child innocents. What do you get out of violating a child mental stability with that perverted shit? Your ass needs to be nail to the cross.

Pervert

I tripped on that shit for a while. This perverted shit was rampant out here. My guy Cityboy told me some shit like that a few weeks earlier. He came on the Met to kick it with me one day. He was also tripping on the respect I had around the crib. We sat down and drank some beers. He told me about this pervert he knew.

He said, "one of the Folks was letting this pervert in the neighborhood suck his dick for a bag a weed, drank and twenty dollars."

We still were only teenagers so it's still, perverted shit.

City said, "other than that dude was cool, but if he likes you." City starts to laugh and then say. "He'll get you high, suck your dick and throw you a few dollars."

City would laugh all the way through while telling me the story. I looked at him funny like and said, "you're bullshitting and then asked, he crack at you City?"

City shook his head quick and said, "aw he knows not to crack at me. Lucky D though uahaa haa! I do know the niggas he cracks on, uhuuud uhudd uhuud."

I couldn't believe, for a few dollars, Lucky D would let him get down.

I asked City, "Is it that bad people will do some homo shit, for a few dollars?"

City answers, "No question it's fucked up out here!"

I look at City in disbelief and shake my head.

City elaborates, "they feel like dude doing the dick sucking is doing the homo shit. They're just getting their dick suck for some money."

I reply, "It's all homo shit to me." One thing is for sure a motherfucka a do almost anything for some chips. I need chips, but I rather hustle for mine.

I'm jump ahead since we talking a about perverts remember Jimmie and Tonya Force. They used to receive the paper so I always ran across them when I used to collect. When I came to collected.

He'd always come to the door and say in a deep voice, "hold on let me get the G." Jimmie was about two three years older.

Well I had started selling weed and I let Jimmie know. Now Jimmie was a Stone, but he always seemed strange to me. He'd catch me in say in the deepest voice.

Colo I need a bag of weed. As a matter of fact give me two."

His voice was deep, but his had a different type of deepness. I used to be happy to see him, because he never asked for credit. He had all the money. I used to love me some Tonya too. I never cracked on her, but I'd kick it with him just to see her. Maybe she would crack on me. Anyway he was a good customer and we kicked it sometimes. He would buy and smoke it with me or I'd match him one.

One day I was with Grimes walking toward the Met from his crib and we seen Jimmie. Jimmie said as usual I need a bag Colo.

I sold him the bag and he says, "y'all want to smoke a couple of them with me." He said follow me to the crib. Grimes and I said fuck it let smoke. We heads back to his house. We get in there and he rolls up the weed. He fired up one and took three deep ass puffs of the weed. He then passes it to us.

He goes over and fucks with the music while Grimes and I took a few puffs. He turns on some house music, which was cool. It was the next thing he did that got me. He changed the lighting in the house to some mood lights.

Grimes and I look at each other and start laughing low-key, but stayed cool. Grimes and I were asking each other with just the look, because he turned on the mood lights. He started moving to the music not much, but it was how he was dancing. His face was looking strange and he started making his lips rigid, trying to look sensuous.

When it came to the high point in the song dude started going crazy. He was tooting his ass in the air then he was touching and rubbing his body like a girl. I was trying to see was he just joking, but he kept on for a full minute.

Once he made a couple of more of those faces at us. We got up at the same time and ran out his house, out the colt way building. We hit Prairie and started laughing and asking each other, what the fuck was wrong with him? We were high and couldn't believe what just happened. We were laughing so hard we couldn't get any words out to talk about it.

Next thing we know he caught up and was walking right behind us. We just knew he stayed in the house. We turned around and we were laughing at him and we couldn't stop.

Jimmie said in his deepest voice, "see y'all niggas be tripping a nigga show y'all a little something about him self and y'all get to tripping."

We both said, "Jimmie what the fuck was that, man we don't do no shit like that?"

Grimes was about the same age as Jimmie.

He laughed and said, "hell naw that was some weird shit Jimmie."

He switched the conversation and said, "y'all want to get some forties I got it", in that deep ass voice.

We like, "yeah!"

We go get the beers and drank the beer in the cut. We didn't go back to his house. Before the bubble was over he asked us to keep the incident between us.

We like, "yeah we don't give no fuck. You just dance strangely."

As soon as we shook him we said dudes is a pervert and told everybody we ran into what happened. He is gay or something, but he wasn't like us. Years later do you know they caught dude fucking with a little boy and he went to jail. I knew back then he was a funny acting motherfucka and called it.

It was something I sensed in Jimmie. I only saw it one time before that's how I knew. When I was in the sixth grade this guy named Tramon Pendelton transferred into the school from Tanner. He hung out with the girls and talked and acted like a girl. Jimmie didn't do that, but he did have some of those characteristics I noticed.

Now this was something new to us in Rock Manor. I paid attention to Tramon, because I didn't understand why was he acting like a girl. I never asked him questions I just watched him. He was out the closet, before out the closet was out the closet. There was no such thing as out in the open as a little boy and he was out in the open. I guess you would call it flaming. Jimmie was in the closet, but he had some of Tramon characteristics before he pulled that stunt.

Getting in the Box

*T*hings had to change. I could sell weed, because they knew I could scrap. I wouldn't get robbed for my sack. That's another reason my sophomore year had little bumps. I jumped in the box.

I felt the pinch of not having my paper route. That little scratch was holding me over. Other than what my mother gives me I am short. I had to get in the box. Instead of trying out for the team I had to get my hustle on to eat. I had been thinking about it a while, while I watched City get down in school. This was a decision I was left with after the fire. It was the only answer that came to my mind.

I went to school and told Cityboy. "Man it time to get my hustle on City. Cityboy sold weed, pills, tac and anything else that could be sold.

He was already schooling me just by watching him get down at school. I see him in class and after class handling his function.

He knew my struggle by shaking his head and said, "straight up man I'm going to help you get started".

By the end of my sophomore year I started getting fuck up at school. That's something I didn't do my first year. I was still thinking I was going to get on the team before the fire. I only got high with my guys around the crib. Transformation was complete.

City took me over on 170th Peoria. I had saved a few dollars and wanted to invest in weed. We copped some big ass nick bags from Romey. Either Rome or his wife would serve us. Sometimes we'd hit Rose up in the Colt way across the street from Rome.

Rome bags were bigger, but Rose bags were more fire. You could roll eleven or twelve joints out of a six-dollar bag from Rome. A joint sold for a dollar. You didn't have to be a genius to see you doubled your money. I think I got about eight nick bags and was on from that point. Colo Dog is in the box.

Cityboy and I would walk across the street from Romey after copping. Chill in the back left side of the colt way building. We would chill in the back one with the four different entrances off to the left and roll up the weed. We went up to the top, because nobody lived in those units. City was drinking beer pretty heavy. This started to be right up my alley.

We'd grab about three forty ounces of Old English and about eight books of tops. We'd get bubbled and smoke, while rolling up about fifteen or twenty nickel bags. We'd rolled them up in a building where Folks used to hang out. We'd sell some right there in the building while rolling.

Slept Rock used to stay on the block. He stayed three houses down from the building where we were chilling. This was a ritual after school for a while for us three. Slept Rock knew we were in the building drinking and smoking.

He would stop and check everyday to see, if we were in the building. He didn't drink much at the time, but he kicked it. He'd take a squig of the forty every once in a while. It was his block so he plugged me to everybody around his house. As a matter of fact they knew me already. Slept Rock told them all about my antic in school so I didn't get no static.

I started selling weed at school and also in my hood. The weed was all right for a minute. All I did with the money was buy clothes. I kept a little eating money and was getting up to snuff, with my gear. Weed was helping me get by mentally and financially.

I didn't have to buy weed to smoke cause I sold weed. If it wasn't for weed calming me down. I would for sure, be in the penitentiary. Mentally I was able to deal with what happened to us. I was mentally fucked up at this time in my life. Now that I looked back on it I just didn't know it.

Busting a Stain

*I*t was not easy to talk me into to doing a stain anymore. For a long while Slept Rock was trying to talk me into to doing a stain. I had weed game and was staying on, but this time I fell off. I fell off this time, because I gotten a bad batch. I bought a bunch of bunk weed. It was at least a quarter pound of bunk.

I was selling the weed and people wanted their money back. I sold a bag to Jerri. You remember Jerri she stayed with her aunt? She went to Rock Manor with us. She's light complexion with shoulder length hair and short.

Emus says, "I think her mother died when she was young."

I then say, "I used to sell to her and her aunt weed. I sold them a bag of the bad batch and I saw Jerri shortly afterwards.

She stayed on 168th & Prairie, in the house by the alley. They caught me walking through their alley.

She started hollering, "Colo this is some bullshit give me my money back."

She had the bag in hand and was running up to me. I took off running and didn't give the money back. I probably would've given her money back, but she was hollering and yelling, "this is some bullshit". The only thing I thought about was getting away from the situation so I ran and she chased me. I was laughing at her, because she was pissed off. I ditched her she couldn't keep up with me. After she did that I couldn't sell to anybody I knew.

I got a couple of more bags off to this guy walking down the nine looking for the bus. I walked by him and he looks at me. I guess I looked like I sell weed.

He just asked out the blue. "You know where the weed?"

It was a tall dude about thirty years old with a long beard. I'm like, "yeah I got it".

He then said, "give me two bags."

That was twelve dollars. I gave him the bags and he walked off. He didn't even crack the seal. I jumped for joy, because I watched him get on the next bus. He was just walking through until the bus came. I felt shitty selling him the bunk, but was happy for the twelve dollars.

Anyway I lost out on that batch and fell off. I didn't want to continue to fuck up my clientele. I had to get more weed and at least mix it good weed. Therefore, I could get some of my money back. I was off, until I got some more money to cop.

Cassius was given money for shoes and he spent it all in the game room. He knew he had a whipping coming from his mother. He did not want to go home without the shoes.

Worst, if his father who didn't live with him found out. He was going to get his ass kicked to the other side of the moon. He told me his father was brutal and fucks him up. I felt him he had some of those same whips on his body that I have.

His father came to get him from school to whip his ass one time. His mother called him after a visit to the school. Mrs. Miskel told his mother that he was terrible and runs around with little kid name Columbus. She told his mother he needed to stay away from me. It was the other way around, so his mother didn't want him around me.

Slept Rock got out of it. Right before he got in the car he dropped his keys on the street to get into the house. When he got home they couldn't get in the house. His father brought him back to the school and said he'll deal with him later.

I looked at him get out the car and said, "you're back already that was a quick ass whipping". Once his father drove off! He went back and got his keys that he dropped and told me how he got out of it. He was petrified of his old dude and he thought he didn't have a way out. He had to bust a stain. He was down to one pair of gym shoes.

Slept kept saying, "I can't wear my plastic shoes no more" and start laughing. He decided, since we both were hurting we should do a stain. I never let on to Slept Rock about my criminal past. Slept Rock was fifteen and didn't know shit about stains.

I never told anybody about how we were cut, around the crib. I'm already bred criminally. This was Slept Rock first time planning to do anything criminal. I tried to side step him a few times. Once I fell off with the weed it was easy. Slept Rock plan was to rob somebody so he could get some shoes. I needed to get back in the box. I needed money to make money. People needed weed and I was out with no money, like a dickface. My dumb ass relapsed and put the rest of the money in the video games.

Cityboy had the missile everyday and I knew he would let me use it. He'd let me get it anytime I wanted it. I told City what I was about to do. He didn't even question my motives. He just gave me the missile for the weekend. I kind of didn't want to do it; no I didn't want to do it. I had to come up off my knuckles though! The pressure was on me to survive and be a major player.

I figured the best place to hit a stain and get some money. It was to do it out of the neighborhood. We needed a spot to lay low too. I decided we would do it around my father's house. My girl Roslyn stayed across the street from my old man. We were real cool so when I went over my old mans house. Slept and I chilled over her crib, until nightfall.

I met 'Ros' at the bus stop on 169th & King Drive. She went to an all girls school, Aquinas. Look like she was a Disciple queen, because she wore butter, but in a sexy style. She had a nice developed body and talked fast.

I pulled her on King Drive to find out she just moved in across the street from my old man. Slept Rock and I got high and chill with her, until it was dark. She was the one who pierced my ear the first time with an ice cube and a needle. We chilled at her house fucking with the gun while showing her, some straight teenage shit. We weren't supposed to show her shit.

It was my plan. Slept Rock ain't never did nothing and I had the gun. The sun went down and it was the moment of evil. We left 'Ros' and went on the prowl. We walked across Western. This means we were going into white people territory.

I figured if I was going to rob somebody with a gun. It's not going to be where I'd be kicking it. When we were out looking for the victim. I still didn't really want to do it. I never ever robbed anybody, before not with a gun anyway. I never confronted someone face to face, to take their money.

Now I'm doing an armed robbery. We are wrong, we are wrong and I knew it. I kept passing people up. I just couldn't bring myself to pull the gun out. I'm thinking all this while were out. Here I am, 14 years old, doing an armed robbery. Cassius was anxious. He kept walking past 'vics' giving me the signal.

Yahweh knows, I know; I am wrong for this, please forgive me. I said to myself again, "here I am fourteen, about to do an armed robbery." Again, I knew, if my situation wasn't this way. I wouldn't be stealing or robbing people. At least that's what I felt in my heart.

Every time Slept Rock would say, "lets get this one."

I would always lag back saying, "not him." He wanted to hit women and old men. It didn't matter to him. It mattered to me. One thing I knew. He wasn't getting the gun and we weren't hitting any ladies. I was in control of that and whatever we did.

I wasn't going to turn into murderers, trying to get a few dollars. Armed robbery carries 7-15 years in prison. Murder carries a life sentence. You might get the chair, if you kill someone during a violent crime. Even though were juveniles. We were going to see some auty home, if caught.

You have no control, over what another person thinks or do in these situations. Slept Rock might think this shit is TV. He might start blasting and now we got a murder case. I was too smart to let him have control.

This is where my I Q kicked in, in the streets. I was being smart not just in the books. You most definitely need to be smart in the street, if you don't want to get caught. Does being smart in school translate to be smart in the street? It does in some situations. Most of the time it doesn't, because smart kids don't do armed robbery. We are putting years on the line, for something that's not for sure. Robbing people is hit or miss! You don't know what people have in their pockets!

Slept could've taken the gun and started killing people trying to get a few scribbles. Now I'm an accessory even, if I didn't pull the trigger. I get the same amount of time, because the vic is dead. I knew that back then so he wasn't going to get the gun. Another thing Slept Rock never got any church lessons. It was easy for evil to take over his body. He was conscious less on these matters of morality. I on the other hand would only go so far.

My boy Eugene Williams we called him Bluski Andrea. The one who could step and was sweet at first base. Eugene was in the system, but he had some up side. He was locked up for an L train shooting and killing. He was with three people trying to rob somebody. No that ain't it. They ran into some Stones and Folks pulled out the gun and shot dude. Bluski knew the guys, but wasn't with them.

When it came on the news. They said he was the triggerman. Bluski got twenty-five years for that! I was going to learn from his mistake. Bluski told me he didn't do it he was just on the platform watching. Anyway, you get the same time for being the triggerman or the man standing next, to the triggerman.

Slept Rock wasn't getting the gun no matter what he said. Slept Rock slipped out of his mind on the prowl. He starts chasing behind this lady asking her a question. I saw what he was trying to do and I almost disappeared. He stopped and came back. Once he got back to me I said, "Cassius we can't hit no women, I can't do it. Do you think I'm going to pull a gun on a lady?" Cassius was getting pissed with me. He damn near was begging me to give him the gun.

He said while looking disgruntled, "Columbus, nigga you bullshitting give me the gun, you scared man." He then told me, "I don't give no fuck, if it's a lady, old, young, crippled or crazy. We out here trying to rob somebody it don't matter. Give me the gun." He asked again, forcefully.

I tell him, "City left instructions don't give nobody the gun especially, not to Slept Rock." Those were his exact words. I was the bridge between City and Slept Rock. He really didn't like Slept Rock like that, because we acted so silly in school.

Slept Rock and I was so silly we should've been comedians. It was this guy in our class, that when you asked him a question. He would look to the side and answer you while looking funny. He'd look at you then he'd answer.

His eye and eyebrows would rise. He kind of stuttered. He'd get caught on his words while cocking his head to the side and say what sounded like, "hut but what." He had those series of words when he answered or asked a question. He said that along with head and eye movement. Cassius and I picked it up and went crazy with it.

Cassius and I would go around the school mimicking dude. He didn't have to be around and a lot of the students didn't know what we were doing. We would just go backwards and forwards with it, doing crazy shit. Slept Rock would grab his bag.

Put his eye in the handle and say, "hut butt, hutt butt, hut but what."

I would in return jump on the wall like spider man and say, "hut butt, hut but what."

Cassius would dive on the floor and after the dive, pose and say, "hut butt what hut butt".

In class I sit down and then put my head on the desk, cover it with my jacket. I pull the jacket up so you just see my eyes. Then say, "Hut butt" then pull it back down, then come back up and say hut butt what."

We'd have the whole class rolling. City couldn't stand it.

He see us acting a fool and say, "y'all be doing that silly shit."

I'll be like, "we just having fun City."

Next thing you know we had the whole school doing the, Hutt butt what. We had thug out Dave doing it.

Finally one day City said it and did it. "Hutt butt what" and cocked his head side ways while doing the eye and eyebrow thing.

I just fell out on the floor laughing and saying, "not you City."

Anyway, I told Cassius, "no I got this, you heard what City said." I didn't know, if Cassius would pop, so I thought. I didn't want him to do nothing stupid and get me caught up. He finally had stopped this guy. He was perfect. He had drifted off the main street onto a side street off Western. Cassius was waiting on me to get to them with the gun.

He is stalling the man asking for directions. The man stop and was trying to give him directions. Slept rock was fifteen, but he looked like an eleven-year-old boy. The man was giving him directions pointing back to Western.

Cassius is waiting on me to get up to the vic. I looked around and peeped the situation nobody was on the street. He was waiting forever on me to get up there with the gun.

I was peeping things out, making sure the twisters weren't around. I got up there and he had an old white man sleeping.

I say to myself before I get up to him, "Yahweh forgive us."

As soon as I get there Slept says, "this is a stick up don't make it a murder."

I pulled the gun out and pointed it.

The victim said, "boys you don't want to do this! Think about it, you don't want to do this."

Slept Rock snapped with a stern like devious voice from the pit of hell. "I'll shoot your motherfucking ass in the head, right now".

It was like he turned from a little boy into the Tasmanian devil. The cloud moved over the middle age man head and it started to storm.

Slept said to me, "give me the gun" and reached for it.

I motioned to dude, "with my eyes, my eyes said dude you better give it up. I had a look on my face like; it's up to you. I'm going to give my man the gun. I gestured to him hurry up, by waving the gun without speaking.

I didn't want him to hear my voice. I was in all black and a hoodie like Big D did. That's how he got away from the train job when every one else got caught. Slept Rock scared the man enough with the outburst I saw it in his eyes. The man reached in his pocket and gave Slept Rock the money.

I was just looking like I was going to give Slept Rock the gun, to the vic. I said to myself, "nope I know what I'm capable of doing. I didn't know what he was capable of doing. I'm going to keep the gun. Nobody gets killed unless it's necessary."

My man came out with the money clip.

Slept saw his watch on his risk and told him, "take the motherfucking watch off."

The old man took his watch without any hesitation. He knew Slept Rock wasn't bullshitting. Slept Rock was too loud though and I knew the police would be coming. We were standing right in the alley in the middle of two houses on each side. After he got the items I give Slept the eye. I broke and became one with wind. I left Slept Rock standing there for a second. After my fifth step in the wind, he took off.

We were sprinting back across Western, running like a motherfucka. I looked up and see a police squad car on the corner. I looked closer and there was a policeman sitting in his car reading or looking down at something. I had the gun in my pocket and the vic was down the block. All he had to do was shout out, I got robbed, what bad luck I thought.

To my amazement! We ran right across Western, right past the police car, without the police officer looking up. The police should've saw us running across Western.

Yahweh was with us during our time of deviousness. We were running from the white people neighborhood. If seen running, he would have jumped right on us no question. He missed us by five seconds.

We ran a couple of more blocks and made it back into the black people neighborhood. We ran until we thought we were safe. We went back to Ros crib, but she was gone.

She probably wanted no part of what we were going to do. Remember we were at her crib putting the plan together. She seen our 22 revolver and knew we were on a mission. She's not answering the door.

We had to get off the street so we went to my old dude crib. He was surprised to see me and I had a friend with me. We came in the house and went straight in the room. The TV was in the living room so that's out the norm. He knew something was up. We're talking quiet and splitting up the money up. It was about one hundred and forty-six dollars apiece.

We like, "yeah we straight for a minute".

The old dude shouts out, "what y'all doing, y'all too quiet? What y'all done did, something is wrong?"

Something we got to work on just in case. Got to play it all the way off, nothing out the norm. I looked at Slept Rock and he looks at me.

The old dude shouts out again, "I know y'all did something you too quiet what y'all done did."

I told pops, "everything is cool I was just showing him something pops". This let me know my old dude is up on game.

The next day we both bought new shoes. I never figured I'd be sticking people up. I know I seem foul, but circumstance, environment and your peers can put you in situations to test your morals. Life is rough, for a fourteen-year-old kid faced with grown up decisions. I wanted a pair of shoes and some recop money to hustle. My answer was to rob somebody at gunpoint to get what I need.

No matter how strong the person is, life is a motherfucka. How do you handle shit like I was going through? I smoked and I drank to not deal with my conscious. Once you start doing stains it can become a habit or a crutch. I hit a few more at gunpoint after that, one with Jimmie and one with Kermit off of 169th my way.

Well, after that day every time I fell short. It was always somebody there with a stain I peeped. Every time I bust a stain I knew it was wrong, but then I had the attitude like Pac said, "fuck the world." I tried endlessly to get a job. At the time I was wearing the carefree curls in my head and not the drippy shit. My curl was short and wavy with a little hang time. A Billie D look, to put it in to perspective!

I'd fill out applications everywhere hoping someone would call. Well no one called me for interviews and I was still on my knuckles. I would wrestle with my thoughts when people wanted to do stains. The niggas scheming knew, if I said let's go do the stain. I was game, but they had to talk to me for a while.

They know I'm looking for the escape route and will abort, if it's not looking good. I'm going to keep us out of jail, because I paid attention to getting away. You know the saying. Dude could've been great in business, but he decided to go the wrong way. He could've done anything he wanted in life, but chose crime. The reasons why smart people choose crime? They fall off or they were poor! Being broke without a way out distorts your thought pattern no matter how smart you are.

When I finished wrestling with my thoughts. I was still coming up on my knuckles. I did a lot of things reluctantly, because of my inexperience with life. I wasn't able to ward off temptation. Don't get me wrong!

I knew it was wrong and I still did it. Look what we did for a 146 dollars and a watch. We put our lives and freedom on the line 7-15 years. I knew they were out patrolling looking for us. Slept Rock and I waited a couple of hours watching TV at pop's house then we breaks to the crib.

He got off the bus at the school after the weekend and said, "I got some new shoes now Colo."

He starts styling in them while walking in the school like he's the shit.

Now with the money I went and bought a pair of new shoes, Kangaroos. I got some Kangaroos, because Emus always had some and I wanted a pair. I copped some weed from my girl, Shannell. I used to go to Rock Manor with Shannell. She was in my fifth grade class. Shannell was fine brown complexion with long hair and a nice shape!

My boy Scott was going with her. Shannell moved in our hood, around about in the eight grade. She went to the Manor, but she lived somewhere else at first. She had a younger sister named Pennie. Shannell saw and knew I was selling weed in the hood.

One day she sees me standing on Prairie corner and says, "Columbus when you ready to cop, come by."

I said, "when I'm ready to cop come by!"

She knew I didn't believe her and shook her head yes and said, "yeah I got some weed and I'll give you a good deal."

I thought about what she said that day. I went by her house after we hit the stain, wearing my new shoes. Shannell's old dude must have been the man. The first time she let me come up in the house. She told me to sit down. I sat at this big brown table in the living room. I look around the house and everything was neat. I only could see what was in that room and her mother's room off to the side.

She asked, "how much you need Columbus?"

I was like, "give me thirty-four dollar worth. She went in the back and grabbed me two hands full of weed.

I was smiling and saying to myself, "this is all mines for thirty four dollars?" It was Cessimillia too.

After giving me the weed she asked me, "is that enough?"

I quickly thought to myself, "she ain't up, she's already gave me twice the amount."

I looked at the weed and say, "come on girl you know this ain't it."

She looks at my hand and says, "wait a minute hold on!"

She goes in the back and gets two more handfuls.

I then said, "yeah that's about right."

I didn't want to fuck shit up and get her killed, by her old dude. I knew she was stealing his shit. I peeped where she was getting it. It was coming out of a big plastic clothes hamper and she's not reaching down in the bag. She's pulling it off the top. That means the hamper was full to the top with weed.

Usually, at her house it was a security gate locked with a pad lock. You had to stay downstairs to talk to Shannell. We used to just come by and kick it with her sometimes. The first time she let me up was to get the weed. I walked out her house jumping for joy. I was saying to myself, "hell yeah I am on." She damn near gave me two ounces and half for 34 bucks. It was some Cessimella too.

I couldn't sell the weed fast enough. When I sold fifteen dollars worth I was back at her door. I burnt her up. For some reason now they keep that gate to get out, pad locked all the time. The girls were stuck in the house.

I always was peeping to see when the grownups were gone. I was looking for the Chevy and the Pontiac to be gone. After a while Pennie, her younger sister put her up on game.

I'd come by to cop some weed. Now Pennie is watching all the transactions.

Pennie used to be behind her saying, "naw that's too much Shannel he straight."

I used to be like, "gone get out the way Pennie."

She'd tell me with sass, "naw, you trying to cheat my sister that's too much."

She reminded me of the little girl D on the sitcom, 'What's Happening'.

This is her younger sister, putting her up on game. They couldn't open the door to get out so she served me through the gate.

I never thought that the reason she was hooking me up was, because she liked me. One day I was getting some weed from her and she told me to come close to the gate. She reached her arms through the gate grab me and kissed me through the gate with the tongue. My first real kiss was not expected. Now I knew what to do even though, it was my first kiss.

I practiced in the mirror at home watching how my lips move as I tongue the mirror. I look around the room and say, "Oh y'all didn't do that Emus and John?"

Everybody laughs and says, "nope no tonguing the mirror."

Anyway, I step back off Shannell after the kiss and looked surprised than a motherfucka. I didn't know what to do after that.

She looked at me like, "how about that!"

Ohh! I was a straight lame, with my game. I said, "ahh right Shannell", and walked out. I didn't get any play from her in grammar school, so I was surprised. This was also Scott girl friend off and on too. I didn't want to get into it with Scott and his brothers, fuck that shit.

The well ran dry, after their old dude got onto their game. She sees me come to the door and shake me off. I knew when to come when those cars were gone. I wasn't the only one she hooked up. She was hooking up the neighborhood.

She was my secret I didn't tell nobody she was selling weed. After a while she got busted and wasn't setting it out as much. She had me rolling for a while and gave me my first kiss.

You know what that was my 2nd kiss. My first kiss was from Pia, Emus's cousin on New Years. The year I was turning 14. We were all down in big momma's basement.

Emus's grandmother brings in the New Year at the house every year. This was the winter before the fire. This is the 1st year I didn't bring the new-year in, in church. I knew momma was going to be gone to at least one o'clock in the morning at church.

I had some money earlier to get high. Emus, Pia and Dina went to the store earlier. We had a little money left for the night and couldn't get much. The only thing we had enough for was a fifth of grain. We had somebody cop us some 100 proof grain alcohol. Yep the shit the used to keep the fire lit to freebase cocaine back in the day. We were drinking that bullshit to bring in the New Year.

We had about eight dollars together on New Years Eve. It was just too many of us to get a buzz on anything else. We got a fifth and a two litter Cola. We snuck the drank downstairs, while holding the pop in our hand visibly. We got these big ass cups for the pop. We poured a couple of nice concoction in everybody cup. I went through the first cup and I am bubbled by 11:59.

We were listening to music and hearing the count down on the radio live. When it got to three, two, one someone turned off the lights.

Everybody said it at one time, "Happy New Year."

Next thing I know Pia comes over and say, "come here Columbus." That's the only way I knew it was her. I heard her voice, but I am bubbled.

I say, "what's up?" She puts her arms around me and lays a wet long one on me.

I'm like, "damn oh yeah, everybody kisses on new years, like in the movies." This is my first New Years in the hood. It was a nice long wet one. Before the lights came back on she stopped.

I had no idea she was going to do that! I'm still clueless to why she'd kiss me. My esteem was so low it was a shame. When the light came back on, there was a shit eating ass grin on my face. A few more minutes went by. I knew I had to get home, before my Mom got back from church.

Now I'm sitting back cool than a motherfucka. I drank one more cup of Cola and grain. I didn't want to leave too early, because they were still shooting. When I finished my second drank it was one o'clock.

"I got to go." I told Emus, "I got to get back. My Mom catches me out. I will be on punishment the whole next year."

He said, "okay" and walks me out.

I wanted to go out the back door. When I go out the backdoor of big momma's house, it's easy and low-key back to the crib. All I have to do is just walk down the alley. All the grownups were in the kitchen. I'm drunk and barely holding myself up.

I can't go through the kitchen and let Emus people see that I'm bubbled. I'll mess it up for everybody. I leave out the front door. I got's to go, my legs are getting weak and I feel like throwing up. I tossed down that last cup of drank while thinking about the kiss. I was on cloud nine.

I could've gone through the vacant lot by Pauly crib, but that was extra walking. I took the scenic route. I bent the corner on King drive and was walking down the 169th St block, wobbling like a motherfucka.

Emus, guess who I see, driving down 169th street? My mother is back home from church.

I am like, "shit" to myself. What am I going to do? She already knows I'm out and I'm not supposed to be out. I am already fucked up, with just her seeing me outside. She rides up and park while I walk up to the car nonchalant. I looked at her face as I am walking up drunk.

I got to hold it together and I say, "I thought that was you, that's why I turned around."

I had to wait until they stopped shooting Mom. I am on my way to the store to get a pop.

She snaps, "Boy you know it's too late."

My reply was, "yeah, but they started shooting early and I didn't want leave and get shot accidentally."

She just said, "get in the house!"

Whew that was close, but I believe she knew I was drunk. Back to Pia, I didn't think anything of it, because it was New Years. She never said anything else about that kiss either. I was slow with the girls. This is the one area I needed some advice.

Pia used to where those skin tight painted on Levis. She had a slim body and pretty face. I watched her all the time, but she was Emus cousin. This made her my street cousin.

As a matter of fact I had some boot cut Levis she sewed into straight legs. I gave her a few dollars. Maybe that was an indicator. Sometimes Pia would hang with Emus and I in the hood. I just was slow or maybe now, I'm just full of myself.

One thing I did know two of the finest girls in the hood kissed me. My self-esteem was low back in the day. I'm not a rocket scientist, but if two of the finest girls kiss you. I believe you have something going.

My momma always told me, "boy you are handsome."

The kid's at school tells me, "I am black and ugly ever since kindergarten."

The things I did to try to get lighter. I remember trying to wash the black off my face when I was young. I'd use kitchen cleanser to clean my skin. I'd use all my mother's skin ointments.

I always remember Lil Rich and Rob singing a song called, "Tar baby."

I used to chase them, but I really couldn't do anything, they were Gooche's people.

You know a momma will love her kid. No matter how ugly he or she is. Her words didn't soothe me that much. That's what a Mom is supposed to say. She supposed to tell you, you are handsome.

I didn't have any girlfriends that lasted longer than two days. I couldn't build up confidence. I had smack kisses before, with girls. Pia and Shannell gave me a grown up kiss. My esteem took a spike upward.

Harold Washington

Back in school I started turning into a menace. I was being used for my boxing skills, until I figured things out. People will do things because they know you are the beast. They'll use you create bad situations for you to activate. Cassius, Ronnie and I were trying to rob this guy for a Harold Washington button.

It wasn't planned or something we set out to do. What type of shit is that? Here it is, the first black man running for mayor, in Chicago. What were we doing? We were taking the buttons from people supporting Harold. The buttons were sweet and they had a cold blue color.

The button said, "Vote for Harold Washington." This is a time, when people wore buttons all the time.

It was like we were goons working for Jane Burn at the time. Jane burn was Chicago first woman mayor. Jane Burn tried to change Chicago atmosphere. She lived n the projects for two weeks. Yep she stayed in Cabrini Greens. She had police protection and rode up in limousines. How can you experience what we are going through, if you have those amenities? Once she saw she was over her head she was out.

We unknowingly were muscle for Jane Burn. We were literally taking the Harold buttons from people. One day we were going home after school. We see a guy I knew with a Harold Washington button. It wasn't that we were helping Jane Burn. We just wanted the buttons. I didn't want the button, but I was with other people who wanted it.

We we're walking down 169th toward Halsted. Ronnie wanted the button from dude he thought was a mark. He walked up to the guy to take the button off. Once the guy saw what Ronnie was trying to do. Dude steals on him, bamm and hits Ronnie in the jaw. It was a good punch too. I looked with astonishment.

Cassius got there first and stole on dude. He walked right through Cassius punch. I ran up and came with a three-piece combination. The combination put him down. Now it's three on one, okay, I faded out.

I just made sure he didn't get on Ronnie. It looked like he dazed the shit out of Ronnie. Cassius and I heads up the street toward Halsted. I didn't want the button, Ronnie did. Here I am now doing something real stupid.

Dude hits the ground and Ronnie starts with the stomping.

I shout and say, "lets go Ronnie that's enough." Dave move out, on the Vicelord my freshmen year, popped in my head. I then saw Cassius older sister's Grewsome and Grewsett walking down the block. I called them that, because they always talk shit about their brother. It's no wonder Slept Rock was so mean to people.

It was no love at home for Slept Rock. I didn't like them. One was dark complexion and one was light. No they weren't ugly, but they had ugly insides. They were yelling at us to leave him alone. They take up for him, which was right, but they always shitted on their brother about anything.

Ronnie was piss though my man stole on his ass good. You could see the anger in his face and his lip was bleeding. Ronnie had a look like he could've killed him. Later Cassius and I used to tease him for that getting stolen on by a mark. I had no idea this was going to happen, if I would've known. I would've stopped Ronnie from taking the button. Once it popped off I had to help.

Now this is a black man, running for mayor of Chicago. Everybody should be pulling together. Why are we taking the buttons from people, representing Harold? We are smashing this guy for the button. We just didn't think.

This guy was representing Harold Washington and got whipped for it. Now tell me what's wrong with this picture. I didn't jump for the button. I jumped, because he stole on Ronnie. Before I knew it, it popped off and was over.

I knew the dude and had a class with him the year previous year. He didn't give up his button though! I just knew he was going to tell. He didn't though and I give him credit for that! Ronnie reached for his button and he stole on Ronnie.

That's something I would've done so I gave him his P's. He did look like a mark that should've just said, here you go, no beating. He stood up for Harold Washington and kept his button. He gets major P's for that!

Ronnie didn't respect neutrons and he fed off of them. He was doing the Ebert to a lot of guys. He got me again with the same shit a few weeks later. This time Ronnie was trying to take this big motherfucka chain. We were walking in the bathroom by the lunchroom just laughing and cracking jokes.

Big dude was standing there looking in the mirror. I didn't know Ronnie was going to snatch the chain. That's how it was, when you riding with somebody. Ronnie was a GD and was a good laughing buddy. You don't know what he's going to do or what he was capable of doing. He transferred into the Robe from another school. You are responsible for the person actions, if he's with you. Right or wrong, you got to roll, when it's going down.

Ronnie looked at big dude smiled and said, "aw this is my chain," and snatched it.

As soon as he snatched it big guy stole on Ronnie, bang. Big fella wasn't having it. Ronnie got stole on again after he snatched the chain off. Just like dude did him for trying to take the button. After he stole on Ronnie he was trying to get out the bathroom.

Now just think Cassius short. Ronnie is a little taller and I'm a little taller than Ronnie. Big fella looked soft, but he wasn't having it. Cassius was holding him from getting out of the bathroom. I started blazing him like a mad man. All the way out the door. Once he got out the door. Now everyone in the lunchroom sees us fighting. It looks like it was just, him and I. Cassius and Ronnie faded out the picture.

He was dazed and I was slinging and swinging. I was wide open too late to call off the dog. When security started coming to the scene all they seen was big fella and I banging. Everybody in the lunchroom watched me go to work. I didn't feel good about what I did. As a matter of fact, I felt bad about what we did. It just happened so quickly.

I never was going to help Ronnie take his chain. We walked in the bathroom together to play get like me. Ronnie saw the guy's gold chain and he went for it. He reached for it like it was his. Oh my gold chain is right here on your neck shit.

How are you going to steal on someone with all these goons in your face? This is when the devil moves and jumps into your body. I was just going to the bathroom and next thing you know my demon was activated. This is not my will to be doing this to this guy.

The same thing happened with the Harold Washington button. I didn't know I was going to smash these guys it just happened. Something took over my body for a second. I'm glad Harold won for mayor, despite us under minding him on a low level.

I reacted to the other guy's aggression for stealing on my boy. I had been on Cassius for laughing every time shit went down. He always stood to the side laughing at other people.

I used to ask him, "are you some sort of giggle box, when shit going on you laugh like the girls do? That was only because people were messing with me, you laugh so they wouldn't mess with you".

Now he's gun hoe for smashing people, only thing though! Nobody messing with us any more, we're starting everything. We are the bullies. I didn't want to be a bully and they were misusing my talents.

Before I knew it, it was over, no thinking on my part. Dude didn't trick though! We went to the office and I do remember getting in trouble. We went to detention and Ronnie still had dude chain. I blew dude eye out ugly.

He was big and light complexion with a super shiner. It was like we had it planned, but it wasn't like that. I didn't want any part of that chain. Ronnie had it on the next day in the lunchroom.

I wish I were strong enough to say, "give dudes chain, Ronnie." Ronnie activated Slept Rocks demon. Both of their demons activated my demon. I knew it was wrong, but shit happens. I tried to rationalize it.

Look what happened to me, I ain't got shit. He'll get another chain. I'm all fucked up and life ain't fair. When you look in the mirror though! You can't hide especially when you have a righteous spirit. At my center, at my core, righteousness is there and I can't hide.

His eye was black for two months. Now the school knows I give out black eyes. One the year before and now he's got one. Don't forget about Ebert, he was knocked out on his feet.

Slept Rock and I started fading from Ronnie. He was getting us into too much shit. He had a treacherous demon in him. You can't be with anybody, who is using you like a pawn. He knows I'm a weapon so he's doing shit, to unleashing me. I peeped his game and faded on him.

He's got our future at stake while he's doing crazy things, of this nature.

My momma said, "she wasn't raising no copycats or no robots. Be your own person and don't let anybody ruin your future. You have a mind of your own, use it."

I was trying to graduate and Slept Rock was too. I don't know what happened to Ronnie. He faded too I just don't know in which direction. I'm glad Mr. Washington won despite our efforts. I remembered before the house burnt down. Mr. Washington came down on 169th King Drive frequently, to dine. He ate at the restaurant called Hel lees.

The Return of the Hawk

*H*ere is somebody from the past. Guess whom I see in the lunchroom at the Robe? Slept Rock and I were walking from the back of the lunchroom. We just got through eating. I didn't know for sure when I saw him. This is the first time I'd seen him in seven years. It was like a chilly feeling that whisked through my body.

I stopped in my tracks before leaving the lunchroom. I don't forget a face. I stopped at the entrance and zoom in and ask myself. "Is that the Hawk?" I couldn't believe it.

Dude sees me look and looked back. He was trying to see why I was looking so hard? Slept Rock asked me, because I stopped and starred at him literally. "Why are you looking at stud?"

I answered, "man Slept Rock I never forget a face. My man sitting right there name is William Hawkins."

Dude is still looking at me as I am saying his name. I continued telling him, "that's dude I told you about. That's the Hawk who used to rob me in the third grade."

Slept smiles a sinister smile and says, "straight up, you want to smash him?"

I look at William and squinted my eyes, like my mother did him. I had to figure things out quick, because I got the ups. He is in my domain and I can sic the dogs on him.

That's all it takes is for me to say, "let's smash this nigga" and he's smashed. Soon as I move, it's about three other Folks standing around who are going to jump, if I move. I don't move like that though, if anything, we could go head up.

The Hawk played it off and turned his head in another direction. He figured out who I am, but he says nothing. I can tell, because he looks uncomfortable.

When he sees me again I'm big, strong and I am plugged. I looked the goon part when he sees me again. Last time he saw me I had tears in my eyes. Slept Rock asked me again while we both are looking dead at him.

He hears what Slept Rock said, "you want to smash him Columbus?"

He was close enough so he could hear Slept talking. Now I know he knows it's me because he heard my name. Slept didn't give a fuck, if he heard or not. He wanted him to hear. Slept Rock was activating my demon.

William had to have just transferred in the school. He didn't know anybody, because he was sitting by himself. He was at the first table sitting as soon as you walk in the lunchroom. You know the goons go straight to the back of the lunchroom.

We were looking straight at him. Something in the back of my head said, "naw that shit happened when we were little kids." I told Slept Rock what the voice says. My emotions wanted to smash him.

Something in my head said, "don't do it. You would be no better than him." I listened to the faint voice and told Slept Rock, "come on let's go." Slept Rock was letting me know now he's got my back on anything now. No more of that laughing like a girl, when shit goes down. He knows how I get down and I was showing him how.

It felt good not to stoop to what others will do. The Hawk introduced me to the rackets. I just looked at him while starring and walked out the lunchroom. It's funny after that day I never saw him again.

He probably said to himself, "this isn't the school for me."

He didn't forget me either. He knew exactly who I was I could tell. It ran through his head what he used to do to me.

The Hawk transferred in and transferred out the same day. The Hawk knew he was going to get smashed, but he wasn't. I let it go. I probably would've put him on the team. When you do fuck shit. You never know when you going to run into that person again and then they'll have the ups. That's the main reason I didn't bother people.

Emus, if it wasn't for the Hawk. I wouldn't be one of the coldest guys in the city with my hands. The Hawk helped with the metamorphous. He helped changed me into a beast. My heart was developed because of that situation in the third grade. William Hawkins got a pass that day when I had the ups! Anybody else would've handled the business, with the power that I had. Emus I wasn't going to be like everybody else.

Where's your Heart Pauly?

*I*t's funny when you expose a bully, who is not really a bully. Pauly pussy ass was exposed to me, John. People gave him a little respect because he knew a little karate. He was a hoe at the core. He bullied the shorties in the hood and put them up on stains to do.

I am growing up and I am vicious with my hand. Pauly hears the damage I am doing and doesn't think about trying me anymore. I was waiting, but as I got bigger he got chill. I wonder why?

After I saw Johnny Howard choke the shit out of him. I knew why! Johnny Howard and Rodell are cousins right. I was standing with Rodell on 169th King Drive Street. Rodell liked Evette Pauly sister and was trying to holler at her.

Pauly confronted Rodell her and was getting aggressive about his sister. You know Rodell didn't have a fighting bone in his body, but he had a nice bark.

His cousin Johnny was walking from his house on Vernon to the store. He sees us standing on 169th & King Drive, right in front of the Leather Lounge store. He was about a block away from us. I saw him first, but I didn't say anything.

I let Pauly go with his flow I could have step in the middle, but didn't. Johnny and Pauly were around the same age. Johnny was plugged and he was a massive motherfucka. He stood about 6 foot 7 inches tall.

Rodell was telling Pauly, "I can do what I want Pauly, who are you?"

Pauly grimed him and said, "you'll get fucked up out here Rodell."

I wasn't going to let Pauly get loose on Rodell anyway, but big Johnny was walking up. I wanted to see what he was going to do about big Johnny. Rodell stood his ground, but Pauly was trying to punk him, still. Pauly was all up in his face and Johnny was only a quarter of a block away. Pauly never saw him coming.

Rodell said, "that's all right we'll see."

He turned around and was about to walk away. He looks up and sees Johnny walking up.

He immediately said, "Johnny this nigga is messing with me."

Johnny looked and his eyebrow crinkled up and his face showed a picture of madness. He took a couple of steps toward Pauly. He didn't say anything and reached out and grabbed Pauly by his neck quick as hell. His fingers engulfed his throat securely.

He then asked, yYou messing with my cousin?" This is while looking him dead in the eye, with the grim face.

Now Pauly for years walked up around with karate gear on! Always doing Bruce Lee kicks and talking shit like Ali. This should've been the time he activated some of that shit.

You don't get a chance to do all the shit you practice on a motherfucka. Johnny grabbed his neck. He should've activated all that shit he used to talk about. I was waiting to see what the fuck was he going to do.

Harold, I never saw a guy back off so quickly. He looked nervous and I thought he started shaking while Johnny fingers were around his neck. He eyes were pinpointed and just like a dog that knows they did something wrong. The dog will try to disappear inside it's own body, when confronted about it.

Pauly nervously said, "Oh no oh no Rodell is cool I'm not messing with your cousin. Rodell is cool."

Johnny told him, "you bet not be or I come down to your house and fuck you up."

He pushed Pauly by the neck and released his fingers from his throat. Pauly backed up looking scared.

I look at him and said to myself, "is this Pauly, looking like a pussy? Now I see why he fucked with kids. He couldn't fuck with nobody his age. Oh he's real tough to kids who are four year younger than him. A nigga bigger than him and he's a hoe.

He lost a lot of respect from me at that exact moment. When you're a bad motherfucka, you are a bad motherfucka. It doesn't matter the size. Todd showed me that!

As big as Johnny was I wouldn't have let him choke me and bow out like a pussy. I thought Pauly was going to put up a resistance or something. That's why I didn't say nothing and let him go with his flow. I saw Johnny coming all the time. I knew he was about to get checked. Rodell and Johnny went in the store after the altercation.

Pauly started crossing the street going back to the crib. I walked across with him and looked him in the eyes. My eyes told him the deal. I looked at him with a smirk on my face. The face I made said, that you were a hoe. I didn't say anything though and he looked me back in my eyes. My eyes said, the gig is up Pauly and he knew it. I saw you wuss all the way out.

He just showed me what a wuss looks like. You don't get any more respect and I should fuck you up. I still had, how he used to do Tiger, fresh in my head. He used to sic his German Shepherd on my dog. He was one of those guys I was going to fuck up when I got bigger anyway. I was bigger right now. I was waiting on the next confrontation, but there were no more confrontations.

After we saw that move Johnny did on Pauly. Pauly faded he didn't come around no more. Once people find out you are a mark, it's over. I wouldn't have let Johnny choke me and wuss out like that! I don't care how big he was, you can't just choke me win or lose. It shot around the hood. Pauly is a hoe, no more respect. He got a pass, until I can get at him. I wanted revenge for my dog Tiger.

Hanging with GDs

*A*fter we botched the job at Mrs. Lane I felt shame. I had to escape the Met for a while. I started to hook up with the Folks on Prairie. I couldn't hang with Emus, as much, because they knew I was a thief, I had to fade.

I knew all the GDs from playing sports around the crib on Prairie. I really wasn't hanging with any of them at the time. I had to go through their whole area goon style. I had to box them all to show them what position I'm ranked. I am ranked the best.

After going at Lucas, Sack's Nino and a few others I got it quick. They were GDs, GDs were more on the grimy hustling side. That was right up my alley. The BGDs King, is Larry Hoover. Larry Hoover set up shop and was spreading through Chicago like wildfire. Englewood is where the nation originated, on 68Th & Green.

We all got close when it was BGDN the nation was all family. They accepted me as I came, a Black Disciple. It never mattered that I was the only BD in this circle. It was the Black Gangster Disciple Nation.

This was a combined force under the six-point star. Larry Hoover and David Barksdale, the nation's founder became as one with both nations as a combined force. This is right before David died from complications from a gunshot wound in 1974.

Both kings reigned together. Before David died he passed it all to Larry Hoover. The BD's and BGDs lived in harmony for a short period. This is the period when I banged.

Doing scandalous shit was starting to be right up my alley. The Met wasn't cut like that! My situation had me cut like that so I had to drift off. I didn't want my Folk's to know how I was getting down. I never talked about any crimes I did.

Most BDs hustled or had jobs. They threw parties or something constructive to get money. The Folks on Prairie were into stealing cars and snatching radios for a quick sell. Pauly and Fonz weren't Folks at first. They were just thieves.

Everybody banging from Calumet back East past Rhodes from 167th to 174th everybody was riding B.D.N except for the Stones that were sprinkled through. Prairie all the way to State was GDs back then, in the hood.

We all got along swell, so to me, it didn't matter which one you were riding. We were all were cool. We all knew each other since shorties and we all were Folks. We used to take pride in saying, "all is one."

Scott German and I were the only BDs who used to kick it with the GDs regularly. I used to kick it with Spider G. Nino Dark, Sacks, Grimes was the main thieving clique. We put Bennies that was on the corner of Indiana, out of business stealing all those forties. We just used to have fun and act wild and we still shot ball.

Now these were the real car thieves. Nino, Sacks, Grimes and Eric off of Michigan were the most consistent. It was Tony Owens from the Robe he stole coach Murry car. Eric would get two, three cars a day. He'd park em somewhere in the hood, until he had a sell for them.

One time I'm at Eric's house and we had a car. Butch told me earlier that day he needed the body parts for his car.

Butch was selling dope so that was money in the bank. I told Eric and Eric went and got the car I needed. He jumped out of it when he got around the crib. The twister was hot.

Eric came and got me and told me, "it's all sweet I got the car and it's parked, low-key."

I told him, "you can have the radio and the tires. I need body parts." I needed the hood and the fender and one of the doors. I was the oldest out of all of them so I was running the show.

This game had no honor. Auto boys would get, auto boys, if they saw the car was peeled. Somebody else would steal your stolen car. He was very worried about somebody getting his stollie. I told Eric, because we drinking forties and listening to Eric's black boom box. It was too hot on the strip and we were waiting till night, to break the car down.

I tell Eric "don't go get back in the car, the police is hot." Butch is Red younger brother. He already told me he would give me two hundred and fifty dollars for the parts. I counted that chicken before it hatched. I needed that money. We were getting blowed and I wasn't paying attention. I didn't even know Eric had left us in the crib.

Next thing you know he came running back through his back door.

Eric came in laughing and said, "we had to leave the car. The police chased us up out of it."

I looked at Eric and said, "I told you not to fuck with the car."

He said "I know but."..

I just got up looked at the boom box, unplugged it and walked out the house. I keep doing these stains and I'm not getting anything. I was fed up and took his box and ran all the way home.

They say he was running behind me with the gun, but stopped when I got to Calumet. I didn't give it back either. I told him to give me two hundred and fifty dollars and he could have it back. I'm not doing crimes for nothing any more. You fuck up you lost out, not me.

Nino was the best car thief. Nino looked like a car thief. He was dark, thin and wore finger waves at the time. This dude was a car worst enemy. The cars would start shaking in fear when

Nino walked by one. His sister Theresa was cold too she was just about as good as Nino. This is how cold he was at stealing cars.

Nino, Grimes and Sacks had cars and we'd all go out looking. He could steal a car in twenty seconds tops. Tilt or no tilt he could get them. I started hanging with them, until things cool down on the Met. I had to get money some how so I started going out with the auto boys. I was selling weed but I could get extra helping breaking down cars and looking out.

We went out of the neighborhood riding and looking all in the suburbs. We would be strapped up. The lookout posted up on each corner low-key. The guy peeling the car would go for his. It would be somebody close to them with a pistol ready to pop. That just in case someone came out shooting.

We weren't getting popped, caught or going to jail. The lookouts and the man on point did their job. The police get on us everybody go in different direction. Nobody knows each other. Get rid of the tools.

I'll catch you around the crib, if the poe poes are on us. Stealing cars wasn't my forte either. When I went I was just along for the ride and quick money. That's why I didn't want to learn how to peel. I didn't want to learn bad habits. I was the help break down man and the look out.

Nino came to get a bag a weed from my house one day. I get the money for the bag and before I get him the bag.

Nino says, "Colo look across the street ooh wee I'm going to get it. If it's a tilt I'ma get it."

He could get anything, but a tilt he was out in twenty seconds. It was a 98 or something old school tilted.

I told him, "Nino I live across the street don't do it."

He replies, "They don't know where you live Colo watch out for me."

That's one thing about car thieves, is that they steal on site.

Nino looked at me gleefully and said, "You ain't got to do nothing, but watch out from the porch ColoDog."

He wore me down and I said, "Nino man, go ahead I got you." Nino goes to his car and gets the screwdriver or crow bar. I forget which one. He slides like a cat over to the car and goes to work.

He didn't have any bearings. This is what we usually used to bust the window. This was a quiet way to break the window. By hitting the window with the bearing it would shatter the class.

The bearing didn't make much sound. It just cracked the glass up in a million pieces. Nino tries to bust the window with the crow bar. Yeah it was a crowbar. He was having a hard time getting under the rain guard. He tried two more times, while bending down next to it. It was good he didn't bust the window.

You couldn't see him from the church side of the street. The church was directly across the street from me. He was on the other side of the car, if you were looking from the church. He was bent low out of site. He was about to try again and the police bent the corner. The police see Nino bent down at the car and he was still working. I give the whoop whoop sound.

Nino looks and hears that car engine revving and coming his way. He breaks behind my house through the alley with the crow bar in hand. When he gets to the alley he threw the crowbar in my yard. Police was on his ass though! They jump out the car and give chase. Once they chased him through the alley. I jumped off the porch ran in the yard grabbed the crowbar and ran in the house.

A few minutes later they were bringing his ass back. I'm in the house looking saying, "damn the got Nino." They were looking for the crowbar, but couldn't find it. After a while of looking they just put Nino in the squad car. I thought he was gone to jail. They didn't have a crowbar and the window wasn't broke.

They let him go, but I told his ass, "don't do it". I saved his ass by grabbing that crowbar. You can always make up a reason why you're running.

Harold interrupts, "Hold on Colo I thought this was a story about three boys?" All I am hearing about is your actions and sometimes Emus."

I reply, you already know John and Emus part already. I'm just filling in on what happened to me. John didn't do stains with me. This part of my life I distance myself from them. They don't know some of this shit either.

We were the real menace to society, Andrea. This is a dark time in my life. Look at the training and atmosphere that I'm around in the hood and at school. Look at everything I've been through and I ain't got shit.

I was selling weed, but I'm selling joints, trey bags and nick bags. I wasn't moving weight. This was a day-to-day hustle. I kept enough to eat and buy a few cloths. It wasn't enough for me and wickedness was taking over my mind and heart. It didn't have my soul yet so I still had a chance.

You get three or four starving guys together and it's a volatile concoction. We give a fuck, but don't give a fuck about nobody, but us. You have to reach down somewhere and touch our heart for us to have mercy.

Each one of my guys had great qualities. It was just the struggle of life and being lost. We were the dark shadow in the street. When we went out to rob people I would try and find a reason not to rob you.

Rob is from NY

We were on our way to the gym to play basketball on Michigan one day. We either play at St Colobanus on 171st & Calumet or we go on Michigan, to the Shiloh gym. It was wintertime so we had to go to gym to shoot ball, because it's cold outside.

We see this stud standing on 169th & Prairie and he's got on this cold ass jacket. We didn't know who he was and as we get closer. We see he's wearing a leather bomber with the fur collar. It was sweet as hell. It was a cold night. I had Grimes and Sacks with me.

Grimes asked while we were walking by him, "look at that nigga's coat. Anybody know him ahh hha?"

Sacks and I said, "nope."

Grimes laughed and asked, "what's up, y'all want to get him he got a sweet ass bomber?"

We say in unison, "fuck it let's get em."

That's how quick it happens. It's nothing planned it's on site. We were on our way to shoot some ball and saw a vic on the block. When you're with goons and thieves at the same time ohhooowwweeeeeeh.

That saying is true than a motherfucka, "birds of the same feather flocked together." Grimes had something to prove, because he was light in the ass. Sacks was mad, because Coach Murry took his dream. He wouldn't let him play, because he gangbanged.

Coach Murry said, "he might get shot at on the field. I'm not going to risk the rest of the team." Folks was a star linebacker for the Robe and he was a sophomore.

Folks didn't know how to pipe it down around season time. He was hardcore throughout. He was throwing pitchfork up on the field of play during the game when he made a tackle. I can see him making a tackle and throwing up the pitchforks after the play.

Sacks didn't know what to do after he got kicked off the team! You already know my story and why. I had some foundation spiritually though and my guys had none. It really makes a difference to at least, understand some spirituality, somehow.

We had one common denominator; there was no father guidance. I was a goon, but I would try and find some space for love for people out in the streets. We all agreed to hit him though!

We turned around and starting walking back toward him. We thought he probably was over there trying to visit. Right before we were about to get in motion, to get his ass.

He spoke up, "oh oh" he called out, y'all know where to get some weed?"

He slowed us up, because we don't ask no questions, when we are about to move. We just move. We know he got some money now.

Sacks said, "go see what it is Colo" since I sold weed.

I yelled back at him, "I got the weed. I whispered to Folks, "I'll check him out Folks". Folks hold up for a second while I checked him out."

I walked up to him and he asked, "let me get a bag."

I look at him and looked him in his face checking him out. I pulled out my weed and sell him a bag. I'm checking his pockets out while he peels me off.

After I sell him the bag he asked, "you know where I can hoop?"

I said to myself, "man this guy is just like us, that could be me."

I conceded the robbery at that point and said, "yeah we on our way to hoop now."

Dude told me, "oh yeah hold on let me grab my sneakers."

Right then I knew he wasn't from here, because he said sneakers. In the Chi we call them jumpers.

Next he said, "we can smoke the bag on the way up to the gym." After he said that he goes and get his shoes."

Yahweh gave this dude the ammunition to confront us. I would say sixth sense, but he didn't sense anything. We were three demons. They say evil come in threes. This stud was cool as hell and Yahweh was with him. We were three demons lurking. Those were the only words that rendered us powerless to move.

He was going to smoke the bag with us. How can you move on a guy who was going to buy and smoke the weed with you? It was no need to take his money, but it still was a matter of his coat. He shoots ball though and we needed another player for a two on two game anyway. He goes in the house and we wait on him.

Grimes and Sacks agrees with what I thought and say, "this nigga couldn't be from around here. People just don't go with niggas they don't know."

He didn't know he was going to go away, with the goons. He bought the bag from me. He had about twenty dollars. My cut was 6 dollars and 66 cents anyway. The bag was six dollars. I'd sell you seven joints for six dollars. It didn't make sense for me to rob him. His name was Rob too, how ironic.

It was all going to be my money. It didn't make sense to take his money. Everybody looked at each other and sort of called it off with our eyes.

Rob comes back and says, "my father stays here."

When he went inside we started laughing, because of how he did not know how close he came to being robbed.

We all say to each other, "that boy is lucky."

He grabbed his sneakers and he walked off with us. Just like he said, we smoke the weed on the way walking to the gym. It wasn't nobody in the gym so we played each other in a game of twenty-one. It was good we picked Rob up, because we needed another player to play two on two.

After everybody else was ball out and tired. I played Rob in a one on one. You know I never quit I'll just keep playing until it's time to leave. This guy wasn't no joke. We found out he was from NY. He was a splitting image of me with hops and different shooting angles. He played defense like he grew up playing in the dungeon. We both were trying to talk each other out of each others game.

It was going back and forth. I couldn't get more than a four-point lead. He never led against me. He tied it up a couple of times. It was intense and physical. I edge him 34 to 32. The last shot was spectacular. He's all in my jock while playing defense. I'm tired, but if I miss, he'll have a chance to win the score was 32 to 30.

I give him my game-winning move. I give him the double crossover with a hesitation. At the same time giving him the shoulder shimmy off the first step. Like I was driving hard to hole.

I've been driving all game. When it's time to finish you. I always ended it with a jumper. Most of the time people gave me room to prevent the blow by. I gave him the fake, step back and pulled it. It would've been equivalent to the three-point line with the hand in my face. Sack and Grimes were watching the whole game and doing the commentation of the game.

He defenses the shot by trying to block it. I looked him in the eyes before coming down and say, "game over nigga", while the ball was in the air. He looked back with me to see the result, swishh!

He was devastated. You had to look back and wait. Once going through the nets I said, "Bango nigga!"

He was pissed and said, "run them back."

I congratulated him on his effort. I wasn't going to run him back I wanted that game to burn him. I did the Lando on him.

I told him, "good game, damn good game Rob." He was pissed he felt he should have won. He thought my skills were primitive, but I didn't show him everything. I was surprise he could play to that level and almost lost.

After the game we all went up to Bennies grabs some forties then shot to Grimes crib. Grimes crib was the spot. All the Folks used to come over and kick it. Grimes didn't have to have no money. People always dropped by with beer and weed and whatever else. Don't get me wrong he put in his share, but he really didn't have to sometimes.

Rob gets to telling us, he's from NY. His mother sent him up here to live with his father. He was getting out of hand.

I asked him, "Rob you don't know how we kick it here?"

He replied, "nope."

We gave him the lowdown on the organizations in the hood. We tell him what the colors meant. We showed him how to wear his hat in the hood since he a neutron. Neutrons wear their hat straight.

We were about half way through the forties. We gave him the lowdown. We told him he was probably three seconds away from getting smashed.

Grimes told him, "you said the right thing at the right time", while laughing. We were coming at the bomber and you would've given it up. You were looking for weed and it saved you."

That's one thing, if you were cool, we didn't fuck with you. If we knew you, we didn't' fuck with you. If you could say a name, we didn't fuck with you. If you came through our hood and none of the above was going on, you had a problem.

When we were bubbled and out of money, you got fucked with or robbed. I'm glad we didn't, because I hung out with Rob after that. His father would let him get high in his room. His old dude also bought weed from me.

It seemed simple to go knock a nigga out and get yours. Now I know we were haters and we were lost. We are all teenagers without fatherly guidance hanging with each other growing into young men. Grimes, Sacks, BoeBoe, Spider G. and Nino all to a certain point, were lost.

We used to trip out together and had love for one another. When we had squabble the squabble was on, on our block. Nobody was coming down 169th St. unannounced. This is some of the regret I leave. Once in power we steered a lot of Folks in the wrong direction.

Rollow House was a good kid he went to Hale Franciscan with Lamont and John. This was Lando's and Stagg nephew. He was light complexion like everybody in their family. You knew it was him when he was blocks away, because he walked slew footed.

Rollow was just a freshman going to Hales Franciscan High School private school with John and Lamont. He got good grades and everything. Emus and I were smoking one in the gangway. Rollow came walking through the gangway trying to get by us, while we were smoking.

I grabbed him and told him, "hit the weed." He didn't want to hit it and was tussling trying to get away.

Emus said, "hit the weed" and put it toward his lips as I held him. He took a small hit and I told him to inhale, because he was just holding the smoke in his mouth. I did him like Lace did me. I showed him how to inhale.

He inhaled it and we let him go he started coughing. After clearing his cough, a big ass grin came over his face, like the rising sun. The smile came up slow, but it kept coming.

We just laughed at the time, because he had to smoke with friends. He was coming up under our belt. We felt like we had to introduce you to the game. After a while Rollow started hustling for Lando. After that he was a regular name with the police. After that he dropped out. After that he started tooting. After that he started preaming. After that he started getting locked up.

I felt I had a hand in his fall off. Had we not stop him that day in that gangway? You never know what he could've done. He got good grades at a private school. This of course is hind site after years.

Now here I am a bonifide goon right, Harold & Andrea. I am equivalent to a player who is about twenty-three as far as respect. I'm known not just in my hood. My name is traveling. It funny that's what we wanted. We wanted our name to be known across the city.

We wanted to know like Flucky Stokes, Don Juan, Jeff Fort, Willie Lord, Don Derky, David Barkdale and Hoover, while getting money. The way you get to know my name is to advertise through the city. All of these names are going down in history for leadership.

This is how it happens. The heads will starts to hearing your name, that means you could get a position. Most of the upper echelon heads were locked up. Word is coming out the joint how shit is to be ran, on the streets. I know my name traveled. Again I never was on any list so the only way was to make a mark.

At first I stayed in the shadows because of the G. Now I see your name was getting you locked up. A lot of my guys were getting locked up in the area. Columbus was too distinctive.

I needed shade for my activities so I didn't want anybody calling me Columbus. It's Colo Dog for now on! I wasn't trying to get locked up. I know my name still traveled. When the guys I know does a bit, they talked about the block. You talk about the street life you just left. My name is in the streets and I am a bonfide street nigga, with major heart. I was known and never did a day in the joint.

CHAPTER THREE

Using Restraint

*W*hen people don't know you this is what happens. Remember Lee, "All is well" Lee, Yeah! This was a trip, because dude happened to move in the neighborhood five doors down from me. Now here it is I'm living in this neighborhood for 12 years.

He had just moved around here and I knew he was a Stone. I don't get him moved on, because he stayed on the block. I wasn't like that anyway. I didn't move on guys just, because they were the opposition.

One cold wintery day this stud comes pass my house. He stops and starts throwing up the five. He's got a red hat on banged hard to the left. Now I never bring drama to the house. That was another reason I didn't pay him any attention.

This is where the G stays so I keep things low-key around the house. I'm looking at the fool throwing up five standing in front of my house. I'm really am astonished looking out my picture window.

I was asking myself, "am I daydreaming? Is this nigga throwing fives up at me in front of my house?"

He does that and walks toward his house. I look at the fool as he goes back into his house. I haven't said a word to this guy, but he must think I am a mark. I shake my head in disbelief. It had snowed that night so I had to shovel the snow off the porch and sidewalk. I walked outside to shovel the snow and see what was up with this nigga.

I don't know what made this guy try to call me out. I'm shoveling the snow and here he comes again.

He walks up while I'm on the porch and ask, "What's up nigga?" and throwing his five up.

I grim him and say, "dude you don't know where you are at and who, you fucking with stud. You are in the wrong neighborhood to be holding it down like that. I'm trying to warn him."

He grims back and say, "fuck you nigga, All is Well"

While doing so he threw the treys and the forks down in my face. I really don't know this nigga. How'd he know me and who put him on me? I snapped, "nigga what's up? You must think I'm a mark."

I'm leery, because I don't know what this nigga got and all I got is the shovel. I ask him, "dude what do you want?" This is while I am holding the shovel.

He looks at me standing there with the shovel and starts to back up.

He was while walking back to his house and said, "he'd be back."

I said to myself, "he said be back." I tell him again, "dude you going to play yourself, fool." He goes in the crib. I'm tripping, because this nigga must be going to call somebody.

I call Grimes first cause I know he's home. It is probably some soldiers there too. He picks up the phone and I say, "nigga I need some aid and assist. This nigga is tripping down the street from me. He came to my house. He came to my house."

That was like an unwritten code in our hood. We have to catch them in the streets we respected the parents. He is not respecting me at all at my house. I tell Grimes "I'm about to see what's up with this nigga, right now. I don't know who he's going to call, but soon as he disrespects again. I'm going to smash his ass."

Grimes said, "I'm on my way."

Now I got the .357 that I got from a stain I hit with Boya. I don't mess with it. I got the switchblades. I don't mess with it. I got my brass knuckles. I don't mess with it. Reason why, he stays five houses down from me.

My mother is inside the house. I don't want to be gangbanging in front of our house. I did grab the heater and put it up under the back porch. I did that just in case some niggas rolled up with heat. I at least be ready just in case I have to blast this nigga.

I figured all he's trying to do is get a little rep off of me. He wasn't going to get one off me. I also didn't want to kill him, because he only stays five houses away. I'd probably go to jail, because it's too close to home.

When you can't get away with it, why do it? I just want to smash his ass for doing all that disrespecting. I get outside and size the nigga up. Now this guy stands about 6'3" and I'm 5'11"& 3/4 at this age. You know I didn't give a fuck, about how big you were, John. I am laughing and fucking with John because he said, "find somebody my own size", when we were playing smash em.

I go back out on the porch after I called Grimes and duff the heater. My momma sent me out there to shovel the snow so that what I'm doing. No soon as I do that! He walks back out the house, straight down in front of my crib. He calls me out again. I said fuck it. It's on! I told him, "come around on the side." We go on the side of Kevin Stroles house. I don't want everybody to see me fucking you up on the block.

The real reason was my mother was in the house. I give her much honor, she can't find out just how scandalous I am. Once I get in pit mode I don't care who is around. We get around to the side

71

of Strole's house and I go at him. I get in my stance while trying to crowd him. He's tall so I got to get under him and knock him out.

He saw I wasn't going to back up. I was asking him, "what's up you goofy ass nigga", and started laughing. "I am about to fuck you up." He kept his distant so I couldn't get to him. I start talking more shit, "you a pussy coming to my house. I'm going to fuck you up for that."

He said, "oh yeah", backed up went in his jacket and pulled out a belt with a big buckle on it.

He did it in one motion swung and hit my ass in the head. I froze for a second, because I thought he had a banger. Bango, he hit me right on the side of the dome. How I'm a let this nigga hit me with the belt? I don't know!

He had to be about eighteen years old. Again, like Ebert I didn't think he would do it. The nigga was way bigger than me that means, an automatic heads up. What was you doing pulling the belt out for me man?

Now, I am dizzier than a motherfucka. My knees are wobbly, but I'm backing up fast. I can't let him get in reach with the belt buckle again. I straightened up and said, "you pussy motherfucka."

He's like, "yeah nigga what's up, what's up?"

I said, "okay you want to go like that huh." I retreated and ran back to my porch where the shovel was laying and picked it up. He was chasing me swinging the belt buckle at me on my way to grab it.

I didn't want to grab the heater, because Moms in the house. I grabbed the shovel and go at him and I chased him back to his crib. He runs up on his porch. I see Grimes out the corner of my eye coming up. I play it off so he could come back out. I started walking back toward my crib.

Just as I thought, he followed me shouting, "all is well, all is well nigga", while throwing up the five.

Grimes is coming up from the cut, with the double barrel shot gun. It was blue cold steel, sawed off. He doesn't see Grimes coming and is hollering big shit. Once he got off of his porch and was coming back my way.

I ran back his way and shouted, "pop his ass Grimes." He sees Grimes and the shotgun. He desperately does an about face and breaks back toward his porch. I could see the change of expressions from fearless to desperation in his face. At first he thought he had the ups. He was looked devious and mean. Like he wanted to do me bad for some reason, I don't know.

I give chase and caught him trying to get in his house. I beat him in the head with the shovel about three or four times. I'm beating him on his porch and Grimes is loading up the shotgun. Apparently he just grabbed it and didn't even load it. Thank God, because Lee would be dead today.

I was just saying, pop his ass, but I really didn't mean it. I just seen the shotgun and that's the only thing came to mind. If I wanted to shoot him I would've just got my gun. He was calling me out head up and I knew he didn't have a win. That's why I was laughing at him. I wouldn't even be beating him with shovel, if he'd fought me head up.

I was just evening the score from the belt buckle blow to my head. I knew one thing I would be locked up for murder if Grimes shot him. You know everybody was in the window watching. This is broad daylight on the block.

Grimes loaded the shotgun he tells me to move. "Colo get out the way, I'm about to blast his ass."

The adrenaline is pumping and Lee is a second away from death. I step in front of Lee and tell Grimes not to shoot him. I saved his life. Just as I say that! Gearl comes running up with a chrome .357 that gleamed and glared when the sun hit it.

Grimes seen Gearl on the way past Bennies and told him what was up. Gearl was a Stone that hung with us, because his guys let him get smashed. That's how tight the hood was it didn't matter what you rode. Gearl grew up in the hood so he was cool to a certain extent. Gearl used to strong arm, with us. His old dude was the police so it could've been his banger. The hood came together on shit like that.

Rob was with him when I called. Rob stayed around the corner out of sight watching how we move. He wasn't used to what was going on and stayed out of site.

Gearl runs up and says, "what's up, what's up?"

He's got the missile on him ready to shoot on command. He needed the nod and he was going to get popped. He had the killer grim and his finger was on the trigger. He also saw he was a Stone and it didn't matter.

I look and said, "don't shoot him he lives here on the same block." I'm steady dropping blows on his ass while I'm saying it. He was trying to get in the house desperately. I grabbed him by his coat and pulled him out of his doorway. I then jumped off the porch spinning in the air with one of those wrestling moves. We were body to body twisting in the air. This was some karate flick shit.

While we were in the air I said, "I am the wrong nigga to fuck with stud I told you."

I slammed him to the concrete off the porch, booomhf. It was about seven or eight steps to the porch. I felt the air leave his body when we hit the ground. Now I could really put the mash on him.

By this time everybody and their mothers were probably in the window watching. Here we are standing outside with those thangs bearing down on him. He's getting his ass smashed in broad daylight. I am banging him to the dome. His mother opens the door and comes outside and begs for us to come up off her son.

She yells, "leave my son alone" and picks up the shovel.

Grimes warned her, "get the fuck back and put the shovel down lady."

Grimes was pointing the double barrel toward Lee and he says. "Your son fucked up he's out here gangbanging with no gang."

His mother backs the fuck up quick and I am watching this as it goes down. I didn't want anybody dead. When you can't get away with it, why do it? Sensing how now the situation was going to another level and getting out my control. Right now I can control the situation.

I get up after beating him for a while and shout. "Let's break! The twisters are probably are on there way." We catch the wind. We all separated and met back at Grimes house. Grimes house was about six blocks away. We get to Grimes crib that's when I found out Rob was with him.

We sent him to go get some forties while we chilled. I smoked some weed and trip out about what happened. I just knew my mother was going to give it to me when I got home. I get home and she's sewing on something without a care in the world.

Nobody called the police or anything. Nobody told my mother what happened. I know people were in their window. They saw I had called the killing goons off of Lee. They heard me say don't shoot him. His mother knew he had started this shit. Nobody was fucking with her son!

That day Lee realized he was just a few seconds away from death. He didn't know he was messing with killers. Next time he saw me. He had a lot more respect for me. He saw a killer in the eyes. All you got to do is have those thangs with you and you are now a killer.

You don't have to kill to be a killer. All you have to do is have the will to kill. Having those thangs on you makes you a killer with a killing device. I got this gun and if need be, I will pull the trigger.

A killer is a motherfucka with a gun, knife, ash tray anything that you can use to kill someone. Killing is pulling the trigger and the taking a life with the bullet. I knew at this point how to kill with my hands. I was just as deadly without a gun. The objective is to take a life I could do it with my skills.

Don't think you're not a killer, because you haven't killed someone. All you have to do is have the will and a reason and you are a killer. Don't worry about killing or could you kill, if you haven't. Carrying heat makes it easier to kill someone. All you got to do is pull the trigger.

You can kill a motherfucka with your hands. You are still a killer. You can kill someone with a glass ashtray. You are still a killer. Cain killed Able with a stone. Manslaughter and premeditation is the difference between the chair and jail time. You can go get a gun after an altercation and kill somebody, that's premeditation. That could land you life or the chair.

You kill them with your hands on the spot, that's manslaughter. You'll be out in less than ten. When he is dead, than it's definitely self-defense, because he can't talk anymore. He tried to kill you first or he said he was going to kill you was the reason why you killed him.

Like I said, Cain killed Abel, his own brother. It's in our genetic makeup to kill so we are all killers. We are hardwired. We just have to have the killer in us, activated. That's how it happens. Someone calls you out, not knowing that he plays himself. You can easily activate your killer button when you've been wronged.

I wasn't messing with this guy, Harold. As far as I was concerned I didn't care what he was riding. As long as he didn't disrespect me, he was cool. He could've gone on his merry way without confrontation from me.

The rest of the Folks in the neighborhood would have sweated him. No, he tried to straight up punk a nigga who would've have helped him and almost got killed. All I had to do was activate my killer instinct and he would've been dead. I used my head to keep us all out of trouble. Some people all they need is a reason to kill. Now I'm trying to find a reason not to kill you and it was my mother.

The love for my Mom and what she thought about me. This wouldn't let me activate the demon. My demon didn't activate so Grimes and Gearl demons stayed put. I knew dude stayed there for a while and I never set him up.

Yahweh was with him on that day, because he was on that line of, life or death. I didn't let Lee activate my demon. Had he been on the next block it would've been a different story. The love for my mother and the pain she would experience for my actions, stop the killing. Lee had done nothing to save his life that day. He showed no respect for his life and he is blessed.

All he took that day was a smashing. He still was alive. I saved his life and he was fucking with me. He hit me in the head with a belt buckle. He called me out at my house and thought I was a mark. Here it is I am saving his life at the end of the day. We later had confrontation again, but not to this magnitude.

He never ever disrespected me again. I believe the girl across the street put him on me. Cindy used to stay across the street from me. My boy Hotdog used to go with her. Hotdog and his brother Jim used to be on 171st balling. Hotdog was a GD, but they had broken up.

She tried setting up a couple of guys up who was trying to talk to her for us. We never got anybody though! I saw that Lee used to go over her house before the confrontation.

Cindy gave me crabs so I didn't fuck with her much after that! I wanted to fuck her up. She probably got mad and put him on me. I jumped ahead with this story a bit. This was later on after I started getting some ass when this happened.

I often throughout the dark times played the mediator, from us going to the next level. I learned that from Emus. We were buck wild, but we had to chill out. I didn't want strong-arming to become a habit. I didn't want to catch no cases. It was obvious it wasn't getting reported, because we stayed on the strip.

Right after we robbed you we wouldn't leave. We probably move on the next block. The police never came rolling up with the vic in the back seat pointing us out. I never wanted to hurt anybody, but I had my Folks back. I ain't going to lie. Even when we were strong arming people, we didn't hurt them though.

One punch and they usually paid out like a jackpot on a slot machine. You hit them first and once they see it's time to fold. The shock gets them when they see the goon's presence. This was probably the worst couple of years of my life as far as hating on the next struggling man. No it was the worst time of my life.

It didn't matter if you were G.D or B.D. When we were hanging I had your back and they had mine. When I was hanging with a Stone. You couldn't fuck with him at that moment. I might as well have set him up, if I let that happen.

You had to respect me on that, because it's coming back to me. I'll have to roll with the Stone, if y'all try to move! When there was any chance for us to squash a confrontation. It was usually I who would try to play it cool.

When you played yourself and took my kindness for weakness. I would handle my function immediately without any remorse for you. I think at that age remorse was a sign of softness. When you fucked yourself, you fucked yourself. "The game was cold but it was fair" is a correct term for what was happening.

Disco

*T*he reason why I say that, "It's cold but it fair" saying. I didn't make it up, but it rings true. I didn't move on Stones on site. One time I did, but we all knew we were about to brawl. As a matter of fact I can honestly say, I never set a Stone up. The only way I got into it with Stones. You had to fuck with my guys or me. I saved so many Stones I knew from getting the pumpkin head.

It was a couple of times my number was up. I ran into Darius on the bus one day. We called him Disco. He was deep with the Brothers at the L station on 169th. One day I'm coming home from the Robe on the bus.

For the longest Disco was supposed to be Sack's cousin. I knew they weren't real cousins. That's how Darius made it through the hood at first before he flipped, Stone.

At first he was Folks back when he was eleven. His uncles from Westside turned him Conservative Vicelord. It was some family shit going on so I can understand that! He still was my man. Even though he was a Vicelord. He was my man's before we started banging. Meaning we played sports and rode bikes together. Him and his boy Marshall were cool. This was before he was Disco.

He went to CZS located on 187th this is the school a lot of Vicelords attended. Folks went there too, but it was known as a Stone school. After school they would ride the L up to 169th and smash Folks. The Folks who were leaving school coming from the Robe getting off at 169th & State. If they were catching the L were getting smashed as they got off the bus. Disco was catching Folks nastily up on State. The Folks were talking about Disco at the Robe during meetings, because he was doing much damage.

They were talking about getting him. I never said I knew him or nothing, because he was my guy. I could've been like I know where he lives and everything. I wasn't that evil. I couldn't set my man out; he stayed in our hood. We were friends before this shit. Setting him out never came across my mind. I was loyal to what came first.

He was just Darius to me. He was cold with the hands, but he wasn't as cold as me. He was the closest as far as reputation. His reputation went a little further, because we were the complete opposite. We were different on how we handled the opposition. He kicked the shit off. I on the other hand diffused things with Stones I knew.

That was Disco's opportunity to catch you slipping, if you were Folks. I used to see Disco in the hood and tell him. "Nigga you got the whole earth looking for you." They never thought to look in Folks neighborhood. He stayed in the heart of the land too.

Disco knew my rep was ranked high as far as a tough guy.

He used always say, "Colo we going to have to see who is the best."

This is why Disco respected me so much. He didn't respect too many Folks at all. He didn't care, if he did know you, he'd set you out, if you were Folks. We were cool and we just wanted to see who was the best slap boxer. I told him, "Disco you sweet, but dude my shit is wicked and you know it."

He was like, "come on lets go."

I shake my head no and say, "Disco you sure, let go on the side of my old crib."

At the time we both wore fingerwaves. I looked at his and his was just freshly whipped. We both used to go to Tonie's. Tonie and her sister were GD queens whipping all the Folks and Stones in the hood. It was reasonable to get whipped over at their house. It cost ten dollars for a fresh perm & lay. Five just to get it re-laid.

I give Disco some credit he had stupid balls. He'd go get his hair whip in the belly of the GD's over there on 175Th. I used to be amazed to see him over there getting whipped up. Shit, I was hesitant to go over in the hood. Every time I saw him over there he was glad to see me though. He was over there by himself getting whipped, what balls.

I could've set him up over there too, but I didn't. That to me, would've been too wicked. I never set any Stones up just, because I knew you. I let the Folks over there know he was plugged with me somehow. By saying what up cuz and embracing him, when we greeted. It was neutral ground over her house even though the girls laying the hair were GD queens. Money came first no banging at Tonies.

Disco was branded up to the max with gang signs. He had all the Vicelord's symbols on him everywhere. He also had all Folks symbols branded on him, but in disrespectful way.

Let me put you in the mind frame of what throwing down the symbols, of a person organization. Just think, if somebody reared back and slapped the shit out of you for no reason, out the blue. This is the level of disrespect you were on when you threw down symbols.

Disco loved confrontation, if he didn't know you and you were Folks. He'd throw those forks or treys down so quick. After that he'd be daring you to throw down the V L. He had some of the Folks spooked. He'll have this mean ass scowl on his face and itching. Disco always told us the stories of all his confrontations when we got bubbled.

Anyway, he wants me and he's been, wanting me, he's anxious. I got him, because I always told him when you ready come on.

He used to like, "I'm already, ready."

I used to be like no you ain't. Especially, if he was with Lord Dave and Loukas I wouldn't box him. These were the other Stones in the neighborhood. They looked up to Disco. I already got Lord Dave in wrestling when we were shorties. He was strong though! We had to be by ourselves when this goes down, because they'll lose respect for him. You want to think your leader is unbeatable.

I saw him coming down 169th from King Drive. I was on Calumet walking his way. It was hot day and it was like the cowboy days. We see each other a block and a half away and we both knew today was the day. All we had missing was the cowboy boots spurs clanging against the ground and the theme music, as we got closer. We were two gunslingers with the hands walking toward each other. It was just he and I this time and I knew he would ask.

He asked and I said, "lets go, because nobody is around and you can save face."

He was like, "Colo you talk real good shit, but we going to see, let's go."

We square up and dude was quick. He was coming at me and was ducking sweet when I fainted. All I was doing though was setting the combinations up.

When a person got excellent slap boxing skills. You don't go straight at him. You figure him out first, how he swings. Find out what did he do, when I fainted? Meaning you throw it out there just to see how dude move. You got to catch him off his moves, if he can go. It took me about forty seconds to figure him out.

You see I was a scientist with this shit now. I fainted, but double up with the right hand bam, bam. I was like, "yeah nigga that jaw is burning ain't it?" He comes back at me and I leaned back with out moving my feet. Left foot was leading out.

This made him come in, when he came. I let him lead again with another punch, but staying out of reach. He swings again and I duck up under the next punch real smooth, which left him wide open. I made the snake sound every time I swung. sssssbam ssbam sssbam a three-piece combo.

I smacked his butter all over his head. I started laughing at him like Dave used to do me, when he had me in the cradle. This was very demoralizing when you can't do anything about it. Dave was laughing and having fun, while I am struggling. I picked that up. It makes the person lose concentration when you're having so much fun.

I knocked the cement loose that was holding the waves in and I saw he was immediately frustrated. He's not used to getting hit and getting hit that fast. I am smiling too like I'm playing it. He was trying to go on the offense, but my defense is so cold. Now the next few seconds he's hesitant, because he was getting hit, too quick.

He was open for the 180-degree reverse smack, cause he's amp. I don't bring this out in front of people. You always need a couple secret moves for those niggas with sweet hands. This was a humiliating weapon to your core, if landed successfully!

I see his eyes squinting trying to refocus, he's determined to get me. Granted he hasn't touched me yet. I do a little of the drunken monkey. I faked like I fell off balance and I'm turning my left shoulder in, and the right side of my back is showing halfway. I'm slowly wincing away with my shoulders, showing an opening.

I'm looking like I'm expecting to get hit. Drawing him in to swing. As soon as he took the bait by lounging desperately, trying to get his licks back. I spent back the other way so quick and backhanded him across the face. Bowww, then came with left on the front side to balance me out, bowww.

I'm smiling with a shit-eating ass grin while saying, "yeah you fell for it. Damn Disco, I got you with that", while laughing at the same time. I looked at his face, because he was light complexion with a unique reddish tone. He was orange as a peach when I finished. I could tell he was defeated. I give him the back door. I say, "Disco", while laughing hard as hell. "I'm fucking you and your butter up its over. You are going to have to go see Toni again we keep going."

He was like, "fuck it naw come on."

I reiterate more firmly, "Disco it over, it no where to go from here I am too fast". On the way out the alley I told him, "Disco I took you in the back while nobody was looking. You got a reputation to protect. I do too, but I knew I had you a long time ago. Your fast, but I am really fast." I never told nobody, how I fucked him up with the hands. Disco not only had the reputation, he was the talk. I spared him humiliation.

Every time we saw each other for years later. We both knew who was the best. I taught him a lesson on friendship too. He would greet me with a smile honor and respect before he said anything to anybody else. He would reach over you to give me some love first.

You know how it goes. You shake the most powerful man hand first. It could be ten people out there, but he's going to find you first. After that then, he would shake and speak to everybody else. This is coming from a nigga who really didn't respect anybody.

Every time he saw me it was, "What up Colo Dog?"

He had respect for how I played him. I don't think he would've done that for me. He would've definitely bragged, because that's what he did. He knocked little Jim out with one punch. I showed him something that day, humility. Before we got to that part, this is what happened on the bus.

I was coming home from the Robe and all the Moes and Vice Lords are up on 169th & State. They were throwing down the forks and treys while throwing up the five. Grimacing everybody on the bus. They know Folks ride the 169th St. bus, leaving the Robe. I said to myself, "this is what everyone was talking about."

The niggas from CZS are up here catching Folks slipping. You're not expecting twenty Stones on 169th & State. They would hit you hard and use the L as their get away when leaving. Folks were coming through Folks neighborhood getting smashed then stomped. I got mad as hell, but I wasn't stupid when I saw them.

I didn't throw anything up at first. They were out there about twenty deep. The bus starts to take off and I couldn't resist. Once I get over the bridge they're not going drift that far down on 169th from the L. The L was their only escape.

I throw the treys up and throw down the five when the bus started moving. I see the bus got a green light at the next bus stop. I only did it, because they were fooling ugly on 169th. This is really out of my character to throw the five down, unless I was stacking.

Once the bus started moving I started stacking and I am laughing too. They took off and started chasing the bus. Do you know they caught the bus at the next stop? Nobody ever gets on at the next stop on State Street. This time it is somebody waiting to get on and the bus stops.

I wanted to tell the bus driver to keep going. My pride wouldn't let me do it. I got warm all in my body once I seen it was about to go down. Once he stopped and picked up the passenger waiting.

They gangstered past the bus driver and about ten of them are on the bus. I thought back to when Dave and the Folks smashed dude and how he was shaking after they whooped him. I said to myself, "it's my turn, but I ain't going out like no hoe."

I get up and take a stand so they couldn't surround me. I stand up in the middle of the bus. It was a little shortie on the bus with a bat, sitting right in front of me. My move is to grab that bat then go ape shit. I'm standing next to shortie while looking at them walk up. They start pulling off their belts, to hit me in the head with the buckles.

The first dude must have been a mark, because he started talking first. Its nothing to talk about after you chased the bus down.

He grimed and said "What's up?"

I reply, in a shaky voice but firm too, "whaaat's up with you?" He was waiting for everybody to get on! He did see me glance at the bat. It's only four feet in between dude and I with the belt.

I was watching everybody who got on the bus. I was locking their face in I was going back up to CZS for my revenge. Disco was the last one on the bus. He got his butter whipped with the gold cane and five-point sprayed on the side. He looked and was like surprised, to see it was I on the bus.

He looked squinted his eyes and said, "Colo?"

I answered, "Disco what's up with your guys?" I was so happy to see him. He was calling it over all those niggas.

He played me like Scooby Doo and said, "why you and Sacks chase me that other day?"

I looked at him and turn my head sideways. All the shaky shit left my voice. I had a look of non-comprehension, rotating my head side to side. I squinted my one eye and said, "Disco you better get out of here with that bullshit. You know what's up. Tell your guys what's up."

I am untouchable right now. If they touched me it will be hell to pay. I might not see them anymore, but I know I am going to see you. He knew he would've had to pack up and leave, because we were family. Disco you from our hood. You live next to my Folk's in the next building, which was Grimes.

When we are getting high, we'd stop and get high at Discos' house. He had three little cool brothers they turned GDs though. It was no question what he had to do. It didn't take him long. He thought about it a second too long for me though! It took two seconds then he made them all get off the bus.

He tells them, "he straight get off the bus, he straight, he straight, let's go, let's go".

They were looking at me like, "fuck that nigga Disco, lets smash his ass." They were jesters made like they wanted to still get at me.

Disco kept repeating, "he straight let's go. He stood there until they all got off and said, "I holler at you later Colo."

He had me worried for a second though! He's going to say that shit, we chased him. If anything we busted stains together, but we never chased him. All man after they got off the bus I was relieved.

People on the bus was like, "dude that was close."

The bus driver was a hoe, he didn't say, not one motherfucking word. The people on the bus saw me stand my ground. It was kind of unbelievable. I just sat down and thanked Yahweh for sparing me the smashing.

I would've gone crazy with that bat, I don't know. They would've killed any goodness I had left, if they would've moved. I would've dog hunted Disco too. It wasn't worth it to smash me. We protected him when he was with us, from the Folks. You couldn't move on him as long as he was with us. You got to catch him another time, that's Folk's cousin.

We went buck wild for a minute anybody walking down any part of 169th street got sweated. We were taking your money and valuables. People we didn't know didn't want to come to the terror dome, because of the reputation.

This part of my life I am not proud of it at all. We were robbing stealing, breaking in houses, stealing cars and just about anything to get money. All we were getting was enough money to get high. We blew it soon as we got it. It wasn't worth it.

I was losing my Soul

*A*ny clothes or leathers we would take off the strip. We took turns in claiming what we got. One time Disco snatched a purse. I didn't snatch purses, but I was with him. I used to hate when you walked next to a lady. She looks you over then clutches her purse against her body.

I would let them know they were okay by saying. "Hi you doing mame" and walk quickly by her. I hated it, but the women had reason to, because niggas used to snatch purses.

I didn't want anybody snatching my mother or sister's purse. My sister got her gold snatched at the bus stop. I was never aggressive toward females on anything. I was not with him, but he did it while he was with us. He busted the move, before we knew it.

I didn't think he was going to do it. I know y'all heard that a lot. I didn't think he was going to do it. He shot off like a cannon.

He said it though! "I'm going to snatch her purse" and then he did it."

No plan no nothing we were bubbled walking down the nine. This is what I mean when you're with thieves and goons anything can happen at any moment.

Birds of the same feather flock together. Disco had a strong demon in him. The Stones loved him, because he moved like Folks. He always hung with Folks too. He was charismatic. The girls loved him too.

His demon activated other people demons. He just told us to meet him at the spot. Disco was spontaneous with his hookup and all we could do was watch the play. After he hit the stain he ran to the building. We had this building on 170th & Michigan where we used to hangout.

They left the power on so we would go there in the winter to get high. I could have said, "no not the lady" or something. I was bubbled and was slow with my mouthpiece. I didn't think he would do it. You can't put anything past anybody.

I see him do just like in the movies. He had a block running start. He ran by and left her holding her strap. After he did it I just went along with it. We met him back at the building. He split up whatever he got, after he did it. That's when I knew I was gone. I am slowly slipping away. I could have made a stand. It went through my mind. I could've said, naw that's all right. I don't want any part of that money.

When he came back with the money and started splitting it up. I forgot all about the lady. When hanging with people their decision, is your decision. You get the same penalty whether or not you knew or not. I should've stopped him, but when you are high and young it's easy to go against morality. That shit wasn't right!

The Demon Within

I knew if I had a job or some money coming in from somewhere. I wouldn't be doing this shit. My conscious was starting to bother me. I must say, if it wasn't for the spiritual up bringing I had gotten in church. I would've been much worst. I learned from Rev Bracken and accepted Yahweh and the savior Jesus Christ at an early age.

I had my knowledge of right and wrong guiding me through hood. Yahweh won't put nothing on you, you can't handle. As a teenager each day seemed forever. If I was broke for two days I was stressed. How would I get some money? I couldn't be a leach. Some guys come outside and leach all day. I just can't wait for shit to happen.

One thing I couldn't let fall off was my butter. It's nothing worst than seeing Folks with a starving ass butter. Some guys would wear their butter out. Me, if a couple of strands got out of place I had to get a whip. I was with Rodell and both of our butter's were starving.

Now, if you couldn't get to Tonie. You would just wash out the waves and slick it back, if it was still a fresh perm. That is the last level of maintaining your butter. This is acceptable amongst players.

Rodell didn't have any money and I didn't either. I had cop fair so I had to hold off on my hair, until I recouped.

Rodell said, "if I got the perm he'd have his girl put it in for both of us."

The perm cost seven dollars. I said, "bet I'll knock some at Harvey Collins."

We walked up to Harvey Collins and I'll get the perm for him. Since I was going to steal it. I told Rodell, "you got to be the diversion."

We go in the store and I duffs the perm in my jacket. I didn't know the butcher was in the back in the cut, watching my every move. You see we went in the store dusty. The store wasn't crowded, but it never stopped me from stealing out of there before. That's what made the butcher look harder at me. We look like we were thieves with those starving butters.

I come out the aisle and start to walk toward the door and see the outside. Rodell did good with the diversion, because the cashier wasn't looking at me. All I got to do is step on the automatic door and the door is going to open.

The butcher comes running out the back with a machete shouting, "don't move nigga."

I looked at him and then the machete. I was about to break, but I couldn't put anything past him. He saw I was about to run and he cocked the machete back like he was about to swing. I froze!

He then said, "run if you want to and I'll chop you up."

I didn't take the chance fuck it and stood there and pulled the perm out and handed it to him. He told me to come to the back and he called the police.

Rodell left the store and was waiting for me by the bus stop on 171st & King Drive. The police came and swooped me up. They put me in handcuffs and took me to jail. I see Rodell standing on 171st corner. I'm in the backseat of the squad car I mouth to him to get somebody to come get me.

I was hoping he could read my lips. They take me to the new police station on 171st South Chicago. Rodell went and got Johnny or somebody to come sign me out. He did it and I got out. I gave them an alias and got out. They didn't take my fingerprints so that I got away with it.

The Creeper

I would do things for money, but I wouldn't do the inconceivable things. My counterparts didn't care as much. A lot of times I talked people out of doing something really rotten. People fed off of your weakness and fears with aggression.

You need people to say, "that shit ain't right." Sometimes that's all you need. It was the alcohol tapping into our wickedness. The alcohol was ushering in the demon to creep in and take control. Most things we did we were drunk and high.

Do you know how hard it is to even say those words in my neighborhood? It takes balls to stand for righteousness in the middle of evilness. I saved a lot of Stones that I knew. The only time I bothered people, it was for money. Any other time I would be the moral voice with my counterparts.

Sometime I would make you think I was mark, if you didn't know me. Being nice to people will make them think you are a mark. They figure the reason why I'm being so cool is I'm scared. If you were a bully, you would try me, because I was so nice.

That's how I could release the demon without being drunk. You had to do me wrong first. Now I'm starting to think I am a weapon for the Yahweh. The only time I moved is when you did me wrong. I am the wrong person to do wrong, because I am so cool and dangerous.

Be weary of a cool motherfucka. Why do you think he so cool? It's because when you blow his cool! You release the pain he was holding back. His pain gets released on you.

I think in a lot of ways, if I hadn't been around to make my Folk's think. We would've been in a lot of other shit. We would be locked up for sure. I was the youngest in all my circles.

It would be a voice in the back of my head saying, "that shit ain't right, that shit ain't right." The voice would be so faint. I listen to it sometime and sometimes, I didn't. The voice was getting distant, more and more, faint.

It takes something small to bring me back to reality. The altercation I had with Lee on the block. The love for my mother stopped me from going to a killing level. I would think about her when evil thoughts crossed my mind.

Emus and John, you know when Grimes gets high; he can get quite ridiculous. One time we left out of his crib and we were high and drunk than a motherfucka. Grimes had this small ax and we saw this cat walking by.

I could get grimey, but I can't stand to see any animals get hurt. Do you know dude tried to chop the cat up? Grimes started chasing behind the cat trying to strike him with the ax. The ax was long as your forearm. That probably would make it a hatchet. That cat had nine lives for real. He used up seven of his lives fucking with Grimes.

It seemed each time he went to strike the cat. Grimes just missed by a cat's whisker. I kept turning my head away telling Grimes, "cool out", expecting to see catguts. I got out his way while he was swinging the hatchet and we were blew out. I didn't want any mistakes to happen. I just knew he just chopped the cat in half. Grimes was winding up with the hatchet and swinging, but kept missing.

Grimes was not trying to hear me.

He kept laughing and said. "Fuck that cat I am about to chop it up."

Have you ever seen a cat climb a concrete wall? I saw the cat escape by climbing a concrete wall, no joke.

I shout out, "Grimes what the fuck is wrong with you?" He was really trying to chop the cat up. He was laughing and just missing. Liquor let's that demon creep out of you. When Grimes laughed it was evil like. Now tell me who wants to see a chopped up cat. When Grimes got drunk and high he was just about game for anything. Only thing though he had the nicest side to him. He would definitely give you his last and make sure you were safe.

Another time, Harold we were on the side of my old crib, on the nine. Grimes and I was high than a motherfucka. We probably were drunk on our feet. I had City's 22 that day. The revolver backing, that held the bullets. Well the backing plate was missing on one side. I carried that pistol all the time when I had it.

Grimes asked me, "let me see it Folks?"

I give the banger to him.

He gives me the heads up, "I'm about to shoot down at the bus stop."

I responded, "yeah right." I look down there and it's a lady down there on the bus stop. I thought he was bullshitting. Grimes aimed, laughed wickedly and pulled the trigger. The only thing that save that lady was the bullet fell out the back. Thank Yahweh it would have been my fault. I gave him the gun.

You see you had to hold the gun straight or in a position so it would shoot. It would shoot, but you got to hold it straight. After I seen him do that I yelled, "Grimes give me the motherfucking missile dude, you crazy than a motherfucka." I looked around and see that nobody saw what happened.

He's laughing, "ahuh ahuh ahuh"

I said it again forcefully, "Grimes give me the missile."

He hands it over to me and we started walking down the alley. I said, "man that could be your mother standing down at the bus stop." Grimes's mother caught the bus everyday just like the lady was doing.

This was his reality check cause Grimes loved his mother. Mrs. Tucker was always at the bus stop going to work. She never drove to my knowledge. Grimes took her everywhere when he got a car.

After hearing those words he said, "you right man I'm glad you was here. I glad it was you. I was going to shoot the shit out her ass."

Grimes would never think of doing something like that in his right mind! It's easy for the demon to take control you when you're drunk and bubbly. Evil sets in and takes over your will. I can see when the demon takes over now.

You got to look closely. The look is in the eyes, deep in the eyes. The person being controlled has the same face, but it's totally different. Grimes weren't present at the time the demon took over!

You got to say something to bring them back. When I said, "that could be your mother", broke him out of it. He gave me the gun reluctantly, but once I said it could be your mother. He snapped out of it. He has mad love for his mother.

Now when Grimes wasn't drinking. When we were just smoking he was the coolest dude on earth. When you need something, if he had it, it's yours. It's really surprising when you see a nigga snap.

When someone is fucking with you Grimes got your back. He's one of the first, to move or add and assist. Grimes was all of, 110 lb wet. You still would always want him in your corner. You need niggas with heart not pounds. Just think we were running the streets. Not running in the streets, running the streets as teenagers. We ran the underground. We had become mobsters. We didn't collect protection fees, but we got protection fees. If a neutron had a problem, you would come to us to handle it.

The neutron would drop some cash. He'd lookout for you buy you something to smoke. Hang out with you while spending his or her money. This would be so he could maneuver out here without getting fucked with by the goons.

I would come around, while he or she is spoiling me. This was just so they could see them with me. I see the goon that's giving them trouble and let them know this is a friend of mines. Look out for him make sure nobody fuck with him. A lot of guys and girls did this for me. I could usually squash shit with no squabble, because of the respect I had.

I never started shit or any beef, but was quick to handle beef. I never cased anybody crib. I would go along, if it were the right stain. It was always somebody coming to me with a lick. I know I seemed scandalous, but out of every stain I hit. I turned down at least twenty other potential stains.

How they used to get me is when I got broke. When I was broke I hate to say it, I could stray easily. The devil knew what rock my boat. I was coming up on my knuckles and scraping for survival.

Too many hard legs

I had no girl friend or nothing at the time not even a prospect! That's another thing I'm around all these hard legs. I'm around guys at school and I am around guys at home. I wanted a girlfriend.

Hanging out with hard legs is okay sometimes. I would like to dip off with a girl too. All of my guys had girlfriends being two and three years older.

I was trying o come at this girl name Missy at school. Slept Rock hooked me up with her she stayed on 169th and Green. I got to first base, but struck out after visiting her.

The girls I like, like my friends. All the girls loved Sacks with his sense of humor. The girls at school and around the crib loved Sacks.

Diago had big muscles and before he got kicked off the team. He was a star on Darobe's football squad. I'd be interested in a girl at school and she'll like him. Diago and I had history class together with Mrs. Van Smith. This was my division teacher too. We would be in her class blowed.

Sacks would buy the weed from me and smoke it with me before her class. He could've bought it from anybody, but he waited to see me. He'll buy a couple of joints and smoked one with me in the bathroom.

We had the lookouts while we blew. Sacks had mad respect at t he Robe. He had much more than I had. He was on the squad and he banged walking in the door at the Robe. He was plugged in the projects on 35th ST with those Del Vikings. That's where his extended family lived. After we finished he reach into his satchel and pulled out some cologne. We spray the cologne on us and then went to class and chilled, until the class started.

Sacks would have on his shades looking cool and hiding his red eyes from the teacher. Mrs. Van Smith would come in the room and tell him to take them off. Once she notice he had them on! Sacks tell her he didn't want to take them off. He would tell her this while laughing sheepishly. The girls would be giggling, because they knew he was high.

Mrs. Van Smith tells him to get out, if he didn't want to take them off.

He just got up and said, "this all it takes to get out of class. I'm coming with shades tomorrow."

The girl loved him. They all busted up. Mrs. Van Smith would put him out though. I'd got this girl number in my typing class named Roberta. I'd be trying to work on the girl. I call her and talk on the phone.

Next thing you know I go by Sacks crib. I see her at his crib after school. I'm sitting on Folks porch and he comes on the porch. He let me know he just bang this broad from school. He says hold on she's coming out. She comes out and cracks my face open. I looked at her funny, because I thought I was making headway. Sacks were running through the girls at the Robe.

Sacks already had a kid when we were in school. I just sucked it up though when shit like that happened. If you liked him, I didn't want you anyway. How can I go with a girl who I know, likes my friend?

Off the Snide

A blessing in disguise is that I stayed a virgin so long. Another thing is I never had a girl friend, until late teens. I could never get myself to say when I was with a girl. Give me that poonany. Let's fuck, can I have some. Lets make love, what do you say. What, if she says yes then, what do I do?

I'll hang out with a girl all day and sex wouldn't come up. I can be grabbing the titties even kissing you. It was one thing holding me back though! I was a virgin. The only way I was going to get me some pussy.

A girl would have to get butt naked and tell me to put it in her, maybe. One time that happen and I still didn't take advantage. It was a different circumstance I'll tell you about that later. I really didn't know what to do.

I used to mess with Darshon and Gwenivere. Those are the girls I'd feel on their booty. I'd go by Gwenivere house and just talk to her. She had the biggest booty in grammar school. I went by a lot of girls house to talk to them.

Evon Cloverton probably would've given me some, but I just didn't ask. I had her upstairs in the vacant apartment above my crib on the Met. I always went upstairs, if I wanted to get high in the vacant apartment. Evon came up there with me to get high when Mom was gone.

I was nervous, but tried to play cool. She could tell, I think, because she was looking at me funny. She then pulled her titties out and I fondled them and sucked them. She had some big titties and she wasn't bad at all. I think after she seen I didn't know what I was doing. It turned her off!

After the drank and the high was gone, she left shortly afterwards. I was straight I sucked some titties I'm getting closer. I just wouldn't reach for the snap on her pants. What was I going to do, once I get her pants off? William was up for action, but my anxiety would take over my mouth!

. It was a few girls like that; it went the same way! I didn't know what I was doing and didn't want to be no scrub. The girls talk about you when you were a scrub. What was I going to do, if somebody got pregnant? I had nothing, my kid's life would be worst than mines. I got a rubber, but what, if it bust. All this shit would be going through my mind.

Finally, one day Rodell and I were hanging. Rodell always told me the girls he had banged. Rodell would have pussy on his fingers in grammar school. He'd have the pussy scent from him finger fucking a girl. Me not knowing, he tells me to smell his fingers.

After I smell it he'd asked, "What do that smell like?"

I would back up and say, "I don't know, it smells funny."

He would bust out laughing, "it's pussy. I just got through finger fucking woo woo woo".

Yeah, it was a time finger fucking was the shit.

Rodell was trying to get me some nookie that day. He knew I wasn't getting any ass, because I told him. Rodell was getting pussy ever since he was in grammar school. All the girls were on

Rodell, old light skin ass, with the red hair. Rodell is my oldest friend. I've known Rodell ever since kindergarten.

When we were younger. His old dude Mr. Ward work somewhere where he got those glazed donuts daily. I would go over to Rodell house at lunch break at school just for one of those donuts. He'd have three or four-dozen boxes of donuts sitting on the counter. I ate at the school, but sometime I would go with him for lunch.

I wanted to get one of those donuts. It was worth the trip. When you little those donuts be big as hell. We had to make sure we got back to the school before the after lunch bell ring.

Rodell couldn't run fast. I had to hold his hand so he could keep up with me. We had to get there and back before the hour lunch had past. When he was a shortie, he split his knee or something. He couldn't run fast at all. This is when we were in the first grade.

I showed him how to hold his fist when he punched. He could skate his ass off though, but couldn't play any sports. When our church had skating parties. Rodell used to go with us. He skate backwards styling doing all the skating moves. He had me in the skating department.

I could only go forward and I fell all the time. I fell in front of one guy and he tried to jump over me. He almost made it, but the wheel clipped me in the head. Bam it almost knocked me out. Rodell came over and helped me off the floor. Yeah he could skate and play the girls.

The girls were on his tip. He was into girls a long time before I was into girls. He had a girl friend named Adrian that went to the Manor for the longest. I was into girls, but he was into them literally.

Anyway Rodell says, "I am about to go get some pussy after we finish getting high."

I said, "oh yeah!"

He then said, "she got a friend over there, if you want I'll get you some pussy."

I looked at him like, for real and said, "how she look?" He looked back at me and started laughing.

I said it again, "how she look Rodell?" Rodell couldn't stop laughing. I said, "I'm straight she must be a boogaloo."

He then said, "naw man she got some ass and some big breast. It's her face, her face" and he started laughing again. Rodell finally stopped laughing and said, "dude lets just go over there and see what happens, if you ain't doing shit."

I wasn't doing shit so we walk over her house. We stopped at the store and grabbed some more beer. We had to wait a while to find somebody to cop. He bought the beer and I had the weed. I get over to their house and she is not as pretty as I would like. After a couple of drinks Rodell talked me into hitting her.

I guess that's why I didn't get any pussy. I wanted me a fine ass women. All the fine ass women are taken. I could've been got me a boogaloo. I expected more for me. We get to drinking beer and I didn't say a word about fucking. Rodell took her off to the side to ask her. I guess he told her my boy wants to fuck you. I am suave I got a fresh butter and a fresh pair of bucks. I am creased up so I do look like somebody.

She stops looks back at and over me and told him, "yeah she'd fuck me."

'Row' comes back smiling and said, "you about to get some ass".

I'm sitting there nervous, because I don't know what to do. Now I know I'm getting some pussy and I am flushed. How do I go at her first, grab her titties? I don't even know her.

I didn't want to kiss her so what do I do? I drank a couple of more beers, while we were sitting in the hallway. We couldn't smoke inside so we were in her hallway. We smoked one more joint and Rodell goes inside to do his thang.

It was just she and I left in the hallway. She basically started guiding me through it. I was laying down with her in the hallway,

I was scared to pull William out. I didn't know I was a catch. My body was chiseled fingerwaves laid. My gear was straight, because I getting my wardrobe back together. She pulled it out and I put the rubber on me. She was aggressive and saw that I was hesitant. She got on top of me while lying on the floor and started riding. I busted quick and didn't know what to do after that! I took the rubber off and pulled my pants up and cooled out with her.

I finished the drink with her and didn't say much of nothing.

Rodell came back all giddy and asked, "did you fuck, did you fuck?"

I was like, "yeah Rodell."

He started smiling and said, "you finally got you some pussy."

I got some pussy, but I did not know what I was doing. The enjoyment wasn't great. I was nervous, tense and scared as hell wondering what she thought. She couldn't have thought much. Now that I know what I'm doing, she couldn't have thought much.

One thing though I was off the snide. I could tell Folks I had some pussy now. It didn't matter, if it was bad or good I had me some now. That part was killing me.

You know when you're a teenager your guys always asked, "have you got some pussy yet".

I had to say no or avoided the question. I hated to be cornered with that question. I be like, "what you think nigga, look at me?"

Usually this would get them off me. This is a way of answering the question without lying. I was one hundred and didn't lie on my dick. I couldn't be a man without getting any pussy I thought. I was doing everything else a man can do, except fucking.

Back in school my junior year though! I was having problems with my English teacher Mrs. Richards. We used to call her "Old Richards." She was a very stern teacher who ran a disciplined classroom.

Now I'm in the third marking period of my junior year. I come in and asked City for some paper and a pen like I usually do. Well Mrs. Richards warned me not to do it anymore. When I came in class unprepared again I would have to leave.

This day I exhaust the little time that we had in between classes. I was trying to sell weed in between the bells and didn't get to my locker. We had a test though! This was a very important test. If we got there late, old Richards would lock the door and wouldn't let us in class. I got to class right before she was ready to lock the door.

I looked at her with a sly grin while sliding pass her. I made it to class. I asked Cityboy for some paper, because he sat right behind me my junior year. He handed me the paper. I sat down and was about to put my name on the paper.

She sat down for about three minutes.

She then thought and blasted loudly, "Mr. George you can leave my classroom."

It was like an after thought. I was writing my name on the paper getting ready to take the test.

I reply, "leave! Why would I do that, Mrs. Richards? I am about to take a test, what I do?"

She looked over her glasses and said, "you're not taking this test. I told you, if you came to class unprepared. You would have to leave my classroom. Mr. George could you please leave so the people who came prepared can take the test."

Mrs. Richards I...

She interrupts, "Mr. George gather your things so we can continue class."

I looked around feeling very embarrassed. Everybody in class was looking at her and I, like damn she's bold.

Even the class was looking and saying, "it okay, Mrs. Richards we all do it." Worst of all though, if I couldn't take the test, I get a zero. I couldn't stand a zero and knew I'd fail the class, if I gotten a zero for the test.

I would have to take the class over! I'd have to go to summer school. I already went my freshmen year to King Martin. My sophomore year I went to night school at Englewood. I had to make up that chemistry class I didn't make. I had all my credits and was on schedule. I wouldn't graduate on time still, because English was a major credit.

I'd have to go to summer or night school again. I won't be able to try out for the team. As I gather my things and started walking out the door. That is what ran across my mind. I got in the hallway and I gave it one more try before leaving.

"Mrs. Richards you know this test...

She interrupts, "Mr. George, if you don't come to class prepared. You cannot pass this class and slammed the door in my face."

I couldn't take it this is an old bitch with no empathy. I exploded, "you old bitch, fuck you" and kick the door as hard as I could.

I couldn't hold those emotions back everything boiled over at that moment. I never said anything like this to a teacher in my life. I never disrespected my elders. I felt she disrespected me and I couldn't handle it.

She came back to the door and said. "You'll never get in this classroom again and slammed the door again."

I started saying to myself, "Mrs. Richards didn't know what I was going through! I want to do right, but all is left, is wrong". She slams the door in my face so the righteous way is out. I can't take the test, because I don't have any fucking paper. I didn't ask her for any paper. I asked my boy City, for some paper?"

Yeah I came to school a lot, unprepared. I asked for school supplies when I got to school. One thing though! I am in school. Don't kick me out when I am trying and passing the class. What got up under the old bitch?

I ran in right before she was about to close the door. She really gets a hard on stopping you from coming in the class late. I could see her face frown up when I slid by her smirking. She thought I was a thug and was making it hard for me. I already got it hard, but it got harder! Thanks a lot Mrs. Richards for being a stumbling block.

Well of course I was disciplined with some detention. I was blackballed from any other English classes. I was too far into the semester. That is the reason they gave me for not letting me in their class. Mrs. Richards probably told the rest of the English teacher what I did. She pigeon holed me. I wouldn't be graduating on time with my class. This was devastating to me, because I hated to fail.

If I transfer to another school I would be able to take the English class. My whole junior year was full of fights and brawls. I was in the assistant principle's office about four times that year.

The Museum

*T*he museum trip was the indicator and the last straw. I was just about to hit my final point with Mrs. Simmons. I had to go. All the Folks were going, if they were suppose to go with a class or not. We knew other schools were going to be up at the museum. This was a pretty big event. I wasn't supposed to be at the museum. My class wasn't giving the trip. I wanted to be, where the happenings. It was going to be girls from other school at the museum. Maybe I can squeeze me a girl from another school

Grimes drove us up to the museum in his green Dodge Charger. I had just bought me some Levi's' creased up to the max. I was wearing a John Wayne shirt that was sweet. I wore a fresh pair of black suede bucks. Grimes's and I had our butters freshly whipped with the finger waves.

Now of course there are gangs at these other schools. They gang bang too. Semion had Folks and Stones. CZS had Cobra Stones, Vicelords, Four Corner Hustlers. All of them ride up under the five-point star. It was Folks at the school too Lace played for CZS and was the man. I knew we might have squabble so I had to be prepared.

I took my missile with me. I had Cityboy's 22 revolver again. Grimes and I rode up there with couple of more Folks.

Grimes asked me, "do you got the missile Colo?"

I told him no and had it duffed away. I knew he was going to tell me to leave it. I must say Grimes used a lot a morality too when he did things. Yeah Grimes was next in line for morality. It was just when he got drunk, he was terrible.

I would've left it, but niggas were shooting now. They ain't just fighting anymore. Folks usually have you out numbered anyway. You even the odds when you got that missile. I wasn't going to get caught, slipping. I got our back. We got bubbled on the way up there drinking forties ounces and smoking joints. We were listening to L'L or something.

We pulled in the parking lot and went in the museum. Never even once thinking about, I'm cutting school. I'm at the museum looking for girls, fresh to death. We get in the museum and I didn't get a chance to talk to one girl.

As soon as we started walking through the museum shit broke out. At first we were gawking and trying to holler at the ladies. We come up to the steps and we see Sacks from around the way with an entourage of Folks.

They are all walking through shouting, "GD GD" repeatedly while throwing up the forks.

Next, we saw Sterling and the rest of the BD's from the Robe.

His crew were all shouting, "BD BD" and throwing up the treys. Everybody met in the middle of the hallway.

That's when everybody gets to shouting, "all is one, all is one."

Everyone was throwing up the one finger, symbolizing unity under the six.

All of a sudden some Brothers came around the corner. They had on red hats broken to the left, throwing the five up.

They were shouting, "all is well."

It was about 20 of them. They were out number, because Folks was mob deep, that day. It was at least fifty or sixty Folks mobbed up in that one section. Sacks and Grimes and I moved first. Sacks blazed the first one that waked up. He spent off and broke my way from the blow. I dropped a blow on him and let him go. I had the banger so I drifted to the perimeter of the brawl. The guys from my hood moved first.

At the same time Grimes went at somebody else and then it all broke loose. Havoc, would be a light word for it. Things were torn down that been up in the museum for years. All type of ancient artifacts was smashed.

Here come the twisters and security, snatching up everybody. They were throwing students against the wall and searching everybody. I had the missile on me and my knees started to shake when I saw the officers. I kept a straight face, but I look like Folks. It was no question I was getting searched on just looks alone.

I had to get out of there or I am going to jail. I started looking for the exit. I walked right past an officer while he was telling people to get against the wall. I see the door and heads right for it.

The officer looked at me and let's me walk outside. Why didn't he throw me up against wall, I do not know? If I seen somebody looking like me after a big altercation. I would stop me. I would've broke out on him anyway. I was too close to the exit!

I get outside and duff the gun in the bushes. That's the reason why Grimes told me to leave the gun at home. It was going to be too many twisters everywhere. Of course I didn't listen. I couldn't locate Grimes so I just went to the car and chilled. I couldn't get caught with the gun on me. Finally Grimes shows up and I tell him about the gun, "Grimes we got to go get the missile."

Grimes looks at me like, motherfucka I told you. I look back like, no argument now Grimes.

He just asked, "where is it at?"

I tell him.

Grimes looked pissed then said, "I'ma let your black ass out and you go get it. I'll meet you at the corner."

Police is everywhere so I had to be smooth. Low-key grab it and go. I did just that I grab it and we shoot back to the crib.

This incident had me at the end of my rope. The incident made the news and heads had to roll. The next day Darobe had an assembly. They called out all the names of people who weren't supposed to be at the museum. They had a list of about fifty people names. I know I ain't on the list. I was in and out. I think I am straight. I guess they went back and checked the cameras. Darobe was barred from the museum for ten years.

We didn't know anything about the cameras at the museum. I didn't get peeped by any of my teachers so I thought I was straight. I was only in the museum max, ten minutes. I was sitting next to Slept Rock when they called his name. He had to see the principal. I was looking like damn they got you. They called everybody name out and when they got to name number fifty. The last name was mines.

I was the last name they called on the list. I could not believe it. You called all those names out and I am the last one. Of course they sent me to detention. I guess they didn't have me hitting the dude. I was just at the museum without permission.

I knew my next move would be getting kicked out. Mrs. Simmons talked to each one of us in private about this matter. When you had to see Mrs. Simmons about your future, it wasn't good.

She told me, "if it wasn't for your grades you would be gone", but I was on the short list.

I would be forced to go to one of those survivalist schools. What I mean by survivalist school. You never know what might happen to you. It was nowhere to go after getting kick out the Darobe. When you can't stay at this school no other school wanted you. The Robe was like the refugees coming in from Cuba, if you got kicked out. No one wanted you in their school.

I was at a survivalist school already, but I knew what was happening. All my friends were at Darobe now. I had been through the hardship of making my name. I was making money hustling weed. I had to make a move for my future though.

I was a made man at the Robe. Rock Manor grammar school was mob training for young goons. Darobe was the highest level of mobsterism for teenagers anywhere. I was rising at the Robe as top mob. They know I ain't no hoe and I fuck motherfuckas up and I had a mob too. Nobody and I mean nobody fucks with you. I would have to start all over again, if I went somewhere else. The Robe was so scandalous it was a shame.

Bonner

I had to get to school early for people who wanted to smoke before class. I was used to getting up early anyway because of my old paper route. I saw a lot of treachery at Darobe being in the mix. I also came out in between bells just in case it was customers, needing weed.

It was the front side of the Robe where people hung. It was also the backside where the thugs lay. Thugs lay in the front and the back, but the back is where the thugs operate. This is where everybody is getting high, shooting dice and playing get like me. All the muscling goes on in the back.

Smashing would take place inside, outside, on the backside, the front and the side of the schools. Now it was some Stones at the school, but they did no representation verbally or visually.

Sometimes you would see a five-point star on the wall. When Dave or Dauk found out it was a Stone in the school. Where or whenever you were caught the smashing took place. If you were in class, it didn't matter; smashzation was going to happen! The teachers can't stop it. They were scared.

Smashzation is the highest level of smashing, on site wherever. A pumpkin head was usually what you were left with afterward the beating. A pumpkin head is when your whole face, is like sitting on top of a big round beach ball. Your head would swell up so bad. Folks would snatch you out your class and whoop your ass. The teachers would just step to the side. This was another level and the teachers didn't want any smoke. They couldn't remember who did the smashing. The peons had to pay peon fees, in order to get to school. Yeah it was rough just getting to school. I never collected peon fees, but it was a lot of Folks who did.

Bonner was so cool you'd swear he had control over those guys at the Robe. The only way Bonner came down on you. You had to fuckup totally. When you didn't give Bonner no respect you might get smashed later that day. I don't know, but if a thug didn't respect him. Next thing you know by the end of the day, he was smashed. After being smashed nobody gets caught or reprimanded.

They might've done it on their own, which is possible. Bonner looked out for me when he could've done me bad. I wouldn't let anybody disrespect Bonner either.

When you made it to Mrs. Simmons the principal office you were through, but she let Bonner run the school. She rarely came out her office. I never got suspended for fighting. I went to detention, but never suspended.

One time Bonner came in the bathroom busted us all. I don't know why nobody was on security. We were in the bathroom blowing like a motherfucka.

He sees me again fucking up and he says, "you see Columbus I always catch you in the wrong spot. First, y'all playing that get like me for quarters."

He caught me earlier in the hall gambling. He doesn't even say anything about the weed smell and smoke. He just made a funny face and waved his hands back and forth to clear the air. He wasn't tripping on us flipping or smoking. He was tripping, because we were cutting class playing, "get like me."

You can bust a nigga pockets with that get like me. Bonner was cool about gambling. He caught us flipping one time and he took a quarter out and flipped it. Bonner flipped a quarter and gambled with us just for fun.

You can win twenty or thirty dollars quick playing get like me. The way you win is, if you're the man. The man flips the quarter and lands on head or tails. Now your opponent got to land on what he or she flipped.

Head or tails on a quarter got you paid. When you matched what the flipper landed on, you pick up both quarters. When you don't match the flipper picks up both quarters and continues to flip. We had the whole school on get like me. We could gamble without shooting dice. What I'm trying to say is, Bonner didn't trip on shit like that. He'll just tell us to get to class.

When he was pissed at us, he'd check up on us. He was pissed this day. He takes us all in his office and pulled up our grades. After he seen my grades I was straight I am passing. I was straight.

He looks at me and says, "damn Columbus you got all your credits. You are passing all your classes too. Keep up the good work and go to class."

Bonner went straight to your grades when making decisions on your future.

Only thing he did that day was say, "stay out the bathroom".

I don't know, if Bonner smoked, but he didn't trip on us smoking weed. How can you suspend somebody for smoking? When you really want to hit it.

CHAPTER FOUR

Leaving the Robe

*Y*ou have to know when to hold them. You have to know when to fold them. I knew the possibility of me making it through Darobe was bleak. I had another year and a 1/4 without getting into any trouble. It was too much in my folder. Mrs. Simmons kept my folder in her desk like I was top priority.

She showed me that day I was being reprimanded for the museum.

Before I left her office she said. "Mr. George your folder is here in a special place in my desk." This is where people folders sit when they are on their way out.

That was after the museum incident. She was ready for my next fall off or my next negative move.

I had to find another school to go to before getting kick out. My grades were O'K. I didn't fail anything and I was in my junior's division. That's the only reason Mrs. Simmons hadn't kicked me out for this incident. A lot of other people got kicked out after the museum.

I had decent grades without trying hard. They would look at my grades and credits and say you have potential and back off me. I knew I had to go or I would not graduate on time. Old Richards and my files in the desk were indicators that my rope was about to snap.

That would be devastation to my mother. I didn't want to transfer to Englewood, because we got into it with them. We smashed a couple of people from that school. Englewood was our rivalry school. They smashed a few people after a game from the Robe and we went back. Englewood was mostly BD's at the time too.

That's all I would need to happen is to get pointed out and smashed at Inglewood. I wanted to go somewhere where Folks held it down though! I couldn't go to the better schools, well I could, but I was Folks. You transfer into one of these schools brand new and your going to get smashed. I was known for banging in other schools so I couldn't just go to any school.

My cousin Todd told me to go to Communication Metro. I said to myself, "that might be the best move".

I agreed and said, "yeah Todd it's a lot of Folks up at that school." I knew a few people from grammar school who went to Communication Metro." Communication Metro was mostly GD's and a few Stones who were mostly on the football team.

I told City, Slept Rock and Dave that I was out. I was transferring out so I could stay on schedule. All of them were still on schedule to graduate. How am I going to be the only one that's going to fail? My guys didn't want me to ride out. I had to graduate that's the only thing I could keep on track. That's the only thing I could control in my life.

I had the pact with Emus and John that I could still keep. I wanted to walk the stage when City walked the stage. I did not want to graduate out of summer school. My back was against the wall. I need a new start and a brand new folder.

I'm so far gone the teacher's aren't going to let me make a new start. They hate to see me coming, but I really wasn't a bad kid. It was my reputation. Well maybe I was terrible, but I wasn't in school. I was terrible in the streets.

Kid got to make it and I got to move before the school, moves me. It's time for another adventure. Right now I got a choice, because my grades are decent. I could've gone to Semion, where my sister Trina had gone. I could have gone to CZS. I even went up to the school and talked to a cousler. My boy Fester went to CZS. I've done damage to a few students from those schools. I didn't want to face the retribution by getting caught sleeping.

My decision to leave and the process of the decision to leave, was one day to the next. That's one thing about me. I was always able to look ahead or around the corner. Life is an adventure.

You have to be able to look ahead and make the right decisions. You might have a chance. The danger out here is real and the pressure is real. It's Folks and Stones getting killed everyday. Learning and seeking to be real, is real!

Ben Wilson

*T*hey knocked off Ben Wilson shot him to death. He was a top prospect for the pros. Word on the street is that he was a Stone. You know you not supposed to touch the prospect, whether they bang or not. Ben played with Juwan Howard at Semion. Juwann played seventeen seasons in the pros. They weren't even looking at Juwan like that! Ben was on a Magic Johnson level as far as skills, when he was in high school.

Ben was 6'8" coming down with the pill, dunking and shooting as a junior. He was the total package. One thing about Chicago to get your street cred, you got to play in all the parks.

You got to have the park street cred. He played at Iron Park a few times. I didn't play with or against, but I wanted too. We heard he was up there and we ran up to the park with excitement.

He was getting mad ink in the papers. He was a star as a junior in Chicago. I couldn't get on the court while he was in the park.

By the time I made it to the park I was seven-games down. To make a long story short anybody head can get knocked off. Wrong place wrong time and your head rolls.

Communication Metro

Since I'm a BD and the GD's and BD's were still all as one, at the time. Oh it makes a difference in Chicago. Go to one of those schools that rides the five and I could have a rough go.

I decided to go to Communication Metro the rest of my junior year. The day I went up there to transfer. I had Sacks's Darobe football jacket on that day. He let me where it and I had his little school bag. He had his name drawn on it sweet with the six-point star on top of his name, Sacks.

Coach Frazier the coach of Communication Metro thought I played for the Robe. He saw me when I came to transfer and he saw me in the jacket. The Robe football team was like stars in high school. We were expected to win. Coach Murry was a star high school coach.

After seeing me in the jacket coach Frazier asked me, you transferring into the school?

I replied, "yeah."

He then asked, "are you going to come out for the team?"

I answered, "yeah why not?"

He then said, "come out to tryouts starting next month".

This could be something to keep me out of trouble. I had something popping coming in the door. Maybe I still got a shot at the pros

They let me transfer into Communication Metro relatively easy. The faculty administration looked at my grades, which was a C average. I was in the school no problem. I am now a Communication Metro Dawg. It feels funny not being a Darobe Raider. It was something missing, but I couldn't fall further behind. I first got there I was put in a demo freshman division.

Darobe wouldn't release my transcript, because of back books I owed. I would be in a demo freshmen division, until my transcripts came. Here I am in here with a bunch of freshmen and I am supposed to be in a junior division.

Everybody thinks I am a freshman too. I look young though, even the teacher thought I was a freshmen. I forget her name, but she didn't believe me at all. I told her, "I supposed to be in a junior's division. I am just here, until my credits come."

She reply's, "yeah right Mr. George."

She stereotyped me from the jump. I didn't fit the MO of a student with all his credits.

Communication Metro wasn't like the Robe. When I went to the Robe the BD's ran it. It might have been 60/40. I let it be known how I was cut, Black Disciple coming in the door. Therefore, the teachers thought I wasn't studious at all. I'd yell it out in the hallways, (Disciple) loud as hell all through the halls.

They'll return the call by yelling GD. I looked to her from what she saw of me to be a demo-freshmen. That's why I was in the class, she thought. I just said to myself, "fuck it, I not going to try and make you believe me. I'll just wait until the credits come."

The first few days at Communication Metro were okay. I was at a new school. Nobody really knew me except for about ten people who went to Rock Manor. Atone Daniels who used to head butt us little niggas at the Manor.

He was on the football team. Manuel was doing just like he was at Rock Manor, trying to run things. That was Atone cousin. I tried to just be smooth with everybody. I got one year and a quarter and I'll graduate on time. At this point Mom was letting me make all my own moves about school.

I met one of the GD Folks in the lunchroom. He was a senior and his name was Pocoe G. I also had a couple of classes with him. He was a GD and introduced me to most of the Folk's that he knew at the school. It was some mix reaction with the Folks. Since the school was predominantly GD's they wanted to flex on me a little.

I could tell I was going to have to get down. When I threw my treys up. Some threw up back with the, all is one love. Some smirked and threw up the forks, like nigga were GD's over here.

I know it's going to go down, but when, I don't know. You know they got to see, if you're the real deal. You can't just have the look of a thug you will be tested immediately. I got into it with a couple of Folks at the end of my junior year.

I was Tested

*I*t was hot outside and I cut my sixth period class. I'm outside with the GDs pitching pennies. We were pitching two for a quarter and liner fifty cents. When you bust somebody line it's double, sisters are double pay out.

It was about four of us playing so you could win a nice little pot. Pitching with Slick Coole, Lace, Todd, Big D and the Folks around the crib had me seasoned. It was much tougher than pitching the Folks at school. Those niggas around the crib were seasoned pros on the lines. It was easy money on the lines at Communication Metro.

I was dropping it on them. It's the strategy that wins not landing in the line. When you land in the line, makes a difference. My first penny I would pitch as close to the line without going in, if I weren't the man. Someone would always jump in and half the time. I would bust their liner and he'd have to pay double.

When I wasn't the man I would call on the man, so I could pitch next to last. You had to be quick calling out your position when pitching pennies. The people who pitch first has a lesser chance of winning. Your opponent's second pitch might go out of bounds. Now all you have to do is pitch it toward the line to win, if you're the man.

I was breaking them on the lines. After making a few dollars I made everybody else quit, but T-bone and Mike. I hit them for about thirty-five dollars quick. I was selling them weed and taking their money on the lines, at the same time. I was getting paid at Communication Metro coming in the door.

This is where things get sticky. I guess they had already talked about doing this, because this is how it went down. I had been talking mad shit to get in the mood on the lines. You can't just pitch; it's a groove you pitch in while you talk shit.

T-bone lost his last dollar and he said he was out. Mike had another pitch and he jumped in the line.

He was happy and shouted, "liner motherfucka."

He said it hard than a motherfucka. I looked and saw I had him pretty charged and I said, "that ain't shit." My next pitch was fucked, but rolled the rest of the way into the line. This type of liner hurts.

It was only half way up the square, before it started to roll. He thought it was his money, because he started walking to pick it up. My penny kept rolling and landed in the line. I bust his liner on a roll. I shout loud, "bust your ass motherfucka, bust your ass." T-bone looks and then steps on my liner.

Mike yells, "burnt money" he then stepped on the other penny.

I look at him and say, "yeah right you can't burn a liner, nigga pay up!"

Mike frowned and looks me in the eyes and said. "I ain't giving you shit, that's burnt money."

Right then I knew the drama was on! He's with six of his Folks and he's clowning looking mean and being demonstrative. I ask him, "how you going to play Folks?"

He said, "fuck you, you ain't my Folk's." He then stepped on the penny again and said, "burnt money" then swung.

He took me by surprise and caught me under the eye, bink. He was coming too hard swinging like a motherfucka. I was surprised and had to back out at first to get my composure.

I kind of knew it was coming, with the elevated tension. Mike caught me slipping again, but not quite. It was glancing, because I rolled with it, but it hit my cheekbone. He kept swinging, but I ducked the next couple.

They must have thought I was a mark or something. This is the shit I love, boxing. I shake off the blaze and started letting them go. I kept giving him two pieces. Left, right combination, until I got my bearings.

He could box, but I could box better. He was stronger though! He was muscling me around when we clinched. Mike had about three years on me. I give it to Mike he was formidable.

His boys were over there shouting, "whoop his ass Mike" urging him on!

I'm shouting back, "Mike going to get his ass whooped." Well, we fought for about seven minutes back and forth. They let us go head up, but that could change at any moment. I was just keeping him off with the one two.

I was watching anybody who got close. Both of us were getting some good exchanges close to the end of the fight. I was distracted I know how they move at the Robe. Once I saw that they really were going to let us go head up. I started putting swag in my fighting style. I was posing and looking sweet with my fighting stance. This is intimidating

He ran up and grabbed me and started banging my head up against a tree. I break his grip by going in between his arms, like I did Robert when I was ten. After that I gave him another two pieces, sweet like though.

I was about to dig in his ass. I staggered him with that two-piece combo. It was an uppercut followed by a hook. You saw his knees wobble. I see that and then say, "yeah nigga, you didn't know, you can't burn no liner?" I started walking him down asking. "You can't burn a liner Mike" while rotating my neck side to side. I was ready to dig in his ass good.

Somebody finally asked, "why Folk's fighting?"

I answered him, "y'all know why, this nigga stole on me."

T-bone finally broke it up by saying, "y'all Folks, y'all shouldn't be fighting."

T-bone was in my division. That's the only reason I don't think they jumped. He jumped in the middle and stopped us. All his Folks were out there cheering him like he won the fight.

T-bone knew he better had broken it up, because I was breaking him down. You can tell it in the face and in the eyes. You can tell by the eyes. When somebody bit off more than they can chew. I was coming hard and getting stronger with confidence. He was fading.

After the fight I was a little exhausted, but satisfied. I didn't get my dollar though! We were out there fighting over a dollar. It wasn't the dollar it was the principal. I had to make a stand for that dollar. Had I not I would be through making money up at Communication Metro. I would be getting rob coming and going.

None of the people I knew were around so I went to the crib after the fight. I left before they thought about smashing me. When I got to the crib my Folks was tripping on my eye. I am a black guy with a black eye. Yeah he got me a little bit. This was my first black eye and it was a small cut that I still have to this day. It was from the first punch he threw.

I get around the crib, Slick Freddie and lil Todd asked me after seeing my eye. Did I need the cavalry to come up to the school?

I said, "naw it was head up. A nigga thought he was just going to punk me on the lines. He stole on me, but I got in his ass. He should have a few bumps too."

Freddie looked at my eye paused then said, "let us know, if you getting more static. We can mob up there and take care of the function."

It felt good I could call on the Folks to move. I reassured them and said, "that's okay, because I still have to go to this school."

My objective is to graduate and not to create havoc. I just convinced them I could take care of it for now. That Monday morning I strapped up and went to school. If push comes to shove I was letting them go. It got through the school that Mike banged me.

I was surprised at the news. I knew and Mike knew; I gave him all he wanted and more. All they had to do was go to the scorecards. I out pointed him and he threw in the towel. He could have easily push T-bone back so he could finish whipping my ass. He was so glad when he stepped in between us. He walked away before I did.

Pocoe G said he heard about the fight and seen the bump under my eye. This indicated to him I got banged.

He asked, "did Mike bang you. I heard Mike beat your ass."

He said this while he was looking at my eye.I responded, "if you believe that you better go look at Mike too." He believed it, because he really didn't fuck with me after the incident. Another reason is, because he was a GD. If it were me I still would've been friends with him. Only person who knew how the fight really went is Mike and I.

I know I handed him some just like he handed me some. I had juniors English with Mike. His lip was busted and swollen. He had knots on his head. He was a senior taking a class he had failed before.

When he saw me he just gave me Ps and said, "what's up?" He didn't want any smoke from me I can tell from the look.

I replied, "what's up?" Things understood need not be spoken upon. He was straight and I knew it. He didn't have the look like I'll whoop your ass. He had the look like, dude you're straight. I had his respect, which means I got their respect.

I didn't say anything about the fight and he didn't say nothing either. Dude could box. I was quicker and faster. I hit him about fifteen times. He hit me about seven and that's good to be done gotten, stolen on first. Usually, when you get stole on, it's the knock out punch, because you're not expecting it.

A nigga stealing on you was the norm going through school. You just can't get caught slipping. I later found out after stealing on other people. They called that a sucker's punch. When Mike didn't want to pay me.

He knew it was either steal or be stolen on. I wasn't getting any money so I had to fight anyway. I pissed him off on the lines, because I was talking shit while winning. He was older and felt disrespected by me talking shit. Like Jason and Red did me when I was a shortie. I am ready now for anybody.

The indicator he was going to steal. When he stepped on the penny the first time. That was an aggressive move. The second indicator he said he wasn't paying me shit. He was out there with all his Folk's, showing off. I wasn't going to steal on him while he with all his Folk's not for a measly dollar. You can get smashed for that, for real. That's calling them all hoes. I should of known he was going to try.

I guess I was getting mixed up with my reputation from the Robe. That wouldn't have happened at this point, at the Robe. I have no reputation at Communication Metro. I should've known what was next. I do the same thing on 169th street! Karma is a motherfucka!

About a month later I get into it with GD Folks name Sugar Bear. Sugar bear stood about 6'3" and about 230 pounds, black as hell and was your classic Bully. He went through the school intimidating smaller and weaker people.

He never fucked with me and always gave me much love. I knew him because he was GD Folks. He was one of the first Folks I met when I came to the school. Sometimes I would shoot ball after school with these guys. Thameus thought he could shoot so I'd shot with him. Thameus was a neutron on junior varsity always shooting at the parkl.

Sugar Bear was with some of the Folks that hung around the Brand Crossing Park. This is where we shot ball after school. Here I am leaving the school going to the crib for the day. I go to push the door and it wouldn't open. It would crack open, but it wouldn't open all the way.

Somebody was pushing the door close when I tried to open it. I kept pushing the release, but it wouldn't open. I'm pushing hard and it won't open so I reared back and kicked the door two times. I kicked it hard as hell and on the second kick the door flew open.

I walked out and looked on the other side of the door. It was Sugar Bear holding the door back. I guess when I kicked the door the first time. 'Bear' was coming up off of it. The second kick the door hit him in the back.

He looked at me when I walked out and said, "nigga you hit me in the back with the door."

I said, "you shouldn't been holding it back nigga." I don't know why I just didn't say my fault. He frowned and came running up the steps swinging at me. I ducked a couple of times with him grazing me across the head.

It was on I had no fear, because it was on before I knew it started. My butterfly warning system didn't have a chance to activate. This was a big black motherfucka swinging trying to take my head off.

I jumped off the steps and started to box. I gave him a two-piece combination. It didn't seem to do any damage. He kept coming. I couldn't get my feet set and he was charging fast. I give him another two pieces. He walked right through the punches and grabbed me. After grabbing me he picked me up in the air and slammed me to the ground.

I grabbed his neck on the way down with both arms locked, while in the air. Before we landed on the ground I started to choke him. I got his neck locked pushing against the ground torquing his neck backwards.

He is on top of me and he said, "let me go."

I said in his ear, "you let me go motherfucka." That wrestling with George and Dave at the Robe came in handy. It doesn't look like I'm that strong, but I am.

I must have surprised him. Bear must have thought I was a peon or I was going to run. You know it got around the school GD Mike, beat my ass. You can't believe what everybody says. He miscalculated my reaction. One of the Folks stepped in and pulled us apart.

I was heated though. I thought to myself, "he tried to straight punk me in front of the Folks." He started to walk away without looking at me. I ran around through the people to get at him. It was a lot of people out there in the mix now. He did not locate me and I stole on him.

After that, I gave him another two-piece. He got me with the same move. I didn't want to keep backing up. I had to make a stand and throw blows. He charged me, grabbed me, picked me up and slammed me again. The only thing is when he was picking me up.

I would immediately latch on to his neck and put the vice on it. When he went to slam me. He couldn't put everything into it, because I had his neck locked. He asked me in a low voice trying not to mark himself out.

He says. "Let me go in my ear", almost whispering it.

By that time officer Johnson came out there and broke it up. He told us to cool out before he took us to the office. Sugar Bear got up and started to walk away. I ran behind him again. Blazed him again with another three-piece combination.

This time he clutched his face. I got some leverage this time and banged him. I was shouting at the same time, "mark, you shouldn't have never fuck with me. I'm in it to win it nigga." I was shouting loud and crazy like, he had me hot. I said to myself while in action. "You are going to find out I ain't no mark along with everybody watching who I am."

I hated to lose anything especially a fight. The fight with Mike I had to eat that one. It was no one there to tell them who quit and the school thinks he won. It was Mike's guys, who called the fight. I was still boxing. He was the one staggered. Mike's guys were the only one's around. I did have a mouse under the eye, which means, loser.

I go at Bear again. I can't turn the engine off. I am in smash mode. The pit is off the leash. Officer Johnson had to grab me to keep me off of Bear. He grabbed my arm then walked Sugar Bear and I to the office. On the way to the office, Sugar Bear was trying to make peace.

He was trying to hold my jock when his friends weren't around. I was like, "fuck you nigga. Now you trying to suck dick it ain't over motherfucka. I'm going to handle my function." His face was looking like; he did fuck with the wrong guy. His eyes were centered in his eye sockets. I can't turn the beast off. How do you turn a beast off? It happened to be Friday when this happened too.

I had gotten so mad that I had it in my mind. I was going to pop this big motherfucka. I wasn't beaten up, but he was just slamming me to the ground. I felt he disrespected to the utmost. I had made up in my mind. I was going to get his ass.

Over the weekend though I had calm down and said, "fuck it." If I had my thang at the time I would have put them in him. My temper at this time is getting out of control, John. I felt it my junior year. I was ready to kill a motherfucka for real.

Once I thought about it, I needed that fight. After they said I lost to Mike, I needed visual conformation. It looked like to the people who saw the fight! It was me who looked like the aggressor. When I came back to school on Monday I got respect.

Everybody said, "I heard you got into it with Bear and I heard you did your thang."

I just replied, "yeah I did okay the nigga just kept slamming me", then I started to chuckle. I fought this big motherfucka and nobody could say, he whooped my ass.

Everybody saw me putting it on him. The bell rang right before we started fighting by the end of the fight. The whole school was out in front. I learned something that day. I should've matadored him.

I should have hit him with an easy step to the right or left. Bang him as he goes by. He would've never been able to grab me. That's the same way Dave kept getting me, but Bear was stronger than Dave. He was easily picking me up. I had to put him in a submission hole to keep from getting fucked up.

It had gotten through the school and then I began to get my respect. I think they were just trying to see, if I was a mark. Since I was a BD and the GDs dominated the school, they tried to flex a little bit. It was more Stones than BD's as a matter of fact. I might have been the only BD at the school.

I didn't fuck with anybody at Communication Metro. You just ain't going to play me like a mark so everybody else could try. My philosophy was to handle your business immediately. For now on, they know how I'm coming. I'm in it to win it!

We were going to fight to the end and I'm not going to quit or lose. I am not going to tuck tail and run. I am not going to stop once you disrespect. Again, Folks let us go head up so I honored the situation. They could've smash me. I didn't call the Folks around the crib. I could've called the Folks from the Darobe. I just cool out because I still had to go to the school.

I still came to school with my thang the next couple of weeks. I never told anybody my intentions. I still had it in the back of my mind that, if he tried anything else. I was going to follow him home. Hang out until he was by himself and take care of my function. Leave a nigga like me alone, because I'm coming hard.

When he saw me again though he apologized, again, then gave me dap.

Bear said, "my fault Folks, thousand pardons! It was just I got hit by that door. I really didn't know it was you Folks."

I kind of sense he knew. I didn't want any trouble, but was going to handle what ever came. I think it's how I look at a motherfucka. I have on my, it's on you, what happens next, face.

It's on you dude to unleash the beast, if you want too. The demon was telling me to kill a motherfucka now. I thought about calling my Folks up to the school. When I call my guys I might as well drop out. I rather pop his ass and be at school the next day.

I felt myself starting to get a killer's mentality at sixteen years old. I had just made another birthday. Being around killers all your life and living in the environment. Slowly it turns you mentally into that of your surroundings. You become numb to people pain.

Whatever environment in which you are around, is what you will become. You have to have very strong will power. I don't care who you are you can grow up with all the values in the world. You still can become brainwashed by your environment.

Boxing is Obsolete

*T*he older we got the more gunplay. The toughest nigga were becoming obsolete. Are you ready to pop that thang? A regular nigga on the block, killed QB, Emus. Quentin Bellamy was calling for the BD's on 171st. I went to school with his younger brother Landress Bellamy.

Landress was about my height brown skin with tiny marks on his face. He was on the basketball team, but died when I was in the eighth grade. He drowned at the lake. Landress and a few guys cut school and went to the lake.

He fell in the lake and the current took him under. This was sad, because Landress was really cool. When we found out the news at school. We were struck in the heart. We had a whole day of memory for Landress playing music and conversing.

A few years later QB got killed. QB was calling it for the BD's. The word on the street and I don't know how true this is, because QB was cool. Whenever I saw him he was chill. He seemed inviting and warm to be calling it. This was before I started banging.

He had been rough-housing the dude that killed him for a while. This particular day dude was ready. As a matter of fact QB wasn't going to bother him that day. People who were out there when he got shot said, QB just said what's up to him? He just pulled out a gun and shot and killed him. QB never saw it coming.

Gunplay is the real power now. When you are scaring a person everyday. By bullying him or taking his money or just making him feel like a hoe. If he's got any kind of a soul one day he's going to raise up on you. It might not be today or tomorrow, but dude is going to get tired of you fucking with him. Even the markest of the marks will one day rise up.

I guess that's how QB got killed. I knew the other side, because me not having a brother to take up for me. I met bullying head on. I had to fend or earn my respect. You know the only thing about it is! You know who is the most surprise when shit like that happens. It's always the bully. They never see it coming!

You just don't know how long and hard a person is thinking about you. Once you bully somebody, you rarely think about what you've done to him. I bet you, the dude that's getting bullied. I betcha he thinks about you, constantly. Everyday he is wondering about how is he going to handle the situation? To all bullies your day is coming and you will reap what you sow. That shit just ain't right. Rip Landress and QB.

Going back on a promise

I would go a month or two focused with my weed game. I wasn't thinking about hitting stains. I was getting down to my last scribbles and I don't have recoup fare. I was kicking it with Boya this day. We went to the store and had bought a bottle of gin. I was smoking on my last few joints with him.

Boya was GD Folks who usually hung with Whiteboy Slopes and Coole Blue. These niggas hit stains and they were good at hitting stains. Now Boya had been casing this joint. He had been trying to get me to hit it with him for a couple of weeks. I kept spinning him. I'm straight I don't have to steal, until I fell off.

Boya was at it again trying to put me up on a stain. You have to be strong to ward off temptation. It's always somebody in your ear when you trying to change your life. Someone is always trying to activate the stealing demon inside me. The devil keeps sending demon soldiers through people who you like can influence you negatively.

We're sitting behind the building on Prairie looking at the back of the laundry matt on 169th St.. We're in the cut out of site getting high. I was on craps after the high was over! Boya said he was going to hit the stain by himself anyway. He was just knocking off the bottle of gin to shake any nerves. At first I was strong and said, "naw man I just ain't cut like that Boya!"

I learned later what to do to get a motherfucka out your ear. You got to get up and walk away. You get stronger and stronger as you get further away from temptation.

I tried to spin Boya by asking him about his stepbrother. Boya was a little guy, but he didn't take any shit. He was small, but he was no hoe, by any means. He could go with the hands too. His stepbrother had just gotten out of prison.

Boya talked about him getting out all the time, while he was in prison. When my brother get out this…. When my brother get out that…

He finally gets out and Boya brought him on the block. When I saw him you could tell Boya pattern himself after his big brother. The only thing about dude is he didn't like how much Ps Boya had on the block. I guess he wanted the same Ps Boya had on our block. He was envious of his respect level and the stud was cock strong. Muscles were budging from his fingertips he was so big.

He wore a long butter and towered over Boya. He was jealous of his little brother swag. We were chilling on John's porch. Dude and Boya get into about nothing and end up body punching. He called Boya out so Boya stepped up. You can't be a dog, if you don't get off the porch. Win or lose, but you got to come off the porch.

They square up. Dude got to blasting him out the gate. He was hitting Boya so hard, I felt it in my body. I went to grab my body parts after he landed. Boya stuck in there and threw back. His punches were like throwing popcorn at the big stud. His blows weren't bothering him at all. After Boya let go his four five-punch combination.

He told Boya, "you hit like a pussy."

He then hit Boya about nine ten straight times, with thunderous blows. I mean thunderous blows boom boom bang boom. He was paralyzing Boya little ass, he couldn't even punch back. His arms wouldn't raise up, because of the pain.

It was about four or five Folks out there watching. This is Boya stepbrother, but he was beasting him. You don't do your brother like that especially if you are in front of Folks, you don't know. He brought you around his hommies and you really saying we all ain't shit.

Another thing you just a stepbrother. All we need is the word. We give Boya the eye and the hunched shoulders move. Boya shook us off he was a trooper. I saw the pain he had absorbed.

After the pain subsided after a minute or so he said, "it wasn't shit we do this all the time."

His brother was still going with his flow. "You see little nigga when those blow come down you ain't saying shit. You see, lil nigga, you ain't shit when a beast coming at you."

He was flexing so we would respect him over Boya. He hadn't gained respect over Boya and now he has no respect. He had just done a ten piece in the joint. He was still in the joint, mentally.

Boya downplayed it and calmed his brother down. His brother just didn't know we were about to smash his ass. I was about to help Boya, you don't come on our block showing out. Two on one is fair when you are that muscle bound.

I asked Boya, "why his brother do him like that!"

Boya was like, "fuck that shit that's my brother", and shook me off.

He changed the subject and went right back to the stain he was trying to hit.

He kept telling me, "I peeped the spot already Folks it's easy money."

I had been doing good warding off potential stains for a long time. The selling point for the job, it was a dirty cop's house. I thought under the bubble and said, "it would be good just to get one of those motherfuckas back."

I don't know why everybody wanted me to go on their stains with them. That was your brother Coole Blue, Boya, White boy Slopes, Pauly and Fonz thang was to hit cribs.

Boya kept saying, "it's a dirty cop's house. He's got all type of shit up in the house."

I think Boya saw the light click on in my eyes, when he said, "dirty cop." He began telling me about his prep work to ease my worry!

"Dude works from eight in the morning until eight at night. Coole and I have been watching his car when it comes and go. When we ain't doing shit we'd walk by every morning. Dude is gone right now and he's got a whole bunch of shit Folks."

I should've asked how do you know?

I had got into it a couple of times with the twisters. The twisters just roughed housed you at will. One time the poe poe hit me in the head with his billie club, hard than a motherfucka. We were in little Lil Jimmie hallway getting bubbled, on Prairie. Like we always do, because this is where Lil Jim stays.

Lil Jim is tiny Folks with bucked eyes with a short butter. He barely had a duck tail, but dude was cut up on the body. Him and his brother Ant moved in the neighborhood when he was fifteen from the projects. They were Folk so we welcomed them to the neighborhood, but they didn't know all the rules.

We see the boys roll up while chilling, we straight. We're waiting on Lil Jimmie or his older brother, Ant to come down.

The twisters come in the vestibule and say, "what the fuck y'all doing in here?"

I was the one who spoke up and said, "waiting on my hommie we are going to shoot ball. Somebody must have called. My hommie stays on the third floor."

They take me up stairs and knock on the door. Jimmie and them wouldn't open the door. He had two sisters. One of them was Spider G's girl Delilah. I know they are in there and they wouldn't open the door. All they had to say is I am on my way down. They didn't have to open it.

The officer comes back down with me and asked me, "why you lie?"

I said, officer they just probably…. thudd across my head, went the club!

I slide down the wall like a snake hugging the wall with my back so I wouldn't fal, dazed like a motherfucka. I looked at him like, what the fuck.

He looked back and said, "y'all get the fuck out of here."

I was pissed at that motherfucka and I couldn't do anything about it, it was the police. I got busted up side my head though! This is the law and they get away with shit like that!

I got Lil Jim back though he should've come down. He could've hollered through the door. I am on my way down. I know they were on the other side of the door listening to every word.

His little ass wanted to wrestle me one day. At first I turned him down he was too little, but then I remembered. They didn't open the door that day I got hit with the billie club.

He was fast, but now I am the ultimate fighter. He was kind of strong. I just reversed his move. I picked his little ass up and body-to-body, slammed his ass on the grass. It was a controlled slam right on the grass. I said to myself, "that's for not opening the door." I did it in front of all the Folks too.

They were like, "damn Colo why you doing him like that?"

I told him, "That's for not coming to the door nigga!"

The next encounter was with the narcos. They slammed me on the wall for dropping paper on the ground. What it was, they rolled up and I honestly didn't think they were poe poes. They told me to pick the paper up I dropped. I looked at them like, "I ain't picking up shit with a smirk on my face." They jumped out the car then I saw their badges hanging from their necks. I didn't even say, I didn't know y'all were the police. They disrespected me bad.

Yeah the Police is scandalous they don't mind putting their hands on you. Another time I was with Daryl and Spider G. We were on 169th & State Street kicking it at the lounge. Spider G was old enough. He also could get us in the lounge so Daryl and I were straight.

I knew Daryl from kicking it with Ros around my old dude house. Light skin guy with a long butter. He kicked it with Ros a while. He was a couple years older than I and I'm not old enough to be in the bar chilling.

Somehow Daryl got into with this lady. Next thing you know. He had picked the lady up and slammed her to the floor in the club.

I looked shocked and said, "damn why you do that Daryle?"

Daryl grimed and replies, "bitch shouldn't been talking shit."

That was Spider G thang too to smack those hoes when disrespected. Daryl looked up to Spider G and wanted to impress him.

He smiled and looked at Spider and said, "I'll pimp slap that bitch Folks."

Spider laughs and says, "we got to go Folks before those boys come.

I'm bubbled and barely comprehend what's going on! I know he slammed her though! I felt and heard the impact of her body hit the ground.

We leave the lounge and go to the store across the street and we picked up a couple of 40's. Spider G and Daryl was laughing about slamming the girl all in the store.

Daryl kept saying, "Folks, I picked that bitch up and slammed her Folks, you see me Folks?"

He said it just like that, three times in a row.

Spider would answer while laughing, "hell yeah Folks you slam that bitch ah hee hee a haa haa."

I wasn't laughing I was wondering why did he slam her? I was looking at him like why did you do it, but didn't say anything. It didn't seem to me like nothing to be so excited about. It was a lady not a hardcore stud. We leave the store and were walking down the Michigan alley, drinking. The boys rolled up on us low-key without their lights on the car. We peeped them coming down the alley so we threw the beers to the side.

Police jump out and tell us to get against the garage. When we get against the garage. The police kicked our leg so far apart we almost did a split. They searched us didn't find anything so they put us in the car. They start to run our names through the computer. We were all sitting in the back seat waiting on names to come back. Spider G and I gave our names first, they came back clear.

It was time for Daryl to give his name.

The driver asked D, "how do you spell your name Daryl?"

Daryl tells him, "D a r y l."

The police say, "that ain't how you spell Daryl. I am going to ask you again and he waits."

Daryl spelled it out again he said, "it is D a r y l."

Cop turns around and whaloop, slaps all shit out of Daryl.

I'm sitting next to him and said, "damnnnnn." Spiders is on the other side of him covered his mouth like, shit. We looked at each other around the back of Daryl cause he sat in the middle like, damn. He slapped the shit out of Daryl. Daryl shakes of the smack after a few seconds.

He asked the officer, "why you hit me?"

Officer replied, "because you don't know how to spell your name."

I knew that was how you spelled his name. I saw his paper work before and notice it was spelled differently.

Police said, "I am going to ask you again."

He said officer that's how you spell my name.

He spelled it again out loud, "D a r y l"

The police turned and slapped him even harder this time, WaloooopPP. If I was Daryl I would've found another way to spell it. We all had butters back then and Daryl butter was longer than Spider and mines put together. His hair whips around and slaps me in the face from the slap.

I didn't say shit, Spider G didn't say shit, either. We looked at each other and thought we were next.

The officer then turned to Spider and me and said. "Get the fuck out the car your friends going to jail. He don't know how to spell his name."

Spider and I get out the car and they rolled off to the station. Once we got out the car. We went back and picked up the forties. We took a drink out of it and looked at each other and started busting up laughing. We started tripping on how hard Daryl got smack.

Spider asked, "did you hear how it sounded off Folks?"

What I think it was, is that the girl he slammed, called the law. They got on us, but they knew she wasn't going to finger him. She knew he was with Spider and nobody told on Spider.

They handled him in their own way. The way the cops treated us even though they had a reason that time. They way they'd roll up on us and stretched us out. The countless times they searched us for no reason.

I'd do anything to get back at them low-key. I wasn't cool with Daryl slamming the lady so he got what he had coming. That was Daryl and Spider G gloating over the slam. I figured you don't get any points for that, not from me.

After thinking about those couple of things I tell Boya I'm in, okay let's go. He then tells me the stain is right around the corner. The stain is down the street from my house. We walked right down the alley. I just came out to kick it and now I'm about to break in someone house. We hit the bell a few times.

When you looked at Boya and I. You know we were up to something. Boya butter is tight, he got pitchforks sprayed in blue off in his shit. I got the six point stars sprayed in my waves. Toni who did our hair had all types of gang symbol stencils.

We both got the black bucks on so we got to move quickly. You know all that's goon gear. We look just like Folks, too easy to identify. Any extra time getting in the house we are going to get spotted.

I can still abort, if I don't feel the stain. This is my rule of thumb, if you don't get away with it, why do it? It was broad daylight, but daylight was the only time you could hit the house, without him being home.

Boya was pro style with his craft. We hit the backyard after the third ring on the bell, no answer. If anybody were watching, they would've thought we were talking to the occupants. Boya played like they came to the door already. He gave the play off to anybody looking, the spin move.

He did this by pointing his finger to the back and saying, "oh okay, go to the back" out loud.

He said it loud enough for anybody in the area looking to hear. This spin was in effect, to throw off anybody. They might be looking and listening from behind the curtains next door.

We shoot around back look around to get our bearings. Boya took his shirt off grabbed a big rock. He goes to work immediately. He pick up and put a nice size stone and rapped it in his shirt. The shirt cushioned the sound it would make banging against the window.

When he banged the stone up against the window. Each time he struck the window without breaking it. He'd he hit it just a little harder. He struck the window three times before it cracked and broke. Boya was striking the window just hard enough so it wouldn't make a lot of noise.

He took all the glass out the window, while wiping his prints off with his shirt. After wiping the prints off he shook the glass out his shirt. He put his shirt back on, then slides in the window to check it out. He was in the house in two minutes tops.

I stay on lookout. You don't want to go in while someone's in the house. You just turned what you were doing into a home invasion. That's a totally different case, if caught. It's a much heavier penalty than an ordinary B&E. A B&E at the time carried one to three years. A home invasion shoots you up to fifteen years.

The people might be sleeping in the house. If someone's in there sleep I'm aborting the mission. I'm sitting low waiting on Boya to come back from looking around the house.

He comes back after a minute and says, "it's all clear", then opens the backdoor.

We get in the house and dude had all type of shit. He had computers, pistols, stereos, cordless phones and money uncut in a picture frame. This dude was heavy whoever he was and stayed right down and across the street from me. I never knew him.

He had the newest shit that technology had offer at the time. People didn't have the latest technology in the hood. A VCR was a new commodity. When they first came out they costed four to five hundred dollars. Microwave hit for six hundred dollars back when they first came out.

I was literally thinking Boya was professional cat burglar. He needed no tools.

I said to myself, "no wonder they hit stains. This nigga is good." We're in and he tells me what to do.

He stops me says, "hit that room and he'll do the one he was standing by. Look under the beds and in the drawers."

Like I didn't know, but if I didn't, he was schooling me. I looked around and picked up this picture frame of money, uncut. Dude got a lot of uncut bills and it blew me away. I never saw the money uncut before in somebody house. I'm looking at the money like wow. There's twenties, five and tens all uncut money.

I opened the drawer it was two brand new heaters. One .357 magnum and a 38 revolver chrome both fully loaded. I grabbed up .357 and put it in my waste. I found Boya in the crib and gave him the 38. I was claiming the .357.

I wanted him to have a missile just in case someone came in on us. I remember Mrs. Lane scream after walking through the door. This dude is the police, if he catches us, he's coming in shooting. That's what I would do, if I caught somebody in my house.

My man had so much shit in his house it was a shame. He had all the newest of the new shit. Granted dude had just got hit about three months earlier. That's why Coole didn't want to go with Boya.

Coole and one of the Folks hit the crib already. They got a bunch of shit then when they hit it. They got a 44 Magnum the first time. He can't have too much more shit I thought. That's another reason why it took him a while to convince me. It already had been hit.

That's Mrs. Lane all over again, sloppy seconds.

Boya gave me the inside lowdown he said, "dude got insurance so he was going to get it right back."

This had to be an inside job Boya knew too much information. He was hoping he had a key of cocaine or something around the house. Something he wouldn't be able to report. We could leave everything in there, if we found the cocaine. Before Boya opened the door. I watched him open the refrigerator and check it first.

We were cleaning dude all the way out. The only thing though its was broad daylight. Now how are we going to get this shit out without a car? We already put the shit we were stealing in black plastic bags by the back door. We got the plastic bags from under the kitchen sink.

We loaded the merch up by the back yard's back gate. He had a privacy fence so nobody on the outside of the gate could see us. Boya leaves the yard and go out on security. He goes all the way out to the end of the alley. The police officer stayed about in the middle of 169th & Calumet.

Boya was going to tell me when it's all clear. I then would have to bring as much shit as I could down the alley. I come with the first load and hid it out of site behind some bushes. When I was coming Boys left for his load. Boya and I are going backward and forwards to the house.

We were criss crossing each other, taking turns on security and getting the merch out. I'm making sure nobody comes on their back porch. I was scoping to see, if anybody's shade move.

When that happens you got to take what you can and just go. The boys will be on their way. We didn't plan to have that much shit. We are kind of looking stupid with all this shit, because we got to flag somebody down, to get us out.

Just so happen one of the Folks was riding down the alley in his blue Pontiac. I stop him and said, "Folks we just hit this crib and we need a ride. We'll give you a hun, if you throw this shit in your car."

He looked at the shit and said, "bet"

I told him, "hold on I'm going to tell Boya what it is. I go back and told Boya and I left Folks on security.

I run back to the yard and tell Boya. First he looks surprise to see me, because I'm not on security, but before he could say something I say, "I got Folks to load us up and we were out."

Boya grabbed the rest of the shit and smiled and said, "you bullshitting?"

I reply, "straight up let's go, we out."

He grinned and said, "Folks that's why I came and got your ass."

We were on our last loads anyway when Folks rolled up.

By the time I get back Folks had the shit loaded up waiting on us. Boya and I grabbed the last of the merch and dropped it in trunk. The timing was impeccable. It was like we planned it that way.

Neither one of us had gloves so we were constantly wiping shit as we go. When I open the dresser drawers. I had my hands underneath my shirt. I was using my shirt as gloves. The only thing I thought I touched was the stuff we were taking. I was hoping I wiped everything. I couldn't risk going back to make sure. We hit the jackpot. We got two missiles, money and a lot of merch.

We shot to the low end to lay low. We kept the merch to sell on the low end, for a few days. Boya sister was cool. As a matter of fact she was fine as hell too. She also cooked for us while we were at her house. We just tore her off a hundred a piece for the storage spot.

I didn't mind hanging over there, until we sold the merch. I spent about three nights over there while we got half of it off. It's honor among thieves, but I ain't no fool. I wasn't going anywhere. We were chilling eating and watching TV and living on the lamb.

The next day while we were chilling at his sister's house. Boya gets into with some niggas on his way to the store to get some beer. He went by himself and it was lucky he took the missile. He had to pop at or popped some niggas trying to rob him. He comes running back into the crib. He slammed the door and hit the window looking out of it.

He was excited while saying, "Folks you hear my shit going off, that was me letting them go."

We asked him like he was bullshitting, "what you pop a nigga for Boya?"

Boya answers, "dude walked up on me and asked for a square. I was going to give the nigga a square. I reach for the square and he steals on me."

"The nigga stole on me and dazed me Folks. It was three niggas coming at me. I stumbled after he stole on me, but I was able to get the banger out. I started blasting at the niggas while I was dazed. I know I hit one of those niggas. I let off three and ran back here. I know I had to hit a couple of those niggas Folks."

I thought he was bullshitting at first. I looked and seen he had some scuffmarks on his jaw from the blow.

He said it again, "they were trying to rob me Folks and I blasted at em."

I opened up his 38 and yep he had four empty shells. I smelled the gunpowder coming from the barrel. The 38 caliber was sweet. It opened up by the chamber and broke in half. It was easy to reload. Boya just left out the door fifteen minutes ago. I couldn't believe it.

We should've gone with him. They wouldn't have tried us two three deep. Boya was high yellow and a good-looking nigga to the girls. You know they think pretty boys are marks. We told Boya to cool out while we go see what was happening.

I know they don't know Folks and I. We got to do the surveillance. I'm trying to see, if they found out where Boya had ran. They will be back blasting, if they did or worse call the police. We got all this stolen merch tying us to the robbery.

I grabbed the .357. Folks grabbed Boya's 38 reloaded it with the shells we got out the house. We needed to know what happened. What if someone is dead or shot? We need to be on our way back to the hood. We had to check it out. Boya told us the path he took and we backtracked.

Folk and I was black ass hell. They're looking for a high yellow nigga. We didn't fit the description. They were looking for somebody light complexion with finger waves. Nobody was out though! We didn't see any blood so we came back. Before going back to spot we got some more bubble and weed and tripped out on the shit.

We sold half of the shit in the first three days at his sister's house. Boya called your brother Slick Coole. He was at the house when we got back. He seen the uncut sheets and was wondering why we didn't try to use the sheets yet? We needed to cut them up straight. We needed one of those paper cutters.

Coole grabbed some scissors and cut the sheets up and went to the store. The edges of the bills were jagged like they were cut up, with scissors. Coole didn't have any problem cashing them.

What are we young niggas doing with some uncut money or money we cut? They got them off though! We bought beers, weed and food, until all those sheets were gone.

Folks who pick us up left after the second night. Boya was calling people he knew to buy the merch. I must admit he knew the people who didn't mind buying stolen shit. We'd jump in cabs to get the merch off. We'd get paid jump back in the same cab and come back. This particular time on the way back from a run.

Boya was like. "I'm a jump out at the light a couple blocks from the crib. Fuck paying this taxi fare."

The fare was about twenty-three dollars. I said, "man don't do it Boya."

He just laughed and said, "I'm jumping out. You can pay, if you want to Colo."

We get a couple blocks from our designation. I was hoping he was bullshitting, but he gave me the elbow. That's the indicator he was about to hits the door break out and run.

I had to do the same thing I hit my door. The cab driver was shouting at us. Come here you motherfuckas. I should pop y'all little asses. He tried to chase us for a while, but we ditched him. Boya was doing too much shit to bring attention to us. We are on the lamb were not suppose to be bringing attention to ourselves. We are jumping out of cabs, popping niggas in the area, while we trying to sell stolen merch.

It was too much going on over on the low-end. After the third day of chilling I took half the stuff that was left, to the crib. He took his half of the stuff to sell to his house. The deal was whoever sold the merch had to split the money when we sold it.

I went to all the dope men and hustlers in the hood and got my shit off. I went and saw Donald Bird, Jake, SteveO, Lando and anybody getting money. I kept the heater. I told Boya he didn't have to give me shit off his and I kept mine.

He said, "bet."

I had enough money to hold me over for a while. I was going to cop some weed while I sit on the shit I already got. When I fuck my cop money up, sell some shit. I ain't in any hurry that's how you get caught. When you got to take what you can get for the merch real quick. Which usually ain't going to be shit, for cash. Niggas know it's hot and are going to lowball you. It's best, if you sit on it to get what you want.

I said to myself, "no more stains Colo." My conscious was still fucking with me afterwards. I went back on my word to the all supreme. I said after Lane job I was straight on breaking in cribs. I didn't feel good about it.

I'm never breaking in nobody else's house again. I got away with it too and I got paid too. This shit ain't right, but I am paid. Even though he was a dirty cop I crossed the line. Going in another motherfuckas home, just ain't right. Tell a starving ass teenager that though! One who has the weight of the world on his young shoulders!

At this age we just don't process the shit right. You're young, but you are facing grown up issues. You got too many people coming from all direction pulling you in the game. Kid make it, has gone to and returned from the dark side. Worst of all I knew I would pay for breaking my word to Yahweh. Right now it all good and I'm cranking my weed after the stain.

Economics

When you are the weed man you are needed in the community. Instead of using, government sponsored drugs that have a lot of side affects. The underground has something that can help when ailing.

There's a dependency on pharmaceuticals making bank on us. This is while shutting down access to a more efficient medicine through law making. They put a stigma on marijuana with a mad negative campaign through movies and propaganda.

Marijuana has properties in it that heals people. It helps with your eyes. It helps with nausea. It helps with cancer patients with pain or any pain for that matter. It is an aphrodisiac when love making. It helps you figure things out despite the popular belief it makes your dumb. I can go

A lot of times in bad situations I'd smoke weed and come up with an answer. It doesn't turn you into a lump of rocks. I wasn't sure, but I knew what it did to me. I began to be more cerebral. It's the alcohol that sends your morals and good values out the window. I figured that out a long time ago. I am the underground medicine man.

Marijuana can be cultivated in your own backyard. This is too much power for poor people to have. This is the only reason it is probably illegal. It's a way of coming up and they don't want poor people coming up. Why would the government let all individuals have this power?

The Mexicans had the West coast and were banging weed. The French had what we know as Middle America. We made a deal with the French and they sold us Middle America with the Louisiana Purchase. We needed the coast in order to control war and trade. We had to have those seaports.

After the war of 1846-48 we confiscated a 1/3 of Mexico. Once the war was won the west perimeter of the land is now in control. After the war the Mexicans was still coming over as vagrants, selling weed in confiscated Mexico. This is now California, Arizona, Texas and spots like that in the Southwest.

Harry Aintslinger head of the DEA did a test on college students. The test came back conclusive that marijuana did you no harm. What did they do? They discarded the results and made it illegal. The results did not reflect the agenda the government had. The government constructed this land off of marijuana.

Benjamin Franklin and lot of other forefathers smoked, wrote on and wore marijuana. The hemp plant was used for paper. The constitution is written on Hemp paper. They made our garments we wore out of the hemp plant. Just think about it, all these thinking guys were smoking Marijuana coming up with how our country would be ran. Marijuana was our national product at one time. What an hypocrisy to keep the 99 percent from coming up.

I know exactly why they outlawed it. Marijuana taps into your thinking process in a positive way. In order to keep you down and stop you from thinking out the box keep them liquored up.

They illegalized it to stop anyone's come up mentally and financially. I have obtained my Bachelor degree and every test I took in college I was high. The weed was unlocking those test blocks you get from anxiety.

The myth that it causes lung cancer has been shattered. You don't get cancer from smoking weed. I don't know, but weed could be a blocker from some diseases. Hey look at Benjamin Franklin he grew to be, an old man smoking weed.

The government still would let you buy and grow Marijuana. You had to have this rubber stamp, but in order to get the rubber stamp. You had to have the weed in hand. This is the catch 22 for people. To have the weed in hand was illegal. Once you got the illegal weed in hand. You would be arrested for trying to buy the rubber stamp.

The government is tricky. Nobody to my knowledge was able to obtain the rubber stamp. Why would the government stop something that's so harmless? The government has there own agenda. They have their own drugs to sell you. The ones with all the side effects and that put your life in jeopardy. I am going to stop with the government, because I could talk you to death. Speaking of weed, fire that shit up Emus.

Emus says, you ain't said nothing but a word".

He immediately starts breaking down the weed and rolling blunts.

John says, "I am about to make a store run, you know I don't smoke. We need more 1738."

Harold looks at me in say, "Colo Dog while Johns at the store what's up with a one on one."

John stops before walking out the door and asked. "You want to play Colo Dog one on one. I already know you ain't got no win. I got twenty dollars Colo Dog runs through you."

Harold laughs and say, "I need some of that action John, easy money."

Once he made the bet he sealed his fate. I told him to immediately go get his shoes. He tells me he doesn't need them for me.

I laced up and we meet on the court. Harold didn't understand what I was going to put on him. I was going to die on that court. I made sure I stepped on his feet after a rebound for the disrespect. He must think he playing his kid out here. I grinded those toes into the concrete and told him my fault.

I jumped so far in his ass on defense he barely could get a shot off. It was one o'clock and the sun was beaming on us like a heat ray. I ran down every loose ball. I ran him even though it was evident he was going to get the ball. I wanted him exhausted. I wanted him to burn the skin off his feet trying to stop and go. After I got him tired I hit him with jumpers with no defense.

Needless to say I won the game 32-12. I didn't say one word to him and just walked off the court and jumped in the shower. Harold and Jackie ended up leaving so he could shower at his house. I get dressed and chill with the satisfaction of changing my status from a loser in Texas. John comes back and I tell him he is a winner, pick up his money.

He then says, "I tried to tell him Colo Dog, you were another level."

I shake my head in agreement and then say, "he was trying to show out in front of his girl. I didn't hear a peep from her when the game was going on!"

Setting them out

When we were young the guys used to set the girls out. It's different now people are killing over these women. Guys back then didn't have any problems with turning you on to a girl.

We grew up in the macking generation so it was no big thing. We weren't pimps on the Met. Macks were different than pimps. A mack just had a bunch of women on his tip. The woman wasn't tricking for him they just wanted him.

A mack can't be tied down and the woman dealing with him knows about each other. A mack is a woman's fantasy, but she can't have him. You only could enjoy him for the moment. A lot of guys ran trains on some of the promiscuous girls. They were some girls who'd let you run trains on them.

I was more private with sex. I didn't think I should go behind a guy with sloppy seconds or third. Exchanging of each other bodily fluids I thought was disgusting. One day John Strong came to the house. He needed some weed.

He told me he was about to run a train on ol girl down the street. It was he and Lil Rich and couple of other guys running the train. I had to come outside the house and serve him the weed so I walked in the direction he was going.

They had already had some drank. I had the weed so I kicked it. I went down in the basement, and yep, they had ol girl. She walked right by me smiling wearing some short, shorts.

I was sitting on the bed chilling and they asked me, "Colo you want some pussy?"

I told him, "I'm straight". She wasn't the prettiest girl, but she had a womb. Everybody down there was hitting her. I am cool and don't indulge. I only wanted to hit the prettiest girls. How can I be picky and I don't get no nookie? She wasn't it and it was about four guys on her already, I was straight.

I just drank a little bit, blew a joint and went back to the crib. A couple weeks later the police came and picked Rich and John up for a rape charge. I see the police at his house and they took them to jail for raping that girl. John gets out of jail and I caught up with him. I asked him what happened?

He said, "she said that we raped her Colo."

I said to John, "John I was there and she didn't get raped. I didn't go back in the room, but she was a willing participant." She went back in the back on her own will and she didn't seem drunk. Now she telling the police they raped her. I was so glad I had my morals and values about sex.

They beat the case, but look at the stigma attached to their name. They didn't rape that girl, but it's on their record somehow I'll bet. Some people in the neighborhood believed that girl, but she lied on them. Of course they could've raped her after I left. They were juveniles at the time.

John was the oldest he was about sixteen. Everybody else was younger than him. That's one thing I was tripping on too the young players are getting pussy!

Even my younger brother was getting more ass than me. He had his little girl friend. He was banging her in the basement at the house when Mom was gone. I come in the house and he'd be sneaking her out.

I'd look and asked, "Walls, you getting pussy?"

He was like, "yeah I smashes her all the time. This had me fucked up, because he's two years younger than I. I ain't getting no poonany except that one time and he is, wow.

Rob from NY was getting plenty too. He had this grown lady he was hitting. We would get high and stop over there and he'd stay. It was right down the street from my crib.

I thought he was bullshitting too, because this was a grown lady. She was straight she had a big ass and big titties. She had short fro, but was cross-sided a little bit. He used to laugh about it.

He used to laugh and say, "Colo I can't look her in the eyes, because I get dizzy."

He would laugh and I'd crack up, because he acted dizzy when he said it. She was about twenty-five. Rob was only sixteen knocking her off. He was with Shannel when he first got here too. For some reason he wasn't sweating her, but she was on him. He comes in from out of town and gets more ass than me.

I wanted a girl out the neighborhood. All the girls in the hood already were blew out. I wanted the girls in the hood, but the pretty ones were taken. Most of them already got guys who were my guys.

I was young with older guys and just couldn't find my niche with the girls. It was just like sports either I was too late or too early. I'm too young to talk to the older girls. It was too late for the pretty ones my age, because they're taken. I didn't want a girl who already been tapped by one of my hommies, anyway.

Banging Hard

*M*y life from fifteen to eighteen years of age I carried the nation hard. This means wherever you go you are identified immediately, because of the battle dress gear. The crew consisted of Spider G, Grimes, Sacks, Lil Tone, and I. Everybody's wore butters long coats and bucks that winter.

Bucks are shoes the Folks used to wear. Vicelords wore them too, but mostly Folks wore these particular shoes. That's how Disco used to get Folks, because he wore bucks and the butter. He'd fly those forks to see, if you threw them back. When you threw them back he'd steal on you.

The shoes were suede and came up to your ankles. They came in blue, black, red and gray. I had all colors except the red ones. Some tied up with the string and some had a buckle. Some had the stitched line up the middle, with the string tie up.

You had to keep buying fresh pairs, because they would get dusty fast. A fresh pair of bucks looked sweet with just about anything you wore. They were affordable too. They hit for sixteen to twenty-five dollars. We'd hit parties everywhere, looking for girls in our battle dress gear. This one night we go to St. Isley on 161st. King Drive

You knew we were together. Everybody in the clique was wearing long cashmere or wool black coats. We call the coats shotgun coats, because you could easily carry a concealed shotgun. Everybody had fresh finger waves in the click.

We go to a party and we see Jamarus Bell he was Folks, but he made it to the pros. He was in the club standing in the six-point stance leaning against the wall. Folks had security, but I wouldn't have been in a spot like that.

He was tall ass hell and was drafted to the NBA in the first round.

I looked at him and said to myself, "there's no way in the world I would be here, if I was in the pros". He had made it out, but he was still hanging and banging. That right their perplexed me. I guess that's why he didn't last in the pros too long he wasn't focused.

This was before Sacks's hair fell out. I come to the front door one day and Sacks's butter is in his hat. He shows me his hat with the hair. I saw him the night before and he had waves. He told me when I looked at his head like, "why you cut your shit, without saying nothing?" He was ball faded from one day to the next so I looked at him surprised.

He tells me how it happened. "It fell out Folks while I was sleep, I had to cut it off."

I laughed and cracked jokes on him. This was one time we all were in unison though, with the look. We're representing the Folks off 169th.St. Grimes knew some girls who were going to be at the party.

We walked to St. Isley down King Drive. We all had a half a pint to ourselves. We were drinking cheap at the time. I had a Gin or a Canadian Mist. I smoked some weed and the crew bought weed from me. We met up with some more Folks, before we get to the joint. Sacks knows everybody so he hollers at em.

He comes back and said, "Folks got a spot where we can drink our shit and cool out, until the party pops."

I said, "fuck it let's go, because it's cold." That's what I loved about being Folks. We could go anywhere in the city. It was like you had cousins everywhere and they all had love for you. You could be in squabble and not know these guys and they would help.

We get to this spot. I was familiar with the area we were sitting in spot around my Godmother's house Mrs. Carmelita. We were with about eight other Folks we didn't know except for Sacks. Sacks busted out a wicky stick. I don't fuck with wickies, but I said fuck it this time. I'll try it once. I'll hit it one time, before we hit the party.

Wicky has a few names. They call it sherm stick or loveboat.

"What it is", Andrea asked.

"It is embalming fluid! It is what they use to preserve dead people. I couldn't see smoking it like people were, because it was for dead people. Sacks used to love those wicky sticks. We crack open the dranks and blow the weed with Folks in the spot. We all offer each other the dranks and passed the weed to the Folks we didn't know. The Folks we met were cool. They bought weed from me and fired it up. We were sitting on the steps inside the back hallway to the apartments. We were sitting on somebody's back step to thier backdoor. Sacks then fired up the wickey after we got a little comfortable.

We were taking turns on security so the twisters wouldn't roll up on us. I hit the wicky twice and passed it. No soon as I passed it to somebody else I look out the door. Here come the twisters coming down the alley slow, with the lights twirling.

We breaks out I can't get caught with the sack. I already scoped out which way to run just in case something happened. That's one thing you got to be on your five P's. You just can't run anywhere you might run into a dead end. When you run, you got to get away.

I already had kicked it in this hood plenty of times. I sprint out running in slow motion. I heard the six million dollar man noise when I was running. Waaa waaa waaaa Waaa waaa waaaa!

You know how Steve Austin was supposed to be running fast, but he was running in slow motion? He had this sound to indicate he's really moving fast, but on TV he's looking slow. The sound represented the speed you couldn't see. I was running in slow motion with that sound playing in my head, waaa wwaaa wwwa wwaaaaa!

I told Folks to follow me and I'd get them out the spot without running into the law. We gave the boys a move, while they searched some of the other guys. We started walking to the hall and blended in with some people going to the party.

Sacks was walking beside me after things calmed down and I asked, "why do you like this wicky shit, this shit gots me tripping?"

He laughs and answers, "that's why I like it. It has me tripping", then he starts laughing again.

That was the first and the last time I would fuck with the wicky sticks. I shelved the wicky stick.

We finally get to the party. It was a Folks party. Only reason we were there is, because Grimes knew some girls coming. We're in the party and I was having a ball. I had a slow dance with this fine looking girl. I pulled her in the dark when the music slow music started playing.

I am grooving with her right. She draped all over me. I started dropping my game on her. She is all in and gives me her number. After the dance and the lights came back on I told her we'd hook up. I didn't want to seem anxious.

I saw Spider G and told him I just pulled a fine young thang. I wanted to show the guys I could pull girls. I walked around the party and came back across her in the light.

She looked like she was bent over walking. I looked closer and I notice a big hump in her back. I'm like, "wow she got a hump in her back." I didn't let Spider know I just kept walking by like I was still looking for her.

I asked myself could I get pass the hump in her back, because she was pretty. I couldn't and never called her. I was wondering why she was so happy to dance with me. She had a hump in her back. No wonder she was draped over me, she couldn't stand up straight.

Everybody having fun, but I could tell, the girls Grimes came to see. They had some other Folks on their tip. Folks were trying to get on them from off 161st but Grimes snatched them up in front of them.

The niggas were not looking cool. They were watching while Grimes was all in the girl's face smiling. I told Grimes, "Grimes watch yourself these niggas are peeping you."

Grimes did the Grimes and said, "fuck those niggas."

I had the weed so I'm trying to sell weed in the party. I was in the back of the hall in the bathroom. This is when I peeped what was going on with Grimes and the niggas.

I zoomed around to find my Folk's and wire them up on the situation. I told them to be ready these niggas are going to try and move. One of his guys was looking at my six-point star earlier. I had it on a chain on my chest.

He looked without an expression and said, "nice star"

I look him in the eye, steely and say, "yep." He kept it moving. No sooner than I said that! One of the dudes that were looking at Grimes got Grimes by the collar. I looked at Folks and said, "let's move." I shoot over there and confronted dude. "Get your motherfucking hands off my Folk's and shouted out 169th ST. D-Cipo."

I'm loud ass hell and ready to blaze, but he let Grimes go immediately. I said it like dude did in the theater in "Warriors", the movie. Once he let Grimes go I said, "come on Grimes what the fuck is he grabbing you for?" Grimes said something, but I am in wreck mode.

I looked at the Folks and said it time to move.

Spider G was like, "I'm a go get the heat."

I said, if you ain't got it on you, it's too late. We got to fight our way out of here". To my amazement all they did was look at us leave.

We did look ruthless, but they had us out number 50 to 5. These were BD's on 61st too. When I said 169th St. D Cipo they must have gave us a pass that night. See that was cool.

All the niggas I was with were GD's. Even though we were all is one. You still will get into it, over those girls. That wicky had me like I could take on all these motherfuckas by myself. Last time I will smoke a wicky. I wanted to stay at the party and everything. The girls were digging me after that happened.

Grimes said, "naw nigga let's get the fuck out of here."

We skated and they didn't fuck with us. Those shotgun coats did look menacing. You just didn't know, if we had the heat. I was talking like we had plenty of heat. That's how charged I got.

On the strip I carried the pistol everyday at this point. The .357 Magnum I got from the stain. I always had it close somewhere stash or in my book bag. Right on the barrel it says Cook County Sheriff. If caught with it, it will be hell to pay. When convicted of carrying it that's an automatic ten years, if caught with it.

All I needed was a reason to use it, but I wasn't looking. I wasn't on a power trip like some people. I was going to just use it for my protection. I'm a known player that means I am a target. I could fight so I didn't have to use a gun. You had to have years of training to confront me physically. You had to have a gun to get the up so I had to have a gun.

I wasn't out looking for drama. It's scandalous out here. I'm around demons that are controlling my guys and I all the time. You got to be prepared when shit pops off. I know we ain't the only demons walking the street. Opposition are riding with bangers and ain't no time to be talking about I'll be back.

That's why I didn't pop Lee that day. Had he shown me or brandished a weapon I would've killed him. It was for niggas who were trying to kill me. I was confident with my hands on the strip. I love to do the man dance with the knuckles. I'll just whoop a nigga ass too. I didn't need a gun, but I wasn't stupid.

You got those guys who talk crazy, but can't take an ass whooping. If there wasn't any guns out here to make guys tough. The only way you settle disputes is if, you had to box and show your manhood. I bet it wouldn't be that many people getting into confrontation.

You know the ones who are ready to pop. They talk like they got a missile. It a different talk a nigga got, when he got a missile. You can tell it, it's in his or her posture. They way he holds his mouth. His nose will flare out with confidence. When you see that don't say nothing out of pocket.

The only people who knew I carried heat, was my Folk's. I wasn't pulling it out and showing people. I wasn't getting charged, because I got a banger. It was for niggas trying to kill my hommies and I. It was never used in starting confrontation or looking for the opposition to kill. I did one-armed robbery with it, but that was by accident.

You had to be my hommie to know I had the missile. You could be Folks and I never said, nothing. Reason why when people know you got one. They get a little more rambunctious. They'll put you in a position so you'll have to use it.

My mother told me, "anytime you pull a gun on somebody. You better be using it."

Some niggas just wanted to flex shoot in the air and act tough, because they got a gun. Real niggas act the same way with or without a gun.

Down for my Hood

You know Boe Boe who used to hang with us. Boe Boe and Spider G came at me while I was walking down the nine.

They said, "the Hooks from the building tried to move on Boe Boe."

Spider told me, "go get the heater Folks."

I told him, "lets ride I already got it."

After I jumped in I asked, "what Hooks was it?"

Spider says, "it was some hooks with Tracy and Ronald."

These were well-known Brothers from the white building. The white building was located on 172nd &Vincennes.

We go get Grimes and jumped in his car. They already know Boe Boe car coming down the street. We ride over toward the white building. Boe Boe began to tell Grimes and me the haps.

Boe Boe got stole on, Harold. Now that's Spider G hommie so we had to help.

He wasn't Folks, but we used to get high over Boe Boe crib all the time. I've known Boe since Rock Manor. We played football in that schoolyard on many of days. I said, "Okay Boe Boe who stole on you?"

Boe Boe said, "I don't know his name. I never seen him before."

I knew a few of the Stones from the white building that were cool.

I told Boe, "We are just going to get the one nigga who moved on you. You are going to smash him." Back then we weren't just popping niggas. It was still some gladiating going on first!

We'll pull the missile out, if shit was out of hand. That was another charge, if caught by the police. Our main thang was to smash you on site. We had to go right back, because they knew Boe was affiliated with us.

That was a form of disrespect to us. We must ain't shit over here. They come over on the nine and move our neutron. The next move is to set up camp. We get back over there to the building within thirty minutes and catch them still walking around. I gave the unit to Grimes, before we got out the car. He was on security. We jumped out the car with the unit out.

We walked over to where they were standing, about five deep. When they seen us coming they didn't run. They weren't expecting us either.

Grimes pulled the banger out and said, "don't move or I'll pop all y'all asses. Which one of y'all motherfuckas stole on my hommie?"

They didn't say nothing.

Grimes was standing in the street, pointing the banger at them. Spider G, Boe and I walks and confronts them. I asked Boe, "which one of these nigga's stole on you?" He points him out.

I said, "smash his ass Boe." Boe walks over and gives my man a love tap on the jaw. After that, he stepped back like he was straight.

I looked at him with unbelievable eyes. I said, "Boe move like a villain, whoop his ass Boe." He swings just a little softer the next time and steps back again. This nigga was a bundle of nerves. If you don't help yourself, I can't help you.

I'm not going to be the one going to jail, while you didn't do shit. He did enough, but I thought he would have put uglies on dude. He was scared of these Stones and I could see how.

He wasn't even Folks so he really didn't want to do it. Spider G really wanted to go back. Boe never said shit about going back. We were over there though and he did make an attempt to do something. He's making us look soft. I saw one of the guys smirk after he saw how Boe Boe punched dude. I had to let them know what the nine, was about.

I looked at Boe with my unbelievable eyes again. I know my eyes popped open to the limit. I push him to the side and had to finish what we came to do. I stole on him, out the blue, quick. We right back at you Brother. He had no reason for messing with Boe he was a neutron.

I banged him with a four or five piece bing bam boom. I threw hooks and uppercuts no jabs thrown. This dropped him to his knees. I blazed him with another three -piece combination. All face shots he took some ugly ones too. He didn't even try to block some of them. He probably was out on the first blaze. I stopped, because he really didn't fuck Boe up either.

I was sending a message to the Brothers. Don't come down on the nine, fucking with nobody. It wasn't anything wrong with Boe. His feelings was hurt, had they smashed him it would've been worst.

Grimes got the drop on everybody and nobody moves. After breaking him down I said, "let's go Folks" I get to walking across the street to the car and noticed my hat fell off while smashing him. Oh you know I am a bad motherfucker. Oh I felt the power.

I turned around and walked back through all of them, while folks walked to the car. I walked through them all looking each one of them, dead in the eyes.

Grimes hollered out frantically, "Folks he coming with a shotgun."

I didn't even look back around I broke wide, shheeewoooOOH into the wind. Grimes weren't parked on the side of the street where I was walking. I figured dude with the shotgun was on my side of the street. I would have to run back across the street, to the car, giving him a shot.

Instead, I break out the other way and hit the corner digging. I hear two blasts. I didn't know who was blasting. I just heard the big booms. I didn't hear the whizzing sound from the pellets going past me, nor feel anything.

The .357 piece might as well, been a shotgun. It sounded like a shotgun. I wasn't hit so I dug into the concrete in my bucks to get away. I bent the corner and hit an alley across the street and was about to hop a gate. Grimes, Spider and Boe jumped in the car by that time. I didn't know how I was going to meet them. The plan was fucked up.

I was thinking to myself, "I got to make it all the way back to 169th" and I am digging, hard. Before I hopped the gate heading that way back home. I hear a car coming through the alley with screeching tires. Grime was coming through the alley like the Dukes of Hazards. All you could hear was the Charger tires screeching and the door pops open.

Before I noticed it was Boe coming through the alley. I was flying and was in mid flight over the gate. My feet didn't touch the gate and I was on the other side when I saw them.

I had to make sure it was Grimes coming through the alley first. It was, thank God, here comes that green Charger. I spent around jumped back over the gate and into the car. We high tail it back to the nine. Grimes was in the passenger seat and Boe was driving. Boe was driving wild and scared as fuck.

Grimes and Spider was shouting at him, "cool out you weak ass nigga before you get us pull over. We over here with your soft ass and ain't trying to go to jail."

I jumped in the car and said while breathing hard, "I had to move cause you made us look weak as hell Boe. When Boe hit dude, it wasTracey who started smiling a little bit. I had to move with your weak ass. I asked Folks, "were they shooting at me?"

Grimes answered, "Naw that was us shooting. I had to start blasting you ran the wrong fucking way."

I reply, "you right, I didn't know who it was popping. I reach over the front seat so Boe could see my face and said. That was your fight Boe we just had your back. I wished I'd known you were going to do that. We shouldn't have even gone over there."

We had to though! You are only as tough as the weakest link. Boe was affiliated with us. That's how they get in through weak niggas. When you fuck with him, you've fucked with me when that's my guy.

CHAPTER FIVE

Back Stabber

I finally got tired of being in a freshmen division. I was used to being around people much older than I. At least two three years older, now I'm around people two three years younger. Ain't that something! Now I want to be around an older crowd. I went back up to Darobe I had to talk to Bonner. I get up there and wait in the attendance office for him.

I still could've come back and graduated from Darobe. All I had to do was finish my junior year at Communication Metro. I got options on the table since I took control. It was an option, but if I was going to play football. I'll have to stay my senior year.

Bonner came out his office looked and said, "Columbus George how are you doing? Are you beating anybody up?"

He had a grin on his face when he said it. I just smiled and answered, "No Bonner I am chilling trying to stay on track. I'm trying to settle into Communication Metro, Bonner. Mr. Bonner, my problem is Darobe won't release my transcripts for missing books."

He shakes he head and says, "Columbus you got to pay for the books and they'll release them."

I pause for a second and made a sigh, then I tell him. "Mr. Bonner you know what I've been going through, trying to go school." I do have a flare for the dramatic!

He knows about the fire that destroyed our home a year ago. He knows about us being wiped out with nowhere to live.

I told him, "I don't have any money. Bonner, those books were stolen from me from my locker. They took everything in the locker." In truth I sold those books to Cadillac on 169th & Wentworth. He had a used book spot in his joint. I sold the books and then put the money in the games he had.

At first, Bonner was hesitant, but I gave him a couple helpless looks. I owed about $186 dollars in books. At the end of my plea I said. "This is the only thing holding me up. I am trying to do the right thing, Bonner it just hard." He finally conceded and signed my release forms and sent my transcripts. I love Bonner he had my back.

This is how I thank him. I kicks it with Slept Rock the rest of the day up at the Robe. I might as well kicked it and have some fun with my guys. I'll sell and smoke some weed then I'll go home. I went to lunch first.

I still had a Darobe ID. After lunch Slept Rock and I went outside the building. Slept Rock doesn't smoke, but I was going to get high and hang a while. While we were outside Slept Rock sees one of his guys from around his crib.

This guy named Charles, who worked in the game room on Halsted. Just a couple blocks from where Slept Rock live.

Slept said, "he's a mark and all you got to do is ask him for the money. He'll give it to you. They rob him easy around the crib all the time."

I told him, "naw I'm straight" I look at dude and dude is big than a motherfucka too.

Slept then says, "I'm telling you, all you got to do is say, "give me your money. He's going to do it. He's just a big ass goofy freshmen. He be having bank, though!"

Slept Rock is pushing the buttons to activate my demon. I then say, "all I got to do is ask him for his money? That's too easy I can do that." We're coming up with this plan while walking along the side of the building.

I said fuck it, stopped dude and told him to give me his money. Charles looked at me like I was a knat.

He looked and said, "you better get the fuck out of my face. I ain't got no money."

I give him the grim look and say. Nigga I ain't playing, give me your money. Charles swung on me. I ducked and looked at him and then I looked at Slept Rock. Remember Adrian, when I said, "a real bully going to come anyway."

Slept Rock looking like he didn't know by hunching his shoulders. My pride kicked in cause he met the challenge. I got to go all the way now. I back up and told him. You should've just given me the money.

The rain cloud moved over his head and then started thunder storming. I put my leather gloves on and started whooping his ass. I hit him about four times fast. I had to reach up at dude cause he was big as hell. After taking four of them upside the head so quick and so fast.

Charles then said, "all right all right. I got eight dollars."

He began reaching in his pocket to get the money. I didn't even want the money after I went through all that. I didn't need his money I had a sack. I felt bad and this is how I repay Bonner by smashing one of his students. I was being a bully. This is what bullies do.

I knew I was wrong and didn't take the money. I told him to go on ahead.

I looked at Slept Rock and said, "Slept Rock you made me do that! I wasn't trying to do that!" Once he tried to steal it was no turning back. The reason why is he could spread the word that he handled me. Slept Rock just laughed at how quickly I went to work.

I didn't expect him to try and steal. I was mad at myself for losing control of my faculties. I told Slept Rock I was about to go. I jumped on the next bus and headed home. I felt bad about what I did as soon as I did it.

I am still letting people activate my demon. It's always Slept Rock too. I didn't listen to the faint voice this time. I am working on it. When the demon is activated it's like someone whispering into your mind. The faint voice is the angel getting drowned out. The demon won this battle.

Mr. Watson

*I*t took a few days, but it was the end of the semester. We were doing the things they do for the end of the year. Teenagers have a lot of energy and we like to test each other.

I was wrestling with my boy Percy in the Hallway. My division teacher Mr. Watson was watching us wrestle.

He looked with disdain and said, "Columbus you try to say you're a junior acting like a little kid."

We stopped wrestling and Percy left and went to class.

After Percy left Mr. Watson kept on ranking on me.

He continues digging in me, "juniors don't act like kids. I don't know who you are trying to fool." He made me feel kind of low.

I responds, "'I'm just waiting for my transcripts they are on the way."

He was like, "yeah right all y'all students do is lie, lie lie lie. Boy you know you ain't no junior."

Mr. Watson had a long salt and pepper beard. He walked with kind of a drag with his right leg.

My reply, "that's okay drag your self on down the hallway and started laughing. I can hear your foot dragging down the hall before I even see you. Pick your foot up. Can you pick your foot up please Mr. Watson. I'm going to be way bigger than you, you are just music teacher!"

He just looked and said, "Okay Mr. George we'll see" and walked away.

The next day my transcripts came. He had to call me up for my division change.

I just looked at him and said, "I tried to tell you, I'm out Mr. Watson."

His response, "You were right Mr. George, but you still need to act your age."

I could honor that! The attendance office sent me a division change and I was in my junior's division.

He then said, "You are in honors division Mr. George."

He had to eat his words, I told him, "I tried to tell you I was a junior. I'm outta here. Where do I go?" He gave me my transcript and my division change and I put Mr. Watson in my rearview mirror.

What I did next, I went around and showed everybody. I was proud I was in my right division. Along with my transcripts, were my test scores. Mr. Watson taught music at the school and was middle age at the time. Look like I got a long way to go, to get bigger than Mr. Watson.

Mr. Watson is on the Hollywood circuit now. He is the one who played Pete in Soul Food. Pete was the one who wouldn't come out his room. Dude is in Hollywood doing it big. I guess he did better than I have so far. Look who is eating their words?

If I met him again, I would apologize to him. He's the dark-complexion dude with a beard, played in a lot of movies. He played in the fugitive with Harrison Ford. He's the black doctor that got killed in the movie.

When I seen him in that movie I couldn't believe it. My eyes almost popped out of my head when I was watching the movie. I said to myself, "that's Mr. Watson" and I went straight back to the hallway incident. He was about fifty when he was teaching music. I wonder did I motivate him, hmmm!

My mother said it is never to late, to do anything in life. You want it bad enough, just put your mind to it. Mr. Watson was a perfect example. He acted in the movie "Good Fellas" he was the bartender when they popped Spider. I guess he gets the last laugh. I was being mean to Mr. Watson, because he hurt my feelings. He hurt my feelings, but he was right. Really, he took the time to even talk to me about my behavior. He had to care.

The Voice

*R*ob from NY was going to Communication Metro too. He was on junior varsity basketball team I see him and showed him my grades. I used to tell him I had all my credits and was graduating next year. I was trying to keep him on point, because he was cutting a lot.

He saw the grades and was like, "damn I thought you was lying too Colo, you are a junior."

I shake my head in modesty and replied. "I know you did that's why I'm showing you. I knew you didn't believe me. Meet me after school and we'll smoke one on the way walking home."

Every morning Rob and I would hook up and stop at Phil's house. Phil was a mack, he had plenty of women. He was tall and cool as hell. When the shade was down he was out of weed early. When it was up he'd serve us through the window.

We had to walk by his house anyway to get to South Chicago to catch the bus. Rob was the first one who smoked a blunt with me. He bought a bag from me that morning. I asked him dude you going to put half the bag in one blunt.

He said, "this is how we do it in NY."

I told him it seemed like a waste of weed. After walking to South Chicago. I'd have to find a cubbyhole and roll the bags quick. I had to get them ready to sell joints at school and that's how my mornings went.

I had a couple of joints left from earlier that I didn't sell at school. It's time to celebrate my credits coming. We hook up after eighth period and left the school.

Rob didn't know I knew he was leaning toward being a Moe. I didn't give a fuck. He was running with guys on the football team. Al Porter and his crew were the Stones on the team. Al was cool, he even talked cool. I could tell Rob didn't really want me to know. I caught him one day throwing the five up low-key to Al. I didn't say anything about it.

Later that day Rob and I were walking to the crib. I fired up a joint and tell him I got the heater so be low-key while smoking. I can't stand a search from the boys.

He smacked his lips and said, "yeah right."

I looked at him and said, "I always got the heater. Rob you know how we get down on 169th. I ain't bullshitting out here." Rob still can't believe, how we are cut.

He asked me, "you had it this morning, let me see?"

I answered, "hold on wait till we get around the crib." We get around the crib on Prairie. We were heading over Grimes's crib. Before we get to his house. We had just walked all the way from Communication Metro.

I'd walk home sometimes, because people would see me and buy weed. We sit on the back porch of one of those colt way buildings. The gangways leading from one block to the next block.

I tell Rob, "It might be a few guys over Grime's so let's smoke and get one under the belt." I pulled out a joint and lit it up.

He still didn't believe I had it and said, "you don't have the missile let me see."

He's standing on the ground looking at me and I'm sitting on the porch. I pulled it out my bag slowly. First he saw the handle and then it kept on coming out the bag. He then saw the barrel next he saw the shaft.

I was carrying a big ass chrome .357 to school with the wood grain handle. He was like, "damn while covering his mouth and his eyes were wide open looking in astonishment. I was just shaking my head up and down. I had the grim look and holding that bitch like, yeah!

Rob just came form NY. I don't why he seemed so naive to the street. First I unloaded it and left one bullet in the gun. I moved the bullet all the way to the left. My only experience with guns is that the chamber turns clockwise. I don't know anything about guns, I see. I thought all chambers rotated to the left.

Wrong answer, because I never shot it. Grimes shot it when we went to the white building. I never paid it any attention where the empty shell was position. I pointed the heater at Rob and was about to pull the trigger.

Something in the back of my head said, "empty or loaded never pull the trigger at someone unless, you're trying to kill them. That's how mistakes happen."

That's what my momma always told me. At that split second I listened to the faint voice. I pointed the banger in the air and pulled the trigger. Boooomm, the gun sounds off echoing off the building and through the gangway. It was fire and shit shooting out the missile's barrel. I looked at Rob and he started laughing.

He was grinning and looking at the gun and said. "Damn Colo that motherfucka is sweet."

I knew I almost killed dude in my mind. He didn't know it. In that split second I diverted the end of his life. I know he thinks I am crazy.

I didn't tell him though! I grabbed my bag and threw the heater back inside of it. I told Rob to come on the twisters will be here quick. We're right outside somebody's house on their porch, blowing one and shooting guns. I didn't expect it to go off.

We didn't run to Grimes house we ran back to the Met. I get back to the Met and hit the gangway. I hid the pistol under some leaves. Rob face had a look of unbelievable on it!

After coming out the gangway he said, "y'all Chicago niggas are out of y'all mind."

I said to myself, "I almost blew your mind wide open." Thank God I listened to the little faint voice.

I am on the Squad

*T*hat summer I tried out and made the Communication Metro football team. I'm still a hustler, a gambler and on the football team. I thought I had a chance to show my skills finally.

I fuck that up before the season even got started. I was gun hoe at first, but once I knew, what it was. I didn't give my all, because I knew I wasn't going to start. It seems like I am always out of place. We had five and six year seniors who were on the team from the year before.

Again, the coach really didn't know me. He saw I had ability, but this was my last year. I should've played defense, but I was trying out for receiver. I'm still trying to be a receiver. Coach already had his receivers. I was so aggressive I should've been playing strong safety. At first, I was gun hoe to play. All summer we had those, two a day practices, in the blazing heat.

The summer drew down and school was about to start. Here come those five and six year seniors. I didn't know they had basically had guaranteed spots. They came to practice with maybe two weeks left before school started. Now I went to most of the practices, but the day they were giving out position. I missed that day. This was the only practice I missed the whole summer.

One thing it did for me by me joining the team. Playing football kept me off the street that summer. After practice I was tired and I had to ride the bus there and back to practice. I would be exhausted. When I got home I didn't do much.

I'd go grab a beer and maybe smoke one with one of the Folks. My next move was to go in the crib for the night. I had to get up in the morning and do the same thing the next day. I had something to occupy my time. I had made the team, but didn't have a spot. I wasn't on any team, not even special teams. I know the reason why? I felt the coach wasn't feeling me the whole summer. I had fucked up royally.

Lace taught me how to pick those combination locks back in the day. Lace was hitting lockers at school and coming back home with a whole bunch of shit. He was selling the merch around the crib. That's all I needed to know. Before school ended my junior year the football team started tryouts and practicing.

I was hitting lockers before and after practice. We had a few practices on the inside of the building when it was raining. I hit a couple while practicing. I was smooth and couldn't possible be peeped. I'll make a quick dip off past the lockers and bam.

I was hitting lockers while in school in between classes. I'd see the mark, with some sweet shit and follow him to his locker. He bet not throws some shit in his locker that I needed. I'd peep and hit him later once I knew where he locker was located. I'd go in the bathroom peer out through a small cracked opening. You couldn't see me and I'd wait until the hallway clear.

Once the hallway cleared I'd look around first, grab the lock and do my thing to pop it open. When somebody enter the hallway even, if I did get the locker open. I'd have to leave it.

I'd grab what I needed and close it back within twenty seconds max. The only way I took something I had to completely finish the job. That means lock the lock back and be walking away from the locker.

I know I had caused some locker partner fights. It got back to me the locker partners were fighting after I knocked them. You know, if the lock and door is not busted. The only person who could have your shit, is your locker partner. I would abort the mission, if someone saw me in the process of knocking you off! I'd pop the lock and put everything back, if I have too.

I was hitting lockers on a daily basis. The football team would practice in the hallway, if the weather were bad. I would hit them low-key in front of everybody. It was easy as cake. I thought of no consequences and no empathy for the people I was hitting.

The havoc I was causing, the insecurity I brought to Communication Metro. I was like a thief in the night. I was ghosting through without getting peeped. Someone is tearing a hole in the security staff. I was getting anything of value, coats, jumpers and sometimes money. I was coming back to the crib selling the shit off.

One day the assistant principal, Mr. Beverly at Communication Metro came up to me and said. "George come here I need to talk to you." He had a stern look on his face.

"What's going on Mr. Beverly?" I asked.

He squinted his eyes and his lips went rigid and said, "I know you are the one hitting these lockers".

My jaw dropped to the ground in disbelief, but I play it. I just gave him the, what look.

He kept going, "another thing, I know your selling weed up here at my school." When I catch you, you are going to jail Mr. George."

He just laid out my whole method of operation. I just looked at him and said, "you've got the wrong person."

His response, "I might have, but if I catch you, you are going to jail."

I reiterate, "I'm not worried, because you got the wrong person. Mr. Beverly somebody is giving you bogus information."

He responded, "George when I catch your ass, you're going to jail", then walked away pissed.

It was like he couldn't bare to see my face. I always wondered how he found out. I never told anybody I hit lockers and I mean nobody. I always went solo dipped.

Mr. Beverly said it with conviction, like he figured it out. "When I catch your ass George, you are going to jail."

He had a disgusted look on his face like he was straight pissed. He was tired of my ass and couldn't catch me. He didn't have any proof. He had a slew of his students who complained about their things being stolen.

Their mothers and fathers are putting pressure on him to find out. Who is the thieves or thief that's ripping everybody off? Again I used my smarts to create havoc and get away with it. Mr. Beverly used his logic to narrow it down to me.

Nobody's locker was getting hit, until I got to the school. The lockers were in the main hallway. I would case my victims, if they don't have on what I saw they had on earlier, it's in their locker.

When I hit them I never used a watch out. I would throw the stuff in an empty locker and put a lock on it. I'd come back the next day and grab the stuff when the coast was clear. I was always hitting them by myself. I didn't want anybody to tell on me, if they got caught. I never hit another locker after the confrontation with Mr. Beverly. If, caught I'd have to take the fall for all the lockers I hit.

That would be a lot of cases against me. A lot of students are going to be mad at me. Anything that was stolen out a locker since I came to the school would've been pinned on me. I would have gotten my ass whooped for sure. I didn't hit no Folks though I hit all neutrons.

I still sold weed though! I had Percy taking the heat off me on that. He smoked as much as he sold. He used to come to me high than a motherfucka and ain't sold a thing. He was selling weed for me, but I had to get my money later.

After they let me in their school I stabbed them in the back. Once people locker stopped getting hit after our conversation. Logically he knew it was me for sure. I shelved the locker job. The shit wasn't right anyway.

Consequences

*A*s I look back it just seemed normal to steal coming from my hood. Mr. Beverly probably had a meeting with all the teachers. He had a talk with coach Frazier so Beverly put them all up on me. He probably told Coach Frazier. I bet not touch the field. The Coach was giving me P's before in practice, because of my work ethic.

He knew I could hit, because I loved doing the alley drill. Andrea, this drill is when you're laying on your back. You got to get up with the ball, then try to get pass the dude on the other side, on the whistle. Everybody lined up on both sides like a tunnel. I wasn't dropping shit at the receiver's position. He could've done something with me.

After Beverly wired me up on what he thought he knew. I felt the teachers and the coaches looking at me strangely. They might not have caught me, but there was no time on the field given to a thief and dope dealer. They let me stay on the team to keep an eye on me, probably. I got no time in varsity games.

I'd go down and help junior varsity, but varsity nope. I still was straight. I was part of a team. I got to wear the school football jersey and did fun things. I fucked up any chance for my talents to flourish. Again, I outsmarted myself trying to cut corners. I didn't get caught, but I would've given all that shit back, if I could've gotten on the field.

I was being greedy. I was already selling weed and making money. I didn't have to steal, but I just couldn't stop with the easy licks. I had a new start and look what I did? I had a chance to chase a dream. This decision to steal when I didn't have to, was a bad decision.

Football Season

*T*he season started and we had a good start 3-1 at the midway point. Communication Metro was having a home coming party. My teammates: Russell Avery, was the quarterback, Bosie was the tight end, Jerry Mallet, receiver, Vincent Price, receiver, Al Porter, runner back, Shaun Payne, runner back, Toni Brown, Linebacker, Walter Readus, runner back, Percy Strayhand, receiver, Steve Cates, Linebacker, Adolpho, tackle, Jimmie Allen, backup QB and starting corner Twilight, receiver Aton Daniels, defensive tackle.

I was a flanker and played the slot. I had an albino teammate and he was cool. I used to go over his house and get high. He was a good weed customer too. He had a fine ass sister, but she wasn't Albino. She had all her pigmentation and eye color. He was a defensive lineman. I could've sworn I saw him in the movie Sparkle. George was a linebacker and Black Stone.

The first week I was going to the school. The Folks tried to smash George. George took off his belt buckle and kept all of them off of him. He got away too, he took a couple of blows nothing major.

I knew right then these guys don't move out like we do at the Robe. It would be no way in the earth dude could have kept niggas from the Robe off of him. I was just watching I didn't know any of the Folks or the Stones at the time.

I don't remember the rest of the team, but those were the major players. We won our homecoming game that we were playing at Gately Stadium. Ooh I felt I should've been on that field. I am standing on the sidelines and knew I wasn't getting in the game. I still sucked it up, because I knew why. Shaun scored the winning touchdown with no seconds on the clock. He ran sixty-yards down the sidelines. Game over!

I invited the Folks around the crib to come up to the school. I wanted to let the school know how plugged I was in the hood. I know Rob from NY already wired the Moes up. I was cool with the Moes at the school.

The only problems I had is with the GDs up at Metro. I remember Charlie Dog, GD Folks with a position was trying to peep my game. He doubted my authenticity. I'm like, "nigga I am authentic all the way and you better check your own squad." He was a GD anyway, back the fuck up. He ended up calling it for GDs around Iron Park. He found out I was not only plugged, but highly favored.

Grimes and I rode the Charger up to Metro. We met Sacks and the rest of the Folks up at Metro. Of course I got the .357 with us. One of my guys from Metro jumped in the car to blow one with us.

He gets in the back seat and comes up with the .357. It was on the floorboard by the back seat. Grimes and I look at each other like how'd it get back in the back seat. I was glad he wasn't scurby and duffed it. That some shit that we would've done, if we didn't know you like that!

Grimes begin to park and I see Jimmie Allen coming to the car. Jimmie Allen had a monster game at cornerback. He had an interception and two good sticks. I said, "what up Jimmie you did your thang today?"

He smiled then looked in the car and says, "is that Grimes?"

Grimes was the one shooting when we went to white building. Now Jimmie is a Vicelord, but Jimmie was cool as hell with me. We got high as hell all the time. He bought plenty of weed from me, then he'd smoke it with me. I always was happy to see Jimmie cause he spent money.

He tells Grimes with an ugly mug, "Grimes, man that was my little brother out there when y'all was shooting."

He said it in a rough tone. Now Jimmie never said anything to me about it, but he came at Grimes. Wrong answer he should've come at me. All this time he was checking me out with the weed smoking. I didn't know who Jimmie brother was at the time.

I was the one doing the damage. When he said what he said. It was like he was saying it, in a checking fashion. Wrong answer, wrong niggas! Grimes so skinny that you wouldn't think this guy is this brave. Grimes wouldn't just shoot your ass. He'll blaze you in a second. Skinny as he was, he was game for whatever.

He looked up at Jimmie while sitting up in his seat.

He started pointing up at Jimmie and began to say. "If your brother was out there, y'all was coming at my Folks with the shotgun. If he got shot, he just would've just got shot. The nigga shouldn't been out there, now what nigga?"

He mugged him back and then it was a pause as they stare each other down.

Grimes looked at me like get to the stash and give me the heater. We got all kinds of signals with just eye movement.

I know what Grimes is on and say, "cool out Grimes this Jimmie, he's cool." I look at Jimmie and shake him off with my head.

Jimmie then says, "naw I was just letting y'all know, who he was, because he ain't about this shit".

Grimes see that he using the backdoor.

Grimes then said, "Oh okay cause I'll fire this whole motherfucka up."

I intercede, "Grimes this my man. He was just letting you know to look out for his brother".

I saved Jimmie he just didn't know it. You know how quick shit gets kicked off. One word out of pocket and shit could pop off one-way or another. Grimes had already popped a couple of niggas before we started hanging. He'd tell me niggas thought he was a mark, because he was so skinny. I already know he is quick to pop.

This is my homecoming though and I am trying to graduate. Jimmie probably told the Brother's and the Folks at the school how we were cut on the nine. Jimmie lived around the white building on 173rd & Vincennes.

Those niggas over there know me quite well. He knows I carry power. He probably wired up the GD's and Moes, because Jimmie was cool with everybody. You know everybody wants to know who you are and how are you cut. They are going to check you out. It was policy.

It probably went like this! Columbus could have this whole school surrounded. I already know how those niggas are cut, he's off 169th St. Those Folks over there don't bullshit and ready to smash and shoot when they get in shit. Columbus is the nigga that's coming down the street to see you.

Jimmy also probably told them I was cool. He don't want any smoke. He's really just trying to graduate. That's the shit I'd kick when hanging with different people getting high.

Columbus don't be starting shit, but don't fuck with him or his guys. We went to the party, but broke out early. I was in my Communication Metro Dawgs jersey #27. I still felt part of the team without getting any time.

We had a good season. We were 7-3 and went to the playoffs. We won our first game against Harper. This is the best that Metro has done in years. The only thing I could do was get my team ready in practice. I still practiced like I was going to get in the game. I knew I wasn't though!

It was times Frazier could've put me in the game. He intentionally looked over me and told somebody else to get in the game. When he did that, Ohhhh it hurted like someone shot me. All I need is a chance I was a ball hawk in practice. I sucked it up, because I knew I was wrong. I was hitting my fellow classmates. It finally sunk in about the damage I had done for a quick buck.

I was playing football though even though I didn't get in the game. I was having fun with the scrimmages. Those were my game days. It didn't matter, because I loved football. Another thing I knew that it kept me out the streets. I had to give up making money, because of practice and I knew I wasn't getting in the game.

Our next playoff game our star runner back, Al Porter. He was a crafty runner with moves. I loved tackling and chasing him down in practice. I was starting to love the safety position chasing him around. One time I had him sized up. I came up and filled the gap.

He was a shifty runner and by this time, I knew when he was ready to cut back. I filled and waited for the cut back and he came. I went air born like a projectile low at thigh level. He spent and ducked up under my arms, but fell down off the contact. I thought I smacked him, but grabbed nothing but grass.

I get up look at him and say, "yeah what happen to that I'm a run you over shit. You were ducking like a prizefighter. I thought we was playing football you're boxing aha hha hha."

He'd laugh and say, "nigga you wish you could get a glove on me."

We both would start laughing. That's all I had I couldn't say nothing, but I stopped him!

Playing safety they don't have to run plays for me and I can make an impact. I get a chance to intercept the ball and I get to come up and hit. We had live practice all the time. I loved this position.

In practice they were looking for me when I played defense. I didn't slow down because this was game day for me. I got our runner back, up to snuff. When he got to the second level I turned the heat up.

Anyway we were playing Phillips in our second playoff game. They had a sweet wide receiver at the time. Al Porter was getting some major ink. Scouts could be looking at him. He was a stud runner back for Metro that year. This game could put him on the map. I was routing for him to have a good game.

We get the ball first for the kick off. We walked straight down the field. Porter carried Metro on his back all the way to the goal line. It was Porter left, Porter right and Porter up the middle. We were going in to score. Al gets the ball up the middle and fumbles on the goal line.

That's okay on the next possession though! Al gets the ball and he scampers for forty yards. On his next run he breaks and was headed for the zone and safety stripes him of the ball.

I was like, "damn Porter." I could keep going, but I won't he fumbled three more times that game. Needless to say we lost, but it was good run. We were the Cinderella story that year.

I never forget Al standing on the sideline by himself. His helmet was on his hip and he was peering out into the sky standing alone. It was a look of sadness and disgust. The biggest game of the year and he fumbles five times.

I stayed out of trouble my senior year. I had no more confrontations with anybody my senior year. I went the whole year without a fight. This is the first time I went a whole year without a fight. I guess those two fights put me on the, don't fuck with him list at Metro. It was a couple of girls I liked, but nothing came of it.

I know Rob was feeding the Moes the stories about 169th ST. Rob probably told him dude is cool as hell. He's got a mob at his disposal and he knows that for sure. This is how your reputation can help. Once they know niggas are going to die behind fucking with you. Unless you fuck with them, they don't want any smoke. I kind of faded off Rob, because he began hanging more with the Moes.

I continued to get my money with my weed sells. I felt ashamed that the staff knew I was the locker thief. I could feel it. It was like they knew they were going to catch me. I was convicted as far as faculty opinion.

The staff kept their eye on me. I didn't steal anything else while up at Communication Metro. Had I kept my word not to steal anymore I probably could've shined at Metro on the squad. I didn't even try out for basketball after that! I messed up everything. What had a profound effect on me though is a picture I saw.

I used to catch the bus on 178th and Cottage. They had a picture of Flucky Stokes son in the restaurant from his funeral. His son was in a casket made like a Cadillac Seville with the steering wheel hood and everything. He was suited up with gold and diamonds. The casket sat upright so you see his body in the casket from a distant. It was like he was driving. His hands had one hundred dollar bills spread out like cards. This reminds me of an Egyptian burial, but in the hood.

He was hustler like his old man, but got killed young. He had all that money and he was a young corpse. This was a powerful picture. I can say that picture help kept me focused on the squad and in school. I looked at that picture every time I caught the bus from school on Cottage. No matter how much money you got. Your head can still roll, is what I took from the picture.

I was scheduled to graduate on time. I didn't want to fuck that up. I had a problem with my computer teacher Mr. Rouser. All year long I was shooting him bullshit. I thought I was getting a work-study credit. I had got a job my senior year working at Burger King for about four months.

That's another reason I didn't have to steal. Metro had me working this job program. My counselor said I was eligible for a half of credit for work-study. I was going to have a half a credit over at graduation time. I am on target to walk no matter what.

I skated by getting D's out of his class the first half of the year. I was totally transformed from a nerd. All I wanted to do was pass. I blew off the ACTs and SATs I took those test drunk.

I didn't care about a GPA or going to college anyway. I really didn't understand how much colleges looked at were your GPA, ACTs and SATs. I guess I thought, if you pass it was just like grammar school. You automatically go to college, if you want to go.

I wasn't doing no studying or anything. I thought, because I was on the team and a senior he'd let me skate. I felt a sense of entitlement. I sold weed during his class outside the school. I came to class a little bit so yeah he'll pass me. I still had a work-study credit anyway. I really didn't need his class the last half of the year to graduate.

I turned in about 25% assignments and thought, because of jock status. Mr. Rouser would pass me. I was a senior too. I go to the counselor to make sure everything sweet. When I get there she tells me. They're not doing work-study credit anymore.

I look at her crazily and say, "what you mean? You told me I was eligible for a work study credit." She said, "It's not just you it's everybody".

She said it like this gives me some consolation that it happened to everybody. I was literally counting that credit. I would just skate by with that credit even, if Rouser failed me.

You know what came back to bite me, Mr. Beverly. Mr. Beverly didn't speak to me the whole senior year. He saw I was graduating and was just keeping his eye on me. He probably went to all my classes and saw all my grades. I was walking a tight rope.

I didn't even know I was oblivious. I didn't steal or have any fights I was breezing through the year. I made sure when I sold weed I was in the cut and couldn't possibly be peeped.

He was still trying to catch me doing something. You can't catch what ain't happening. He went to the rest of my teachers and at Mr. Rouser. He saw that I couldn't pass no matter what I did. He probably made sure Mr. Rouser knew, he knew, I couldn't pass. I was a rock in a hard spot.

I've gone on prom and did all the thing's seniors do. I went to graduating practices, trips to different places. I was on schedule to walk. When it was time for the grades. Mr. Rouser flagged me in the last marking period.

I was in rage and knew my mother would be disappointed to the maximum level. All this time I was telling her I was graduating. She could hang her hat on at least that! I found out the last few days of school I wasn't graduating. Mr. Rouser cracked my face open I failed his class.

I go to Rouser about my grade all I wanted was a D to pass. All Mr. Rouser did was showed me what I had done the last part of the semester.

Mr. Rouser said, "George, I can't pass you with grades like this. This isn't how life is, you are not even close."

I looked at my grades and he was right. I basically did nothing in his class. I still was mad and could've slapped the shit out of that man. My little voice I hear told me not to do it. It did cross my mind. I thought he was a push over, because he passed me the first marking period.

This was another example of trying to slick my way through things. I could've done what I was supposed to do. It was no reason I couldn't easily pass his class. It was too easy and I didn't produce. I just didn't put the work in and thought wrong. It was my fault and only had myself to blame, for my total fall off.

Mr. Beverly couldn't have come in to play. I let him in the game. I had to pay some way for making him look bad. The little money I made off the stolen merchandise was not worth it. I lost on the field and in the class. I was not walking in June all because I was greedy and thought I was slick. This was an unimaginable hurt and humiliation to know, I did it to myself.

Walking across the Stage

I had to graduate out of summer school. I was envious of Cassius and Dave they both walked across the stage at Darobe. Dave Sterling graduated and I didn't, wow. Dave was smart and went to class, gangbanged in between periods and he made it. Everything we did we were competitive and I lost. I had to tell them I got to go to summer school, after me working around Mrs. Richards. She still came into effect.

I still had to graduate out of summer school. This was disappointing to the highest degree. I called Slept Rock and told him the deal.

He tells me in a gloating voice, "oh I am walking across, baby."

I went to the prom and he didn't, that was my only consolation. No he went, but went by himself. I was able to get a date and he didn't.

It was cool though City boy and Lil' Gooch had to go to summer school too. As a matter of fact a lot of people went to summer school that I knew. It was like summer camp from Darobe and Metro. The only thing bad about it was, not walking and going to summer school. Again, I had something to do that summer and that's graduate.

We went to Percy Julian on a 103rd & Vincennes. The Stones and Vicelords held it down over in that school and neighborhood. When you get off the bus and walked across the street. Right in front of the school is a big ass five-point star on the ground.

I hung out with Cityboy that whole summer. Sometime I would stay with my sister Regina, she lived on 103rd and Cottage. She'd let me stay with her a few weeks while I was going to summer school.

The script flipped with City and I. Now I was the one with the weed and the connects. City was selling for me. He was getting his on, but Cityboy used to like to get fuck up. What I mean by fucked up.

He pop pills, tac, smoke weed, drank, shermstick and would do it all at the same time, if he had it. If he had money, he was getting high, no, fucked up. He used to have this saying he said all the time.

"Colo I am fuuuccCKK uuuuPP" and he'd be smashed.

You rarely saw me fuck fucked up. I got high, but fucked up in the streets was a no no. Some people like to hog the high, but it usually catches up with them. They end up throwing up for being so greedy. The bubble will have you out of control and I like to stay in control.

For instance one night one of his own guys, blew City's eye out. I was still going to the Robe at the time. He comes to school with motorcycle shades on the next day. When we greet we greet with the Folk's handshake and then he takes the glasses off. I see his eye bubbled and was surprised. I'm like, "dAAMMNNN we going to kill whoever City."

His eye was black with a half moon bubble surrounding the eye area. His eye was super swole, closed shut and black. He tells me how it happened.

He paused looked and said, "I was fucked up the night before and Bob stole on me."

That's all he said he remembered. I asked him again, because I couldn't believe he said Bob.

He answered quickly, "Bob did this and I am fucking going to kill him."

I asked City, "why what happen and why would Bob do this? I can't believe he got you like that!"

I know Bob can't box and I know City can.

City mumbles under his breath, "I'm going to kill Bob."

City eye was so swollen I don't know, if I could've come to school. It had a big ass circular bubble on the bottom and the top of the eye. You barely could see his eyelashes. The lashes were tucked into the swollenness of the two eyelids. The dark shade couldn't even conceal the swollenness. Another thing the eye was leaking a little.

I told him, "City that's your man. You just got to suck it up. You lost the fight." City pride was hurt. He has protected Bob since day one he enter the Robe

His response, "Fuck that nigga I want to kill him and I am going to do it."

City's emotion is at a high level. We go in the school and I knew his pride was hurt. City was known for his hands. I know he wished it would just disappear, but it wasn't.

When we went to the bathroom. He stayed in the mirror looking at the bruise.

Almost in a meditative state he would say. "He is a dead motherfucka! I'm going to kill him and I need your help".

I say to myself, "I'm going to agree with this nigga and figure things out later. I tell him, "all right City, if he's got to go, he's got to go". I liked Bob he was so mild manner. You couldn't fuck him over though!

In order for Bob to hit City, City had to be fucking with Bob. Bob loves City. I know how City gets when he's bubbled and starts playing with you. Waving his hand all in your face and fucking with you, just pawing at you all the time. I kept asking, "what you do to him City?"

He responds quickly, "it don't matter what I did. He shouldn't have blew my eye out. I'm a kill his ass."

I said to myself, "he was probably punking Bob in a drunken state. Bob just got fed up and hit him." He only hit him one time. He was planning to kill Bob though and he wanted my help.

We had to get a ride first. His plan is, he wanted me to get in the trunk and when it opened, blast Bob. City was going to put some time in between the hit and the incident. He said he was going to invite Bob over to the trunk to talk to him.

Bob would think things were cool after a while and then get him. He said he was going to ride up and call Bob to the car to get in and ride. He was going to have some beer and kick it. Once they parked. He would go to the truck and call Bob to check something out.

When he pops the trunk and it opened. I was supposed to jump up and blast Bob. Once I popped him I jump out. City was supposed to grab him and push him in the trunk. I close the trunk and drive off and dispose the body. He said he knew a spot to drop the body. We had to get rid of him, because Bob was close.

I went with it, because we had to put shit in motion. First of all we weren't ready to do it. We had to get a car. He was working on that! I hung out with City a couple of day getting high and figuring it out. He calmed down like I figured after a couple of days and called it off. City was a good guy, but his emotions had him going crazy. His eye went down a bit just a bit.

When I hung on 7 Deuce with City. We used to go over to Bob house and hang. I met his mother and everything and she was nice. She offered us food and everything. I couldn't do Bob like that! I'm glad he changed his mind.

Those couple of days we hung, all we did was had fun. Now you want to kill your hommie, Bob, you got to suck it up City. It was just a fight and real friends don't kill each other. I could be Bob one day and now I got to go or I know you got to go, cause I know I got to go.

We caught him a few days later in school. We were outside by the side door. We slide off in the cubbyhole. This is a spot where you couldn't see from the streets. We were behind a ten feet wall.

Bob tried to apologize to him saying, "City I kept telling you, to leave me alone", when they squared up.

City wasn't trying to hear it. He stole on him a few times and threw him to the ground. Bob tried to fight back, but he had little boxing skills. City beat his ass cause he wasn't drunk this time. City was one of the coolest guys on the Earth. Drinking turns some people for the worst. City was one of them.

When City was smashing him that day. You could tell he didn't want to do him ugly. After throwing him to the ground he could've stomped him. Bob didn't have a chance and he was looking up for mercy. You know like when your mother is whipping you.

City didn't bang him like he could've though! I don't know, if he would've done my eye like that though! He would've got stomped, at least stomped. He let him slide once the love crept back in his body.

His demon that was pushing him to kill was deactivated. I'm glad I was around for you Bob. After that incident City wasn't the same anymore. That took a lot out of him. He wasn't the hustler he had been and he started getting too too drunk.

Anyway that summer I spent nights over City's house too. His Mom was nice and also looked good too. When we came in late she often fix us something to eat. He was just glad I had the weed and I was close.

He didn't mind selling for me when he was out. I'd just cut him in on the pros. We would bubble out at his house and go to school the next day. I kept a change of clothes over his house so I would be fresh.

City would freeze the 40's the night before school. After freezing them he wrapped the beer in aluminum foil. The beers would stay cold until we were ready to drink them at lunch break.

Sherm who was Folks off 7 Duece used to be with us. He didn't have fresh gear and his shit wasn't stable at home. I felt him so I gave him a sack to roll. I let him sell weed for me while Cityboy and I went to class. He didn't go to the school, but he rolled and hung out and kept the bangers. Folk's was kind of starving and we were looking out for him.

All the time we were up at Julian I was expecting a war. Folks and the Brothers symbols were written all over the building. You know I did damage all through the school. I had Colo Dog from 169th St. with the heart and the wings everywhere in the school. If you were looking for me I wasn't hard to find. The Vicelords knew who I was, because everybody was calling me Colo Dog.

I had BDN symbols marked all through the school and on buses and trains. Both organizations were disrespecting each other all on the wall. Most niggas shit gets crossed out, but my stayed up without getting crossed. I never disrespected the other organizations with my graffiti. Most of them were buying weed from me.

Cityboy and I always had our thangs on us, but nothing ever broke out. Except one time, we were all sitting on the catwalk where everybody gets high. This is where I make my money. We are the popular cats at the school. For the first time in my life I felt like that guy. They knew me from Metro and the Robe. I had respect at both schools.

I had fresh gear and shoes at this time. I had about seven silver ropes with charms on each one. My butter stayed whipped so I felt good about myself. The girls and the guys gave me my P's. They know Cityboy and I, because we sell the weed and we knew all the goons.

The girls and the guys came to us for weed. I had me a little shine, as the man that summer. My butter was getting long. I was still getting the six-pointed star dyed blue in the back on my head, while riding the shaw. All this was representation of Folks.

At this point I don't think I was too much scared of anybody. When you step my way I'm coming at ya, hard. I had my guy City riding. This is a guy I know going to go hard. I wasn't stupid I kept my thang and nobody knew I carried, but City and Sherm.

What nigga want to see me, for what? I was making money and never started anything! That's why I got a lot of respect. I was cool with the opposition and they respected me for that, already hearing of my reputation!

They saw how all the Folks would gather around me and I didn't have a spot. I could've misused the power, but I know right from wrong. Some people kick shit off just because they can. You won't get it from me unless you do me wrong. Do unto others, as you would want others, to do to you. You know things don't last. It's always somebody to break the peace.

One of the Folks from the Robe snapped, thinking he was on 169th & Halsted. You know Folks will snap anywhere, but we were on a mission. It was about ten Folks and six Stones in this graduation class.

We were some of the exceptional Folks from 169th St to reach this plateau. Tone was cliqued up with Savanne and his Folk's from the Robe. This is when City and I started to be recognized as those guys at the Robe. Something happened on the 7duece block and it carried on to the school. City wired me up for a week to ready, because the beef is on!

We had got into it with Savanne in the, A lockers at the Robe. City and I were on our way to English class. Ruff came up to us and told us that it about to go down. We run up the steps and met in the A lockers.

It was about eight of us and it was about ten of them. I was helping City andt hey were all BGDs. It was like in the movies when Wyatt Earp went at the Clantons, but this was knuckles. We we're on one side of the hallway and they on the other. There was the stare down then the shit broke out. Bing #*@bam#*@#*@ boom boom. I really can't tell you what happened. I was squared up with Savanne.

I was about to go at Savanne the leader. He sees it's me and pulled his belt off quickly. He swings just as fast. Dude hits me in the head with the belt buckle. Harold, Jackie, I am always getting clocked with the belt buckle.

By that time, security was in the locker area and everybody scattered. I was going at him head up and he got me just like Lee did. My reputation precedes me and he knew I would've knocked him out.

Right after he hit me the police officers came. We had to disappear, because you get kicked out for a massive gang fight. By that time my reputation was, don't fuck with his hands. I never got him back for that, but it's funny how things workout. It was like you brought Bruce Lee to the fight when I squared up.

Anyway, we were all cooling out on the catwalk. The catwalk gave us great shield. It was a bunch of bushes four feet high lined along the catwalk. When you sat on it, it shielded you from the school. In the summer we could sit there and get blowed and drink our beers.

I could also duff my weed in the bushes, just in case the boys rolled up. The bushes were so dense you couldn't see the sack. I would sit the sack a ways away from wherever we were sitting. You got the lookouts looking out for you. I'll fire up a few joints for the lookouts so it was real cool up at Julian.

Like I said out the blue, one of Savanne Folk's snapped. He saw some Brothers walking by the school. Tone snapped out. The same Stones that have been buying weed from me are coming down the sidewalk. Tone was in the middle of the sidewalk in the pathway for the pedestrians.

Tone started mean mugging.

He shouting out, "GD" to the Moes walking up while throwing up the forks".

We are on the catwalk watching like this is a movie. The Brothers started throwing up the five, walking dead in his direction. I had on my Frank Fotis' that day, but had my jumpers in the bag. I started to grab for the bag to put on my jumpers.

City stopped me and said, "fuck em, these niggas, they're always starting trouble."

Well before we knew it and to everybody amazement. Tone stole on one of the Moes that walked up. He blazed my man a couple of times, good. My man grabbed his face from the blows. After he did that it was down hill. His guy moved first, then dude Tone stole on, shook it off and then he moved.

It was two niggas that Tone attacked. They both put a whooping on him quick, bing, bang#*@ boom#*@ bink, boom boom. After the light smashing took place. The Moe Tone hit, hat flew off, when he got hit.

Dude picked it up and he told his guy, "let's go."

They didn't smash him bad, but they were on him for about ten seconds. Tone hit the ground, but they didn't stomp him.

Tone got up after the Stones left and was dazed. He looked at his Folks and his Folks looked back at him.

Tone face said, "I don't believe y'all didn't move out. Y'all let me get whooped?"

That's what his face asked. He stood there for about fifteen seconds. He was shaking his head while dusting and shaking off the smashing. Tone fingerwaves were all over his head.

He was looking like he stuck his finger in a electrical socket. Tone's clique that he rolled with didn't even help him. Train and them just watched him take the smashing. They were the Folks that clique together. Tone looked at his crew and they looked at him like why did you do that! He didn't say a word and walked away.

Everybody was trying to graduate we were all seniors. Tone was a senior too. That's why we were in summer school banging and hanging. We did our banging and didn't walk already. We all talked about it the first day of school. Folks were here to graduate so don't kick the shit off. The faculty at the school was letting us know, all throughout summer school.

Any gang violence and you will be kicked out immediately. Any hint of banging and we're kicking you out immediately. It was two Brothers smashing his ass, no aid and assist. While he was getting smashed I asked City what's up?

City was like, "this is a bad group can't follow niggas with no vision. I don't fuck with niggas who demonstrate power just, because they have it. We got into with his clique anyway. He just wasn't there at the time. Once he said that was Savannes hommie I was straight on Tone.

I said, "oh that's one of Savanne soldiers." Thirty seconds later Folks had a slight pumpkin head. Before he left Tone was standing there shaking it off.

City said, "you see what I'm saying. His own clique didn't even help him, so fuck em."

We kinda had a truce with these guys at the school. The Vicelords were trying to graduate, too.

I knew Tone was a senior he bought weed from me all the time up at Julian. He was happy he was scheduled to graduate that summer. He only had a week and a half and he would be walking. He had a lapse in judgment for 45 seconds and his future changed. Tone should've been focusing on the books, but he rather kicks the shit off. They got on him for about twenty seconds.

He didn't tell his Folks anything. He just saw the situation and made his own decision. A decision that would've affects others future. Folks didn't tell him to do that!

He went with his flow trying to kick shit off. He got fucked up and never came back to school. What did that prove? City was right, we were all getting along okay the Brothers and the Folks.

We were all representing our organization by having our hats banged, but it was no friction. When you're wrong you're were wrong. City wasn't going to risk his health or his life for you. I picked that up from City and added it to my game.

You can't let a person make his destiny, your destiny without a conversation. He didn't say Folks I am about to move. Folks y'all got my back, cause I going to move. He went with his flow. Somebody would've told him, not to do it. He was bringing that 169th St. to 103rd. His ass was out that day he violated himself.

We came to Julian to graduate out of high school. That meant putting up with what you have to, to graduate. Our future is on the line, for what? Those guys weren't bothering anybody. They were helping me by buying weed. Follow that concept. One thing about that literature, say what you want. When you followed your literature you would be morally sound. The literature guided you into being a man. Especially, if their was no man to guide you.

After the altercation, everybody stayed ready, because we were in their hood. Anything could've jumped off going over there to school everyday. We continued to stay strapped everyday coming to school.

Summer school was relativity easy. All you had to do was come to class. Do the assignments and you would pass. Lil' Gooch from the crib, City, Train and I all passed. Folks passed the mandatory requirements for a high school education. We are now eligible to walk across the stage.

Graduation Day

I am seventeen and I have strived to have this day come true. I basically took care of myself ever since the house caught on fire. My Mom covered the food and roof the over my head. Mom gave me money, but it wasn't enough. I was a major player. I needed gear and a car to represent the player that I am.

I saved up my money for graduation to buy me my first tailor made suit. It was midnight dark blue. On the pants back pockets I had a flap with the button to close the pocket. The jacket came up to my waist and had my initials on the front handkerchief pocket. That was common in those days. I had a pair of baby blue and dark blue Frank Fotis that I wore on my prom. I had hustled all year to have my gear straight for graduation and prom.

Graduation day came and I was so happy. I felt like Joe Pesci when he found out he was getting made in the movie, "Good Fella's." I had my tailor made on with my Foti's complementing the made, to the max. My butter was whipped with the fresh perm and finger waves.

I looked in the mirror and said to myself. "I'm walking across the stage today I waited seventeen years for this date." I kept up with my goal to graduate. I made my mother happy too. Lately I wasn't giving her anything to be happy about.

I accomplished this on my own. After everything I've been through and done. I persevered and graduated through all the obstacles. I felt good that morning and actually patted myself on the back. I was beating the system. I was so slick even when caught I'll slick my way out of it. It came at a lot of people expense.

City came to my crib that morning, suited up. He had a tan suit jacket and brown pants hookup. He had fresh carefree curls in his head and wore shades. He was looking dapper for the occasion. It was about nine o'clock that morning. We had to celebrate early before graduating so we hit the store.

We went to Bennies on 169th grabbed up a Martell. After that we went down the street to get Gooch. We knocked on the door and Gooch came down.

Gooch smiled and said, "What's up fellas? Time to walk across the stage."

He saw that we had the drink already.

Gooch looked at the bottle and said, "Martell let go in the back Folks."

His Mom Marge looks us over and says, "you boys look nice for graduation."

We smiled looked at each other and said, "thanks" and headed to the back.

We went in the back yard to his garage and got fucked up. We drank the Martell and smoked about six joints. We did it on an empty stomach that morning before the graduation too.

We all said that morning, "we were going to throw up the nation."

I told them what Spider G said he did when walking across the stage.

I told them, "we should let them fly when they call our names to walk. Let's represent the nation while walking across the stage."

We all agreed, "bet" and starting tripping on how we were going to do it.

Freddie, Spider G and Dickey Lee impressed me in that way coming up. They bang and they still graduated. I kind of knew Freddie was going to graduate. The one who amazed me the most was spider G. He was scandalous as anyone of the GDs.

When it was time to walk across the stage both of them had on the tailor made. Spider G had a brown one with the pin stripes. Freddie had a gray one on with a square pin print. I saw their accomplishments when I was a sophomore at Darobe. I saw them both at the Robe on their graduation day.

I asked Spider after looking him over, "Spider G you are graduating?"

He replied, "hell yeah Folks I'm a real G. Nigga didn't nobody know, but look at Spider G. walking across the stage. I'm throwing up the forks too, Folks. Let everybody know a real G graduated high school Folks."

He said it with a chuckle, "let's go get fucked up."

That's where I got the idea from Spider G. I already knew I wanted to graduate and this gave me extra motivation. I saw three real Folks, put it down on the strip and still take care of their function. After rapping the bubble up we got on our way. We rode with Gooch to the graduation.

We get to the graduation hall on 95th & Halsted. We saw all our parents. We were bubbled than a motherfucka. I wanted to get there early for those who wanted weed. I wanted a few more ends to kick it with after the graduation. We got there kind of late. When we got there everybody was getting set up to walk. I grabbed my cap and gown and put it on like, "yeah." I still didn't eating anything that morning.

We all lined up to walk down and took our seats in the auditorium. After that point, everything started to become a blur. The Martell had started to creep in me, on the empty stomach. I don't even know who was speaking at the graduation. We should've at least waited, until we ate.

I looked back to locate my family. They were sitting almost directly behind me. I took a position where they couldn't see my face and dozed off. The next thing I knew they were calling the graduates up to walk across the stage. I wasn't that bubble once they started calling names. I perked up.

Gooch name got called first. Just as we had planned, he let the treys fly as he walked across the stage. He threw up with both hands with his swagger and grabbed his diploma. About fifteen minutes later it was my turn. I came behind him throwing up three fingers. Bob and I were representing the treys, our organizational symbol.

I walked slowed then stop stood and looked at the crowd and then let them fly.

Lil rich Gooche's cousin was in the crowd heard somebody said. "Ain't it a shame these niggas gangbanging while walking across the stage."

This was my thinking to give Folks inspiration and show them we did it. City threw up the forks as he walked across the stage. He smiled and strutted cool than a motherfucka.

I realized this was the first big accomplishment I made in life. Which in a way, set the pattern that I would take from that moment forth. Always finish what you start or why try in the first place? My Mom always told me that!

The satisfaction I got from achieving something people thought I'd fail. This drove me just like, if I was playing ball in the dungeon. When I was playing strikeout or in the street; trying to score a touchdown. Don't forget the challenges I took slap boxing and boxing in the hood.

The tragedies and obstacles I had to hurdle. Some self inflicted and some were just continuing to living a grown up life from a teenagers perspective. All these sports I played aided me in my drive to graduate. I hated to lose and a loss is a loss in whatever you do. I lost my opportunity to make a splash in athletics.

Sports, transcends into your life's journey. You have to learn how to lose and you must learn how to win. When you lose attack your weak points. In order to win you have to put in the work. That is the same thing about school, if you want to win, you have to put in the work.

I accepted the challenge and nothing took precedence of my graduating. I wasn't excellent and I didn't do my best, but I did it. I was the first to achieve this goal out of the three of us. I did it ahead of schedule too that was magnificent. My mother preached and preached how important it was to have it.

Mom would say, "persevere and hurdle those obstacles that are thrown in your path."

There were teachers I had to hurdle, because of their insecurities. This was probably against the odds for a lot of people, who came up my way. Gooch, City and I made it. I've known Bob, since the 1st grade. I kicked it with City everyday at the Robe every since freshman year. I remember when we were freshmen and it went by so fast. Now were walking across the stage together. All three of us were bonifide intellectual goons now.

I got a lot of satisfaction from people, just coming up to me saying. "Colo you graduated out of high school."

They had a look of amazement on their face. They would then ask, "Aren't you just sixteen or seventeen?"

I answered, "I just turned seventeen." They had the same look when I saw Freddie, Dickey and Spider G graduate. I guess people couldn't understand. How could a person who was out doing the same thing they were doing. He still graduate before his time? A lot of people around the hood knew I was just turning seventeen and I'm Folks. That was impressive!

I still came out a year earlier and fuck Rouser and Beverly. Rouser taught me a very important lesson in life. Never leave it to anybody else to determine your future. Beverly taught me a lesson, because hitting those lockers weren't for survival. I was being greedy. I fucked myself out of maybe an athletic scholarship. You win some you lose some. I had to figure it out.

I still hoped I gave others inspiration like Freddie, Dickie Lee and Spider G was to me. It didn't make sense for me to leave grammar school early, if I couldn't finish high school early. I just turned seventeen and didn't need an extra year of school.

You have to grab inspiration from wherever you can get it. Now Aaron did something I could've, if I had set my mind to it. Aaron was valedictorian at Leo high school. This was a private school not public and he still was the valedictorian. This was absolutely amazing.

Aaron was on the stoop with us getting high just like we did. I asked how after smoking weed could he go home and focus studying. The light bulb went off weed assisted him in his studies. Aaron failed in the eighth grade and made a miracle comeback.

I couldn't believe dude had a 4.0 on his graduation day. Harold Washington was the speaker at his graduation. He was shaking Aaron hand as he received his award. He's got all the pictures to show at his Mom's house.

I just knew he was on his way with the scholarship to Howard University. That's when I learned about scholarships, but it was too late for me. I bet they didn't know Aaron was Folks and tops academically at Leo High School. I was almost as proud of Aaron than I was for myself. This is something I could've done, but he did it. He was at the right school to prosper.

Karma

I could've gone and had dinner with the family. We did that at my eighth grade graduation. We went to Ponderosa and celebrated. I didn't want to do that I wanted to hang with my guys! City Boy, Gooch and I said we were going to this graduation party. The graduation party was on a 103rd. I went to my old man house to get the car so we could roll. Gooch dropped me off and he went to the crib to chill with his family.

My old man had City and I rent the car from him. I thought that was real scandalous considering he didn't get me anything for graduating. My old dude stop giving me any money, when I turned sixteen. The older I got, the stingier he got. He wasn't letting me be a bum on his watch. He didn't even come to the graduation.

He was our only alternative for a car. My old dude knew I was hustling so he hustled me on my day. I was getting money up at Julian. I'd roll a couple of hundred joints and roll through the whole sack before leaving that day. I was to school early and left after the last joint was sold. I hit 169ᵗʰ reload then go to City's house chill and roll up the sack and do the same thing the next day.

They old dude knew I was hustling, because I was too fresh everyday. We had no choice so we paid him to use the car. I come in the house and City and I were dressed to the T. Pops was sitting in his chair smiled and said, "you boys are sharp Jack", then congratulated us on graduating.

I wanted to say something about how he was playing me, but City was with me. After getting the car I went to scoop up Gooch. Gooch had bubbled out from earlier. He was still on athlete status playing for the Robe. His system wasn't used to it. Lil Rob and Lil Rich tried to wake him, but they couldn't get him up. We had to leave Gooch. I went and picked up this girl I met in summer school named, Kim.

She was pretty with a nice little shape and was light brown skinned. She had a little sexy scar right by her lip. She had some nice lips too. She was cool about a year younger than I. Kim, City and I used to get high on the catwalk at lunch together. She was one of my best customers.

I kind of think she liked me too. We just kept it kind of cool, but I think we could have hit it off. I used to go check her out, but nothing ever happened with her. I still didn't know how to make aggressive moves.

Anyway, I go and pick her up. She was looking lovely with a big smile on her face. That smile made me feel real good when I saw it. This girl was trying to look good for me. I was impressed. I meet her parents and they were nice. They were young and up on game. They smoked weed and everything.

She had a nice big house with up to date furniture. It was a nice stereo in the corner and the carpet was a light brown and clean. I said to myself, "she's from a good family with some money." We said goodbye to her Mom and we left for the party.

Next it's time to pick up City's date up. Somehow we didn't catch up with her. We were driving here and we were driving there, to find her. There were no cell phones or pagers back in the day. City got stood up. He should've taken somebody else anyway. His girlfriend was a GD queen acting like she was all that! I could've dropped him off at the crib, but City and I come a long way together.

We were freshmen together and we graduated together. It was only proper we celebrated together. About time we got to the party, it wasn't shit. I'm thinking this bitch was going to be tight. It wasn't shit and I didn't sell any weed! We stayed for a while and then we broke out.

We get to the car Kim and I roll up some weed. We started getting our high up. We steady smoking weed and drinking on some Golden Champale. That's the closes I was going to get to champagne.

This is where thing go bad. My father had a cut off switch on his brake pedal. He showed me how to switch it on to keep someone from stealing the car. Well I had been fucking up with it, all night. I couldn't remember what position I had it. I kept trying to start the car while it was engaged. We were in and out of places all day and night.

If you fucked up, you could drain the battery or mess up something internally. I kept trying to start that car with it in the on position. City had to keep reminding me on several occasions to turn it off. I was bubbled and high and kept forgetting.

Trying to be cool with this girl was throwing me off. The reason why I kept engaging the cutoff switch? I didn't want anybody to steal the car. I was driving pops 1980 sky blue Oldsmobile Cutlass.

It was at high risk for being stolen. I had to keep engaging the alarm no matter what. All it takes is ten seconds and your shit is gone. It was a tilt too. Believe me I know. It was about one or two o'clock and Kim had to be home. I get in and start the car in the on position.

The cut off switch had to be tricky it wasn't just me. It might've been going out. This time it wouldn't start no matter what we did. I tried to jump it off and do everything else that I could possibly do in my suit. I got frustrated and sat in the car for a while. We finished knocking off the drinks and smoked the weed.

I cut my losses and flagged us a cab and took Kim home on 119Th & Halsted. City rolled with me to her crib. I told Kim I'm sorry for what happened and gave her a kiss goodnight. She gave me a nice long kiss though and that was the best part of my night.

I fucked the car up so whatever chance I had for some ass it was over. My plan was drop City off first and hang with her the rest of the night. After dropping Kim off we told the cab driver to drop us off on 195th & State.

That away City could catch the 195th street bus going west, to his crib. I could catch the L going South and it would drop me off on 169th & State. The cab already had me up to twenty-six bucks. Once on 169th I could either wait for the bus or walk to the crib. City bus came first. We gave each other love and he jumped on the bus.

Disappointment set in once he bus took off. I was walking through the terminal shaking my head. This is how my night ends up with me waiting on the L fucked up. I wished that were the case. Right then, I began thinking to myself. "This would be the perfect time for me to get peeped sleeping by the opposition. I am tailor made up, with my baby blue, dark blue leather & suede Fotis, bubbled. I don't have no heat so I'm naked."

I was swaying backwards and forwards from the bubble. We really had to do guzzle the dranks fast, before I flagged down the cab. It was our only chance for Kim and I to kick it, really. I knew I wasn't driving anymore and was depressed and took the drank to the head.

I began to be up on my surroundings, until the L came. I had to keep my eyes open at this spot 195th St. is smashville. This is a major bus and train depot. Every gang member who lived out that way had to stop here. The L came after about another five minutes. I got on and rode to 169th & State.

Whenever I get to 169th & State it was like a relief. It was a sense of I made it home safe. I am really worried about pop's car. The old dude was going through my mind and how he was going to react. He's going to explode when he finds out. I get off the train at 169th and starts walking up the stairs. I stand up there waiting on the bus, still bubbling. I could've gone toward the old dude to let him know about the car.

Really I was waiting on which ever, bus came first. It was a few people up there waiting for the bus. After thinking awhile I asked myself. "Why should I go to pops crib without the car? I am drunk and coming in the house with no car. This is not good."

I decided I was going to walk to the crib. "Kid make it", made it across the stage though! What an adventure! I was going to savor the rest of the night without any drama so I'm going home. The only bright part to the day was throwing those treys up and looking into the crowd. Oh yeah and that kiss from Kim, because I still was feeling it. I was thinking about how her tongue and lips tasted. How soft her lips were. I was bubbling thinking about that kiss and how my plans went sour to spend time with her.

This night was supposed to turn out right. It was my graduation night and here I am walking home. No car, no pussy, can't get no worst. My intention was to get a room and hang out with her. City had a fake ID and was going to get the room for me. I am in a bubbly deep thought walking to the crib.

All of a sudden someone shouts, "My man can I get that transfer."

I turn around and it is three dudes running up behind me. I was sleeping at first since I was on my own strip I felt safe. My transfer was still good so I was going to pass it to them. The only way I could've slept, is trying to look out for somebody, bubbled.

I should've peeped three guys coming at me. You don't need three guys to run up from the L for one transfer. They got that close to me, because I slept.

I reached in my both pockets searching for the transfer to give to them. That's when the biggest guy slipped behind me and grabbed my arms. The other two went for my silver ropes. I had on all my silver. They snatched them off my neck while trying to blaze me. The other one was trying to go in my pockets.

I got away from the big dude somehow and threw my hands up. It was on. They charged me a couple of times to no avail.

I was shouting at them, "come on motherfucka, come get what your looking for." I was shouted hoping somebody would hear me on the block. It was about three in the morning and nobody was out.

The bigger guy looked at the other two guys and gave them the eye to break off. They started running back toward the L. I ran the other way up the nine trying to find somebody out. I look down at myself to see what they get.

They got my two longest ropes and my cocaine spoon charm. Worst of all I ripped myself out of my tailored made suit. I had a rip from my buttonhole all the way around to the back of my jacket. My suit was ruined I got even madder. They didn't get any money though! I had a couple of hundred on me at the time.

I ran to the Met and nobody was out. I went to Lace crib and knocked on his window. He answered looking sleepy as hell. I told him to give me some jumpers and come on I just got robbed.

Lace didn't believe me at first, until I showed him where I was ripped out my jacket. He was sleep, but he put on his shoes. I took off my Fotis and my torn jacket real quick. He gave me a shank and he had something. I can't quite remember, but we took off in the direction they went.

We ran looking for them, but we knew, I knew, they were long gone. I had to make sure that's when a sinking feeling came over me. We jogged all the way back to the L station. While running we were looking down each block all the way to the L to no avail. I said, "Lace lets go these motherfuckas are long gone." We headed back to the Met and I'm feeling as empty as a person could feel.

Lace started asking me questions about the incident as we walked back to the Met. He welcomes me to smoke a joints and I take him up on his offer. We smoke a couple of joints and I tell him about my graduation day and night.

After that I gathered my things with disgusted and started walking toward the crib. I get to the crib finally and reminisce over the whole day while sitting on my bed.

I went from having a feeling of euphoria to disgust and emptiness. Before the day and night were over! I had two totally different feelings. It kind of reminded of when the house caught on fire. How quickly things change. I'm sitting on the bed looking in that same mirror. This morning I was happy like Pesci getting made in Good Fellas. The good part is I didn't get one to the head.

This time looking in the mirror I am frowning and sad. This was supposed to be my day. I still have to worry about the car my father rented me for graduation. The next day I called him and he had it towed to the dealer. He gave me an earful and ended it with I'd have to pay for it. Now my graduation night is officially over.

That day I think a little more compassion for people, left out of me that day. I was in the, fuck the Earth mode. I think I felt as, if every time I try to come up something disastrous happens. "Kid make it", was up in spirits. Now I am back down, mentally. This all happened in the same day. I was reaping what I sowed. It doesn't feel good when the shoe is on your foot.

Little did I know! This was just the beginning of me learning about life. The strong survive and the weak fall and this was just the beginning, Harold. I went down hill after that!

The same things we were doing to other people, on 169th St happened to me on 169th St. My graduation day was also payback day for me! I'm out here doing evil things and this is what happened when I'm trying to cross back over.

Change

During this time my mother had met her somebody from the church. He came over a couple of times, bought us dinner a couple of times. The next, thing you know they are getting married. He was coming to live with us, until he house was ready. The fact of my mother getting married didn't bother me, as a matter of fact, I was happy. The problem came when he tried to regulate.

I knew it would be a change. Here I am seventeen years old. This motherfucka was trying to tell me what to do, while raising his voice. He was trying to help my mother enforce what time I came in and I was like. "Fuck you dude, you ain't got nothing to say to me in my house"

I believe his opinion of me at the time, was, I was scandalous. He didn't know anything about me. He shouldn't have had that opinion. I wasn't scandalous to my family or friends. This would lead him to believe that when some money came up missing a couple of times. It had to be me who took it.

A couple of his pistols came up missing. I was the target of the investigation in his eyes. I didn't even know what was missing.

He just came at me like, "I know you got my stuff and I want it back."

No matter what I said, he thought I was the culprit. This would strain our relationships for the next ten years. I wasn't trying to here him after that, nothing he had to say.

My mother knew it wasn't me who was knocking him off. My mother knows me and she knows I don't steal from the house anymore. I thought she took his side, because she didn't say anything.

I never ever took a thing from him not one quarter. I'd never make my mother's son look so weak. He was from the church so I respected him like that! Now dude is accusing me of taking from him. I am getting accused for shit, I ain't done. It didn't go over well with me.

All the shit I do, this ain't one of them. I don't steal from my own house. Who do that? How can I take from my momma and I know she's on her knuckles. My comprehension level was high. You don't take from people who love you. I was seventeen not ten or eleven. I knew all the time it had to be my little brother, because it wasn't me. I didn't find out, until later for sure.

Walley was a straight clepto every since he was a shortie. He didn't steal from momma, but everybody else was fair game. Oh yeah by this time Walley had flipped GD. A couple of his Folk's came by looking for Walley one day.

Walley was fifteen, but he was coming fast and hard behind me. Walley fights anybody so he was power in his crew. Walley wasn't home so that's what I told him. I shoot the breeze with young Folks cause he was still standing around. While chilling he asked me, "where did Walley get those pistols?"

I looked at dude crazily and my heart starts to race and I said, "what guns?"

He replies, "the guns he carries all the time."

I told him to hold on while I ran in the crib and checked for my missile. My heater was still there so I come back out. When I come back out his boy gives me the lowdown. The young Folks all looked up to me. No Andrea, they really looked up to me. They always gave me the information on the street. I knew my brother was getting dude money. I knew nothing about the pistols.

The things that he was accusing me of I had no idea was missing. No wonder he was so hot. He couldn't believe it was my younger brother. I didn't even know he kept a pistol in the house. I was a hustler and had stopped the petty pilferage from my family a long time ago.

I knew my mother was having a hard time. Especially, after the house burnt down. I was trying to ease the burden by getting my own money. It sort of hurt me that she would take his side. She didn't take his side, but dude was talking to me. Talking to me about shit I don't know anything about. I rebelled in a negative way.

She wanted me to give him honor and respect, but in the same token. He was disrespecting me by coming at me with that bullshit. I was like fuck him. Now I'm glad my brother took the pistols, but I took the heat for it. I never said anything about what I knew, because I was no snitch either.

When things got real heated I'd just break out for a couple of days. I'd go and chill at one of the Folk's crib. Grimes, Spider G or Todd's crib usually. Mom would see me on the street and tell me to come home when she got worried. Maybe I'd hear through the grapevine that my mother was looking for me.

Those times were critical, because I saw she still had love for me. It's okay chilling out here with your Folk's. Only, if its just for a couple of days. I didn't want to over stay my welcome: Eating up the food. Using up the soap. Taking up space, which is usually empty! It's no place like home. I didn't mind chilling for a couple of days and accessing the situation. It was good I didn't have to be there when things were heated in the home.

When I got back home. I always would lay around the house a couple of days. You just can't be on the corner all the time. You got to give it a break. Take some days off work. I had to get some things done for my mother. I'd do some things for my mother and then cool out.

When they left home I would shoot upstairs and blow some joints. I was chilling high as a giraffe. Lying down in my room, doing my do. I was watching TV tripping. I had my room hookup from the different stains I hit.

My room was the enclosed back porch. I had a door to get in and out. I had my music and TV and a twin size bed. I had a long rack to hang my clothes so I stayed neat. My room was organized and clean.

This was my space to rebuild my comfort after the fire. Most times, if you wanted weed you'd knock on that back window. You had to be my guys or family. I had to keep the traffic down.

My mother had accepted the life I was leading. She didn't accept it, but I could be doing worse. I was just half as bad as everybody else. It was the environment and surroundings of life. She knew

I was drunk coming in at night. She didn't condone it, but what could she do? I am a street nigga, but I am still her son.

I cooled out getting drunk. One time she had to pick me up off the bathroom floor. After coming in after a night of getting bubbled. I go to the bathroom and fall in between the toilet and wall. My pants were still down half way and I was passed out. I probably pissed on myself. She had to help me up and carried me to my room.

I get up the next day and asked her what happen and that's what she told me happened. I didn't want her to catch me like that, but she didn't say anything else. I expected a sermon. She knew I was selling weed, because Nino busted me out. I was talking to my mother on the nine while she was on her way to church.

Nino ride up and say, "Colo I need a bags of weed."

I look at Nino like be cool. He didn't notice my mother was in the car.

He said it again, "No Colo I need two bags of weed."

I looked at my Mom and she looks at me.

I told Nino "I'd holler at him I'm talking to my mother." Nino's mother didn't care, if he smokes or sells weed so it was no big deal to him. We got high on his porch, while his mother sat in the front room looking out the window.

My mother frowned and said, "I'll talk to you later."

I then, go and serve him still and tell him, "never in front of the G Nino."

He said, "my fault Colo your mother don't know you got the weed."

I gives him the bags and say, "you know my mother don't condone shit like that!" Check out what Gearl did. Gearl wasn't my guy, but he hung out with us. He figured cause he was older than us that meant something on the strip. Gearl jumped out his skin one day with some weak ass shit.

This is why you can't put anything past anybody. Gearl comes to my house. He knocks on the door. My mother answers the door and came and got me from the back. It was a Sunday so she was going to church.

I go on the porch and it's Gearl. My regular guy's knows to respect the G to the utmost. I tell them to say nothing about anything you or I do in these streets. I give him the weed and he gives me the money. My mother got her things together and she coming out the house going to church.

I told Gearl, "keep it on the low. You know my momma don't want me selling weed."

She comes out on the porch and speaks to Gearl. "Hi are you doing young man?"

That's when Gearl get's to tripping.

He looks and paused then said, "I'm okay, but I want my money back this weed ain't no good."

I looked at him like I could've strangled him. He looked back grimed me and stole on me, smack. He did it right in front of my momma. After he stole on me he jumped in the wind like a bitch. Who does that, steal on you and run? He didn't get me good I rolled with it. I just couldn't phantom him doing that! I ran after him and killed him with anticipation of killing him. He was already dead.

My Mom was shouting my name saying, "Colo come back."

I paid her no attention. Can't call off the dog when he's been bit.

This nigga hit me in front of my momma like I am a hoe. I chased his ass all the way to 169th St. and he got tired. I knew he would he was never going to make it back to is house on Indiana. I knew he was going to tire out before he got home. I was digging into the concrete trying to catch him.

I still got plenty of wind from football training. I still play basketball all the time too. He was not going to make it home or to his heater. He stopped and started running around the car in front of the sub spot on 169th. This nigga is literally running around the car so I can't catch him.

I couldn't catch him so I grabbed a pole. It was hanging on the inside of the gate in the back of the sub spot. I was swinging the pole over the car trying to take his head off. He was ducking like a motherfucka.

Gearl face looked like he bit off more than he could chew. I'd have beaten him with that pole to death I was so angry. Gearl knows I'm a beast. He knew he couldn't stand there and fight so why did he do it? He knows he doesn't have a win with the knuckles. He paid for the bag already. He saw it in my face I could kill him, but I couldn't get at him. My mother drove up and told me to get in the car. I still listen to my mother and he was lucky I respect her like that!

I looked at Gearl and told him. "You're lucky and I'd be to see him." I jumped in the car and we took off. I didn't see Gearl anymore for a long time, if I ever saw him again. I don't think I've seen him since that day.

CHAPTER SIX

Killer Mentality

Do y'all know how many killers were around us when we were shorties. When we were just ten years old. Mr. Reef and his guys were straight killers. They went to Nam and they killed a lot of people. They killed for our government so it was legal, but they were killers. Mr. Reef was so cool you wouldn't think he was a killer.

He opened up a game room for kids. His wife Mrs. Reef worked at the Manor in the lunchroom. Mrs. Reef would help him in the game room sometimes. We saw Mrs. Reef at school and in the hood all in the same day.

Mr. Reef made sure we didn't stay in the game room during school time. He was one dude that cared what happen to us. He laughed with us and sometimes roughhoused us a little. That was only because he cared.

Sometimes he would kick us out for no reason. He would get a hazed look over his face. This is when he just got fed up with all us kids. He might have had post-traumatic syndrome. His faced didn't look right. We knew not to fuck with him when he was like that! He started getting aggressive didn't he Emus.

Emus shakes his head in agreement and says. "Yeah he did get aggressive out the blue. He'd kick us and then throw us out and lock the door."

His guy with the one leg opened up one across the street he was a killer too. He always gave us quarters and the good word. How can you tell when there's a killer around? You don't know, because anyone can kill.

It was killers across the street from me. We've known Butch Travis and Black John for years. I always shot ball in dungeon with his brother Chris Travis who was a little older. Butch went to school with my sister.

Black John used to go to the Robe with us. He got kicked out for moving on somebody my freshmen year. Chris ward Rodells brother and John moved on somebody right by the lunchroom. I didn't know John was a killer.

John was cool, but when he moved that day in the lunchroom. You could see killer in him. I was standing right next to him when somebody disrespected and he snapped. Butch and John were BD's. They used to sit on my porch before the fire all the time. They were killers and you'd never know it. Butch lived across the street in the building with big booty Diane, next to the record shop.

Remember Diane Emus and John?

John eyes get gleeful and he smiles and says. "Big Booty Diane had the biggest ass on the Southside ahh hha ha."

I smile and say, "No I was talking about where butch lived, but she did have the biggest shapely ass on the South side."

Andrea looks at John say with a smirk and sass, "what you saying you like big asses John?

John hurrys up and says, "no baby I like your ass I don't like big asses."

Everybody starts to laugh and I jump back in cause I see it didn't ease her. I say, "naw Andrea, a killer doesn't advertise what they do staying on the subject." She looks but she let it pass. I then say, killers were kicking it with us playing basketball, sitting on my porch or walking down the street. Every killer on 169th &171st camped and hung on John's porch.

John says, "you right Colo I knew all the killers before the went to jail just hanging on my porch."

I then say, "Butch and John killed somebody a few days earlier and we didn't know. I heard they killed them in his their back yard. When the police picked them up for the murder, we couldn't believe it. After that day I never saw Butch Travis and Black John again. I think they gave them twenty five to life."

Brain Jackson was found in the dungeon under the snow in 79'. His mother was my mother friend in the hood. I remember when Mrs. Jackson called and told my mother over the phone. They had been looking for him for months. Once the snow started to melt they found him under the snow shot dead.

It had to be somebody we knew killed him. It was too close. Word on the street is he had a bad smack problem and somebody solved it. I was conscious of and knew it was killers around me.

People were getting killed and nobody knew who killed them before that! It was people who killed for the government and people who killed for themselves, all around us.

I figured it out everybody is killers. It just what reason will you kill a person. I started to wonder where was my line. You have to know your line. I said I will kill for my family and I will kill for my friends in all righteousness. I know I am a killer I need guidelines to kill someone. You just can't go around just, because you can kill people and kill them. I had morality and valued the life of a person, until threaten.

I am chilling though this one night and the grim reaper was about to activate me. This is at a time when my guidelines weren't clear.

I am chilling in the back watching TV and my Mom yells, "somebody is at the door for you Colo."

I can't hear anybody knocking at the door from the enclosed back porch.

I tell her, "here I come Mom." I get up and go to the door and it was Sacks. I come on the porch and say, "what's up Folks?"

Sacks wanted to use my banger. He had got into it with Reico. You know Reico John. He was an older Vicelord who opened up a store in the hood. He took over Mint Orient on Indiana from the Koreans.

John says, "yeah I remember them cause I went up there to play games."

I then say, "he turned it into a little food joint. I heard he was one of the original twelve for the Vice Lord Nation. They had to be about twenty-five or thirty years old at the time. They owned a couple of stores on the block. They drove big yellow Fleetwood Caddies. They were the kind of guys who look down on you, I thought.

Reico is a black ass nigga like me with a drippy Jerry curl. He wore nugget rings and herringbone gold chains all the time. He was Westside, straight country, with all that gold in his mouth.

Reico would talk to you like you weren't shit. They would be serving you from behind the counter.

He cock his lips up with a slight grim and say. "What you want little nigga?"

He probably thought I was a little nigga. I learned from the older guys, back in the day. Now I am bigger and I'm knocking big guys off. He would answer like you were bothering him. I didn't like him, but up until then, we had no problems. I observed how he treated other people. I even used to go to the game room and play the games.

Like I said Folks come to my door. It was a raining that night. I let him in the corridor before you actually get in the house. He was talking low, because he sees Moms was sitting in the front room.

"Let me get the missile Folks I'ma kill Reico, tonight."

I look surprised and asked, "What he do Folks?" Sacks looked like why you asking me that. I really didn't care what he did. If he's fucking with you, let's go get him. I told him to hold on let me get dressed.

I went back to my room and jump in some all black clothes and a black hoodie. I grabbed the heat and was dressed to kill. We were about to do a hook ass nigga tonight. I get back to the porch to put the plan together.

Sacks said, "you stay here Folks."

I look at him like he was out of his mind and replied. "You know I'm going to roll, let's go."

Our plan was to sneak up Prairie and shoot down the alley and pop up on 169th. Hoping to catch him sleeping.

I asked Folks while running, "Folks you going to kill em or this for protection and you just going to smash him?"

He replies, "Folks I'm going to pop him."

I look at him nod and reply, "let's do him then." We had our hoods on and running up Prairie. It was a perfect night to do him, because it was drizzling raining. People are inside, instead of on the street.

Now we sneaking down this block low-key. Here comes Reico around the corner perfect like. I peeped him first and say in a low voice, "there he goes Folks." We ran across the street where Reico was walking and Folks pulled out the .357. We were supposed to run up and he was done up.

Instead of popping him he says, "what's up now Reico?"

Emus, I looked at him with the Scooby Doo face. That wasn't the plan. We got the drop on him give it to him. Nobody was around or anything. We caught him in front of Lil Jimmie and Kim Richards building. Folks looked back at me for the clear.

Reico looked at me and said, "man call your man off, don't shoot me."

I look him in his eyes then looked back at Folks and give him the nod with the grim look. Meaning blast his ass with my eyes. My face got the grim look and my head is nodding yes. I didn't want anybody to hear my voice.

Now twenty then thirty seconds have gone by. Reico is trying to talk his way out of it. He's talking not loud, but loud enough for somebody to hear.

He kept saying "come on y'all don't do it."

People in the building are hearing dude talking about, "put the gun down."

He continues pleading for his life. "It ain't that serious, man don't shoot me." They're hearing all this shit, instead of the blast sound is what's going through my head.

Right then I knew it was too late. I back up and stayed on security just in case the twisters were rolling. I look up and around. People were coming to the window and everything so I called it off.

I come back and tap Folks and said forget about with my face, shaking him off. Let's go we can't get away with it. People are in the window. If were not going to get away I don't want to do it. Let go Folks with the nod that says let's get out of here.

Do you know he just kept the missile on him.

He kept saying over and over again, "I should pop your ass, what up now?"

I looked at him and said to myself, "Folks must be on that wicky." I know Folks will move 100 percent of the time so I am bewildered.

By this time Disco his street cousin, Spider G, Boe Boe and few other Folks came around the corner.

Disco seen what was happening and immediately was like, "no Sacks, no Sacks, don't do it, don't do it."

That was one of Disco's Lords. Disco saved his life, but honestly he should be dead already. He shouldn't have had a chance to save his life. Nobody would've known we popped him.

You don't pull a gun on a motherfucka of his stature and don't use it. I should've grabbed the gun and popped him myself, but it was his beef. I would've popped him. It's too late and was too far to go back.

Disco continues to tell Sacks, "Give me the gun, put it down Sacks."

Disco goes over to Sacks and pry the gun out of Sack's hand and then gives it to me.

I know the twisters are on their way. I ran across the street. I put the missile on top of the front tire of a car sitting on the corner. The car was sitting on the other side of the street. I slide it under the wheel well on top of tire. The fender covered the top of the wheel so you couldn't see it at all.

I trotted back across the street to the scene after I duffed it. Once I crossed the street, about twenty squad cars converged on the set their heaters out. They came from every direction that you could use to trap us.

The police jumped out shouting, "get on the ground everybody. Where's the gun, where's the gun?"

We all answered, "It ain't no gun officer we just out here kicking it."

Reico kept quiet. All while I'm laying on the ground looking at him. I'm thinking to myself, "we fucked up, this is bad. This shit ain't over, dude is not going to let it go."

After they searched us and checked the whole area. They checked everywhere, but where I put the heater. I kind of got a sense when the police is coming. This is the only thing that kept us from getting caught with it. The gun carry a ten years bit off the top, if caught with it.

After they couldn't find it the twisters leave. Everybody dispersed and I go get the missile. After the altercation we go get 40's and sit on Boe Boe porch. I start tripping on Sacks I say. "Them niggas play for keeps Sacks. We fucked up! You should've popped that nigga. Nobody would've known nothing cause we were in and out".

"They got to retaliate now. These Vicelords were made and came from the Westside. I knew that was going to happen, there will be retaliation. I'd have did him myself, if I had the chance to get away".

I knew it would be repercussions behind this debacle. At the time I didn't give a fuck about killing nobody. Now I thank Yahweh Folks didn't pull that trigger. They would've caught us. Dude gets popped after confrontation with Sacks. It was people who seen the first altercation. I wasn't thinking about that!

To my surprise they didn't come right back at us. I know it ain't over. Reico walked off with Disco and I know Disco put him up on me. I know Reico wanted to know about me. I knew Disco wouldn't tell him, but he had to tell him something.

Dude saw me give Sacks the nod to kill him. He'll never forget that, I know I wouldn't. You just can't pull that pistol out and don't shoot. This is not a robbery.

Folks gave him mercy I thought he wanted to kill him. I guess it wasn't that bad whatever Reico did, because he didn't pop him. Harold, I should've investigated further before I gave him the pistol. Now Reico knows three things about me.

He knows who I am and he knows I gave Sacks the missile. Sacks came back with me to kill him. He left without the banger and came back with one. He knows I gave the go ahead to pop him. Sacks still should've hit Reico across the head or something. We ain't no hoes and you lucky we let you live or something.

Right then I had to reevaluate the reason I'd kill someone. I didn't have an criteria at first. This is something to think about. It's got to be discussed, before I just go out here blind for a friend. I won't kill over money, unless it's mine. I'll kill for my family. I'm not killing over any girl. I'll kill, if disrespected on a high level. I'll kill for me, if my life is threatened, that's disrespect for my life. I won't kill for someone who doesn't value these morals.

You will be tested and you have to make a stand when you cross that bridge. One time we were at the park. The Vicelords jumped out with the assault rifles and started letting them go. Nobody got hit, we scattered, but we went to get those thangs. We knew where one of the guys lived. Well some of the Folks were going right back at them and I was one of them.

We avoided the main streets. We worked the alleys and gangway all the way to the guy's house. We were hoping to catch him coming in or out house. We were going to ambush him, but he took too long. We were all in the bushes and out of site trying to catch him sleeping. We were out there a few hours laying for him.

One of the Folks got impatient and said, "fuck it let's shoot up the house."

I was like Folks, "I ain't with shooting up no house, but we can wait and catch his ass. It could be a mother, grandmother, child, baby or anybody in there that doesn't have anything to do with his actions. That's taking off the gloves".

I'm here to get that nigga who was trying to kill us. I was out voted so I faded. It wasn't my Folk's we were just at the park together. I head on back and they lit that motherfucka up. I don't want anybody shooting up my mother's house. What we do in these streets is left in the streets.

He should have been hit in the streets up close. I thank God nobody was home at the time. I prayed for them. "Yahweh I hope nobody got hit." I checked the next day low-key and nobody got hit. That was inconceivable for me to do.

Cooling Out

I kind of stayed on the Met after the botched attempt on Reico. When Reico come at me, it would be on my own land. We are the type of niggas that's going to come, right back. I can't put nothing past anybody either. If it could happen to QB it could happen to anybody. I was waiting, but it didn't go down right away, I kept the banger on me.

I told Todd and Slick Freddie what happened. They'll put the word out for security for anything out of place. When Reico or somebody out the ordinary start riding by looking out of place. Let me know and I was going to do a preemptive strike by myself.

I wasn't waiting on shit to happen. I was going to let it pass, if they were. I'm no fool so I'm going to shake and move. I wasn't hanging with Sacks and them for a while. He pissed me off with that shit. Another reason is Disco knew my method of operations. I to changed up just in case he told them something.

I'm cooling out back on the Met. I stayed in the dungeon when I'm on the nine. I never saw any of the Vicelords come back to the dungeon. I started sitting in the middle of the block, if I was on the Met. I didn't sit on the edge on John's porch. I wanted to see them coming, can't get caught slipping.

A few days later we're playing twenty-one in the dungeon. Slick Freddie, Todd and I were playing each other. Donald Bird walks down the alley from his house and said. "Me and my brother against anyone of y'all meaning, Freddie."

Todd said, "come on me and you cuz."

It was only the three of us in the alley. Donald Bird could shoot his ass off. You just can't let him shoot. Freddie was super at football, but was very competitive at basketball. He had a drive game and a decent shot. He used to misuse me when I was little on the court. I am a beast now.

Lil Todd and Freddie got something festering from the past. They had a few fights throughout the years. I always tried to be the peacemaker between the two. From time to time they would be at each other, saying slick shit. They were cool sometimes and other times not so much.

Neither guy wanted to give the other any P's. Some days are good and some days were bad. We start playing and it was a good game at first. The score was like, 10 to10. Freddie came to the hole and dropped it off, in the bucket.

Once he scored on Todd he said, "Todd lil ass ain't shit, keep giving me the ball down here Bird."

I saw it in Todd's face he didn't like that part. They had been talking shit all game to each other.

Bird did what Slick Freddie said and was dropping the rock to Freddie in the post. Now you know Todd got this Neopolian complex. The line was drawn in the sand when he said those words. Every time Freddie started backing down or tried beasting Todd in the post. Todd would hard foul him across the risk or arms.

Anytime he tried to muscle him, Todd would hard foul him. Freddie began elbowing Todd on the back down, because of the fouls. Every time Freddie got hard fouled. Todd was swinging going for the ball aggressively. The next thing that happened I guess, I guess Todd accidentally smacked Freddie. He hit him across the face going for the ball I guess.

Freddie was like, "damn Todd you ain't got to do all that."

Todd reply, "damn Todd my ass, play ball nigga."

Slick Freddie said, "Okay do it again."

It was like a replay, the same exact thing happened when Bird gave him the ball down low. This time Freddie retaliates and mush smacks Todd in face. It wasn't a smack and it wasn't a mush it was in between both. It was on, like Donkey Kong.

They started swinging at each other and some how gets locked up. This was a perfect time to break it up.

I say to both of them, "cool out y'all" and started trying to separate Freddie and Todd. I'm trying to break it up.

Bird says out the blue, "let my brother go" and swings on me.

I ducked and started swinging trying to knock his head off. I just missed by a nip off the counter.

Here I go and I tell him, "I am the wrong one Bird." I had to reach up while swinging at Bird, because he was tall. He backs out the way, but sees the bad intentions and the precision. I looked over and Todd and Freddie were wrestling on the ground. Freddie was on top, but he couldn't do anything, because Todd had his neck.

Now Bird is about twenty-five and I am seventeen. I was lining him up bouncing and ready to pounce. I'm looking sweet because I'm bouncing and I ain't backing up. I am trying to make my move.

Bird said, "Nigga I'm just saying don't put your hands on my brother."

Bird was using the back door.

I let him out by saying. "I was breaking it up and you swung on me Bird what's up with that shit. Freddie is my guy too."

We kind of faded, because Todd mother came out and told Freddie and Todd to stop.

She said in a stern voice, "Todd and Freddie get up, right now. I mean right now."

Mother is on the set and she says, "it's over both of y'all get off the ground, it's over".

She then tells the both of us, "break them up pull them apart."

Bird and I say, "Okay Mrs. Stables then Bird and I started working together to pull them apart. After pulling them apart Freddie and Bird walked back down the alley to the crib. They didn't say much to each other, because Mrs. Stables was governing the situation. Respect what came before you. It didn't get messy, so it was all-good.

Harold, Adrian life on the Met was live. I didn't know that our block was one of the most unique blocks in the city. The whole block was like your blood family. It never got messy with family members.

The Stables and the Small brothers and sister have lived the same block for years. All of the older brothers and sister interacted with each other. When people came to our block to hang out on our block. They literally didn't leave. They came to our block to hang for years.

You could stay as long as you obeyed block rules, you could kick it. When you didn't you take a smashing, but you could come back. As long as you understood what was happening on the block.

I never remember anybody on the block going hard, trying to kill each other. We fought, we played ball, we chased girls, we signify and we sold dope. We gangbanged, but it was still always family first. You couldn't fuck with anybody on our block with out us riding.

Bounce

*Y*ou know me Emus I am the adventurer. I can't stay in one place for a long time. I didn't want to be a sitting duck for Reico. Reico sold dope and information is easy to get for the dope man. When I wasn't on the nine I was on the 171st at Iron Park. I started kicking it with Butter.

Butter was calling it over the BD's in that area and at the Iron Park. They called him Butter, because he had the longest finger waves on the South side. When he came down to the nine we always kicked it. He had an older brother that was cool as hell.

I forget his name, but he used to be at the park, above the rim. He used to dunk all different type of ways. I remember going over Butter's house to get them to play basketball. It was nobody at the court playing.

We all had just played the day before and we were on the same team. He went to work and left Butter and I on the court. They stayed right across the street from the park. One day his brother was here and the next day he was gone.

That night he was killed at work. I didn't know and I go to get them to play. I rang the bell and Butter came to the door and he told me what happened.

Butter said, "he got smashed by machinery or some machinery hit him."

I was like, "damn Butter you straight." He sat on his steps in the hallway a little stoic while telling me. He wasn't falling to pieces. I give it to him he was holding it together. Had it been my brother I would have fallen to pieces. Those two guys were close. They were always together playing ball. RIP my man

Butter was older now and had respect on 171st. I kind of like how Butter had control over his regime. He didn't rule with the iron hand he was more diplomatic. That's why the niggas love him in the hood. I didn't here him violating his soldiers all the time. If you fuckup bad, he'd have to do something. If it wasn't that bad, it was either or. Take the violation or do some other community building task.

I was thinking about coming down to the 171st and hanging with Butter. It was my second home anyway from home. He and I would make a good combination. I got goons and he got goons. It was just something I thought about. I was thinking about holding a position too.

The reason I didn't at first was, because of the O.G. Now I could, if I wanted too. Only thing about a position is that you are the head. The heads usually get killed or go to jail. I'll just stay incognito, it seem to be a good way to survive. I know my history. Dr. King, Malcolm X, Fred Hampton, David Barksdale and QB were all dead leaders.

I had power still, Harold, but it was a different power. I had a low-key behind the scene type of power. When the goon, goons have respect for you, that's power. I was a smart guy who could fight better than most.

I carried the banger all the time, but they knew I didn't lean on the heat. That is what gave me mad respect. I will use the heat, if necessary, but I could fight. It was totally up to you how you played yourself.

I often boxed one on one and the heat was close. I will kill, if I feel threatened to be killed or you fucking with family. That's power too, if you know the guys in control and the guys in control are at your call.

Those are the guys I had respect from, because they knew I was 100. You couldn't get me to do nothing dumb anymore. I had my own mind. I would often offer better ideas when fuck shit happened.

I could get people together, because I knew and was cool with the whole hood. A lot of guys just stayed in their own area. I bounced because I had the weed. I couldn't sell out the house like that! I did, but you had to be my man's. I sold weed at the park. I'd go to Rock Manor for a while to sell. I even get on the bus with a joint in my ear. I'd sell weed on the bus. I was always moving trying to get money.

I could bounce, because I knew all the players who were in play. They were happy to see me come around. I didn't start anything and controlled no areas and still had power. I figured out a long time ago. The police and the opposition are looking for the heads. I can stay low-key and not be known to the law for, banging.

I had the weed and often smoke, if my custo got the drank. That was the trade off. You can bounce, but you can't just stay around for a long time. The Met was the only block like that in the city. You could only hang out in someone else's hood for just two or three days of chilling then bounce. When you stay too long sooner or later somebody's going to try you for something.

Let them get to know you, but don't let them know you. My rep preceded me wherever I go. I'd bounce in and out and that's how you stay cool. People don't get tired of seeing you all the time. You are not a threat trying to talk to their girls and shit like that.

You can't let people pinpoint your moves. Not even your own guys. People are looking for the chink in your amour. They're looking to find your weakness. Once they find it and everybody has one, they'll exploit it. Remember in grammar school when you said, you hit me in my weak spot, cool out. That's how you get got they'll go right at your weakness.

On the way back walking home from the Park. I see Lee and his little brother on 170th & Calumet. I'm by walking by myself across the street from Gooch's house on the Met.

My Lil brother wired me up that Lee and his Moes chased him. They pulled out the heater and chased them. Wally did say it wasn't Lee who did it, but he was with them. He should have called it off. Especially, since he knows it's my brother. Lee knows not to chase my brother anywhere.

I couldn't wait to catch him. Here it is, he's walking right towards me. His Lil brother all ready knew what was up. Once he saw me he face told the story. I see it in his face they didn't want to see me. His brother started crossing the street as soon as he saw me.

His mother probably told him not to get involved with his older brother's affairs. His brother goes around starting shit that will get him killed. As we were getting closer to each other Lee tries to veer off in the streets.

I asked him, "what you walking in the street for?" He already knows what's up he knew I would be looking for him. I give him the look and say, "I heard you chased my brother with the missile", as I get closer.

He looked and said, "It wasn't…..

I played it off like I was going to talk to him and blazed him, bam. Back him up with the punch. He tried to kick me. That karate training kicks in and I hit him with the downward block. I blocked it and stole on him again. I didn't get him good, but I got him good enough.

Lee started running around the car next to us and I couldn't get at him. His little brother was just watching me chase him around the car. I looked at Lee like, "uggh you running with your big pussy ass." I stop chasing him and said, "you a big ass pussy don't fuck with my brother no more" and I walked to the crib.

Before leaving I said, "anything happens to my lil brother and the Folks coming to kill you. You won't even see my face." He didn't say anything after that and him his brother walked toward 171st.

I didn't hear about Reico looking for me. That could be good or that could be bad. They could've said fuck it or they could be planning to strike low-key. I started hanging with GDs again. That whole year Sacks, Spider G, Grimes and I used to hit the parties all around the hood.

It was a lot more of us, but this was the inner circle. We used to be ten or twelve deep before we got to the party. Guess who I ran into while we were hood-hopping parties?

Emus says, "who Colo?"

I ran into Ebert from the Robe who used to try and rob me my freshmen year. We were going to a house party over around Slept Rock's crib, on 169th & Sangamon.

It was a party on Peoria I forgot exactly, because I was high and bubbled. We were twelve deep coming up the steps of the party. Ebert was coming down the steps.

He stopped me and said, "what's up?"

I looked at him and something said to me, "you got his ass you're here with all your Folks." He was Folks too, but he used to fuck with me. I quickly thought to myself, "I should fuck this nigga up." He put his hand out though and I just looked at him while thinking. He didn't know I was here with my Folks and offered me his hand. I was the first one up the stairs. You never know who your going to run into so that's why I stayed righteous.

Ebert looked and felt the coldness and said, "awe man you ain't going to shake my hand Folks?"

I shook off the devil and said, "what's up man?" I gave him some love. That's when he saw who I was with nothing, but goons. I was with niggas who were known all through the land.

To be honest I think he was glad to see me. Maybe I changed his life. Lil Dave probably told him, dude whooped your ass. Ebert didn't know what happened to him once he got his bearings. It happened so fast. He thought he was in control and then he was sitting down asking what happened.

Lil Dave had to tell him he was knocked out on his feet. He was literally staggering walking down the hallway. He probably stopped that bully shit. He really thought I was a mark. I changed his life for the better never underestimate anybody. That's what my Mom used to say.

Guess who else I gave a pass? You will never believe this one. This is when we were scandalous on the nine. I had gone out one more time with the Folks strong-arming. We'd catch the bus on Sunday with that Super Transfer and pop motherfuckas off in different spots. We hadn't been able to see nothing worth grabbing the whole day. We were waiting at one of the bus terminals. We were about six deep this particular time.

I see the nigga who robbed me on my graduation night. He was hanging out the backdoor of the bus. He probably was out doing exactly what we were doing robbing people. We catch eye contact and he sees I'm with my mob. He knows I know who he is, because I squinted at him with the, you motherfucka look. He played it off and faded back onto the bus.

It ran through my mind to grab him out the door. I thought though, right then nope. I was out there slipping and they got me. This is what we do to niggas and it was just my turn. We were out here doing the same thing he did to me, right now.

I could've continued the cycle and smashed dude into a coma. Dave just kept popping in my head about what he did to the Brother in my freshmen year.

Man Emus, it was a battle at my core. I was touching whatever fraction of love that was left in my body. I thought and said to myself, "Folks will damn near kill this nigga right here in the bus terminal." I told the Folks and they were so pissed off about me getting robbed more than I was.

I'd a said Folks that's dude who robbed me that night. They would've gotten on the bus and drug dude off and smashed him. I did bad things to people. Now I'm going to kill him, because he got me. I bet somebody out here looking to kill me too. I give him a pass and didn't say anything.

You couldn't have told me I was going to do that! I was actually looking to run across this guy and I wanted to kill him. Once I saw him and giving him that pass. I aborted the missions to rob and never strong-armed anyone else.

We really never hurt anyone during these robberies. Just seeing the goons coming will make you give your shit up like a slot machine paying out a jackpot. You might take a blow just to let you know, we ain't bullshitting.

We had knives, brass knuckles, numb chucks everything, but a heater. You can't go to jail, if caught with these items. Most of the time they'd take your numb chucks or brass knuckles, if you had them. A knife you could keep as long as it was under six inches, it was legal. I used to practice throwing my knife into a trees and became quite good. I could hit you in the chest on the fly. I kept that motherfucka sharp too.

Those numb chucks were cold. I could work them good, but I wasn't as good as the best guys. When I didn't have a pistol on me. I definitely had a knife and those brass knuckles in my back pocket. I can't be caught totally slipping. When they come three or four deep at me, I still got a chance.

I'd cuff the knife and slip on the brass knuckles. Let them see and know I ain't playing. Tell the motherfuckas to step up, if you want too. You had to be ready in the streets of Chicago for whatever. That motherfucka is scandalous to a motherfuckas health. I know, because I'm riding everyday with these goons.

I was dishing out the bad medicine too. I know what another human being will do to another human being. It gives them joy to fuck you over! I was in it for the money. I never enjoyed doing people bad.

I was young and broke and that's a volatile concoction to combust in my system. I felt life wasn't fair to me and lost control for a second. That's why I let dude on the bus go. I was trying to gain control over myself again. I didn't have to rob and steal. I had a hustle! I shelved the strong-arming when I saw my assailant again. That shit ain't right.

The Spots

*I*t was either Sacks crib or we were at Grimes crib. Mrs. McGraw, Sacks mother wasn't having it, but we could hang. She had three other sons Faye, Tim and Mike. She didn't want them destroyed by his influence. We couldn't be as wide open at Sacks's crib, as we were at Grimes's crib. Grimes was the only child in his family.

Mrs. Tucker would close her bedroom door and we were straight. It was like she wasn't ever at home, unless we got too loud. We can smoke and drink at Grimes's house. While watching TV, listening to music or playing cards. A lot of times we would go in the hallway to smoke weed.

We had this girl we used to play strip poker with Grimes and I. You win once we get her down to her panties or she our drawers. We were playing cards one morning and watching the prelude to the shuttle take off. We were watching it, because they had a teacher and a black person on the shuttle.

It was regular people going up in space. You know I got the weed so we blowing early.

Folks say hold on, "let's watch the shuttle, it's about to take off."

We stop and we're watching the shuttle's countdown and everything. We caught it at eight, seven, six, five, four, three, two and one.

The shuttle blasted off into the air. Seven seconds later it exploded into smoke and fire. I knew something was supposed to drop off after it got so far in the air. I am thinking this, before fourteen seconds pass and it's in a ball of fire. I was thinking that, but then I knew that was supposed to happen, closer to leaving the atmosphere.

I looked at Grimes then Grimes looks at me. We looked back at the TV. We were blowing some good weed so I'm still processing. You could tell after seven seconds, we were all processing what just happened. It took five seconds for it to sink in that it exploded. Even the broadcaster didn't say anything for a long time.

Before the broadcaster says something Grimes says, "uuh was that supposed to happen? It looked like that motherfucka blew up to me."

That's when the broadcaster comes in and says, "it seems to be a problem."

I said, "no shit Sherlock, that motherfucka blew up." We stop playing cards and put our shit back on was glued to the television.

Mobsters for Real

*F*olks were up on their current events. The five presidents that served during our lifetime were Nixon, Ford, Carter, Regan and Bush. Let see what happen in that period in time.

Nixon will go down as our most controversial president. They called him Tricky Dick. Now he opened up the trade routes to China. He was the first to invoke environmental laws for air and sea. He did his part in subduing the Russians in the cold war. They say he had a brilliant mind. The lost to Kennedy in the 1960 election left him bitter. He felt they stole the election from him in Chicago. This stuck in his craw and it festered.

Hate was Richard Nixon downfall. He hated his enemies and this was his undoing. It says in the bible love thy enemies. It was said that he knew in the 1976 election. He was the incumbent and would not be reelected to office.

No sitting president has been relieved of duties during wartime. It's a given he will be reelected to finish things up. He also knew they had to get out and they wouldn't win the war, still the war continued. It was said that he let the Vietnam War continue so he could stay president. In the mean time, 25,000 more people were killed. Most of these people are draftees and were from poor communities, black and white. Power is a motherfucka in the wrong hands.

I was four years old when the Water Gate Scandal broke. It was nothing else on TV to watch. My mother was glued to the TV set. Mr. Nixon sent his cronies to plant bugs in his enemies whereabouts. After they caught the fools planting the bugs. He tried to cover it up with payoffs. This sounds like mob shit to me. This is what you call obstruction of justice.

This act will lead to the impeachment process, to oust him from his presidency. He let all his boys take the fall and go to jail. After seeing the writing on the wall Richard Nixon resigned August 8th 1974.

The Vice President Gerald Ford assumed office and pardons Nixon for his wrong doings. His reason was that the country needed to heal. He did not want what handcuffed the country for the last few years to continue.

Richard Nixon would have been the first president to go to jail. Gerald Ford spared the country. This act of understanding will kill him in his reelection bid against Jimmie Carter. The people wanted Tricy Dick to go down. Squeaky Fraum tried to assassinate President Ford. He finished up his two years and Carter won the presidency in 1980.

What killed Carters reelection bid, was the hostage crises in the Middle East. The embassy was over ran and they had about eighty hostage. This gripped the country each day that passed. He tried to get them home before he lost his presidency. Ronald Reagan was doing some back door dealings and the hostages weren't to be released, until he took over office.

This left a stain on Carter presidency, because Regan got the credit for getting them home. Carter tried to do some different things, but he was consumed with the hostage crisis.

Regan was trading guns for dope and his Vice President Bush is now in office. He was the head of the CIA before he ran on Regan's presidential ticket. It's right in our face, but we can't see it. Bush is the guy in control of all the black ops that goes on in the world!

He is our top spy so he knows the underground circuit. How did all that cocaine get on the corner? You got to comprehend how scandalous things are cloaked to deceive you. This is all a conspiracy theory but 2+2 =4. I don't know shit I just comprehend shit. Somebody else will comprehend it differently

The guys who make it all the way to the top are true street niggas in suits. On the world stage though! Street niggas do good things and sometimes, you have to get your hands dirty, to survive. The saying is, "for the greater good."

I know a street nigga when I see one! A street nigga will gangster what he wants, if it's not given. Which presidents do you think were gangsters in our lifetime y'all? These are the people we aspire to be. This is what I call trickle down mobster game? You learn from the best. We learn from the guys in leadership how to be beast.

This mob shit trickles down to the kids learning in school. They teach us how to be mobsters. They mask things, because they write the history we learn. What did they do to the Indians and the Mexicans? They killed gangstered their land and resources.

They got this day called Thanksgiving we celebrate. Why don't I see any Indians celebrating this day? I never see an Indian in a commercial celebrating this day.

What would they be thankful for? Let see thanks for taking our land and killing our people. Thanks for setting us up in a little spot called reservations. This is when Indians roamed all over North America. What do you call people who takes what is not theres? I call them Mobsters!

What did they do to us Africans? They slaved us and stole our God given freedoms. To read write and the pursuit of happiness was not a given. They made a mint off of our back and we can't get a slug for respirations. What would some of these guys be with out the presidential seal? They would be mobsters in those suits! One thing about it! The way they did it spring boarded this country to greatness. Now this is the best country in the world for some people. I'm telling another story I didn't mean to get side tracked. When logic hits you it is a motherfucka!

I snitched

*A*ll the young Folks who looked up to us would always come by Sacks. They would bring drinks and buy weed from me. My brother used to come and hang with Grimes when I wasn't around. I did not want my brother around us. These guys were three and four years older than me.

Now my younger brother is going to hang with me. My mother would never forgive me. She already had put me in the hands of Yahweh. All she could do was pray for me. My mother wore her knees out praying for me.

Walley was cutting school and getting bubbled all the time. He was getting out of hand and wouldn't listen to me.

I'd tell him, "Walley you only suppose to cut one day out the week. You're only going, but one day a week, if that! Walley you got to go to school." He would play me off and continue to do his do.

Now I understand why my sister told my old dude on me when she saw the beers. I was getting out of hand. I called my mother after wrestling with myself for a couple of weeks. I was wrestling with whether to tell her or not, because he was fucking off school.

I had to call her before he fucks off school. I called on the phone by the alley across from the laundry matt. I dropped a dime on my brother and was feeling funny. I have never done this before, but he was fucking up in school.

I call anyway and she answers, "hello George resident."

I say, "Mom Walls is in the game room and he's always in the game room. He is not going to school".

She says, "what game room?"

I tell her, "down the street at the sub spot on 169th St". It had a few games like, Pack Man and Galga in it.

. She says, "okay I'm putting my clothes on and on my way."

I skate right afterwards from the sub spot. I leave so he wouldn't know it was me who told. She drives up and sees him and tells him to get in the car. I watched from a distance as he gets in the car. I wanted my brother to go to school. I gave him bad examples, but I did show him that I did graduated.

Doing dumb Shit

*A*ll the young Folks looked up to our crew. Most of the time they didn't know I was the same age as them. I was either the same age or no more than a couple years older than they were. I already was known in the game and put in mad work.

One of the young Folks was checking out the blue steel sawed off shotgun Grimes had.

Young Folks asked, "is it real?"

Grimes was like, "hell yeah it's real, nigga" while laughing. Grimes was talking on the phone and ironing his clothes when he asked.

I ask Grimes, "let me take it outside and show them how it works?"

Grimes said, "go ahead."

I go down in the alley next to the playground. I jacked it, aimed at the sky and pulled the trigger, Boommm.

After shooting it we were standing around looking into the sky like we were watching fireworks. We were admiring how it sounded and the fire that came out of it.

Grimes came on the back porch and hollered from upstairs, "get y'all dumb asses in the house you know somebody going to call."

We come up stairs all giddy and tripping on the fire that came out of it.

Grimes was like, "hurry up. Y'all done fucked up we got to get out of here. Y'all were supposed to pop it on the back porch and run on back in the house. You know somebody seen y'all dumb asses."

Grimes hurried up put his clothes on and telling us, "let's go."

He knew the neighbors were going to call the police. He didn't want to be there when they came. We walked out onto the back porch, while Grimes started locking up the house and the security gate with the padlock. He was talking shit to us while he was doing it. That's what got us caught, locking up the fortress and him talking shit.

We started walking down the stairs and the twisters were coming up the stairs. Their guns were drawn out at their side while asking. "Where's the shotgun?"

We look at them and say, "we don't know nothing about no shotgun." Grimes couldn't get the pad lock on in time and the keys were still in the lock.

One of the officers sees the keys in the lock and asked, "whose inside and who house is this?"

Grimes answers, "it's my mother's house and she's at work."

The police grab the keys in the lock and opened the door then told us to get inside. After we all get inside, they handcuff us to each other and began searching.

One of the officers says, "tell us where it is or you are going to jail?"

Grimes had a let out couch he slept on in the front room. He threw the double barrel inside the couch before leaving. Police kept searching and we didn't say anything. One of them looked at the couch, opened it up, bingo.

He looked at Grimes, smiled then slaps the shit out of him and said, "you're going to jail."

Grimes took the blow and asked, "to jail for what?"

Officer smelled it and said, "yeah it's just been fired let's go smart ass nigga", and put Grimes in the car, locked up the house and took Grimes to jail.

I felt fucked up cause Grimes is in jail and the police got the shotgun. It was my fault. He got out on a I bond. Grimes retained a paid lawyer with money from his college fund that he didn't use for college. The sawed off carried a ten year bit. It was sawed off too short and he was facing time.

On court day Grimes was nervous. We smoked a couple of joints and drunk a brew before court. Grimes and I walked in courtroom while we were waiting on his lawyer. We were listening to the other detainee's cases.

The judge was sending everybody he saw to the clink. They called everybody locked up in the back first. Grimes was out on bond so he had a better chance. It means something when you out on bond vs. you locked up in the county. It's better to fight your case on the street. The judge needs to see that somebody loves you.

Grimes started getting more nervous, because his lawyer wasn't there at first.

He was like, "aw shit this judge ain't bullshitting. Folks I should leave."

I reassured him and said, "cool out Grimes we got a lawyer." They called his name while his lawyer wasn't there yet. He had to stand up and tell the judge nervously, his lawyer was on the way.

Judge says, "okay" and tells him to sit down.

His lawyer finally came in and addressed the judge. After he addressed the judge we walked out in five minutes. Police didn't have a search warrant to search the house. We did not invite them in the house.

This was an unlawful search and seizure of the property. That's the difference from a paid lawyer and a public defender. A public defender is working for the state. He is not paid to get you off especially, if you're guilty. Grimes paid the lawyer about twenty five hundred dollars to represent him. They dropped all charges.

A paid lawyer is working for you guilty or not, get me off. This is called Capitalism. Grimes had a college fund he dipped into to get him off. Grimes was still worried though! He was twenty years old. His lightweight ass was going to have to go to jail. This wasn't his first case and all because of us.

He would have to hang out with the big boys. It would've been my fault. I had to walk him through the process. I had to drive the car back just in case they kept him. I had his keys and everything. After court we jumped in the Charger and got bubbled. He was happy than a motherfucka. He was like let's go Folks we out of here. My stupidness cost him twenty five hundred dollars.

Going to Jail

Harold, the next time it was his fault that I went to jail. I'm riding with Grimes and Boe Boe. We are going to do something, but not steal, because I wouldn't have gone. I'm along for the ride this time and wasn't in control of my situation.

You can't change totally unless you change your surroundings and can control your situation. I can jump in the car with Folks at anytime. What am I supposed to walk while my Folks got a car? I wasn't going to go that far. You must change the people and the environment you are around, if you want to change. There's no other way.

I know at anytime, Grimes would bust his screwdriver out. Grimes was driving and rolled by this strip mall on 187Th. He started to slow down to look at the cars in the parking lot. I'm like, "oh shit", to my self. We could be rolling do something totally opposite, until Grimes sees something to steal. You can't stop stealing, if you're hanging out with thieves and thugs. At anytime something could go down.

Grimes get so happy when he sees the shit that he likes to steal.

He spots something and says, "Ooh Folks the bitch got fresh meat, fresh meat."

When he said it twice that means he is about to hit em.

It would be in the back of my mind, "here we go again."

Grimes started drooling and say, "Folks he's sitting on ¾ inch white walls and the 30's." When you didn't have vogues you rode ¾inch white walls or royal seals for style. That's a quick, three hundred not to mention the radio.

Grimes start saying kind of in a low voice. "I got to get it, I got to get it."

Grimes grabbed the screwdriver under the seat and jumps out. I'm like, "damn damn damn", like Florida did on good times. When she found out James was dead.

He then tells Boe, "jump in the driver seat and drive my car."

John, I already said I wasn't going to be doing shit like this anymore. The only way that will happen though is, if I stop hanging with thieves. The thieves were my hommies so I couldn't do that! We waited until the lot cleared of the immediate people who saw us roll up.

Grimes was posted close by the car, leaning on a pole and fucking with his shoes. The first opportunity he had he busted the window with the screwdriver. He looked around then knocked the glass out the way. After that he hit the lock and jumped in the car and busted up the ignition. He went to work and peeled it in twenty seconds.

. Sometimes Grimes couldn't break the steering by himself.

When it doesn't break he'll say, "this bitch won't break, help me break it Folks." Now I'm an accessory. I had to help him before, because he was so skinny and frail.

I was praying he could break it by himself. Grimes put his feet on the door and leveraged his butt on the seat. He put the whole 120lb on that steering and broke it. Once you break it one way, it's easier the other way.

Once he broke the steering he pulled off with the car. The alarm was still going off as he was driving down the street. He had just popped a 1980 Park Avenue.

Boe Boe drove off in Grimes car following him till we got to the hood. He pulled over a couple of blocks away. He then jumped out and snatched the wires to the alarm off! He then jumps back in the car and drives back to the nine.

Grimes stopped on 170th & King Drive alley. This is right down the street from my crib to break the car down. All he wanted was the tires and the radio. He could get a quick few hundred dollars and drop the car right in the alley.

Grimes popped the trunk and grabbed the crowbar out of it. He bends down and start breaking the tires. I was just watching him from the passenger seat of his car. Grimes tell me to find a brick to drop the car on once the tires are off. I get out looking for bricks to set the car on!

Grimes suddenly looked up and say, "somebody in the window."

Next the dude in the window comes on the porch and was watching us.

Grimes jumped in the steamer and says emphatically, "somebody looking let's go, let's go."

He skirts out. Now the passenger door is stuck and doesn't open. I ran to the other side of the car and had to crawl over the driver's seat, to get back in the car. I look at the steering column and no keys. Boe jumps in the car.

We hear the police siren and the revved up car engine of the car, speeding down the alley. You couldn't see us, because of the horseshoe in the alley. The police was riding down the Calumet side of the horseshoe. We were in behind King Drive and Calumet alley. Boe hit his pockets for the keys. After he heard the sirens he got nervous and breaks out. He jumped over a gate in into the wind and was out of site.

I see he ran and at the same time my dumb ass, hits the passenger door. I forgot that quick it was stuck. I climbed out the driver side costing me precious seconds. I get out the car and before I could run. The car screeches to a stop.

The officer jumps out shouting. "Don't move don't move!"

I walked to the front fender without running and didn't move. I made sure she knew I was no threat.

It was a lady police officer, out the car, with her weapon drawn on me.

I asked her, "what's the problem officer?" Had I gotten out the car on my side she'd have never caught me.

She was in the prone position leaning over her driver's door window.

She yells, "put your hands up and get on the car. Where's the car?"

I answer, "what car?" I could've still broke and ran, but the car was gone. I'm in a legal car so I didn't have to run, once the steamer was gone.

I looked at her badge to see her name. Her name was officer Hayes.

She asked me again, "where's the car y'all were striping back here?"

I looked strange and said, "I don't know nothing about stripping any cars.

She then tells me, "put your hands behind your back," while she put the cuffs on me.

I was thinking to myself, "that was fast, within 90 seconds of the man calling the police, the police was on the scene."

I keep playing the dumb role for a while. After cuffing me she put me in the back seat of the squad car. She kept asking me questions and I'd spin her. Once I knew I was going to jail I stopped talking.

I was the only one who got caught. I know the game. You didn't catch me driving the car. I was in dude who ran, car.

Officer Hayes asked, "why'd your friend run?"

I answered, "I don't know why he ran. He must got warrants or something."

She then asked, "who was driving the car? I don't even know dude who was in the other car and don't know why he squirted.

She says, "yeah right and takes me to jail."

I was seventeen so I went to lock up. No more Mom coming to get you. I can't call Spider G to come get me. He needs some dough to bond me out. They get me in the prescient and charge me with a stealing a car.

I'm in the bullpen and see about five or six guys I knew from Rock Manor. I saw Todd Smith in there and a few other people from Rock Manor. It was like a class reunion from grade school. I had a fresh pack of New Ports so I set them out.

It was good I didn't have any weed on me that day. I passed out a couple squares to guys I knew in lock up. I left the weed at Grimes crib, because we were riding. Police were always pulling young motherfuckas over! When you two three deep, in a green Charger, it's automatic.

I didn't have any money to bond out from the station. My bond was five hundred dollars and I didn't have a college fund like Grimes. They shipped me to the Cook County Corrections. I called my mother and told her the deal.

She came down to 26^(Th) & California, Cook County to see me. When she got back there to see me. I said, "momma they got the wrong person. I need five hundred to get out."

Mother replies, "I know your friends are coming to get you."

I asked her, "why would you say that, I'm seventeen now and they can't sign me out?"

She responds, "That's the people you listen to, tell them to come get you out."

She continued to talk for a minute. I blocked everything out after she said, "get your friends". She might as well been mumbling to her self. She sounded like Charlie Brown's mother when he was on the phone with her waaaaa waaaaa waaaaa waaaaa.

I didn't have one number to call that had five hundred dollars to get me out. I wasn't going to call my old man, because I was shamed. I didn't really want him to know how I was cut. He had no idea what was going on with me in the streets. When I was around him it was nothing, but honor and respect.

My mother knew me so I called her. That's right she knew me and walked right back out the County.

After she said, "I see y'all having a party in the back. I hope you're having fun."

Her jokes weren't that funny to me and neither one of us laughed at them.

She then says, "I was just coming to make sure you were all right. I can go home now" and she walked out.

I'm standing behind the glass and I watched her leave me in jail. I stood there for a second hoping she would come back.

I thought again and said to myself, "you know she ain't bullshitting." This right here was a ground shaking moment for me. She was right like most of the time. I can't get signed out of jail any more I was seventeen.

I went back to the bullpen and sat and thought. I started praying in the bullpen, "Yahweh, no more stealing cars, no more breaking in houses and no more thievery of any kind. Please let me get me out of this jam." I did not like being locked up. I am locked up for something I did not do.

I was telling the truth. I was locked up for something I didn't do. I couldn't stop Grimes from stealing the car, if I wanted to stop him. I had no control. I had a little control, because when they stopped the car.

I could've walked to the crib at that point. My house was ¾ of a block away. I thought about it, before he asked me to get the bricks. Once he had it and he was going to cut me in I couldn't walk away. Again being greedy because I already had flow.

All I had to do was get the bricks and load the tires up and I'd get fifty bucks at least. I should've followed my first mind. Officer Hayes rolled right by my house on the way to the police station. I just shook my head.

I had already been locked up for three days when she came down to see me.

I had to go through quarantine. When I first got to lock up we undressed, butt naked. They checked us thoroughly.

The rent a cop was giving us instructions, "bend over, cough, pull your butt cheeks open."

Dude who was in there with me was hiding something in his mouth. He showed us, cause he didn't know what he was going to do with it.

Next the officer told every body to open your mouth and move your tongue side to side.

He get to dude and said, "open your mouth."

The officer look, squinted to get a better look and saw what was in his mouth. He tried to swallow it once the officer peeped it. The officer grabbed him by his throat so he couldn't swallow it.

The rest of us were just looking over our shoulder at dude, while we were butt naked. Dude swallowed it anyway. Once the officers seen it was gone they whooped his ass and I mean whooped his ass. This is while dude was butt naked.

I was like, "Dammm they are whooping his ass."

I thought my mother was coming to get me when she did that move. When she walked out, for the first time in a long time. I didn't know what to do. Once she left and I went back to the bullpen depressed and prayed that prayer. Do you know twenty minutes later, I was getting out on an I bond?

They're letting me go on my own word and signature. I had forgot about an I bond, stressed out about the situation. I figure out what work for Grimes didn't work for me. When Grimes was locked up his mother had him out the next day. How was I going to get five hundred dollars?

I thought you have to pay to get out of jail. I just got to sign and come back to court. I could do that! A lot of guys would get out of jail and just don't go back. Now the judge is going to issue you a warrant for your arrest.

When they catch you the next time and they are, going to catch you. You got to pay to get out. You better have at least five thousand the next time they catch you, cash. Not to mention it does nothing for your case you already had.

When they catch you doing something else illegal. They are going to run your name and there will be a felony warrant for your arrest. You know you're going to sit down for a while. All you got to do, is go to court. A lot of times they don't have their case together.

It was just a catch, for some guys. They couldn't see they were giving you a rope and letting you hang yourself. Once you didn't come to court, now they get paid. The jails were so crowded they couldn't keep me. I wasn't going to miss my court date either. They let me out and I caught the bus home. You get a free ride to the crib when you show them you just got out of jail. You just show them your bracelet and you could get to the crib.

I catch the bus from California up to Western. I got on the Western bus going south to 169th then caught 169th street bus to Calumet. I'm back on the street. Lando was the first person that saw me when I got off the bus.

He yelled all the way from down at his crib, which is a block away loud as hell. "Jaiiiiillllllbird, here comes the jailbird."

I was salty and replied, "shut the fuck up with your fat ass Lando." He wasn't fat but he carried a little weight.

What I say that for he got even louder. "Jailbird Jailbird Jailbird."

Lando was a character. It flew through the hood I was locked up fast. Grimes and them were trying to get my bond up. Lando had a light blue Chevy van and it had mad sounds in it.

It seemed like he drove around the block every two minutes. I always wondered why he didn't go somewhere out the neighborhood? That's when I used to live on 169th St. sitting on my porch. I didn't know at first what he was doing, but he was selling dope.

Lando talked mad shit all the time. Him and his brother Stagelee, talked the most shit in the hood. That saying something, because we all talked mad shit. He just knew he could shoot ball and he could.

Emus and John agree and say, "yeah Lando could shoot!"

When we were shorties he used to get us on the court, but now, stick a fork in him. That's where I got the walk off the court after busting your ass, from Lando. He used to hit that shot from the corner by Santo's gate for the game and walk off the court on us.

He'd then say, "y'all ain't even worth playing" and then walk into the crib. He could dribble, but didn't have handles, but he could shoot that ball.

I always talked shit back to Lando. When I was a shortie Lando was in his yard. I was living on 169th St. then, he was drinking some kool aid. I was in my yard talking shit to him.

Lando finished the kool aid then launch the peanut butter jar. It was at least eighty yards from his house to mine. It landed about six feet from me and busted all over the ground.

He started laughing and said, "you lucky I missed."

Harold, Lando was getting money on the block. This was Stag's little brother. He had his nephew Rollow selling for him. Anytime the police got on them they ran in the house. Once in the house they were good.

It was a time Lando said the police was chasing him and he ran in jumped in the bed with his mother and father. They bust in behind him going room-to-room looking for him. They made it to Mr. Mrs. Houses's room.

Once in there Mrs. House went off, because they were in their pajamas. After snapping so hard. They left not knowing he was in between them under the covers. The other reason they left was, because Mr. House was a thirty-year vet on the force.

They were twisters chased Lando in the house all the time. Back then the poe poes couldn't just chase you into your house, unless they saw a crime. Lando was hot and he'd slide in the house every time he saw them coming for him.

Mr. House would see what was happening and come to the door with that gold shield. He was a retired police officer now. The officers would see the gold shield and you didn't hear another word. They just got in their car and rolled out.

Bryant Keith

Lando was talking shit to me and he sells dope. He's calling me a jailbird. It hurt though, we prided ourselves on the Met for not getting caught. When they used to sell dope on the block. The law boys would roll up and never find the spots. The guys who get caught and go to jail, don't plan it out. Every time I got caught I didn't plan it out.

Once they caught me doing a certain crime. I wasn't going to get caught doing that particular crime anymore. Ohh I was glad to be getting out though! I came home took a shower first. I just thought while the water rolled down my back.

I sat on the bed and said to myself. "I do not like being locked up. I do not like being locked up." This kept going through my mind. Some people like when they go to jail like it's a stripe for being hard.

Jail is not for me. The plan was not for "kid make it", to make it to jail. I learned my lesson. You can't ride with thieves, if you're not a thief anymore. At anytime, thieves will steal at any opportunity.

My court day came. I made sure I had it marked on the calendar. I was going to beat this case. I didn't steal that car and I'm not telling on my hommies. Once at court I was hoping the vic didn't come.

He got his car back and nothing was wrong with it except the steering and the window. To my dismay dude came to court. My fucking bad luck is continuing. Usually on shit like that the vic wouldn't come to court.

Especially, if he seen it was goons trying to steal his car. He got his car back anyway. I had about three of my guys sitting with me. You come with five of your friends and they would look at the victim real good.

You have to spook them. Once the case is called. Three of them leave once the case is called. They'll get a good look at the vic and leave. The three guys would wait outside the court for the vic. Once the vic walked outside. They'd follow them for about a half a block and stop. Most of the time on little shit like that! They would get spooked and wouldn't return to court. It wasn't like a murder or an assault and battery.

Most times the vic will say to themselves, "it ain't worth taking the chance."

They see you're plugged into the nation and it's not worth it. They figured these niggas might pay my family or me a visit. My vic came to court, but dude was deaf and dumb. I am standing in front of the judge and he can't talk or hear.

They needed somebody to read sign language. This case was going to cost too much and take too much time. I kept wondering though, if dude was deaf and dumb. Why did he have a fresh ass Alpine system in his car?

I was sticking to my story I don't why the driver ran. I didn't have anything to run for so I didn't. I could've been just clueless to what was going on! I had no warrants. I don't know who were the guys in the stolen car. It was two cars on the scene with me and the other guy.

We were pulled over drinking on a beer in the Charger. Dude saw you coming and broke. Who was in the stolen car? I thought dude was working on his car. I don't know. My story is solid once time is under my belt. I made sure there were no loopholes.

I lived down the street and was getting a free high. We were down the street so my mother wouldn't see me. You see I just got out with no resistance. I didn't know what was going on! They continued the case for another date, because I didn't plea out.

They continued the case so they could get an interpreter. My next court date, same thing no interpreter. They dismissed the case. You see what I'm saying, if I didn't come to court. They would've slammed me for the same thing. I had a public defender too. I was really my own lawyer, because I was sticking to my story.

They didn't see me in the car. I didn't steal the car. My fingerprints weren't in or on the car. I didn't run. I was just drinking beer. I didn't know the guys in the other car. I lived down the street. I wouldn't be stripping a car down the street from my house.

It was no jury that would convict me on that. Oh Grimes squirted out once dude came on the porch. He got out that hot bitch. Six minutes later they had the car, but Grimes was gone. As long as Grimes got away I was straight. I am not guilty.

Everything I said was true except about me knowing the driver of the steamer. If they'd caught Grimes then they would've found out we went to the same school a few years earlier. I still would've said, I still didn't know him. I never said I never saw him before. It's not my business. Another thing these guys out here will kill a nigga for running his mouth.

I said to myself as I am leaving out the court. "I ain't stealing any more cars. No, I ain't riding with any more thieves. No more look out or anything. I just can't ride with my guys, because they could get loose from one minute to the next. I can't mess my record up just along for the ride."

Oh believe me I would've got paid off those tires, but it just wasn't worth the risk. I have to be smart, if 'kid make it', going to make it. I committed a lot of felony crimes and still don't have any on my record.

Out in Limbo

*I*n regular life I had a dilemma. I didn't register for college since I graduated out of summer school. I didn't want to go anyway I wasn't prepared. After I got out I was going straight way with my hustle game.

I still had my weed game, but I need a career. My mother was giving me money in the morning to look for a job. I wanted to get a job, but nobody in the city was hiring me.

I filled out applications everywhere all across town. I put in an application here, a application there, a application everywhere. I filled them out for the city, banks, industrial, restaurants and a sky chef, on a plane. I even filled out an application for a high beam sky walker for those skyscrapers. Now I am scared of height to the fullest. I said, "fuck it I'll walk the high beam I need a job." I couldn't get a job that even risks your life.

Nobody would even call me for an interview. No I can't say that, I had a few interviews, but once they saw me. I didn't hear from them again. My mother always told me. Your appearance will keep a lot of doors close to you.

I was too stubborn to cut my hair. Everything else was okay, but I would not cut my hair. You couldn't see my gang tattoos and I took my earring out. The fingerwaves had me stereotyped in the category of a thug and rightfully so!

I decided to go to this school call Entech. This school helps you develop office skills. Don't get me wrong this was a very good school. It was like a four-month course in the clerical field.

Upon completion it would polish you up for interviews. They taught me how to master my resumes, type on the computer. They also taught us how to fill out applications and a lot more things. I figured I would do this, to keep my Mom off my back. At least for a little while and get some communication skills.

I met a cool dude name Jeff at the school. He had just ETS out the army. He was doing the same thing. He was getting him some communicational skills. We also got paid some money for going. Some type of way we got money. Jeff was about twenty-one at the time.

I always could hold my own with people older than I. I had to adjust to the class. Everybody in the class was way older than me now. It was some students forty years old in the class. I had to figure out a way to gel.

A lot of times being good at sports transcend your youth. We didn't play sports at this school. People will fuck with you, because you are sweet at sports no matter how old you were. Knowing how to fight also helped tremendously. I was exposed to lot more things at a younger age than most people my age.

Well anyway, Jeff and I hit it off well. We were in class cracking jokes with each other, not about each other. Our jokes just touch the surface. We were the youngest males in the class. He had a car and I didn't. I was catching the bus downtown to the school. It was located a block or two down from Columbia.

Columbia is the school I was thinking about going attending. This is before I found out I wasn't walking that June. The school was located in the 200 or 300 South block on Michigan Ave. I caught the bus back and forth for about couple of weeks.

One day Jeff and I got to kicking it after school. After getting to know me Jeff offered me a ride home. He said he was going the same way and was practically riding by my house. Of course I take him up on his offer.

On the way home I offered to buy some dranks since he was taking me home. He was twenty-one so I didn't worry about looking for somebody to cop. We stop at the store and he grabs the beers.

We got to the Met and started chilling over a couple of beers in front of the sub joint. I see Spider G. You know Spider G is 6'5" tall with finger waves and looks like the Grim Reaper with his shotgun coat. Spider G rarely smiled only when he seen his Folks.

Spider sees me and started to stack them and I stack back. We give each other love and I jump back in the car with Jeff.

Jeff looked and said, "that's one of your guys", when I got in the car.

I said, "yeah."

He looked as Spider walked away and said, "I'm glad you know him. He looks like you should cross the street when you see him."

He was right too Spider is no joke. He began telling me over the beers he just got back from Maryland. He had just completed two years in the army. He talked about all the fun he had. He spoke about the girls he ran into while in Maryland. He said he was the man on base.

I put him up on what's happening in Chicago while he was gone. Who was holding what down and what neighborhood he was living around. The reason why I liked Jeff was because he had been to different places. He had some other adventures that kept me captivated.

Now that I think about it, it was something different. He was stationed In Maryland and was pretty popular. You could tell he was trying to be on top of things in class. He was confident and he had a man's disposition about himself. He had other things to talk about other than gang stories. What's the latest on somebody humiliation in the hood, is what we talk about.

He had some content to himself. Meaning he had been somewhere and had something else to talk about. He was experienced with life at twenty-one. You must remember I hung around a lot of twenty-one years old guys too. We hung out for a couple of months.

He finally gets around to asking me. "How old are you Colo?"

You know I never tell people my age unless you ask. I answered, "seventeen." I never lied about my age either.

He looked in amazement and said, "your just seventeen? I thought you were at least twenty. You and my brother are the same age. I can't kick it with my brother like I can with you."

"I look that old? I asked.

Jeff answered, "no it your conversation and how you chill."

Somehow we lost contact a little while after we finished the course. It's funny how people can spend a few minutes with a person and make a life's impression. He doesn't know to this day how influential he was to me at that time.

Even after all that training at the school. I still didn't get a job. We graduated from the course and that was it. I had the knowledge though! Again I was getting up everyday to look and couldn't find a job anywhere.

My Mom is ready to move out 107th & Racine to my stepfather's house. This was cool since I never did like living at 16959 Calumet. It was a step down from where we used to live at 356 E

169th St. Mom made it comfortable, but we were starting over from scratch. It was better than the streets. I did so much dirt on 169th. St. I said it would be good, if people didn't know where I lived.

My Mom put so much love in that house on 169th St. It was a change of pace to move to the hundreds. We were moving over there by the Racine Courts. I needed a new atmosphere to build up resistance from my criminal activity. I get to meet new people and new girls. A new adventure is always good.

We move that summer and we slowly move everything out the house. Now Emus lived out there in the hundreds too on a 103rd & Wallace.

Emus mother got married to her new husband Lemmy. Lemmy and her used to work together at CTA. I know y'all know this! Lemmy was cool he just talked all the time and never stop.

He always would stop us and give us the good word. Mrs. King aced her new house out. Everything in there was brand new. Glass, brass and wood floors the place felt like you were in a hotel. By this time Emus told her about me graduating. I'd gotten back in their good graces.

They probably had discussion about me that went this way. The boy can't be that bad. He graduated a year early.

I was a good example for Emus in that way. I wouldn't fuck that up ever again. I spent many nights out in the hundreds at Emus house.

Slick Coole

We would come in late and his parents would leave early for work. Emus's brother Slick Coole was so cool. He'd get up and make you breakfast in the morning.

Coole would ask me, "you want something to eat Columbus?"

After getting bubble and high the night before this is right on time.

I answered, "hell yeah Coole."

Coole would hook up some shit that looked like a gourmet restaurant did it. That was Coole calling he should've been a chef. He loved to cook for you. He'd have your plate looking all pretty with the eggs and sausages. Sometimes he would fix us omelets with tomatoes and parsley on top. You see people didn't know that side to Coole.

Coole was very hospitable when at his house or just in his presence. Coole had just got hit by a car the week before, I was with him. We just left the Pantries on Prairie and we were about to drink some forties. Coole was next to me and I made it across the street.

Slick Coole didn't make it and got hit by a car. I hear the impact of the car, but didn't see the accident. Next thing I know Coole was coming down out the air, boommph. The fortie in his hand busted and hit the ground, first. Mike got up and was wondering where his fortie went deliriously. I looked and said, "damn Coole you fucked up."

Mike just kept saying, "where's my fortie where's my fortie?"

I told him, "it's busted, Coole are you all right." The driver that hit him took off. He was laid up, but still got up and fixed me breakfast.

After a good breakfast Coole would bust the drink open. They had a VCR so we'd watched the "God Father" while getting bubbled. They kept a small bar in the corner. It was half of gallons of liquor sitting on the floor, unopened.

Coole would open the bottle and we would drink half the bottle.

I used to be like, "Coole you know the G is going to snap. How you going to replace it?"

Coole would respond in his squeaky voice. "Don't worry about it Columbus, just drink up. I'll worry about that shit"

Coole would fill the bottle back up with water and lick the seal back closed.

You couldn't see that it was opened already from a distance. When he hit a stain he would replace the liquor. He always tried to replace it, before they found out. Now since I moved Emus and Coole don't stay that far from me. I chilled over there a lot when I was living in the hundreds.

Coole was like, "Columbus I'll be back on the court in a couple of minutes this ain't shit."

Coole was good at playing basketball. He didn't have a cold dribble game, but he didn't get ripped. He could shoot that ball though. He had this funny sidewinder shot that spent out his hand when he released it.

Coole had a payday from the accident. We got the license plates from the car and he had a court date. Mike never went to court. It seemed strange to me that he wouldn't go to court. I began to think the accident was not an accident. I believe somebody hit him on purpose.

I couldn't see how he got hit, because I was right in front of him when it happened. The cars wasn't coming that fast. This was probably retribution from one of his stains. Slick Coole did a lot of dirt on 169th. As far as busting stains I was in kindergarten and Coole was a college professor.

Emus gets a little upset and says, "Okay y'all get off my brother he wasn't that bad."

I say, "you right Emus, but he was nice. While were talking about getting hit Emus had gotten hit by a CTA bus head on while crossing the street. I thought he was hamburger meat. I was watching from my porch on 169th and gasped. It was winter-time and he slid on the ice, up under the bus.

Emus replies, "hell yeah and I got right back up from under that bitch and took off."

He had plenty of money coming and he ran. He wasn't hurt, but it scared the shit out of him.

I then asked Emus, "did Coole dropped you out the second floor window like Todd said he did?"

Emus answers reluctantly, "he he..dropped me, but he wasn't trying to he was just trying to scare me and he lost his grip."

Emus still take up for his brother.

The wild Hundreds

When I moved to the wild hundreds I met this guy name Reg he was cool. I liked his sister, but didn't know how to come at her. The next-door neighbor Eddie was gay and sold weed. He was the only gay guy I met that I spoke to and that's, because he had the weed. I stayed on the 169th a couple of extra weeks by myself, until we got everything out the house.

Before we could move everything out. I get into it with my mother's husband about some money. No it wasn't about any money. It was about a job I did for him. I was supposed to wash his car. He had a Fleetwood Cadillac gray. I washed the car for him every Sunday and he'd give me fifteen dollars to wash it.

He was just trying to keep a few dollars in my pocket I must say. The last time I washed it. I just ran some water on it and smeared the dirt. He always paid me to do the job before I did it. After running the water over it, I just left with the chips.

When they came back I saw the job I did after it had dried. I had smear marks all over it. I said to myself, "damn that is a terrible job." I was even embarrassed that they went to church with a dirty smeared up car. A car they paid me to clean.

I know my Mom was embarrassed about my work. He was probably pissed, because he paid me first. I did a bad job and felt bad about it. I didn't want to face the music or do the car either. This time I break out and leave for a week. Mom catches up with me and tells me. She needs me to stay at the house while they were at the new house. She wanted me to stay, until we got everything out.

I was like cool and decided to throw a party before I moved off 169th. I thought I could make some extra money throwing a going away party. I had little Rich and Lil Rob DJ the party. It mostly turned out to be a Folks get together. The women who did come didn't stay long, because it was just too many Folks.

It turned into a get high party with music. Lil Rich and Rob did a good job. They did it for free. They had the new tables in the neighborhood. They had all the rap jams going all night. We all cooled out though together as one. I sold weed to the people who came to the party so I made a little money.

Nobody started fighting. BD's and GD's chilled all night. After the party was over early that morning. My brother Walls, Scott German and I just got high the rest of the night and fell out asleep.

Do you know my mother was at the house at seven o'clock the next morning? I see her pull up. I shoot Scott out the back and my mother was coming through the front. She already knew about the party to my amazement. Someone is still wiring her up on what I do, ain't that a bitch. You already know she was giving it to me. I didn't want to hear too much.

I spat back at her, "Mom I was just throwing a going away party." I started walking out the house, because I didn't want to hear it.

She tells Walls to get in the car. Walls get in the car and she calls me over gesturing, come closer. I get closer and she swings, swooosh. I duck and she almost topples over to the ground. She caught herself with her hands before falling. I just looked at her making sure she was all right.

I then asked her, "you are alright Mom", still keeping my distance as she got up. I would've helped her up, but I was scared she'd start man handling me. The look on her face was that she couldn't believe she missed me. I kind of giggled to myself when I turned and walked away, that was to myself, you heard.

I caught up with Scott and we got high some more. I couldn't believe she was so mad. I never had a party before in my life. I wanted a party for once in my life, a going away party. At this time in my life! My Mom and I were getting more and more distant from each other.

I'm out of high school and I've graduated from Entech. They were accomplishments, but I still can't find a job though! My Mom is putting some pressure on me to do something. She knew I was selling weed and just wasn't having it. I wasn't going to the army. I hated the army ever since I was a kid. I heard all of those Vietnam stories from the vets from the war. Who would take ROTC in school instead of physical education anyway? I used to damn near laugh when I saw a classmate in the ROTC uniform.

I never would've joined an organization like that in my life. I like freedom on the streets. I liked being with my Folks. I like the struggle of just holding down my neighborhood. I like the respect that I had obtained on the street.

I was seventeen and my name was circulating. I hate to say it, but you're main objective is being known. My outlook on life was tunnel like. All I could see was what was around me. Now I've been taught well on not being a follower.

It's getting rough day after day. The same atmosphere and the same surroundings will crumble a monk. The monk vowed to silence, but after a while 169th St. He'll have to say something about the fuck shit that's going on!

Super Bowl Shuffle

*E*nter the transition from smack to cocaine. You know coming up you just didn't see the smack man. It wasn't, until years later that I found who were the smack dealers. The smack dealers sat in a car at the end of the block chilling. We didn't know what they were doing, because they were so low-key. Mrs. Hugh's son Leggs had this tight ass Caddy that sat in the alley all the time. He was selling dog food, O boy. I walk by that car everyday and never knew what he did.

I never knew he was the smack man, until I got older. The smack dealers were telling us to go to school. Now I see why Mrs. Hughs had that store running for years. Everything in the store was the best. The ice cream and those golden chicken wings.

I'd wonder why sometimes they'd tell us to get from around the area? The smack dealers hid everything from us on the block. It wasn't until later when people just didn't give a fuck about the kids.

As members of the organization we weren't suppose to sell that shit to our people. Once the girl show up all bets were off. The Movie Scarface was Hollowood and the government, marketing tool. Scarface played at the movies for five straight years. There was a theater somewhere playing Scarface for five straight years. The movie came out when I was thirteen and I couldn't see it.

I could've waited four years to see it on my seventeenth birthday. It was still somewhere playing at the movies. This movie is entrenched into our psyche. It had me fooled and I am a smart guy.

My mothers wouldn't let me see it, but of course I got around that! Anything rated R she wasn't having it. All I had to do was wait, until my seventeenth birthday. Now they've just schooled another generation on dope smuggling. Video stores were just coming out in our neighborhood around 1985.

This was the perfect movie to learn how to fuck over friends, business partners and family, because of self-absorption and greed. The line that gets you is when he's in the oval tub and he's mumbling to himself.

Scarface says, "I don't need nobody and fuck em all."

This is a very powerful scene. This is the scene that got me. This was the perfect movie for people who were brainwashed into being "the man" quote unquote. Cocaine hit the street heavily in 1983.

SteveO was the first on the block to explore setting it up like a business corporation. First SteveO worked for United Parcel and went to school at DeVry. After learning marketing and business structure from DeVry. He set the Met up as the Mecca center for distribution of cocaine.

He was banging that girl, but what made him explode. It was 1985 the Bears were on there way to the Super Bowl. The Super Bowl Shuffle was out in week ten of the season. The Bears hadn't even won the Super Bowl and it was out.

Jim McMahon and Walter Payton finally won a super bowl that year. The only thing that hurt me is Walter Payton didn't get a touch down in the Super Bowl. The touch down William the Refrigerator Perry scored on should've been his. Hold on I am getting sidetracked cause that was a shame.

Anyway, SteveO had this innovation to market cocaine during that time. It went like wild fire SteveO's cocaine Super Bowl special. This was the beginning of the end of the love on the Met. For now on it would be a slow degradation to money over love.

At first Folks followed that concept. Folks weren't supposed to sell drugs to our community. That's how the players took over the game. SteveO, Jason, Lando and Phil were some of the players on 169th.

Once that cocaine hit the street all bets were off. I saw black Shaun who went to Rock Manor and played on the Cardinals with me. You remember Shaun, Emus. I think he graduated with you.

Emus say, "yeah I know who you talking about. He was banging in grammar school".

I say, "this was the first time I heard that Folks were about to enter the dope business. Shaun was off 75Th and was hard-core GD Folks. He kept his shit banged hard to the right no matter what. We greet and show love and he told me he was looking for SteveO.

I looked at him and said, "SteveO."

He looks back with that look and said, "yeah I heard he got that weight."

I looked at him again and asked him. I know he knows we're not supposed to indulge. I ask him, "you about to get in the game Shaun?"

He answered, "hell yeah, it too much money in this white powder Folks."

Now this was one of the building blocks for the organization. Don't sell dope to your own people. To be honest it was a double edge sword. It's either get in to drug game make money and flourish. Don't get in the dope game and continue to starve in the struggle.

The organization would've been extinct in about ten years. Mass money rules in a Capitalistic system. Individualism is what is conceived out of this system. On the Met the love faded.

Before cocaine hit our neighborhood. It was so much love, because we didn't have money. Everybody was about in the same financial group. It wasn't that much division as far as the gap, between individuals, financially. Everybody's mother or father worked for a living. They weren't too many CEO owning any company on the Met.

Most parents worked for a check. Some were on financial aid, but it wasn't that much difference. Most families had between six to ten children so it equaled out. Once you feed and clothes, that many kids, you still are poor. That's working or not working for a living.

Our parent's dream for us was to go to school and make something of ourself. What we shot for as youngsters was futile in one-way or another. The Calumet athletes wanted to get famous playing sports was our dream. Nobody made it.

Our family wasn't the only ones eating mayonnaise, ketchup, sugar, government cheese and butter sandwiches. I saw a lot of families waiting in line for that government food. The Evening Star Church was a distribution center for it. I saw everybody getting some at the church. It was only three doors down from me.

It was tight and most people got clothes once or twice a year. That was during school time and Christmas time. Other than that there wasn't that much styling day to day. When you had a function to go to you'd shine, but no, it wasn't that much division.

The cocaine money brought division and individualism into our world. It happened so fast. I saw from what it seems to me one day to the next, niggas with money. The money bought artillery to protect the drugs. Now with the money and the power you can buy goons. Where you get the goons from, in the hood!

We never considered weed drugs. I considered drugs, drugs. Cocaine, heroine LSD and angle dust, shit like that! I smoke weed everyday and seem like it helped me through the struggle. I was selling something that I took daily. Ethically I was in the clear. My first recollection of drugs being used I saw when I was shortie, shortie.

I was selling subscriptions for the newspaper, for Gino. I worked for him about a couple a weeks. I quit cause I just didn't like doing that soliciting shit. This was a dry sell knocking on people doors. You never know what's going on in the house. I would knock on the door to give them my presentation.

Someone would come to the door and I give them my spiel. I am selling subscriptions bla blaa blaa. I'd look in the kitchen and see that the people are burning something in a spoon.

They would free base right in front of me. I didn't know what it was at the time. It was just creepy inside. It was dark in the house and everybody looked like ghost. I shelved that job.

The powder was another thing. It had us brainwashed through film. Mostly white people sniff powder at first. It was supposed to be the rich mans high. When it became accessible to street hustler it changed the game.

This was the ultimate shortcut. What am I trying to do in life? Make money! Am I going to be an athlete? When the answer to the question is no, the short cut provided was taken.

Here is another opportunity to make more than your parents in one month. It takes them all year to make that money. What do you think a teenager goal going to be? Why go to school, if I can get all this money right now? Why do any of those things that my momma is talking about, school etc...?

The young dope dealer's perception is to get money now. How do I know that I'm even going to grow up? I get this money now and can enjoy myself, fuck school. Mom is out of touch she doesn't know what's going on!

It's a quicker way to get rich. It's a catch to it though! You might shortcut your freedom. You will shortcut your community. You will shortcut your education. Most of all you can shortcut your life.

You start to see street niggas with brand new cars. People in our neighborhood didn't have brand new cars. The girls they loved that cocaine. Anyone who sold it was the man. I saw a lot of girls go south quickly over that girl.

You were a hood superstar, if you were getting money and had that girl for girls to toot. Big had it easy. His brother used to hook him up. Big had a painted up Pontiac Lamans two toned brown and beige coming out of grammar school. I watched his father do the bodywork on it and then paint it.

Big and Lace was blessed by their older brothers into the game. They looked like hood stars. They got on dookie rope gold chains on and chilling filming themselves with a camcorder. It was some girls walking by that thought they were rap stars. We didn't have shit like that! This wasn't any regular shit that goes on in the hood. We take still pictures.

After they drop the guns and dope in the community. We started shooting at each other like it was duck season in the hood. We were shooting at each other over money and you better duck. We used to share with each other. Now we got to have all the money.

In order to operate, it can't be any love in the dope game. It can't be any loyalty, because this game is money driven. It's not a movement anymore. That was the first brick that crumbled the building block of the six-point star.

Replace those L's with Money and Power. The first L got to go when it's money driven. It's money over love now. Get what you can get and fuck everybody else. 2nd brick was the loyalty, can't be no loyalty when your loyalty is to money. Money is the root to most evil. Replace that 2nd L with the P for Power. The only reason I don't replace the last L is because this is life that we all are living.

We didn't know it at the time and it blind sited us, and the whole organization. This was a brand new destruction for our community. This stems from the Iran Contra Scandal. The government, CIA was giving the Contras guns for dope. Ollie North and Ronal Reagan use the plausible deniability defense.

Where do you think that dope went? The dope went right here on our cities street corners. It's all a plan to return us to the Willie Lynch style of thinking again, but money driven. Teenagers were selling to the older folks. We didn't respect you, if you were freebasing!

Before cocaine hit we'd shoot at people, but it was rare. A lot of people honored the man dance. Now with all this money being generated you must protect it. We are a direct product of that experiment to enslave us mentally. First the dope and guns flood the neighborhood. We had revolver back in the day. We used shotguns and rifles. Who dropped those assault rifles in our community?

My assumption is the same people who were trading guns for dope. This plan will suck the life out the community. No more respect for the generation before us or after us. This didn't happen in just Chicago. This happen in every major urban city with a concentration of black folks.

The young dope dealers are feeding it to the generation before us. This tore down the infulstructure of the community. The older folks on and off dope, now don't get any respect. Once a lot of killings take place in the community. It's time for the police to come in and clean up the scourge.

The next move is to lock up the survivors. The ones on dope and the ones selling dope. Take all the money, cars and jewelry that they've accumulated.

Once their locked up they can't make babies. The ones they made will be fucked continuing the cycle. What do you have a strong nigga out the way? You have to be strong to look-over all this and still make money on their weakness. Willie Lynch all over again! After cocaine hit, killing became the norm. I look back at that time as the Shaun Jackson moment.

After a few months every hustler on the Met was selling cocaine. I was cool with my weed so I didn't fuck with it at first. SteveO was a mastermind. He had three shifts and never closed down.

Once he had the Met set up. He expanded all throughout the community. SteveO crews, had crews, but it hit the Met first, hard.

The players on 171st were selling smack. Some of them were nodding on it too. SteveO blew 169th out with the cocaine. It was the Mecca center for distribution. Emus this was the embryo of a lot of people getting killed or locked up.

We didn't know at the time, it was a glorious time for the Met in the beginning. Everything came to the Met, money and the merch. My weed sells went up. Everybody was getting money.

When Scarface came out. Al Pachino portrayed a picture of the ultimate individual. He killed the ones he loved directly or indirectly. After that movie came out cocaine hit our neighborhood like a tornado. Now they reintroduce it to you every five years. This is to make sure that next generation is tainted.

The movie New Jack City was the black mans concept of Scarface. Everybody including myself wanted to be the character Westly Snipes played, Nino Brown. They do give you a clue to the movie though! Both main characters friends and family ended up dead. The moral to the main part was overlooked. Scarface and Nino died young along with their friends and family.

There is a reason why people don't even think about that part. You figure it's not going to happen to you. You are willing to take the risk. I figured this out, 90 percent who indulge and stay in the drug trade ends up on dope, locked up or dead.

You maybe have a four or five-year run in the game, if you are smart, then you are going down. The other 10 percent will have demons to chase or the demons are chasing them. You have to do a lot of dirt to be prominent in the cocaine game. There will be plenty of killings and lives destroyed, if you are the quote unquote man.

Now the cocaine has added another negative element to hood. In many movies they show what you need and how to cook cocaine. We weren't no chemist in the neighborhood they marketed crack before it hit our hood. Respectable people turned into to hypes and feigns. Hypes are people who are up late at night to early morning, walking the streets looking for a come up. Their goal in life is trying to score some good dope.

Along with that on the Met you have: auto boys cliques, home break in artist, pickpockets, scam artist, stick up people and straight killers. Some of these people fit in all categories. I am out here everyday and these are my guys.

The people I knew, I know they didn't start out like that. Dope was heroine that shit that have you nodding. Cocaine is for players who got those chips. People were rationalizing that girl.

Folks were supposed to obtain jobs and seek education. We had to understand politics and economics. This is what controlled our neighborhood and the world. Before cocaine the people whom didn't have jobs had to do something to eat.

We had limited knowledge on how to make money the legal way. This is what spurred a lot of teenagers in this direction for the quick cash!

We were doing stains, but it wasn't condoned. You always say I won't do it again, until you see it was so easy. Once you do it the first time its much easier the second time. When you fall off and you ain't got no chips. I know how to get on again. There will be stains that you peeped out, but don't hit. Saving them for when you are low.

Now everybody is rolling cocaine. We started feeding dope to our women for pleasure. The girls loved that cocaine and it took them straight down the gutter. These are the mothers of our future kids, sprung on cocaine.

Before cocaine! You could be anyone of these types of criminals and on the Met you were accepted. When you're born in crime and around crime, crime became the normal. Law abiding becomes weird and out of place, in our land. While on the land, you had to respect the land or you got your head cracked.

You would get a warning, but you had to take heed immediately or it was on! The only thing you didn't get respect for was being a hype. You could toot, but once you became a hype people looked at you totally differently. You're not a hustler anymore, you are a hype. The dope controls you now and you are not to be trusted. You will lose your identity.

Ever since I was sixteen. It was quite normal for us teenagers to take a sniff of cocaine. Lace some on your weed, that's what we called a 3750. You could toot as long as you didn't freebase cocaine and you held your hustle down. It wasn't nothing for us to toot cocaine like in Scarface. He showed us how cool it was to do it.

Our knowledge of the drug was limited. Once you do something the first time. The next time it is much easier and then it becomes habit forming. Lace would set out a pack every once in a while. The niggas couldn't hit stains anymore. We weren't stealing from the community now. They'll give it to you now for the low lows. It was a cakewalk with that girl.

Now the people are bringing everything they own, to the dope man. You don't have to steal anymore they're bringing it to your doorsteps. You can get it all for a little of nothing. I was seventeen years old and thought I knew everything about the streets.

Before cocaine hit the set, niggas busted stains to get money. You got to feed the underground somehow they have to eat. Tell me this what are you to do after high school? When you couldn't find a job. A lot of teenagers had kids already. They had to eat. This is a blessing in disguise that I didn't have a girl friend.

Once you got a girl friend then the baby comes shortly afterward. You didn't have enough money for your self. Now you got a family and this is where a lot of bad decisions came about. My family got to eat what was I going to do for money?

I've been selling weed for about four years. Now I was known for weed. I kept a few dollars, because of my clientele. Most of my guys didn't have a weed hustle. What were you going to do for money? Most of us, didn't sell smack so before cocaine. To get money you had to steal or you don't have any money.

Momma can't peel you off what you need. You need more, because you want more. At this age most people money went toward getting high. The only teenager that had a job constantly, if he wanted was Todd.

It was a couple of stains people hit that I couldn't bring myself to doing. It was some moral type shit going on with me. This was before I stopped stealing. Remember when they hit Zells Cleaners, twice? They took all those clothes and all of Mr. Zell shit. I couldn't go do that stain. When I was a kid Mr. Zells used to give me money for my birthday. I used to deliver the paper to Mr. Zells and he would tip me.

At Christmas time I had extras from Mr. Zells. He got the Sun times, but I would leave him a Defender too. When they hit him it was like they were hitting my uncle. He couldn't sustain the losses he was taking. That is one person I wished I could've warned. This is another black man out of business. That shit wasn't right.

They hit the Currency Exchange Coole and Spider went through the roof. They got some bank. I couldn't do that one either. I knew the lady who worked there for years. This was federal too. This ain't nobody house, this is federal currency, it will be an investigation.

I was scandalous, but never pegged in any of those categories of criminality. I was just a person who couldn't find a job and does criminal things. I'd do a couple of stains in each category and leave it alone and go to something else. My main thang was to keep my weed game in effect.

I wasn't no big time weed dealer. I was doing joints and bags. In my mind though things are not shaping up for, 'kid make it'. Kid make is looking lost. I am not a ball player. I didn't go to college. I don't have a job. I'm not going to the pros. I don't steal anymore. What am I going to do to get over the hump?

CHAPTER SEVEN

Pushed to the Limit

*H*ere I am living out here with my stepfather and Mom. I'm living in his house and have to abide by his rules. I had been living on 107th & Racine for about two months. I tried kicking it with the Folks in the hundreds. Of course I end up getting into it with them. I was an outsider just like, if they moved in on the Met. I am an alpha type guy and there's only room for one alpha.

This dude name Lemmo was the one calling it over there in that area. Reg hook me up with them, he said they were cool. I'm trying to plug since I am out here. Instead of me riding back and forward to the 169th St. to kick it.

I never and I mean never stayed in the house. When I was living in the hundreds. I came in when it was time to go to bed, but I had to give 169th a break too. When you don't come around all the time. People will miss you a little bit. I tried to stay gone a couple of weeks at a time. While I do that! I'll hang with these niggas in the wild wild hundreds.

These Folks were cool at first, but they switched it up. I used to go over to where they hung, get high and watch wrestling. That's what they like to do watch wrestling. I used to love wrestling and watching it with my mother. My mother put me in my first submission hole. Yep, until the day, I found out it was fake.

The winner was already predetermined before the match started. I'd watch it with them, but had no interest in watching wrestling anymore. We'd order a pizza and cool out and get bubbled. It was a spot to go and get out my stepfather's house and hang. It was this dude name Larry and his girl house.

One night something came up missing or something. I hadn't even been over there long. They didn't even know I was a thief. I never would steal from niggas I knew, point blank, anyway. I knew the deal though they were coming at me. I know the game let's see how this nigga cut. One of his boys grabbed me and was trying to throw me around.

I stood my ground and didn't give. I didn't drop any blows, but grabbed him back. He thought he was going to beast me, little nigga style. He felt the resistance and a certain calm about myself.

What's going through my mind at the very exact moment? My mother stays over here so I didn't let any blows go.

Once I get loose on this nigga and do him bad. It's going to get deep out here in the hundreds for me. I don't want anybody blasting in the crib and hit my mother. I got to live over here, but I ain't no hoe. I'm new over here and they don't give a fuck about my family or me.

Dude is trying to sling me and I am slinging him. I was figuring they're going to try and move on me any second. We let each other go and I just looked at him while he was breathing hard.

Dude who grabbed me, pumped his chest out like he did something. He didn't throw any blows. I guess he was doing the wrestling shit on me. I couldn't have held back, if he had thrown just, one blow.

I said to myself while they're getting hype. "I better leave and go home before they get the courage up to move."

As I was leaving Lemmo said, "yeah you better get the fuck out of here."

I just watched my back and didn't say anything. I could've fucked dude up. He just didn't know it. It's funny how you have to restrain yourself, because of the fact of wisdom.

It wouldn't have been over, after I fucked him up. You know how you visualize the act of punching dude in the face. Usually, when I do that, it's like a hairpin trigger. Shortly after visualization I usually blaze. I had to use my 360 degrees.

In order to be a beast out here I got to come hard. Somebody will have to die and I am going to jail. Once I do what I am going to do to this stud.

I then say to myself, "you know what I'm going to do, I'ma fade. I stayed too long anyway. I should've bounced a long time ago." They figured they knew me, but they didn't. I don't have to kick it with these niggas so I faded.

I had to bite it for the family and put my pride to aside. I could've called the Folks from the 169th. They were GDs out in the hundreds. I could've gone to the nine and got a mob of GDs and BDs and did some ugly shit.

My Mom had to live here though! Dude didn't really do shit to me. My pride wasn't really even shaken. I did feel funny for them trying me, but I was straight. For my mother safety I chilled.

I was new and didn't want to kick up dust for her. I had my banger and I could have come back blasting. It wasn't worth it as long as they didn't move. I'll play the mark role just until they try me again. The next time I'll kill them, but I got to get away. I don't warn them or nothing! I just waited for the next encounter.

Sometime when you have power to create damage you can't. You have to use will power and not use it. Especially, when it won't have a positive outcome. You have to be able to win or at least make a stand.

I could've brought pain, but to harm one hair on my mother's head would've devastated me. Now I got to kill up everything, so if that's all I get, is a sling around, I'll take it. I sucked up my pride, but I ain't no fool. I stayed ready for action.

I had to get a car though! I can't get caught slipping on the bus stop or going to the store. I can't get caught slipping when I know its static. Fat Cat stepfather was selling a 77 Cadillac. I was eighteen now and getting me an aid check. I had hustled some money up to buy a car.

My Mom was like she needs that money for the house. I said, "Mom I need a car. I can't be standing on these bus stops. I mess around and get killed out here. This ain't my neighborhood. It's my neighborhood now, but we didn't grow up around here".

Mother does not know that a car is critical, for life preservation on these streets. I am a street nigga. I can't be on these corners waiting on shit. She kept putting pressure on me to give up that money.

I had to choose survival so I chose to get the car. My response to her demand, "I didn't get a car for graduations and I graduated. I bought everything I had on for prom and graduation from my hustle game. I had to rent a car from my pops for graduation. Y'all just ain't got nothing for me. I got to get it on my own."

My adopted father left me his social security benefits. I knew I was supposed to be getting money every month. Everybody else's whom pops died, couldn't wait on the beginning of the month. They didn't have to steal, because they just waited on their check. My check was going to the two colt way buildings. My pops owned and left to my mother on 61ˢᵗ and King Drive.

She also used it for the attempted reconstruction of 356 E. 169ᵗʰ St. My mother wanted to rebuild our house on 169ᵗʰ St. Other than bus fare to school and some for clothes and shoes during school time. I wouldn't see that money on a monthly basis.

Now I didn't get my check like other kids got. Yeah my Mom dumped a lot of money in saving those buildings. We didn't have insurance. She slowly was trying to rebuild our house. She was trying to secure our future and have something of our own. I needed something to secure my right now. I am eighteen now and my check has stopped. I applied for assistance and now she needs it.

I had to get right now, on my own. My mother showed me determination and drive. She got us up early to go to the buildings. We cleaned them out, painted and did the up keep. It wasn't helping my self–esteem.

My mother didn't go to high school. She had no idea what I was going through at school. She had no idea of what I was going through in the streets. My mother worked and went to church and that's it. She didn't know how hard it is for a teenager in Chicago. It is absolutely madness out here.

Mom used to tell me that saying. "Sticks and stones will break your bones, but words will never hurt you."

You can tell yourself that, but words hurt. Words will get you fucked up in school and in the streets. Words will have a motherfucka drop out of school. Words will get you kill.

My mother said a lot of true things that came to light. The statement, "words will never hurt you" is not a true statement! I don't know about her, but words hurt like a motherfucka. Words will get your ass smashed or killed with sticks and stones. Using that analogy words will hurt your ass. Say a word a nigga don't like and they'll try to fuck you up.

I needed a car and Mom wasn't feeling me. She had no idea of what standing on these bus stops, got a nigga like me. I am a target. I ain't just a regular nigga I am Colo Dog off 169th in these streets. My name is traveling through the, 'All is Well circle'. I can't be standing on the bus stop.

Niggas will serve my ass up slipping out here. They'll give me a grade A pumpkin head or worst, killed. My mother didn't listen to me at all. I would try and tell her how it was in the streets. She would tell me how it was going to be. I started moving in the direction for survival. I couldn't let her control me anymore. She's going to get me killed. She's moved us out here, but I ain't got no car to get around.

The stores weren't across the street anymore. While living on 169th I didn't have to walk more than two blocks for anything. You had to walk on 111th & Racine or 115th & Halsted to the liquor store. That is six or seven blocks in both directions.

You know how many goons you walk by to get to the store. I got squabble with these stupid niggas. Now I must walk by these guys going to the store everyday. I am not going to let these marks catch me slipping. I can't walk to the store any more and if I did I took the unit.

When you're in someone else's neighborhood even though they were GD's, shit can pop off. You just don't know it could be a deception. It's no question you can get smashed on site. It was no question that when you saw me. You knew I was Folks. Here I am riding the bus like a goofy everywhere.

I was on 79Th & Halsted at the bus stop going to the hundreds. I was in the terminal. John & E you know the 79Th St. terminal is in the back of Halsted, off in the cut. You see shit like this I wouldn't even tell my Mom about.

Two guys walked by with their hats banged to the right. They looked at me and kept walking. I just didn't throw up to everybody, if I didn't know you. I threw up, if you represented.

They got a few feet further and threw up the forks. I threw up the treys. They bang the treys to the ground and started walking back towards me. I know the move, but you ain't smashing me back here. Let me get on the main strip at least so somebody sees me going at it. It's only two of them and this would be a good time to test my skills.

I started walking to get out on Halsted's main street. I hurried up to Halsted when I hit the Ave dude follows me

He shouts out, "All is Well."

I turn around it was just one of them.

He asked, "what you be nigga?"

I looked smirked and yelled back, "you already know" and threw up my treys again. I began walking back toward him while saying, "BD nigga", just as I was saying it and concentrating on what he was talking about.

The other guy ran the other way to trap me, but I wasn't running. He ran all the way around the front side of Halsted. He snuck up and stole on me from behind. I swear I didn't peep him. He hits me, dead in the ear and my shit was ringing.

I was locked in on the nigga shouting, "all is well." I took the blow and looked to check the atmosphere. It was just the one other guy. I shake it off and jump in my stance like, "whats up?" I got lucky or maybe they got lucky.

I kind of wanted to know, if I could take two at once. I would've played coy for the first one. Once the element of surprise got one of them out the way. I could concentrate on just smashing the other one. One on one you don't have a chance. Willie German whooped about ten police officers at once. He knew that karate shit.

My hat fell off after he steals on me. I'm still getting my bearings from dude who hit me. He picks up my hat and walked away. It was a Detroit Tigers navy blue major league hat.

The D was a representation for Disciple. I wasn't going to chase them in their neighborhood for my hat. Right on 79th it used to be a clan of Stones in the middle of all these Folks on the South side. That's one reason why I kept the heat on me from that point on!

I wasn't going to get smashed waiting on the bus again. I was lucky they could have been five or ten deep. What kept going through my head is when Dave and his guys beat dude into a seizure. I needed a car to get around niggas who don't like me for whatever reason. Mom is telling me to put the money in the house. The house of my stepfather, no bet!

I bought the1972 Cadillac for $250 and it runs, but the gearbox is fuck up. The steering wheel would be shaking like a motherfucka while driving it. It didn't have any power steering, but it started and moved.

I would just ride it to the hood and back. Just until I could get the gearbox fixed. Most of the time I left it at Grimes house. When I got around the house I was riding with somebody or just walked the hood. Grimes knew how to work on car and said he was going to help me fix it. He would always tell me to leave the keys just in case he had to move it.

I hadn't had the car a whole month just using it to get back and forth. What Grimes do? He gives the keys to one of the Folks in the neighborhood? You know how Grimes is Emus? He'll give you not only his shirt off his back. He'll also give you my shirt. I didn't have my own shirt after that!

His reason though! "Folks I was bubbled and I told him to go to the store. I didn't feel like driving that shaky motherfucka. When I turned the corner all my strength would be drained. He was right about that, that's why I didn't drive it around the crib. Once I got out I would be dripping with sweat from trying to maneuver the car.

He gave it to young Folks to go get something. Folks drives the car and smashes it into something and left the scene. The whole driver side fender and hood was bent up. Folks made it to snake alley and left it and now it's not starting anymore.

Folks who took the car was just about homeless. They lived in a crib, but they had to be squatting. He was taking care of his two little brothers. I still had to get my money.

What Grimes say about the incident? John asked.

Grimes said, "my fault, but don't trip though! You, Kermit and Emus drove my Mustang into a wall."

I couldn't say a word cause we did.

Kerrmit kept asking me, "let me drive Folks, let me drive."

Kermit didn't know how to drive, but wanted too. I thought he could drive, because he said he could. I let him drive and he was doing okay, until he had to turn a corner. Kermit didn't know he had to turn the wheel back to straighten the car out. Something that happened to me the first time I took Moms cars on a joy ride.

He was turning right into a parked car. I see what's about to happen and grabbed the steering wheel. I spent the wheel away from the car. What flashed quickly in my head was when Robert ran into the back of the van with the steamer.

I spent the wheel back and Kermit panics. He hits the gas and loses control, jumps the curb and drove across the grass. He still didn't stop and I was trying to get my foot on the brake. He runs right into the side of someone brick house. Of course we gets out and run and left the car. Grimes had to go back and get his shit and say somebody stole it.

I couldn't go at Grimes for any cheese. Especially since I cost him $2500 for a lawyer. I go at Folks he had to pay me three hundred for my car.

Folks looked sad and said, "Colo I don't have all the money."

He promised me he'd pay me. I told Folks with the, I'm going to give you one chance look, because you Folks and say. "I am not bullshitting I need my money." He gave me 100 on the spot in good faith.

Grimes probably told him he'd better have something for me, when he saw me.

Now I don't have a car and I am stuck in the hundreds again. I have to ride the bus late at night, which is not good. When I am out here I got to walk with the heat. These niggas ain't going to get up on me, without getting blasted.

I'm Stuck like Chuck

I had to go back to my old tricks. When Mom goes to sleep I would sneak the car and make a couple of moves. I'd put the gas back in so she wouldn't know the car was gone. I didn't even have a license. This went on for a couple of months.

I'd park the car back in the same spot and I am straight. I believe she knew I was taking the car or maybe she didn't. She kept leaving the keys on the table. This isn't the first time I've taken the car.

This particular evening my Mom asleep as usual, it was ten o'clock pm. I walked into the dining room and there are the keys to the car. There sitting right on the table as usual. I am already fucked up, but I said, "I'm going to the store to get another drink." I grabbed the keys and take off in the car.

I ride and pick up a buddies in the hood and drove up to the store. I think we went in and got a wine or something. It takes a couple of seconds to get somebody to cop. We get somebody to cop finally. We got the drink and were leaving the store. I come outside and we're on a slow leak on passenger back tire.

I tell Reg, "jump in I got to get the car back before it's flat."

I didn't know how to change a flat at the time. He gets in and I take off! I was driving around the bend by the expressway on 107^Th Place.

Reg said, "Colo you on a flat you got to slow down."

I'm like, "shit I got to get home before the air goes all the way out." I drive a little faster on a rim in the drizzling rain. This shows how inexperienced I was at driving. I was just a couple of blocks away from the crib.

I was coming around the curve and I couldn't straighten it out. The brakes wouldn't stop the car either. The rim was sliding on the ground for about ten feet. I hopped the curve and slid across the grass and into the guardrail, bammm. I look over the steering wheel and see the cars down on the expressway.

The rail was the only thing keeping the car from going over onto the expressway. Reg and I jumped out and looked at the car. The front fender was smashed up. I couldn't move the car so I had to leave it. I can't bring it back smashed up.

I told Reg we were out before anybody sees us. I ran the rest of the way to the block. We get to Reg house first and I finish the drink. All I could think about is what am I going to tell my mother? We finished the drink and I feel fucked up. Reg was looking at me like I done fucked up.

I told Reg "I'll holler don't say nothing to nobody and ran home. These ain't my 169th St. guys though and I was worried! I got to the house and jumped in the bed.

Five minutes later or what seemed like five minutes later. My Mom comes in my room downstairs, turns on the light.

She asked me, "where is my car?"

My reply, "I don't know I just came in."

She said, "I seen you drive off with the car."

I look like what and said, "you didn't see me drive off with it."

She could see I was drunk and talking belligerent.

She then says, "If I find out you took my car. Your ass is out of here tomorrow. You will have to find some place else to live."

I said, "yeah all right", sarcastically. Of course I slept late, because I was bubbled. Moms got up early and went and found the car that morning.

She comes back and tell me she found the car. She then said, "some of my friends or one of the neighbors told her they saw me running from the car."

It was Reg who told her, I was out and I knew it. Once she confirmed it was me, who was in the car.

She was in war-path mode.

She starts shouting, "get up, get up and get out."

I was hoping it was a dream what had happened last night. I rolled over from the bubble and looked at her. She has the one eye squinted with the meanest scowl on her face.

She said in a stern, but low tone from the bottom of her belly, "pack your shit and leave this very moment. She sounded like the girl in Excorcist when the demon had control of her.

She said, "have your ass outta here by the time I get back down these steps."

I brought you in this world and I'll take you out saying, ran through my mind. This is probably the time to activate on that saying. This is the first time I ever heard my Mom curse. Anything after this moment is not known what she'll do. I knew not to test her so I grabbed everything I could and left.

I was hurt. My Mom was kicking me out. I rebelled and said, "I am out anyway. You believe what people told you." That's all I could say and I knew I was wrong.

She looked at me with disdain and said, "just get out before I do something to you."

I hated to lie to her and wished I would've just come in and went to bed. I was already straight and didn't need another drank.

Mom is kicking me out, overshadowed those feelings though! This was the only thing I did to really mess up at home. A lot of my stress came from my little brother. I felt she shouldn't have kicked me out for that. She'll find out about my little brother once I'm gone. All my deviousness was left in the streets. Home is home and you shouldn't fuck home up.

This was my first big mistake and I was out. Well I don't count the party, because everything went smooth. I often said to myself, "she was taking my stepfather side." I tried to convince myself this was really his decision, but it was hers 100%. I knew I was walking a tightrope with my mother. I bought that car and now I don't have the car. Now I wrecked her car.

She had a very low tolerance level for disobedience. Mom wasn't going to let her kids run over her. She put me in the hands of the Yahweh and let me go. I felt abandoned, left to the dogs. It took me a long time to get over that Emus.

Well, I wasn't totally in the streets. I went over to my old man's house to live again. I figured, if someone's going to boss me around. At least it's my own father, anyway. I was closer to 169th & Calumet too. He had moved on the second floor the year I graduated. My room was the enclosed back porch.

I'm living at pops house so I only have to catch one bus to get to 169th. I was constantly riding through the opposition neighborhood living in the hundreds.

Now to get to 169th St. it was only one bus straight down 169th. This is the Mecca for Folks. Before I went to live over pops house. I traveled only on Sundays and Holidays. You could ride all day on one Super Transfer.

Now I could use one transfer during the weekday. Now, the CTA had it where you could only get three rides within the time it was stamped. Another thing you only could go in one direction. You couldn't travel back in the same the direction you left. Those bus passes was the shit. Emus always had the bus passes for me. This is how I traveled and sold weed. When Emus wasn't using his bus pass he'd throw it to me.

I'd stop at Slept Rock crib on 169th & Sangamon. Sell some weed over on Peoria. When nothings popping, I can still get to 169th & Calumet on the same transfer. I would stop and kick it around 172nd around City's old spot.

My prom date Dorus had moved around into City's old neighborhood too. That was the reason I really stopped over on 172nd. While I was over there I'd get a few bags off. I was bouncing in out.

That's the reason why a lot of my dirt wasn't known. I didn't burn up my set. I could go to other spots and kick it. When I did stains I'd disappear for a couple of weeks and set up a weed spot. As long as I had weed I wasn't going to do a stain.

I had to stay on regardless, because I made that deal the Yahweh. Not only that, I didn't want my father to know how scandalous I am. I had to change my method of operation. I had to keep money in my pocket.

Check this out though! Anytime you try to change something someone tests you immediately. Whether it's a friend or a situation. I hadn't done a stain in a long time. I was keeping to my promise. I was just selling weed. This time I am doing okay I'm focused. I'm not falling off as much. I was being tested and passed the test by passing up stains.

My guys used to say Folks ain't even smoking with us no more. He's acting funny! I used to smoke one, if you bought the drank, that shit adds up though! After the bubble I got to get something to eat. I was spending too much money when I got high.

When I get bubbled I get easy with my smoke. I just start firing up weed, because I am the weed man. I stopped that and tighten my grip up on my money. I'm starting to get my gear back together. I'm getting my butter whip every week. When I came to live with my father it was my sister Trina, my nephew Harvell and I living together.

Well shut the Front Door

Now I am hustling well, about the best since I started selling weed. I didn't have to go to school so I hustle all day, all night. The nine was popping from increased traffic from dope sells.

I am not a burden to the old dude I carry my own weight. I really just come home to sleep and change clothes. I do my do to help around the house. I kept the grass cut front and back yard. Once I made sure the house was straight I was in the streets

I hit the buses and different hoods with my hoodie on and my weed tucked. I had rolled joints ready. I wouldn't get them all crinkled up. The pullover I wore concealed the weed and it was stylish.

It was lightweight so I could where it in the summer time. The pullover hoodie had a zipper on it. You couldn't see the zipper, because it had a flap that covered it. When I took it off to shoot ball. You wouldn't know the sack was in it. I had about six of those jackets, all different colors.

One day I come home with a little outfit I bought and a pizza for everybody. We were busting the pizza up. I asked my sister Trina how does this outfit look?

She looks at the outfit and says, "that's sweet Colo."

Next she tells me something missing and pops thinks I took it.

I was astonished and said, "he thinks I took it I don't even be here." My face dropped like are you for real! I asked my sister, "what's missing Trina?"

She said, "I don't know, he just said, you got his shit."

First my stepfather thinks I steal his shit. Now my old dude thinks I stole his shit. I was perplexed. Here it is again, I don't know what's missing. I wait to see what was he talking about and he comes home. He makes a B line to my room and confronts me. He was looking like he's going to knock me out.

Once he saw the new clothes on my bed and peered at them for a second. That was the clincher in his mind. He frowned up and bucked his eyes and had ridged lips.

He was pissed off and asks. "Where's my shit?"

I looked at him bewildered, because I know I haven't taken anything. I don't even know what's missing.

He swells up and shouts at me, "give me my gold chains, nigga."

I looked like what, and said, "gold chains, I have no idea what you are talking about. I don't have your gold chains." I was looking at him with unbelievable eyes.

He didn't buy the eyes and swung on me hard as hell to be an old man. Of course I ducked sweet and calmly stepped out the way. He thought he had me clocked and was surprised he came up empty.

Now he had the same bewildered look on his face that I got. I back up and said, "pops you tripping I don't got no gold chains. I don't be here half the time." I guessed he seen how easily he missed and didn't swing again.

I looked at him in his eyes and said, "pops I don't steal from my family." I don't even steal any more and I still have to carry the tag. I used to steal. He looks at the new clothes on my bed, because they still had the tags on them.

He then says, "you bought this with the gold you stole."

I'm trying to get him to understand by saying, "I never stole anything in my life from you, except those beers. I didn't steal those I took them and was going to drink them. Just like I would, if I would've gotten a six back of pops. I just wasn't supposed to have them."

Pops response, "you are a lie, you are lying and you are nothing but a thief. Get your shit together and get out."

Those words sucked the wind out of my sail, what am I going to do now? I look in disbelief and asked, "I got to get out for something I didn't do, are you for real?"

He yells back as he walking away, "yes, I know you did it get out."

I wasn't even there two months and I have to go.

He said it again, "you did it nigga, get your stuff and leave."

This time I didn't do it and I get kicked out, still. When you known as a liar and a thief it follows you. You are the first person to get blamed, if something's missing.

My sister Trina and my nephew Harvell were in the house too. I didn't even go that route to defend myself. I just took the fall.

I was so embarrassed helpless and hurt. I almost couldn't control my emotions, but I kept calm. I called my boy Slept Rock. He had just got a 76 Cutlass from his father. He bought it for him for graduation.

Just so happened him and David Sterling were kicking it together. Sterling was sitting on his porch when I called.

Dave told Slept Rock to tell me. "He was on his way. He'd be there to pick me up in fifteen minutes."

I gathered all my things and wait for Dave on the porch. I'm fucked up in the head about this situation. Dave drives up and blows. He was in a brown Deuce and Quarter, he just bought for his graduation. I came down with a couple of plastic bags full of clothes.

I threw them in his trunk and jumped in the car. I get in the car and looked back up. I looked back up to see, if the old dude changes his mind. No Bet! Trina and Harvell and pops were looking down on me from the back porch as I left. I will never forget that picture it was engrained in my head!

I get in the car and Slept Rock asked me, "what's up what's happening?"

I tell him, "I don't know. My old man thinks I stole something from him."

I try and play it off and said, "Sterling take me to my car so I could put my clothes up, fuck em." I put my clothes in my car by snake alley. I kicked it with them for a couple of minutes. I really wanted to be on the nine. I got to figure this out. My crimes came back to haunt me in a different way.

Slept Rock was like, "you can stay at my crib, if you want too."

I was like, "that's cool, but I will be straight." I couldn't stand his sisters they always talked shit about him. I couldn't let them see me hurting. We kicked it on Peoria a while, but they knew I was hurting.

I didn't want any sympathy I wanted to know my next move. After that I told them to drop me off back on the Met. 'Kid make it', is on the street literally and that is a bad feeling. Now that shit ain't right!

Smack me in the Face

I called Doris my prom date. I met Doris up at the Communication Metro High school one day. I dropped game on her. She didn't go to the school. She was up there waiting on her sister Alice.

I knew her sister Alice from grammar school. She was smiling at me when I came out the school. I had a black leather jacket on and my butter was whipped. It was probably March of the year I graduated. I needed a prom date.

I didn't want to take anybody from the school. Everybody worth taking had dates or they were too young for me to ask. I wanted somebody my age or older. After I asked her who you waiting on!

She tells me who, I knew Alice so this gets me in the door. I said, "my name is Colo what's yours?

To make a long story short! I got the number hook up with her and we went on prom. I never hit her, not even on prom. I was still sort of scared to be aggressive. I did not know how or how to ask for the poonany, still. I found out later on how easy it was, but that's after I knew how. All you got to do is ask for the poonanny. Half of the time, I got the poo poo when I asked.

I called her up, because she had her own crib. I would spend nights over there sometime before being kicked out. She knew I was a thief. She didn't know I don't steal from loved ones. I had to let her in on what I do. She let me keep some merch at her house.

I'd sell the merch and drop her a few dollars. I chilled there a couple of weeks. We would hang out getting high and shit. She didn't smoke, but she did drink. I would sleep on the couch sometimes. She was cool, but she was crazy and I knew it. I didn't fuck with her and she wanted me too, but I knew she was a little crazy. Something she did to me when she stayed on the North side. That's another story

I called her up. Give her the deal on what was going on.

She said, "come on over you can chill for a while."

I was like, "bet" but I couldn't have any keys. Some of my clothes was there, but if I wanted to shower or get in the house. I would have to wait, until she came home. I come home with drinks and something for us to eat, while staying. I'd drop her twenty here and twenty there on some things.

I did my part to come to the table. I used to be sick when I bent that corner and she wasn't home. Sometimes what I would do, if she weren't home. I would just walk over on the 17 Deuce and hang out.

She stayed close to Lucky D and Snake. These were my guys from the Robe who was riding BGN with City. This day that's exactly what happened. I bent the corner and she wasn't home.

I go get them and we get a couple of 40's and blow through them. Nobody got any more money so I said, "walk with me over to ol girl's crib. I got a couple of dollar in the crib. If she home, we'll get a couple of more 40's."

We get there, she still not there, so we wait about an hour. I had a Super Transfer so I told them, "I'll catch y'all later, she's taking too long to come home. I am about to skate back to the Met. I'll holler, ain't no use of sitting around, not doing shit." At least on the Met one of my guys will reach for me. I fell asleep right!

They said "okay" and I break out and jump on the bus. Snake and Lucky D went back toward their way. I go hang out on the Met and came back a few hours later.

I see the light on and she's home and I am like, "bet." I hated to bend that corner and she wasn't home. You had to walk three long ass blocks, after you got off the bus to get to her house.

I come in hallway walked up the steps and I see the gate is twisted back. She stays right on the first floor so I looked at the bars a few seconds just tripping. I then knock on the door and Doris comes to the door. I asked Dorus, "what happened to the bars?" I was thinking maybe she lost her keys and had to get in the house. I told her, "I just left a couple of hours ago and they weren't like that!"

She snaps back with sass and pisstivity, "somebody broke in the house. I bet it was you."

First I was surprised and said, "what", then she said that last part. "I bet it was you", that part. I was astonished and told her, "Doris I wouldn't break in your house. It's nothing in here anyway, but a small TV. I gave that to you. This is the only place I can lay my head. I'd never break in your house."

I come in the house and chill for one minute and tried to figure this out. I was telling her I came earlier and she wasn't here so I left. Before I could finish the statement I hear the door opening in the hall. Next thing you know I hear walkie-talkies in the hallway. I go to the door and listen and I said, "it's the police."

She was talking real jazzy and said, "yeah I called them!"

She goes to the door opens it and looks at the police and says, "he's here now officer, he came back."

I got the Scooby Doo look and ran it back through my brain what she said, "he's here now officer. He came back."

I told the officer. "I don't know what's going on I just got here. She's accusing me of breaking in here." She smacked me in the face with that one. She was my girl!

Doris then asked the officer, "can you check for prints."

The officer turned and asked me, "have I been in here before?"

I answered, "she's been letting me stay the last couple of weeks."

He tells her, "mame well his prints are all over the place."

Doris then said, "they kick the bottom of the door can you get his shoe print?"

I took my shoe off and give it to the officer. I tell them these are the shoes I've been wearing all day. The rest of my stuff is in the bag in the corner. The officer took my shoe and did his investigation. It was not a match to the shoe print at the bottom of the door. They took her TV and the radio. She had some nice furniture, but I don't know what else they took of hers. That's all I could see that was gone.

They left all my stuff. I even had the money I was coming back to get. My money was still in the bag. Why didn't they take this shit? Police goes through my things and tells Doris.

The police couldn't connect me to the robbery and said, "I can't take him in for this, we don't have any proof. His bag is in the corner so that's why he's here. Unless, you seen him take it, we can't do anything, you can make a report."

Doris is pissed and says, "I know he did it let me fill out the paperwork."

The officer gives her something to fill out.

First I'm sitting there just looking at Doris while she's making the report. I'm looking at the police like I can't believe this. I am getting accused of some more shit I didn't do again. Here we go again, because she knows I used to steal.

You can't just wish away what people think of you. The thief tag is following me everywhere I go. I can't shed it. My family and friends won't let me self-rehabilitate. I am the first on the list accused when something comes up missing. I gave Dorus a couple of things from the stain Boya and I hit. Now she thinks I would hit her. I don't hit anybody I know.

Except for Mrs. Lane, but I only knew her, cordially. That was years ago, that I tried to hit that stain. Hitting people I really know, this ain't what I do. I knew I had to go this is a bad situation. I get up grabbed my bag then asked the officer, "can I go?"

The police agreed with me about me leaving, "yeah you going to have to go."

I look at Dorus while walking out with a look of betrayal and disgust on my face. I shake my head to let her know I was displeased. This is the last time I would see her in my life.

I walked back out to the bus stop on 169th & Racine. I still had my Super Transfer. I waited on the bus to head back to the Met. I'm sitting at the bus stop trying to figure this out. I was sitting on my bag and I was feeling low at this point. I was asking myself in a depressed mode. "Why do I keep getting kick out or accused of stealing?"

I don't take shit from people I know. My own family and friends think I will steal from them. Just then the police, who was on the call, came riding up. They noticed me first. I looked up, because I hear a car running, sitting by the light. They were looking at me sitting on my bag with my head in my hands, waiting on the bus.

I said to myself, "I hope they ain't about to fuck with me." They saw the way I was looking while Doris was snapping in the house. I honestly believe the police didn't think I did it. The driver hunched his shoulders like he was just doing his job.

I looked back at the officers and hunched my shoulders. I had the, I don't know look on my face, with the gestured. They looked at me with the same look and rolled off. I am back on the street, is what's going through my mind. I said to myself, "I know what happened after I thought about it. Snake and Lucky D came back and hit the crib.

They knew it was nobody home and they came back. You see, on the Met that would not be tolerated. That was one of our rules, don't do your guys. We don't scheme on each other's people.

Not only that these niggas know how I get down. They know I don't bullshit. That's why they didn't take my shit. Over here Folks didn't have any honor and even though I didn't see them. I knew it was them who broke in Doris house.

I knew it was them, because they were known for B&E's. It was Lucky D. I felt bad for her things being stolen. I should've known not to bring them niggas where I was laying. Since I brought this on Doris I was still responsible and I knew it.

It was just like I broke in her house, if I brought the people to your house. I wished she could've waited, until I got back. I probably could've gotten her shit back. Right now I got to figure out where I was going to lay my head. Even though it was my fault. I was still was mad at her, because she knew I had nowhere to go.

Kick out on the streets
Spider G

The first person I saw when I got off the bus 169th St bus was Spider G. I saw him on Michigan and I got off. Spider G and his Mom were the coolest. Spider G father passed away a few years earlier. He had a brother, but they were years apart and never hung out.

Spider G was feared. He had shot a few people already. He'd almost chopped somebody arm completely off. He robbed the train station of 169th. He was urban folklore. Spider G didn't have hands, but he was dangerous. He was quick on the trigger in the streets. Spider G walked around in the summer time with his trench coat on all the time. When he had that trench on! You knew he had a shotgun or a rifle.

Spider and I got real cool a couple of years earlier. We were hanging at Sacks crib. People still was thinking I was a shortie even though, my age, was on shortie status. I wasn't a shortie, because of my skills. My skills were older than me.

We we're on the second floor in the front room. It was no furniture up stairs at the time. Spider G was doing his bogart the little shortie shit. He knew my hands were special so he came at me with the wrestling shit.

Larry Driver and Dave Sterling prepared me for this moment. He thought he was going to run through me. He found out I was quite formidable. I was stronger and I had moves and holes I could use. Spider G was on Darobe wrestling so he had skills too. He knew sweet wrestling moves. Spider used to always be walking around with that Darobe wrestling cover on his head and wrestling jacket all the time when he was in school.

Anyway we locked up. He was slamming me and I was slamming him. As a matter of fact! I was slinging and slamming his ass as good as I got. When he got up he just looked at me. I know that look. I see it all the time. He under estimated me. I know why I fucked his head up. How could this young, skinny, little guy be this strong?

If you were Spider G hommie though, he'll give you the Earth. I told him, "Spider G I'm out here on the streets, and I ain't got nowhere to go."

He seemed happy and said, "you can stay with me Folks."

I said, "cool at least tonight I am straight." I spent a few nights that lead to a couple of weeks at Spider G's. I ate, what he ate. He would split whatever he had with me. He broke bread when we were at his house.

I turned around and broke bread with him in the streets. I turned Spider G on to the weed game. We put our checks together and bought some weed. Now we both had weed on the set. He didn't smoke, but he drank like a fish. He turned me on to mixing the Kool-Aid and White Port together. Since he didn't smoke, he couldn't smoke up the weed for sell.

Now you got two black ass niggas with butters and weed on 169th St. You couldn't miss us coming down the block. We often would be out all night drinking and selling weed. He'd come in and cook after all that. Most of the time, Moms would cook or he'd cook.

He'd tell me to chill while I'm watching TV. While I'm cooling out he'd hook us up a big ass plate of potato French fries. After eating a plate of potatoes. We would crack jokes and trip on guys in the street, until we fell asleep.

He loved talking about how he had his women in check. He always brought up how I couldn't drive that good.

Spider and I would laugh and reminisce, "Folks remember you couldn't park the steamer in the garage."

A couple of years earlier I wanted to drive so bad. I jumped in a steamer that they had. Folks let me drive just like Kermit was doing me. Spider jumped out and let me drive. I drove it a while hitting corners.

Spider told me, "shoot through this alley and park the car in garage. We were in the middle of the block on 170ᵗʰ & Michigan." That's where they were going to break the car down. I didn't crash it, but I couldn't get it in the garage. It was something else on one side of the garage.

The car they stole was a 98 Oldsmobile or a car big like that! I tried twice the first time I almost hit the corner of the garage. I stopped just in time. Spider just looks at me crazily bucking his eyes and shit. The next time I almost hit the other side of the garage.

Spider yells at me, "Folks you can't drive, get the fuck out before you get us caught. What the fuck is wrong with you?"

I get out and he jumps in the driver's seat.

Before he moved the car he looked at me and said, "this how you drive Folks." He backed it up cut the wheels, pulled forward and banged it in the garage.

I was like, "okay Spider that's a big motherfucka."

Next he'd go into how he robbed the L station.

He said, "Folks I had the trench coat on and walked up to the L station. Once everybody got on the train I walked up to the man in the booth pulled out the shotgun. I told dude, you know what this is, give me everything."

Spider said dude eyes popped open like saucers. When he saw the double sawed off. He dropped everything in the bag and he was out.

Spider had tokens, bus passes, money and a lot of change. He was selling tokens and passes around the crib. He was walking around a week with a pocket full of change in both pockets. Let him tell how he got away.

He said, "he grab the bag and ran up the steps and ran home."

You know he only lived a block in a half away from the L station. All he had to do was hit an alley and disappear.

Spider said, "I made it through the alley to my back door. I could hear the sirens and they were coming. He got in the crib laid on the floor, while the police was scouring the area. They were all in the alley and knocking on doors. Spider mother went to door and told them she was the only one in the house. They left and he got away with it.

I kind of kept, Spider under the radarscope while we hung. I brought him back to morality on some shit. Spider G didn't play. I don't think Spider G ever went to church. He only had one way of looking at things.

This was his saying, "If you're a Stone, be gone, cause you wrong, fuck with Spider G and you won't be living long."

Sacks and Spider G bleeds Gangster Disciple blue blood, through and through. Like Christians love Jesus that's how much they loved being Gangster Disciples.

Spider mostly loved talking about his woman while chilling. He had Delilah, Lil Jim sister and he went with Nino old girl friend, Lisa. He'd tell me about all the position he had them in and the noises they made.

How they were hollering while saying, "you're too much Spider." He tells me when he was about to cum he'd change positions. This would hold him off a while. He also would tell me how he'd dispose of a body, if need be. Mostly he talked about girls.

This one time he comes back from 171st. He went up there to sell some weed. I stayed on 169th, because we were branching out. He'd go to the park and I stay on the nine. You could get us mixed up from a distant.

Spider started selling weed at the park. It was no need for us both to be in the same spot. He came from the park one day and said, "Lynn Oldson threw the five up in his face." Lynn Oldson and her sister Tangy had flipped flowers and was riding with the Moes at the park. I've know Lynn since the Rock. Her and her sister came in the fifth grade.

Spider said, "When she said it Folks, I had to get closer to her so she could do it again. She did it again Folks".

I was astonished and said, "wow she did that to you Folks?"

When he seen how I looked he said, "Folks you know I slapped the shit out her Folks for the disrespect. I backhanded her Folks and said Bitch, this Spider G you don't know, now you know bitch, bow."

While telling me, he did his reenactment. "Bow, bitch while he's laughing. She walked away talking about I'm a get mines".

I don't leave I just stay at the park hoping somebody got something to say to me. She comes back a couple of hours later. I'm ready too Folks, but it wasn't that. Now she wants to give me some pussy Folks.

I looked at him like he was crazy and said, "not the Lynn Oldsome I know."

He then said, "for real Folks she went back and told the Moes, Folks. They probably told her that's Spider G, we ain't fucking with Spider G. We ain't fucking with Spider G, why did you disrespect that man?"

He laugh after giving me his spin on what he thought went down. After she came to her senses and the Moes didn't move.

A couple weeks later he comes and tells me. She was looking for him and saw me Folks at the park.

Lynn walked up and said, "Spider you are a real motherfucking G. How can a bitch holler at you?" Again Spider is laughing while telling me.

He then says, "She's coming through later on today she just called me."

I didn't believe him. Lynn gets slapped and now she's coming through. Lynn came through too. I was super surprise to see her walking down the nine.

I thought the nigga was bullshitting. I was like, "yeah right she probably trying to set you up Folks."

Spider while smiling said, "I'll holler" and they walked toward his crib. I don't know, if his story was true, but she walked off with him. She was another one I like, but she liked somebody else.

Lynn Oldson was mean in grammar school, but had some big titties. I love big titties. She was pretty to me, but mean. It kind of turned me on!

She always used to tell me at Rock Manor. "Shut your black ass up Columbus."

I was a little nigga to her and I didn't mind when she said it. Lynn and her sister Tangy used to fuck some girls up. Tangie was just as black as me or darker. They lived right on King Drive, down the street from the park.

It was cool hanging with Spider. It's only two things that can happen with guys with our characteristic together. Havoc! All they had to do was see us two guys coming.

His reputation preceded him all over the land. My reputation was known all over the Southside. I had to keep it moving Spider G didn't give a fuck about jail. He didn't give a fuck about doing time or none of that shit. He had already been to jail a couple of times. Those couple of days I was locked up was enough for me.

Spider would drop you just as quick as he talking to you! He better love you or have love for somebody in your family. You cross him and he's going to get you. He was just all Folks 100 %. I was 100%, but I did use morality in my decision-making.

Spiritual Foundation

*M*y spiritual foundation helped out in the streets and I didn't know I was leaning on it. It was a good resource to draw strength! I built up a resistant and would never let Spider activate my demon. I already had good practice warding off Slept Rock and Pauly. I had to be strong and not be influenced by his demon. I had gotten plenty of practice of falling off. I had to create space.

His demon was strong. I could control his demon with love and reason. You can't tell him what to do, but he'd listen. You had to speak up though and say. "Spider cool out that ain't right." He would think of the most devious thing to do to you while laughing at the same time

It was evil all around that was permeating all throughout the hood. One thing about it! You could sense and feel the evil, when it was around. Evil can jump off one person into another person.

You have to be strong when confronting evil or warding off evil. When you have goodness in you. You'll get this feeling in your stomach, which feels the evil around! When you have goodness in you, it's like, an alarm system.

Evil can't stand to be around any light. When evil can't contaminate or control you, you are a threat. When evil sees any light. Evil will hate and try to gain control. Spider had much good in him.

He never tried to control me and had my back so he had love in him. He never be-little me or use my falloff against me, because I was in the streets. People will try to flunk you out, when you are on your knuckles. Spider opened his arms and took care of me. He thought of me as a little brother.

I believe that's the only thing that help me ward off demons sometimes. I had a spiritual foundation. A lot of these guys ain't been to church. The only time they'd go is when it's was a funeral. I had extensive teaching while going to church with my mother. This is what got me about church.

Where did fake end and real begin it got confusing to me? You want me to believe and have faith. I believed these stories only to find out it wasn't true. I was only six when I found out Santa Clause and the fairy godmother wasn't real.

I was getting money for teeth under my pillow. I'd wake up and gift are under the tree on Christmas. We never piled them up before Christmas at first. We got presents on Christmas Eve so I thought Santa brought them to us.

My Mom came to me when I was about six and told me there was no Santa Clause. That fucked me up!

She told me, "momma and daddy is Santa Clause."

It was tight that year and we weren't getting any presents. That's why she told me. Now you want me to believe in giants. This little guy Joseph with a slingshot took down a giant named Goliath.

Daniel was in a den with lions and he didn't get ate. Moses parted the whole sea with a wooden staff. Jesus turned water into wine and raised the dead. He got killed, but came back after death. My daddy died and he is not coming back. It rained for forty days and forty nights. Noah and his family took two of every creature and repopulated the earth.

All Santa did was ride a magic sled with flying reindeer and came down the chimney to drop off some gifts. I was good that whole year and Santa is not coming. My thinking was she should be coming to tell me those stories ain't real either, sooner or later.

Back then it was no air conditioner at the church. We had hand fans to keep us cool. On every fan was a white man with straight hair and blue eyes.

When you read the scripture it says, "skin of bronze and wool like hair", okay. It was hard to believe. That means he was black and I didn't believe it. I was brainwashed.

That's how my demons could be activated so quickly in me. I began to think as long as you didn't get caught. What ever you did was cool. There's no repercussion as long as you got away. I knew it was something higher than us I could feel it, but not to the extent they were talking in church.

My Mom used to tell me it is demons out here. You know I read comic books religiously. What's the difference in the stories in the comic book and the ones in the bible? When I was a shortie I would ask in disbelief, "momma there are real demons, demons you can't see. They can control your body."

It was a demon battling for mines as I was talking to her. The best thing the devil got on you is to believe he is not real. Once you think that he's got you. It was conceivable though, because I had no control over stealing at first. I like it and I did it and I nurtured that demon by being a willing vehicle for it.

My Mom answered, "If it's your will, yes that's why we have the Ten Commandments, the commandment tells us how to live together." Learning the stories of the bible would aid me in these streets. My hommies didn't have that Ace! The only love they had was for their Folks and their family.

I sat on the front seat when I was thirteen. I was an usher, in the choir, on the junior deacon board. I was being groomed in the church. I played the bongos, the washboard with the fork and the tambourine during broadcast. Not at the same time, but I would be cold, if I could.

The day I got baptized I was thirteen. My mother got me up that Sunday and told me I would be responsible for my sins. Today I would be baptized in the name of the spirit. I will be reborn today.

She told me, "I know the difference between right and wrong. She would no longer be responsible for what I do."

By this time I was doing wrong despite being aware that it was wrong. I was doing my will. We get to the Greater Harvest church early before Sunday school and Reverend Bracken baptized me.

Here's something I did not know all this time I was going to my church. The pulpit where Reverend Bracken taught on Sundays is where I was baptized. You can open up the floor and there was a small pool that held the water.

We got dressed in these long white gowns in the room underneath the choir stand. One by one we came out to accept Jesus Christ as our savior. It was my turn to be baptized and I get in the water. Reverend Bracken said something and covered my mouth.

I went down underneath and when I came back up. I felt totally different. I felt the difference from when I entered the water. I felt difference when I came back up. My whole body and mind felt refresh.

I knew something spiritual had happened at that moment. I had tapped into something that will guide me back to the light. I felt electricity flowing in my body. I knew right then that something has taken place. I was born in sin and I'm trying to find my way back from that point.

I really enjoyed church when I was in attendance. The devil had a hold on me somehow, still. I would be in church taking money out the plate or trying to figure out how. When I was on the usher board I went through everybody pockets. The ushers' were in charge of the coatroom. Nobody left money in their pockets, but I did check.

I was a bonified thief two times, but I was working on that demon the last three five years. There was a spiritual warfare still going on in my body. Those traumatic experiences I blocked out. I was riding on automatic pilot. My adopted father's death my dog's death and the house burning down. Now I am on the streets. The last four years has been mentally murder on my psyche.

This is hard for a teenager to comprehend, but I didn't go back to thieving. Once I started to change for the better. I got caught for somebody else's thievery and I didn't even want to steal. Something comes up missing I am the culprit. I lost my family, because I stole or was known for stealing.

My environment and surroundings were sucking me down with my family. My emotional traumas were weighing on me. The struggle to succeed in life still festered. The devil and I or one of his demons, walked closely together.

Now I know there's real demons from my own experiences. When you are around demons, if you watch closely. You can see when a demon takes over a person. Have you ever did something and you say to yourself, why did I do that?

You knew it was wrong from the beginning. Still, you couldn't stop yourself from doing it. That is the time your demon is activated. You have to pay attention and you can see the transformation. Had I not been aware of what was happening to me. I would've been all in or even more scandalous.

Spider G would have brought that devil out more, cause I loved him like that! When people help you, you feel a sense of gratefulness, gratitude. Whether it's evil or good you appreciate the help. Whether, if it's love or what you think is love, you appreciate it. You love who loves you and if you can't distinguish evil love from good love. You can get sucked in fast. Love brings the devil out more in this case.

The devil will use love against you. How can you not love a person who takes you in and feeds you? Depending on the individual he can use it against you. You'd do anything for that person at least I would. The only way you wouldn't is, if you've never been hungry or didn't have your church lessons.

This is how Jeff Fort the leader of the Black P Stones, came to power. I heard his mother was feeding all the street guys in the hood, is the story. Once you got guys eating, you got their ear. This is when you can get things done.

You feed a person when he's hungry or not, he'll never forget it. I had to get away form Spider G. I didn't do this consciously, this was going on in my subconscious, it was spiritual. I was in and out, until I was all the way out at Spider G's crib.

Grimes

I just faded out somehow. I stayed with Grimes a few weeks that summer. I thank him and his Mom for letting me cool out I needed it. Grimes didn't have siblings and I think his Mom was happy when I was around. He had a cousin I think liked me, but she wasn't my style. She worked at Mickidees on 169th and when I came through, she'd set me out free food.

I could be Grimes little brother. That's one thing Mrs. Tucker looked out for me too. She did the same things as Spider G Mom, Mrs. Ivy. They made me feel welcomed.

I kept things clean so I wasn't any problem that way. I think the parents liked me around, because they saw the respect factor I had. Being gracious by saying thank you and always being courteous.

Do you need me to do anything? This is why everybody's Mom knows me. I would be the first to jump and help out.

My mother told me. "If I ever have to stay at people houses and you don't have money. Don't be a burden. There's nothing out here free. You don't have money. Help out and keep everything clean. See if theirs anything you could do, don't wait to be told. That's how you can pull your weight."

I knew Grimes from the hood, but I plugged with him at the Robe. I was a freshmen and I was walking home. I see Grimes coming from the old building. I stop and talked to him.

I don't know what happened, but Grimes probably said something smart like he always do. I look at him and said to myself, "this skinny little motherfucka." Grimes was laughing so I took his hat off his head and started running. Grimes starting chasing me down the street. I was laughing and shit so he knew I was bullshitting, so I thought. Grimes chased me all the way to Michigan from Parker's parking lot.

I knew he stayed on Michigan so I stop there and gave him his hat. I give him his hat and he just looked at me. He was out of breath and I kept laughing. I said you know you can't catch me playing like a little kid. He didn't tell me then, but later he said he wanted to fuck me up. Until he really knew my dumb ass was playing.

He said, "I kind of figured it out when I would get close then you turn on the motor, while laughing."

I stopped on Michigan and gave it back. I found out he liked playing baseball. We first plugged by playing strikeout and football at Brownell. Next we would play whole court at the inside gyms.

After the game I'd kick it awhile. Once Sacks got kicked off the team we were the three amigos in the hood. That's how we got to hanging and hitting licks.

Grimes was just about game for anything, if you could get away with it. Don't fuck with his Folks and he had much love for you. Grimes would protect you and everything. He was the littlest guy with major heart. Grimes took care of the girls.

You know, if he'd look out for a hard leg. Now just think what he'd do for the girls. Grimes made sure the girls were happy. The girls always came by Grimes's house to hang.

I was staying with Grimes at the time. Spider G and Grimes got into over this girl while I was at his house. Spider and Daryl brought the girl over to Grimes's to chill. Daryl was low-key pimping he had a few women on the track.

Daryl left the girl with Spider G to do what he pleased. Spider G took her over Grimes's to cool out. He had to put things in motion. I was coming through the gangway and peeped the girl. I saw them when Spider and Daryl walked up with her.

The girl was homeless and Grimes let her stay. I forget her name. She was a pretty girl and she shouldn't have been in the street. You can tell I looked at her fingernails. They were clean and her teeth were bright white. She could've been my woman.

She had pretty brown skin with long hair and it was real. This was before weave took over! She had a nice body too and she was a looker. Spider wanted to pimp her and get money. Daryl was on pimp status and was turning Spider G on to the pimp game. She laid the game down on Grimes when Spider left.

She told Grimes, "I don't want to be out here."

I understood her, because they walked up with her. They didn't get out of a car. What type of pimp is that? A pimp that doesn't have a car! That's why they were at Grimes's. Don't you at least have to have to have a car to be a pimp. She wasn't feeling it.

Grimes was soft on the girls. He told her not to worry about it, before she could get the words out. He said he would talk to Spider and she'd be cool. I'm thinking to myself then said to Grimes, off to the side. "Aah Grimes, Spider is going to pimp her. What do you mean don't worry about it?"

He answers quickly, "just what I said, the girl said she doesn't want to trick, she ain't going."

My response, "okay, but I know Spider ain't going to want to hear no shit like that!"

Spider came back later to get her. He got her a couple dates lined up. Spider had already counted them dollars, before the eggs hatched. That's what he said he was going to do before he left. He had to get her a couple of customers, before they got to walking.

Spider knocked on the door and Grimes wouldn't let him inside.

After he knocked a while Grimes yelled through the door. "Ain't no use of you knocking she ain't coming out. The girl don't want to be pimped."

Spider started knocking hard on the door and shouting, "send my bitch out Grimes" over and over again.

My mother didn't raise any pimps. I was on Grimes side. Spider G started turning the heat up with the cussing and the banging on the door. Grimes told him to stop banging on the door.

Once he cooled out I went out there to talk to him. By this time he walked down the steps. I walked down the steps in into the alley. Spider was in the alley pacing backwards and forwards. His eyes are bucked and his mouth is ridged with anger.

I pause look and say, "Spider you snapping", then I paused.

I took a few more seconds then I told him, "she don't want to do it Spider. I heard it out her mouth. That's why she ain't coming out. That's what came out of her mouth Spider, it ain't Grimes."

Spider look frowns and says while shouting. "Grimes is trying to take my bitch."

I tell him, "I heard the girl say this Spider, "they're trying to pass me around and I don't want to do it."

I asked Spider, "Spider you going to make her sell her pussy? Don't she has to be willing to do it Folks? What's that a kidnapping and a rape charge?"

Not only that, you're going to fall out with Folks, over this shit. You know his ol G is in her room. Show some respect Folks".

Mrs. Tucker is in there asking, "what's wrong with Spider G?" Spider looked at me, but I could tell he was pissed he paused and thought.

After that he said, "all right Folks" and walked away.

I go back up stairs and told Grimes. "I don't know how long it's going to hold him. If he starts drinking, it won't be long."

The girl was so appreciative that I talked to him. She thanked me and gave me offered me the poonanny.

Grimes was like, "gone take her in the bathroom Folks, if you want to hit her."

I almost told him no, but she was bad. I look at her and said, "yeah she can get it."

I didn't want Grimes to know I wasn't strong in this area. He was getting plenty of nook nook. He gave me a rubber and I went in the bathroom.

She was like, "come on you can hit this" with a smile on her face. I guess my face was looking funny so she reassured me. She was bad so I put my fear of not performing out of my mind.

As a matter of fact she showed me what I was doing wrong. For some reason I thought I had to be gentle and careful like in the movies. She closed the top on the toilet and she sat me down. She was in control. I unzip my pants and pull them down around my knees. She knew how she wanted to handle me she lifted her shirt and the beautiful hangers fell out. She grabbed and maneuvers my throbbing stick inside her.

She liked my swag. I didn't know she was listening from the window and heard what I told Spider G. She was ingratiated to me. I'm in the bathroom sitting on the toilet seat top and she goes to work. She showed me what I was doing wrong. She got on and was sliding up and down filling herself up. Once I got it I turned strong and rolled with her.

Grimes mother was in the other room asking Grimes, "what's that noise?"

You could hear the toilet seat banging against the toilet. It had a cover over the top, but you still could hear the vigorous shaking.

Grimes started knocking on the door and saying, "cool out I can hear y'all out here."

We move from there and she bent over the tub. She guided big dawg on in and finished me up.

That was Grimes though he always had a soft spot for the girls. I'd gotten me some poonanny, for being me. I felt better about sex after she schooled me. She was a pro but gave me some free nookie that means she likes me. I didn't even ask for it. That was my problem not being aggressive and assertive.

Most girls like you to take control, but she was a pro and she was aggressive. I like that! The girl was no older than nineteen or twenty. She didn't look like she should have been out there in the streets.

Grimes got the girl to safety. The only thing is Spiders upset about his money. Since the girl was at Grimes's house I left. It was too much going on now. I know it's too many mouths to constantly feed. I didn't want to be in the middle of Grimes and Spider so I faded. She didn't stay long either somebody had to be looking for her. She looked too good.

Sacks

I drifted on down to Prairie and hung out with Sacks a few days. He has three little brothers, Fabian, Tim and Mike. These were the coolest little guys. Sacks didn't hang with his brothers much in the street. He loved them all and always talked about each one. His mother didn't want Sack's streetness to leak over to the younger boys.

Sack carried his shit the hardest. He was known all over for banging and his football time at the Robe. I'm telling you when you were on the squad at the Robe, you were a star. He played linebacker too. Sacks was tattooed with the pitchforks all over his body.

I'd ride with him and he'd take us in the belly of Stone neighborhood. He'd jump out of his little rabbit he bought, with his hat bang hard to the right. My stomach would bubble up, but they never moved. I wore butter so you knew what it is.

When we were together we never got any static. He'd take us on 35th to the projects where his aunt Gracy lived. She had two young daughters named Keisha and Washetta. We'll stay down there and get high, while meeting some of the Folks in the jets. He got his hustle on selling weed, but his thang was to bang out radios. He really didn't steal the cars he snatched radios.

Sack's brothers really didn't have to put in work in the hood. Just like my brothers and Harris's boys. They all got passes because of our respect factor.

All they had to say was, "you know Colo? You know Sacks?"

Niggas would immediately back off. Our brothers would get respect, because of our respect. It was easier for the younger brothers. They knew we were coming, if you fucked with them. We set the precedence of, these are the goon's little brothers.

Sacks knew how to kick it. This how we got cool. His old dude used to give him his burgundy 1983 Park Avenue. He'd ride on the Met and scoop a nigga up.

He'll ride up and say, what you doing Folks?

I'd say, "I ain't doing shit but chilling."

He then says, "jump in and lets kick it. When I got in, he'd have a six-pack and a bag of weed. He'll say, "ride to the car wash with me and get high."

We'd smoke one and ride up to 187th & Halsted to the car wash. We get up there washing that boy up. He tells me to get in and pull it up. I get in and pulled the gearshift and looked to see was it in drive. It didn't work so I guessed I was straight. I gave it some gas and went backwards. I hit a car behind me and cracked the backlight. I get out and say, "damn Sacks I fuck up I thought it was in drive." It wasn't anything wrong with the other car.

Sacks looked and said, "damn Folks you cracked the light. I'll tell the old dude it was me don't worry about it."

We finish the car up. We drank and got high like nothing ever happened. That was my man from that point on!

Sacks reputation was worst than mine for banging and stealing. Everybody loved Sacks, the girls and the guys on the block. He was ride or die. He would keep you laughing all the rest of the time.

When rapping came out it was he and I trying to rap, in the neighborhood. He played all the sports too and could box. He wasn't as good as me, but if he stole on you, you were going out. It was like Mike Tyson coming down.

I chilled for a while, but didn't want to impose. I know I can eat, but people will start looking at you grabbing too much. Most of the time I bought my own food I just needed a place to lay my head. You don't bring anything to the table. Sooner or later you get a side ways look from people.

It will be addressed or people will eat in your face. This never happened at Sack's, but you got to know the situation. Half the time Mrs. Mckenzie didn't know I was in the house. I myself don't want to over stay my welcome. I rather sleep in my car than to be overbearing.

CHAPTER EIGHT

Back to Where it all Started
The Met

I finally made it back to the Met. My sister Barbara didn't move to the hundreds with us. She got her a house on 168Th & Calumet. She stayed a few doors down from Todd. I would stay with my sister a few nights, but she wanted me in early.

My sister was just like momma at this point. She went to church every Sunday. She was singing in the adult choir at church. I gave my sister respect like I did my momma. I never let her see me doing much of anything. I never let her see me smoking weed or drinking. I'd come drunk, but I wouldn't drink in front of her.

I didn't have any keys so I didn't bother her, if I was out too late. She had to go to work. The nights I did spend the night it was terrible. My nephew Deshaun, had this dog with fleas. The fleas had infiltrated where I slept in the basement.

I'd wake up with about twenty tic bites all over me. The tics were sucking my blood while I slept. I'd have little suck bites all over my legs and arms. This was crazy living to me. I would wake up depressed about my situation and life in general. That's the only reason I didn't go over there more. I couldn't stand the tics all over in the basement

Sometimes I would stay in the basement of the crib on 356 E 169th St. We still had furniture in the basement. The basement was the only place the fire didn't destroy. I wished my comic books were in the basement.

I'd go down their some nights and sleep. It was a window I could slip in and out. I come in and lay down on that green paisley couch we had. The only thing is in the morning I wake up smelling like burnt wood. I slept there very little. It brought back bad memories or memories I was trying to forget.

I took the Folks in the basement to get high one day. It had to be raining or we had to get off the set for something. It might have been the latter of the two. It was about seven of us and I told them we can chill out down here. We were getting bubbled and high as hell for a while in the basement that day. We made a couple of store runs for drinks. We come out the basement a couple of hours later, blowed.

We come out the alley squinting, because we just came out the dark. We had our hands covering our eyes, until they adjusted to the sunlight.

Todd hit the block first and said, "look at that hook riding through here on a ten-speed." He was a half a block away and riding towards us.

He had a red hat on and it was banged ugly to the left. He looked at us and we're deep, all banged out to the right.

The fear immediately hit his face when he sees Todd pointing at him. It was perfect timing for his destruction. He starts speeding up trying to get by us. We we're on the sidewalk and he was riding with traffic on the other side of the street. About time he gets to us.

Lace had this push broom stick in his hand. He reared back underhanded and propelled it toward him. He slung it at the front tire. Dude is on the bike and digging hard trying to get away. He standing up torquing the bike pedals in a 360.

Do you know he slung the stick and it went through the spokes of the tire? After I see it protrude the spokes. I said to myself, "dude is about to get flipped." Lace couldn't have thrown it any better. As soon as the stick hits the forks of the bike, he's going to wipeout, right.

The stick goes all the way through right before hitting the forks. Clears the spokes and hits the other side of the pavement. This was a miracle to me. He had to pray at that moment.

Dude looked at stick hit the ground and busted ass getting out the hood. He was digging hard on those pedals. I was so happy that the stick went through the forks. I didn't want him to get caught.

I was just looking, but everyone else was moving in his direction to smash. Once the stick went all the way through! Everybody stopped and looked in amazement. Everybody said at one time. "Damn you see that, it went all the way through!"

Big Darrin

I was making my rounds around on the Met. I stayed at Big D's a couple of days. We were always cool we never had confrontation. We never slap boxed or anything of a physical nature. We did have a confrontation a few years earlier when we lived at, 356 E 169th.

My brother came home and told me Darrin took his baseball glove. Walls tried a lot of people bigger than him. As a matter of fact my brother rarely came and got me. He handled his own business and had his own reputation. This was before he joined the GDs. Big D though, was something else. Big D really didn't fuck with anybody. Big D was told who to hurt.

I was working on a put together bike in the yard when he told me. I stopped and asked my brother, "Big D took your glove?"

He shook his head and replied, "yeah it was Big D."

I started asking myself, "why would Big D take your glove?" He knows better we are cool. Big D would see me in the alley and walk down and play ball with me all the time. I put the bike up in the basement and came back up and I'm thinking all the time what the fuck is wrong with D.

I asked my brother, "what did you do to him?" I know my brother can get under your skin

He replied, "we had words on the court and he picked my glove up and took it"

My brother just didn't back down to nobody. Big D was out his league he had to come get me! Shit, Big D was out of my league. He was in a league of his own.

I told my brother to come on and grabbed the bat. We walked down the alley and I'm thinking what am I going to do? I'm going to ask him for the glove and if he don't give it up. I am going to wear his ass out with this bat. I felt like he was calling me out. That's how it works he's really saying fuck you and your brother. We get down the alley and Big D was in his backyard.

I said, "Big D what's up with my brother glove?" He looked and sees the bat in my hand. He didn't say anything. He just started walking toward the glove to pick it up. He picks it up and tosses it to me.

After that the only thing he said was, "your brother got a big mouth."

I said, "thank you Jesus! Yeah Big D was a beast!"

The night I spent over Big D's. His mother Judy made a big pot of chili. Big D and I busted it up good. Big D used to get kicked out all the time. He was at home this particular time. After tearing into the pot of chili we just kicked the breeze. He might have been on house arrest.

I was tripping with him about when Craig Jake and Juice moved on him. Big D was working with Butch, Dirty Red's brother and he was a Stone. I think Big D was going in that direction of being a Brother at the time.

John says, "yeah he was talking about all is well. He was about to flip "All is Well." He'd been Folks all this time. Now he was flipping.

I say, "It didn't matter what Big D was he still was my hommie. I just didn't understand it. I can see flipping when you were a shortie, thirteen or fourteen. When you a shortie you are trying to survive and find a way. I can even see flipping from BD to GD for the opportunity. Big D was nineteen and flipping "all is well" that was way too late to be flipping. He put in too much work by that time.

It felt strange not seeing him throwing the treys up way down the block. He'll see us on John porch. He'd start walking down that long ass block, to greet us with the treys flying. We give each other love with the BD handshake.

Now he's throwing the five up. Now what we going to do when we greet? It was strange to see him throwing the five up. I'd just quit, if I didn't want to ride under the six. To me he was riding the eleven-point star, he knew too much.

You know both literatures and switching sides so where's your loyalty. This ain't like flipping GD to BD or vice versa, this was joining the opposition. Most of your friends are Folks so why would you do that?

You're going to get violated too. Motherfuckas are going to be coming at you. Why do it? Just retire and don't be anything. It was Big D so you know how that goes.

Anyway Criag Jake and Juice, that's Kermit older brother caught Big D on 169th & Calumet. This is right across the street from John's house.

John jumps in and says, "We were all sitting on the my porch. Colo, Emus and I were watching it all go down. Craig and Juice was like we heard you flipped. Big D threw up the five up, in their face. Juice and Craig has been known in the hood for years. They were goons controlling the streets when we were going to grammar school.

Craig Jake sees him throw up the five, after he did that! Jake pulled the stick from behind his back. Swings and hits D in the head with this wooden plank, cracCCCk was the sound it made. Big D tried to go at him and Jake cracks him again.

Big D didn't see the stick at first. He had it concealed behind his back. Juice jumped in and dropped about four blows on him after D grabbed his head. He hits the ground clutching his head. Once on the ground Jake hit him in the head two more times. I said to myself, "why subject yourself to this? I knew this was going to happen!"

Everybody who was on the porch started yelling. "Stop hitting him he's down Jake."

Jake and Juice breaks off and headed toward Prairie. Big D gets up holding his head.

We all went over to him and asked, "are you straight Big D?" He just walked back toward his house saying he was going to fuck them up. This is family and he just got some discipline. He didn't get smashed smashed.

I then say, "a couple days later the police had just harassed us for sitting on John's porch. They jumped out the car and were asking us. "What we were doing on the corner?"

I used to love when Josephine would come out and shoo them away. John's Mom always sat in the window so she saw when the police jumped out. When they jumped out she'd be at the door and tell them to leave us alone.

She'd be like, "these boys ain't bothering nobody leave them alone."

The police officers would look funny at her. They were surprise to see a white person or whom they thought, was white taking up for us.

She would then say, "you heard me leave these boys alone."

We could be on the porch eight deep and she'd get them off us. They knew we had work, but you couldn't come on her property. We wouldn't say anything to them, but if you got caught on the sidewalk, it was another story. The police circled our block like vultures looking for a carcass especially since SteveO blew it out with the yeayo. We got searched at least once a day.

Here's their procedure on searching us. They'll jump out quick and tell us to put our hands on the squad car. Next they would kick your legs open one at time as far as they could. When they kicked your legs. They did it aggressively to get a reaction from you.

To stop them from doing that! I would put my hands on the car and then I damn near, did a split. You didn't have to kick my legs. I didn't like them kicking my legs like that! It pissed me off so I just assumed the position. This stopped them from kicking my legs.

Next they'd ask, "where's the dope? Where's the guns?"

I tell them what they want to hear, but tell them nothing. Most of the time they wanted to feel power over you. I give them the, yes officer, no officer and I don't know officer. I just walked up officer. I just came out the house to any questions they had.

When we were on your porch John, we were untouchable. Josephine would come out and clown the police. I know she knew we were selling weed and dope off her porch. I didn't know how Jughead was cut, so that's why.

The twisters left. We got to talking about the smashing that Jake and Juice put on D.

Emus shake his head and says, "we saw Juice walking up from Prairie that's why were talking about it. Juice stops on the Met and was waiting on SteveO to come out the crib.

Big D can looked out his window and see all the way to the corner of Calumet from his house. Big D must have been sitting and waiting, because he came out of nowhere.

He rode up through the Met alley on a ten-speed. Jumped off the bike and threw it to the side and was on Juice. They square up.

We all jumped off the porch saying, "Oh shit Big D caught him by himself." Juice was bobbing and weaving and telling Big D he didn't want none.

Big D had his guns cocked up with his elbows by his ears. His fist was crossing his face. He was doing the peek-a-boo style of boxing.

Big D starts talking, "I got your ass now" and swung two times and connected. Big D hits Juice in his mouth with some big thunderous blows, bam, bammM. His lips turned into hamburger, instantly.

Andrea Juice eyes were all over the place after the first two blows. Juice nose, eyes and lips everything was blown out. He tried to stick in there, but big D hit him like five times the same way he did the first two times."

He didn't knock him out, but Juice faded out and went the other way. Juice was known for fucking motherfuckas up too. Today he was fucking with Big D by himself.

Big D yelled at him as Juice skated, "tell Jake I'm fucking him up worst."

He didn't catch Jake, but he did pick up the sewer top and slung it at Jake when he saw him. Jake jumped in the wind.

Big D was boxing. This wasn't the pick him up, slam, then stomp him. He fucked Juice up bad. Juice had to fade out he had nothing coming. Big D could've done him way worst, but had mercy. He did blow his eyes, lips and nose all the way out. You know when you get your ass whooped. You don't come back on the strip for a while. I didn't see Juice too much more after D smashed him.

Big D does the same thing to Slick Freddie with the five. We are in the sub spot on Calumet. He kept throwing up the five, fucking with motherfuckas on the Met. You know niggas like me, wouldn't even entertain him and play him off.

Other niggas wasn't going to do nothing to Big D on the Ace boogie dance. He was definitely too big to see by yourself. This time it was Slick Freddie, Big A, Smiley and I all sitting down eating in the sub joint. We spotted him coming across the street with his hat to the left.

Freddie watches him across the street before 'D' walks in the sub joint.

Freddie says. "Look at Stubeen he got his hat to the left. Man I don't believe this!" You see Slick Freddie brought D up and felt he showed no loyalty.

Slick Freddie said, "He needs to get violated."

Big D comes in the sub joint.

Freddie was like, "man Big D what's up with this, all is well shit."

Freddie reached and tried to straighten his hat out while it was on his head. Big D pushed Freddie back up off of him and threw up the five. Bow, boww Freddie stole on him two times.

It was like he didn't even connect. Big D walks through those punches and picks Freddie up in the air. He carries Freddie about twenty feet on the run to the back by the door to the kitchen. He was about to slam Freddie, but before he could do that!

Big A and Smiley jumped up immediately smashes him on the spot. Bang#**@* boom bang#**@* boom boom#**@* boom. I just sat there and watched. I told everybody to cool out once Big D curled up. Cool out he straight. Big D wasn't following block rules. He got tapped up a little bit, but not a pumpkin head. Big D knew how to curl up and protect himself.

It broke out so quick I kept eating my sandwich like I was watching TV. It was a smashing you would get from your brothers when you stole something from momma. He took ten or twelve to the domb and they got off of him after I said that's enough.

Big D was known and we had love for him. You couldn't do him bad and he was off the Met. Big D had been doing it a while, irritating Folks, it just boiled over. He was breaking the Met rules.

This bewildered me about Big D. From one day to the next you are throwing up the five. You know a violation or a smashing is coming anyway. I always told Big D, "you know, you stirring the pot."

After the smashing I asked D, "you straight" then picked his hat up and gave it to him. Big D got up and walked toward Indiana.

He's said, "he'd be back",

He went to get Butch. Like I said, he was my hommie and he was straight. I wasn't going to move and he never disrespected. A man going to be what he going to be so I didn't trip on it.

He went and got Butch this time. Everybody who moved on Big D got up off the block. I stayed in the store and finished my food. Butch was getting money and he was carry weight with the Moes. Butch stayed in and out of jail so he was plugged to them upper echelon Moes.

Big D comes back with Butch walking and asking, "where those niggas at Colo?"

He had the heat with him too. I saw it on his waist. I was like, "what up Butch?" He didn't acknowledge me speaking.

He asked. "Where's Slick Freddie and them at with that bullshit?"

Like I said Butch was a Stone, but his brother dirty Red is Folks. We all came up together in school or on the block. It wasn't no smoke coming to or from Butch. It was like Big D went and got our cousin on us.

You see, before we all were gang banging we all played sports or got high together. It was unwritten, but if we knew each other before we started banging. You were still my distant cousin. It didn't matter what you was riding. It went back to who got who back.

Well Butch had D's back. Just then Aaron popped out. He dropped a couple on Big D when they moved. Butch walked over to him with the heat out. Wallop, smacked the shit out of Aaron. Aaron took the smack and faded out after he saw the heat.

Once Big D saw everybody else was gone. Him and Butch just walked back toward Indiana. Big D was really just fucking with motherfuckas. I think he got tired of being look down on by the Folks. He never really gave a reason why he flipped.

Big D still was my Folk's. He used to sell fat ass dime bags of weed. Listen to house music and go to all the house parties down town at the Box. He kept changing styles and that's why niggas were tripping. One day he was like this and one day he's like that! He was the only child so he was kind of like me, looking for guidance.

He didn't have an older big brother or father at the household. He needed someone to show him how to get through these streets. His father had gotten killed on 169th & King Drive when he was a shortie, shortie.

I never even saw a cousin come and kick it with D. He had this auntie who was on heroine bad. She would be passed out in the alley on the pole in the dungeon. She let morning catch her sometimes. We be out there trying to play ball and she's pass out on the pole.

We'd go get Big D from the crib to let him know. He would go get her and put her on his back like a feather and take her home. He was the man of the house and looked like a man at fifteen. He had no idea of how to become a man. He had a man body, but a child's brain. When Big D was thirteen he was big ass fuck. I never saw him work out, his physic was all-natural. He was Deboe for real in Chicago in 1981.

He used to practice with Darobe varsity when he was in grade school, crushing niggas. If he would've focused I know Big D would have been in the pros. He was trying to find his way. He just wouldn't go to school trying to fit in the hood.

He'd be coming down the street shouting all the way from his house, "boota, boota, boota, Colo." He used to try saying it with the Jamaican accent. "Guuuuud guuunja Colo!"

You got some papers and he'd stop and smoke one with me anytime. He kept the weed in the battery box of his boom box. Those couple of nights hanging with Big D, was cool, but I kept it moving.

I didn't let everybody know I was on the street. Most of the time I would cool out until it gets too late. Play it off like I'm bubbled. One of the Folks will end up offering me a spot at their crib for the night. They knew I had a long way to the crib or so they thought.

During this time of sparrow, I got love from my guy's mothers. I will always give them credit. They played their part and helping raising me. They will help me figure my next move out. This gave me a little time so I wouldn't make desperate decisions. I knew now I had to find a way off the streets. These parents showing me love, is helping me ward off the devil. It could've been easy for them to say, "that boy got to go", like my family did!

The wake up Call

*I*t was sort of an adventure staying with different families. I became part of my guy's families. I stayed at Lil Todd's a couple of days. Staying with these different families was getting on my nerves though! I can't even go around my own family.

I miss my family the more I was with other people families. Mrs. Stables was family anyway, but I did not feel right. I'm not standing on my own two. 'Kid make it' is on his knuckles bad. I didn't want people looking at me like the boy needs help. I didn't want to be a leach. I still had weed and I was staying in the box. Even though, I'm living on the streets.

Mrs. Bilkins Lacey mother used to always cook. You always smell the Sunday cooking when you walked down 169th St. She always had the house smelling good with food aromas. A few nights I slept in the back with Lace on the floor. Like I said I made it around the Met kicking it with everybody.

Anyway she was a mother figure to me, because it was Lace's mother. She went to the church next door to me, Evening Star Baptist Church. Every once in a while when we lived on 169th Mrs. Bilkins and my mother would have conversations. She had a bunch of boys and my mother had three. She knows my mother and knows how I was raised.

Mrs. Bilkins caught me early one morning. I had been drinking all week. I know I was in the streets hanging all week. I was in and out my car this week. I drink, but I didn't drink everyday, before I hit the streets. She comes out on the porch and looked at me with disdain. She kicked her leg out and held on the banister.

She shook her head and said, "you know Columbus I'm hearing what you are doing up and down 169th St.

I looked at her and shoot it through my brain again, "I'm hearing what you are doing up and down 169th St."

She goes on, "I expected more out of you Columbus. I know you've got very good upbringing Columbus. You know you are wrong! I know your mother didn't bring you up that way."

I said, "your right Mrs. Bilkins but…

She interrupts and says, "I can smell alcohol on you from here Columbus. It's coming through your pores and that's bad Columbus. Columbus you are going to wind up in jail or a bum like Co Co. I can see it."

I was shaking my head no and asked, "you see that, I can't see myself like Co Co the wino, Mrs. Bilkins."

Co Co wanted a quarter for his wine.

His favorite line was, "Give Co Co a quarter."

Once he got enough quarters he would go get his wine. This is while he's already scum bubbly. He'd go in the store and get another red Irish Rose. He takes the whole bottle to the skull two steps out the store.

He'd leave just a little bit left in the bottom. He'll be licking his tongue outside his mouth like aagghhhh.

After he takes the bite from the alcohol he'd say, "Can't drink the poison."

Next he'd throw the little bit that's left and the bottle in the alley right next to Bennies.

I always said, "I never wanted to be like Co Co all while I was a shortie." I used to roll by him all the time when delivering papers and he'd be terribly drunk. She hit me in the head with that one. I was mentally fucked up.

I said, "okay Mrs. Bilkins I'm going to be better."

Now here her sons are no angels. SteveO and Dave at this point are supplying the neighborhood with dope. Lace teaches me how to smoke and pick locks. She still goes to church every Sunday morning, while they bang the crib out.

No matter what they were doing she was right. She sees jail or she sees a wino. I don't even drink like that nobody ever sees me drunk. I get bubbled, but not drunk. You got to stay on your toes out here. You can't get caught slipping.

All I needed was a place to wash up and change clothes. I had to keep my pride up. I never wanted to overstay my welcome. Who want somebody telling them they got to go? I already know how it feels.

On those nights I sneak to the car and chill. Lock myself in the car for safety. Most of my night in the car ended up with me smoking a joint. I'd look up at the stars at night before I passed out. My room was small, but it was my room. On those nights I grabbed the .357 out the house on 169th and slept with it. I'd clutch the missile and pass out.

During these times I often ponder before I went to sleep. I'd talk to myself, "I am sleeping in my car that don't run. I'm in a lot next to an alley. I am at the next to lowest step in life. If I didn't have that car I would be on the street or in a hallway."

I'm still good, but I am one step away from being what I never wanted to be. That is a bum in life. At this young age and I am already a bum. It used to weigh on my back the whole day, until I laid my head down. Where was I going to sleep? I knew while I was hanging with the Folks and getting high. I knew, after it was all over I had nowhere to go, but my car. It was stressed thinking about where I was going to sleep those nights.

Emus and John had graduated and were going away to college. Even Lil Rich went to Texas. I began thinking I was failing to achieve my goals. Emus and John came to me a couple of years earlier. This is what was really at the core of helping me stop thieving.

They were like, "Colo what's up man you out here foul. Word on the street you are out here wicked."

I look, thought and spat at em, "Yeah, but this is all I got what the fuck else I'm going to do."

John looked at me and said, "Colo this ain't you I know you."

I spat at him, "well at least somebody knows me."

Emus said, "Colo you got to stop this shit it ain't looking good."

I look at both of them and ask, "are you going to fill my pockets", they didn't say anything, I then said, "well what the fuck are you talking about?" I told them I would holler and walked away.

Those words were frying me and I couldn't take it. They were right when they confronted me and I had to look at things differently. They were the only two guys on the block to talk to me like that! Everybody else was using my talents and nack for getting away with things.

Emus and John were leaving Chicago and going to Texas to college. I was happy for them, but I was depressed. My guys were leaving me behind.

I didn't even want to kick it with them. They were staying on the pathway for success. I had broken off and success didn't look like it was in my future. All I could do was fuck up what they had going.

I was bringing nothing positive to the table. I was ahead of you guys. Now they had caught up and were passing me up. Y'all went to school in August to settle in school and left me behind. I was the smart guy, but who is looking stupid? Mrs. Bilkins just sunk me deeper into depression.

I hit bottom

*J*ohnny Howard threw a party in the backyard on Vernon later on that night. His house was next to snake alley. I wouldn't go to the car, if someone were standing on Vernon. At night I would wait, until everybody was gone in the house before I jumped in the car.

I did not want anybody seeing me sleeping in the car. I had plenty much pride. A lot of guys were kicked out the crib and you could tell. When you see them they look like yesterday and day before that and so on.

You could tell they were out all night or sleeping in a hallway. The mornings I woke up in my car. I went to the laundry matt on 169th & Prairie. It opened up at six in the morning. I would go in there and move my bowels. I had my toothbrush and brushed my teeth. Next, I would wash up. I kept my clothes in the trunk. When I needed to wash I would wash my clothes.

It was a move I did on the washing machine so I didn't have to pay. When you hit it hard enough it would begin cycle. I worked that machine for years. It was a certain spot you had to hit it.

I used to have the attendant asking, "what's up with that banging noise?"

Most of the time you got to do it when a lot of people are washing. They can't hear the banging over the other machines noises.

Early in the morning though nobody washing, it's just me. I stayed clean and fresh. You couldn't tell I was out all night or slept in my car. I knew how to fold my clothes so they wouldn't be wrinkled. That was one of our chores.

My mother had the kids wash the clothes for the week. They clothes better be folded up correctly, corner to corner or we have to refold them at home. Before they open the Laundry matt up on 169th. We used to walk to the laundry matt on 171st & King drive at first.

We'd have one of those carts walking the clothes backward and forwards. A couple of times the clean clothes fell on the ground. When that happened my mother was hot. We'd have to walk home in the snow with the cart before we had a car. I knew how to wash. I'd buy some detergent and some bounce out the machine and wash.

During the day I would bounce to different neighborhood. I didn't want my guys to see me posted in one spot. I still had the matter of Reico still looming. In the morning I'm there, at night I'm here. Last week there and this week here.

When on the street you bounce from here to there so you are not a burden. Don't nobody know you are in the streets, unless you tell them. I kept a few clean outfits in the car. I changed my clothes daily so nobody knew I was bouncing. I also kept some clothes at my sister's house.

This night, life was weighing on me. I go to the party. I was sitting down not having much fun. I sat there looking while everybody was mingling. I kept looking over in the alley at my bed. My 77 Cadillac and I was thinking, "damn I didn't think it was going to be like this. I thought I would be well on my way to being famous."

I know I should be playing some sort of sport. I'm getting low on my ends. I was thinking while on security, if something breaks out, the missile is close. I kept it in the trunk when I was living in the car. At night my routine was to get the missile out the trunk. I'd look around to see if anybody was watching. Next I'd get in the back and lay across the floor. The party was going on and on!

It's about three and I want to go to bed. I'm buzzed and ready to lie down, but the party won't end. I left the party and walk to the Met. I sat on John's porch for a while hoping somebody would be out. Nobody was out.

I'm sitting there saying to myself, "this shit right here, is for the birds." It's too late to knock on my sister's door. I went back to my car after a while and everybody was gone. I get the missile jumped in the back and lay down.

I was feeling bad mentally. What Mrs. Bilkins said kept ringing through my head.

She saw my future and it read, "A bum like Co Co, a bum like, CoCo, I see jail for you Colo."

I looked up at sky and asked Yahweh. "I know this couldn't be what you got for me? I've done bad things to survive. I don't want to do these things no more. I don't know what to do."

I really didn't, I was at wits end and was looking for a way out. All my doors were closing and summer is almost over. It's going to be cold in a minute. What am I going to do when it's cold? I need a crib and a job so I don't have to worry about food and a place to stay.

I had some papers in the car. I started looking through them for some reason. I guess I was cleaning my room. I see this card from my mail. It was a recruiting for the army showing the address to the station. I said to myself, "I want be needing this." I kept the windows cracked, because it could get hot, while sleeping. The sun and the birds wouldn't let you sleep once it came up.

I would wake up drenched in sweat and I hated that! That's probably what Mrs. Bilkins smelled. I got drenched from sweat the night before from sleeping in the car. Anyway, I was trying to toss the recruitment card out the crack in the window. I couldn't do it for some reason. I tossed it about three or four times trying to get it through the crack.

It was a small crack, but with my skills. It shouldn't have taken so many times. It kept bouncing off the window and back toward me. I grabbed it again and was frustrated and was about to ball it up. I said to myself, "this motherfucka keeps bouncing back off the window back in the car."

At that moment I stopped. This is what you call an epiphany. I looked at the join the army card. I looked up at the sky and said, "this possibly couldn't be the answer Yahweh."

My whole life I always said, "I'd never join the army." I think back to the commercial, "be all you can be." I think about Jeff from Entech school who went to the service. Jeff used to tell me how much fun he had in the service. All the women he'd banged. All the places he had been. I used to tell him it sounds fun, but that shit ain't for me though!

In the Army I wouldn't have to worry about those things I was just thinking about. Jeff told me, "I get three meals a day. I get a bed to sleep in and roof over my head." I didn't have to worry about bills.

Right now I thought it just didn't seem like a bad idea. I was eating cheap. I hit Harvey Collins barbecue joint at nighttime. He had the four wings and fries with mile sauce for a dollar. I'd hit K C for one of those super tacos and fries on 171st between Calumet and King Drive. They were the greatest for a dollar fifty.

KC used to be the spot girls and the guys used to hang up at the restaurant. It was like the Happy Days Arnolds, but it was hood. We didn't have nowhere to sit down. When I didn't want to walk. I'd hit Mrs. Hugh's for the wings. She had the best wings. You had to pay for them though! She had the best shakes. Mrs. Hugh's shit was the bomb. I had to watch my pennies though! Some nights I had to walk to 171st for those wings Harvey Collins. They were four for a dollar and some fries and a piece of bread.

I rather sell dope, if I have to, for survival. I'm going to the service and just that quick, I made the decision. I can't keep doing shit like this it's going to get cold in a minute. I have nowhere to live.

I didn't want to operate from weakness. People will use you when you operate from weakness. The percentages are against me now. The probability goes up greater and greater. Every time you get away with something your probability of getting caught goes up. You got to know when to hold them. You got to know when to fold them and I fold.

Either I was going to get me a job rolling with SteveO. I knew I wasn't going to find a job I had given up on that! That was a waste of my money, but it was an experience. I knew I couldn't go that route. I'd call them periodically and all I heard, "No there's no openings Columbus. We'll call you Columbus."

How could they call me while I'm on the streets? My other option was going to the service. At least now I do have something else on the table. The boys in the hood were rolling for SteveO and he was the man. I knew personally who was holding all the dope and money on the strip.

It game was accessible to me and I knew the crew. All I had to do was go get a job. Fat Cat was working for SteveO at the time. I watched how Fat Cat came up so quick when he started selling dope. He pulled the girl at the sub spot and she was pretty.

Emus brother Coole robbed him he was getting so much money. We used to go up in Fat Cat room and get high than a motherfucka. He sold dope out the backdoor of his upstairs room.

Coole would go up there and get high with Fat Cat all the time. This one time he laid up here and stuck the heater to him. He told him to give him the dope.

Let Coole tell it he said, "Raymond didn't believe it."

He was like, "yeah right Coole sit your ass down."

Coole said, "Colo I had to let him know so I shot in the floor." Coole starts to laughing, because sometimes, he doesn't believe the shit that he does.

He said, "Smoke and gun powder filled the back room Colo. I stuck it back on him and said it again with the grim on my face. Give me the money and the dope ahha hhaa. After that Colo, Fat Cat knew I wasn't bullshitting."

He then says, "Colo Dog he was like a slot machine after that!. He got all the dope and the money for me quickly. It just like I told him before I shot in the floor, it wasn't his shit."

I said Coole that's Raymond, Fat cat.

He said, "man those niggas are from Parkway."

I say, "but it SteveO dope."

He was like, "fuck Steve he won't let me work", and started laughing, then says, shit. Fat Cat ain't one of the originals and SteveO got him rolling. Fat Cat from Parkway anyway. Steve got plenty money. He ain't worried about that shit."

Coole just stayed off the strip, until the money ran out. SteveO didn't want me to sell dope for him either. He didn't want Lacey selling dope. Lace went to school at Washburn and learn carpentry. I went down there to check that out too looking for a career.

Lace had just got married at Evening Star church to his sweetheart Donna. This was strange, because Lacey is in the church getting married. We were in the back of the church playing basketball. Lace never said a word. We come out the alley. We see Lacey and his bride coming out the church. I always wondered why didn't he tell us?

Anyway he was working good in the construction field. I had asked Lace before when we were having a session. "Lace what's up man? You're going to have to tell SteveO to put me down. Y'all video stores are opening up and I need a job. I used to come over and see mounds of cocaine and piles of money.

I don't think SteveO wanted any goons working for him. He needed people he could control. He really needed goons, because if he would've put us to work. He would have had muscle too.

Things are changing the nation has enter the drug trade. That means the Folks and the Stones will shortly start to control it. Renardo used to work for him. SteveO come up with a plan for Renardo to take a bullet.

Renardo was my lil brother's hang out partner when they were younger. He paid Renardo some thousands to say he was short. SteveO was suppose to have gotten mad and popped Renardo in the leg. It was some bullshit. This was so people would stop trying SteveO and pay him all his money.

To me he really punked himself out. I would've shot one of those niggas who were coming at me or not paying me. I know I said I wouldn't kill over somebody else's money. When it's my money, I coming for your head, because my money is part of me.

You don't give me my money you've disrespected me. Nobody gave him respect for that! He really lost more respect. He was paying for respect and not putting in work.

He had all the guns, but SteveO wasn't like that! He tried to maneuver around a situation. SteveO wasn't ready to kill to make money. He was in the wrong game because that money, breeds envy, jealous and treachery. SteveO had the money.

SteveO was so cool he'd see us sitting on the porch and buy us all drinks. He would throw Emus and us money to go get bubble. Sometimes when we were broke as shorties. We knew SteveO would be coming home at a certain time.

We were the lookout not knowing it at the time. When something happened we would see it. He was the first dope house they hit, like that hit them now. At least in our hood it was the first time I saw it. That was some new shit when they came with the battering ram to bust the door down.

John says, "yep, used to be sitting on the my porch waiting on SteveO. When Steve came home he sets it out. He probably knew that. He didn't pay us like lookouts, but we were the lookouts. When he came home for the night. We'd tell him everything that happened while he was gone.

SteveO felt he was untouchable with all that money he was making. One time the twisters rolled up on him. He had two packs of cocaine in his hand. They rolled up and looked at him. SteveO was paying the cops off so he felt invincible. They told him to come here.

Steveo looked at them and said, "fuck you."

He emptied both packs of cocaine on the fat back part of his hand.

The police looked and jumped out the car and was trying to get at him. I'm sitting on the porch with Colo. Before they got to him he tooted it all and the rest hit the ground.

StevO then asked them being real smug, "What the fuck y'all want?" They searched him and rough him up. He didn't have any more dope left so they let him go.

Yep John, I knew I would've been one of his best workers. Once they taught me the cocaine game. I was already out selling weed. I knew everybody. It was so tempting. My only thing is, I didn't like working for anybody. I often saw people who worked for others and was short on the money. It was nothing nice.

I tried to sell before for myself. It wasn't my game. I bought some of those Super Bowl specials and tried to break them down to make some money. I didn't know anything about it. I ended up tooting it all with John Lingo at his house. My game was weed. Lingo said he was going to give me half on it later.

He never gave me anything so that was a loss. I didn't even sweat it. I left his crib early in the morning after blowing through it all. I was walking home and my nose opened on one side and clog on the other.

All that fucking manitol is clogging me up. I said to myself. I blew 120 worth of cocaine in three hours. I would have never smoked up 120 worth of weed in a couple of minutes. This was a realization don't fuck with that shit. I need much more money. I didn't fuck with it any more, because financially it didn't make sense.

Weed was keeping me fed. I had me a few clothes. I didn't have to beg on the strip. Selling weed got me what I needed without busting anybody in the head. I still was getting my hair whip. I was on the line of survival mode though! It can all change in one night.

If, I got on with Steve or something I would be straight. He already had the customers. I would be off the hip, in the street or in a spot. I would be on thousands quick if I was down with him. I'd open up me a spot once I got enough to cop. Roll the spot and don't look back. I was leaning toward that plan. The only thing Mrs. Bilkens is SteveO Moms. She is the one who said it is bullshit in my future.

I saw with my own eyes how quick you can come up selling that girl. Fat Cat was shining and he was on his knuckles at first. Half the guys off my block worked for him. All of them had money Corvettes, BMW's, Run DMC dookey ropes. Niggas wasn't even thinking about stains anymore. It was too easy selling dope. They had all the best women in and out the hood. They had a whole lot of other shit that a nigga would want.

Another option was to go to the service. This is something I said I would never do. Yet, it was the best decision. Do to the fact. I was mad at my parents. I was known in the hood as a wrecker. We would go put the mash down on anybody who disrespected.

The opposition was looking for me. I heard through the grapevine people were looking for me with those thangs. The police knew me by name on the street. My reputation was too well known in the hood to be living on the streets.

I still had the magnum that I carried with me like a credit card. I kept the unit with me. Never went anywhere without it. I was carrying ten years, if caught with the Cook County Sheriff gun. I didn't even try to file it off.

There was the girl that I was living with some of the time. The one who called the police on me and tried to have me arrested. That's why I was strictly with my nigga's. They were the only people who knew, I was real. The real pressure to leave was coming from my family. I felt abandon and I'm all alone.

Here I am with this decision that's going to dictate the rest of my life. It is on the table. I didn't want to go to the service. I rather stayed and rolled. By doing that I was going to have to face all these other consequences. I was hot and I really needed to cool off.

After I weighed the probability of success. I had to go to the service. Even if I got a job with SteveO. I would still be on the streets. I still need a place to stay. I thought about it all night and could barely sleep.

The next morning I get up and said this is it. Surprisingly, I felt the same way. I cleaned myself up that morning. I caught the bus to 91st & Commercial, to the recruiting office to take the test. I was a little excited too riding up there on the shaw. I thought I found a way out. That was the first step to making my come up.

The card says 9-5 and I wanted to be the first person in the office. The army people weren't in the office and it's 10 o'clock. I sit down and wait while reading the literature. The marines weren't in their office either. The marine's recruiter came in first and saw me waiting.

It was two big brothers marines who stopped and asked while walking by, "who are you waiting on?"

I responded, "I was waiting on a army recruiter."

The marine recruiter told me to come in his office.

Once in the office he said, "I could get you set up, right away."

I was ready and anxious and told him to hook me up. I took the test and was getting set to push out with the marines. I left the office and the army recruiter still hadn't come to the office.

Slick Freddie flashed in my head. I came back home and talked to Freddie about it. I remember when he was going. Freddie was supposed to ship out. He had his date to leave and everything. He decided not to at the last moment.

He said he was about to take the oath but before he did it. He asked the sergeant was he in the army yet. He had his orders to his designation for basic training.

The sergeant was like, "yeah as soon as you finish taking the oath."

Slick Freddie said, "so right now I'm not in the army."

Recruiter says, "you are in the army, but to make it official. You got to take the oath."

Freddie said, "well I'm a change my mind. I'm not going."

The army recruiter was upset, but Freddie didn't care.

He told the recruiter. "You don't even have to take me home, I'm gone."

The recruiter said, "no the policy is we have to drop you back off."

He drove Freddie to the crib and he didn't go to the service. The man didn't say one word to Freddie all the way home. I used to see the recruiters come pick him up and take him to the Meps station.

Yeah, I better go ask Freddie what up with the Marines. Especially, since he's been through the process. I caught up with Slick Freddie on the Met. Just so happened he was sitting on John's porch when I got off the bus.

What a coincident when I see him I say, "I was looking for you guy and you're right here when I get off the bus.

He said, "what's up Colo".

I said, "I just took the test for the Marines."

He bucked his eyes and said, "you bullshitting Colo you ain't going to the Marines are you." He started shaking his head and then said, "the Marines. Nooo Colo nooo, not the Marines. My brother Marvell went to the Marines. The Marines play those mind games with you. Nigga's like us will probably snap".

"I'm telling you my brother Marvell went to the marines. You know how that nigga is now. He beat his sergeant up and got kicked out."

I said, "yeah you right." One day we were playing basketball in the alley when we were shorties. Marvell came walking by and said, "watch out little niggas."

He then jumped up on the rim and pulled it down and then took the rim to the crib. He left us shorties looking like what the fuck just happened? We didn't question him though! We just watched him walk down the alley with the rim.

Freddie asked me though, "why you want to go to the service Colo?"

He had to go get another sack. He'd just served his last bag, while I was talking to him. Freddie asked me to walk to his crib with him. We get to his crib and go down stairs. He had a couple of beers already so I fired up. Right before I was about to say something. The Big O comes down and smells the weed. The Big O is Freddies father. He was about sixty-five at the time.

He looks at me and says, "let me hit that shit Columbus, that shit smells good."

Everybody in the room starts laughing.

Y'all thought he was about to snap. I give it to him and he hit it two times.

The Big O said he was straight and kicked it for a minute then went back upstairs. After he left Freddie started hooking up the work.

After he got everything together Freddie looked up and said, "okay Colo now why are you going?"

From appearances you couldn't tell I was hurting so Freddie has no idea. I thought for a second trying to see, if I was going to unload. Up until now I've been keeping everything in and to myself. I took a big breath and said, "Freddie it's getting tight out here and I need a break. Everything is coming down on me. I don't want to leave, but I'm on bad terms with my family.

My heart and compassion for people is getting smaller and smaller. I don't fear death the more and more I was around it. The more I got used to the idea of being dead. I guess I prepared myself for it. I'm only here for a short time. That's a sign of hopelessness Freddie.

Freddie response, "Colo if that's what it is, that's what it is! You got to do what you got to do, to survive."

I said, "you right Freddie I'm going to push out." Freddie and I go get a drink and cool out the rest of the day, while he got his sack off.

Don't get me wrong I didn't want to die. I really think we here predetermined. When your clock runs out, it runs out. A lot of people are scared to live for fear of dying. I thought I was too slick to go to jail, until I got caught.

Most of the time I'm stealing from people of the struggle. I also made that deal to not do thievery things, with Yahweh.

Another reason, I knew it was wrong. I would have to pay double for it down the road. I would have to pay more than everybody else around me. I had a spiritual upbringing so even, if I did get away with it. I knew I would still pay and I would pay double. At the time I called it survival.

I was just trying to keep from starving on the strip. I rationalized what I did by saying "they ain't hurt worst than me. He can get it back." I was doing things at a lot of other people expense, because of my pride.

I knew no other way so I thought. It was plenty of other ways. I known, if shown another way or had more opportunities. I wouldn't have been doing these evil things. My situation and my young mind, couple with a nigga who thought he knew it all.

It wasn't in my makeup, but it was. My mother brought us up to appreciate other people things and have love for people. At this point in my life I think I strayed the furthest. I was no longer in touch with the some of the values and morals that my mother taught us.

I am now a product of my environment and surroundings. The good in me was overshadowed, because of my situation, environment and also a lack of knowledge. All those smarts I had in school. Now I was using or used my smarts for criminal things.

It's coming to the end of summer. I wanted to be gone before it got cold outside. I planned to be gone before the fall was over. My mother planned everything down to the last detail and this was rubbing off on me.

You got to look ahead and not get caught in the moment. The next time I went back to the recruiters. I told the marine recruiter it wasn't going to happen. Those marine mothrfuckers got so pissed off.

The sergeant was like, "what, let's do this" with a mean face.

I looked smirked and told him, "it wasn't going to happen I guess he thought he could scare me." I almost laughed but said, "I was going to join the army anyway. They just weren't in the office and you swoop up on me."

I can see frustration in their faces. They were pissed off. I had taken the test for them and already passed. The marines were ready to swoop me up. It was just one thing wrong my reading scores on the test. They were very high and the math was under average. That's how it always is when I take test. My math was always up under my reading score. Therefore, it was a discrepancy. I had to take the test over to be sure I didn't cheat.

The next time I would take the test it would be for the Army. I think the marine boot camp was twelve weeks and the army boot camp was eight. It was self-explanatory after that fact. The army pumped me up like it was going to be a breeze. I was going to be a truck driver.

I wouldn't be subjected to supervision like everyone else. You just get in your truck and go. That was one great deciding point for me. I wanted to be a truck driver and I wanted little supervision. I really didn't know what I wanted to be. I thought truck driving would be cool. It was a lot of other jobs I was eligible to do. I scored high enough that I didn't have to be a grunt.

I had to get my license first. I needed somebody with a car so I could take the test. I got Jessie off the Met. He was about thirty-five years old and he sold weed. He was an older guy who wore a beard. I used to talk to Jessie about certain things. He gave some advise on a few occasions. I used to buy all his bags then roll them up. He was cool and had a fine daughter.

Anyway he's the one who took me up to the Secretary of State. The one located on 99Th & King Drive. He had a two tone Pontiac at the time, fairly new. Everybody was trying to help get me off the block. That I appreciated Jessie just didn't know how much I did. Thank you just didn't do it to show him how much. I got my license and I was one step closer. He seemed happy to do it. I passed the test and I'm one step closer.

After I went through a series of test for the army and passed the physical. I set the date I wanted to leave which was Sept 9th 1986. My mother birthday would be a symbolic jester. Here's your birthday present, me leaving town. The only thing though! I was waiting on my police clearance and the drug test to come back.

The police clearance was another thing. My prints had to come back clean. If they came back fucked up. I am stuck, like Chuck. It could be anything I wasn't sure. I was waiting on my prints to clear, it took a couple of weeks. I had to get other paperwork in order. I needed my birth certificate with the blue seal and my high school diploma

I tried to enlist for six to eight years. I wasn't going to tell my mother or father anything. I was just going to be gone. The recruiter said, thank God, "you only can do a three years enlistment at the Mos that I chose.

It's only a two, three or four year enlistment in the service. The recruiter insured me that at the end of your original enlistment. You can reenlist for another three years, if you want too. I was like, "bet."

The only reason my mother found out I was leaving. I had to get the birth certificate with the blue seal before I left. The recruiter drove me to pick it up and that's how she found out. The recruiter was in his light green Chrysler with the army recruiter sign on the side.

She looked at me with the squinted eyes while saying, "you were going to leave without telling me anything?

I think my reply was, "what's there to tell? You don't care anyway."

My older brother had gone to the service. He made it through training, but he chapter out after that! He told me it was the worst thing in life. It was like hell on earth was how he described it. He told me he would never suggest anyone join.

I tell my Mom, "I'm just doing what I got to do to survive."

She go gets the birth certificate and that is the last time I talked to her before I left. I didn't tell my old man anything.

Leaving

I had the rest of the summer to kick it and say good-bye on the strip. I was set to go. I got me a sack and a few dollars in my pocket. I just got to ride this out. I wasn't as desperate mentally from one day to the next anymore.

This lifted the boulder I was carrying on my shoulders. There was an expected end to this type of living. I knew, if I could keep out of trouble, I could turn things around. I still had the pistol. Since I wasn't doing anymore stain I needed to sell it, but I was reluctant to sell it.

I felt I had to sell it to make sure I didn't do anything stupid. I don't need anything to hold me back. I can't get caught with it especially since it's a Cook County Sheriffs gun. That was a felony by itself, so that's two felonies; it's already one felony for carrying the gun. I didn't want to sell it to nobody who knew me.

Someone might want to use it or anything. I just got to get rid of it. They get caught now their facing ten years. Now the question for him from the police is where did you get the gun? I know where the gun came from too. I couldn't have the gun come back on me. It was stolen out of a police officer's house.

I ended up selling it to Eddie the Arabic guy who owned the submarine shop on 169th St. He gives me two hundred and owed me two hundred. That was cool! I don't want to blow all my money anyway. He said he'd give me a hundred dollars next week. He'd give me another hundred a week after that.

Eddie wasn't going to fuck me he was probably the coolest Arab I knew. He knew that wasn't the only gun on the street too. I told him though, "Eddie don't bullshit with my money I know how y'all get down." I sold him the gun with no bullets.

I also got a few scribbles coming from my car. Folks owe's me scratch. He already gave me a hundred dollars. Every time Folks saw me on the strip. He said he was going to pay, but didn't. That was playing out real quick. He kept apologizing over and over again. He knew he was just one wrong word away from getting fucked up. I knew he was struggling though!

I was mad at Grimes, because he gave my man the car. I wasn't fucking with him much after that move. I am off to the service, because of that move. Everything transpired, because of that car.

I got kick out, because I didn't have the car. I wouldn't have taken my Mom's car, if I had mine. I wouldn't have got accused of stealing. I got accused of stealing from two different people, cause I didn't have that car. My old dude and Dorus shut the front door.

None of this would have taken place. This nigga takes my car and smashed it. Now I'm living in the car. I made the decision to go to the service in that car. That 1972 Cadillac changed my life. I only had it for three months. I realized that I had to sell the car anyway when I left or give it to Grimes. Everything happened, because the car didn't move anymore. That car played a major part in my decision.

I was going to give it to Grimes anyway. I fucked him over with his Mustang and I cost him $2500 for his lawyer. When I knew I was going to join the service I was giving the car to Grimes?

He always let me ride his cars. Grimes always kept a car. Not for long, but he always kept a car. The Folks used to be in Grimes car creating havoc. His cars either got smashed or confiscated by the police or something to that effect.

Scott German

*N*ow I feel little better, but I still have no home. I hooked up with Scott German. I chill with the Germans family the rest of the way. The German's always took in the people who were living on the street. They took in Big D, Otis and now me.

Their house had just burnt down too. They were living across the street in a garage like house. They were on hard times, but still they welcome me. They knew I was on hard times. They took me in until I went off for the service.

Since the German's house caught on fire. Scott and I had that in common. We knew how it felt for your shit to go up in smoke.

Of course sometimes I still stayed with other people. I mostly kicked it with Scott German the rest of the way. The German family showed me love. They were known to be one of the most scandalous families in the neighborhood.

Andrea, the Germans showed up for fights twelve deep. It was bunch of brothers and if you fucked up and the Germans you had a problem. It was my suggestion you leave town, because when they catch you, it was nothing nice. They'll try out shit they seen on TV. They'd try new fuck things on you, to see if it would work.

Their family had all types of gadgets and weapons to fuck you up. They'd order bow and arrows, a blowgun or a guillotine. What is a nigga doing with a guillotine? They just had all type of shit to fuck you up, but legal. You ordered it out of the back of those weapon magazines and they would order that shit. Scott and I were cool at first, but we didn't hang.

Scott was notorious for kicking something off. Scott had a real flaky temper and I didn't want to clash with him. A few years back we were in the dungeon playing one on one. He got mad cause he was losing. Rome started getting aggressive, but I wrestled him down and held him. I didn't throw any blows. Once he calmed down I let him up.

He got up and said, "okay he'd be back."

I said to myself, "aw shit, I knew I shouldn't have played him." I just watched him as he walked down the alley home, while bouncing the ball. I didn't leave the court I just kept practicing, wasn't any use of running. They were going to catch me anyway. I might as well face the music.

Just like I knew, here he comes with Ramont back down the alley. It's only two of them Ramont was the older brother next in age.

Once he got down the alley I told Ramont, "look I didn't touch him. I was just stopping him from getting on me. I put him in a wrestling hole. I wasn't trying to fight him, but he ain't going to beast me."

Ramont was diplomatic and told Scott, "let's go he ain't trying to fight you."

Scott is the same guy a couple years later. He's over Lil Tone house messing with the rifle Tone stepfather, Love had. He accidentally popped Mook in the chest when he was fifteen.

At least that's what Mook said, "it was an accident".

You know Mook was a Stone so that could have played a factor. Once he lived he had to say it was an accident or move out the hood. I knew, if we got into with Scott. The whole family was coming down on you.

Don't get me wrong Scott would get the best of a motherfucka. He definitely could fight. He'd still come down with his brothers after whooping your ass. Before, we'd kick it, if we had a bubble session. We'd kick it when we had to move out on somebody.

We just didn't hang out together after that incident. I used to ring his bell to come out and play when we were ten and eleven. I went in his basement before the fire to play when we shorties a couple of times. After that move he did I wasn't going to ring his bell anymore. We had another confrontation when I was living with Grimes.

Grimes bought a pizza that was delivered to the crib. We were busting it up. We had an equal amount of slices. Scott and I already had finished ours. Grimes said he was straight and one of us could have the last pizza.

I hurried up and snatched the pizza up and ate it, before he could get to it. While he I was eating it I could see him burning. I was smiling eating the pizza cause I got it first. It wasn't enough to split.

Scott got pissed off and said, "yeah your ass laughing I'm going to shoot your ass".

I laughed at him while still chewing the pizza and this infuriated him more. Scott knows he can't handle the knuckles head up.

He walks out the crib and said, "do not to walk through the gangway nigga, now laugh at that".

Grimes shout at him while he was leaving, "cool out it was my pizza how you going to shoot him over my pizza?"

Scott look back at me and reiterated, "don't walk through the gangway", and walk down the steps.

Grimes was laughing and said, "Colo Dog you know you hurt his feelings and you know how sensitive he is, I hope he calms down cause he's going to shoot your ass.

I didn't say nothing I just grabbed my banger. Of course I walked through the gangway, but he wasn't out there to my surprise. I was peeking to see was he camped out somewhere lurking. I was walking slow as hell watching anything that moved. I know he'll shoot your ass. I was betting he had more love for me than that! Oh I was nervous, but if it's going down, it's going down.

During my time of need though! The person you least expected to show love. Scott showed me some love. If nobody else knew, I know Scott have some heart. If he ate I ate and vice versa. Since Scott was showing me some love the rest of his brothers did too. I will never forget that. They would bring us both something to eat.

Eric German used to show me how to reverse holes to get out of when fighting. Kenny German was always laid back and kool. Ramont was the quiet before the storm. He had to be the meanest of all his brothers, but he was cool. He'd talk to you in a low tone and fuck you up. You know how people got to get, loud to get amped up.

Ramont never got loud he just got busy. You didn't want to be on Ramont's bad side. These were the brothers close to my age and they were the most scandalous. When I was hanging with Scott I got to know all his older brothers. The older brother were June, Willie and Johnny.

Everybody knew Mike German he drank, but he was a goon. His younger brothers were Sickma and Marvin. I know I missed a couple of his brother's names. He had some sisters too. This was the crossroads of my brief life.

I believe the closer and closer I got to straighten myself out mentally. The more shit was coming my way. The more obstacles I had to hurdle to get back. It was nothing but love at the Germans in that tiny shack. We were striving for a come up.

I would be up thinking at night about my struggle when everybody fell asleep. I was along for the ride and got an auto thief case. I beat it, but it taught me a lesson. It is still on my record and can be used against me. If I catch another auto case they will use it against me. They'll bring it up at sentencing or something.

People are looking for me to kill me. The police are asking around about me. Yeah one day I am in Eddie sub spot on Calumet, eating a sub.

This lone police jumped out his squad car and walks in the sub joint.

He looked around then asked. Does anybody know Colo Dog?

I look up at the officer and answered, "no."

The police asked me my name. I said, "my name is Columbus Cody."

After that he turned around and walked out. I could barely eat my sandwich after that. What does he want with me? My prints cleared so I am straight with the law so I thought. The prints hadn't came back yet, but if they were bold. The recruiter would tell me immediately. I haven't did anything but is something catching up with me.

The process stops immediately if your prints are bold. I wondered did Dorus press charges on me? My car was still stuck in the alley and sometimes I would give Scott a break. You can't just be leaching all the time.

All my clothes and shoes were in the trunk. I still was fresh I got up in the morning and went to my trunk. It could've been very easy to lose my focus. The roof Scott and his family provided had a wood burning stove in it.

At night we would keep the fire going so we could stay warm. We'd wake up shivering and have to find wood to keep it going. Scott loved him some Charade. I would be listening to Charde and looking into the fire. He would play 'Smooth Operator' all the time.

It was getting cold at night and my thoughts would wonder. I was sleeping sitting up on the couch. It was only a one-room house. It had one couch and a hammock to rest on. Willie would come in late and sleep.

Scott and I would share the couch. I got an arm and he had an arm and that's how we slept, sitting up. I'd say to myself, "Kid Make It" got to leave and come back on something else. This is cool, but my struggle is so great at this point. I need a come up.

I sweated my man who crashed my car for that $200 before I left. He didn't have the money for a couple of more weeks and my pockets are empty. That's not good for my man. I had to turn the pressure up. I popped up on him walking down the nine.

I don't even give him no love I just begin talking. Dude I got to have my cheese. You got me out here starving. I don't got no car and I'm walking. He senses he doesn't have much longer. He tells me to come by and get his VCR, that's all he got.

I asked, "does it work?"

He said, "yeah."

I tell him, "if I sell it your ticket is clear." We walked to his house so I could get it immediately. We go upstairs inside his crib. He plugged it up and that bitch worked. I immediately got happy. I saw his little brothers were chilling watching a movie on TV. That is until they saw him unhooking the VCR and giving it to me. They looked kind of sad.

I tucked that bitch under my arm and left. I feel for you shorties, but I got to have this! I take it down the street and goes over Slick Freddie house to see, if they needed one.

I left it with Freddie, until I got a sell. I couldn't be walking up and down the street with it.

He said, "my brother Bird was looking for one, but he wasn't around at the time."

I asked Lando and Steve and they said they were straight. These were the niggas getting money on the block. They already had too many VCR's.

I caught up with Bird and he said he would buy it. We go back to his crib and he hooked it up. It had a tape in it already. I told him two hundred and Bird said one fifty. I said sold.

I felt much better with a Franklin and a half in my pocket. I went right to Eddie submarine and got me a big sub combo with double meat sandwich with fries and a pop. Oh how it feels to go get something you want to eat.

The date is August the 15th and I got three more weeks to hold out. Everybody I saw I told them I was leaving. All the Folks celebrated with me, with free get highs. I told them I was leaving in a week, but really it would be three weeks. They would see me the next week and the same thing. I said they pushed it back a week so I got another week to kick it. The next week they saw me.

Folk's was like, "Folks you ain't going to the army."

Some of the Folks began to wonder, if I was going. I assured them I was going and it was a major party. I won't be back for three years. I told them that so Folks would get me fucked up, all up until the day I left. I won't be able to get high throughout boot camp.

I had to handle some things that was coming my way. It seems as, if the White building niggas were still pissed at me. That's what I'm hearing on the streets. They're pissed, because of the move I did for Boe Boe.

Tracy and Ronald was the Moes calling it over at the building. Word on the street is these niggas been asking question. Riding through with heat looking for me. It could've been Reico. It could've been anybody. We were doing or did treacherous shit on the strip.

Now the word is coming from a few guys, neutrons and the Folks. I took it serious. The next day I meet all the Folks up at the park and the subject comes up.

Someone asked me, "What about Tracy and Ronald, Colo?"

Now we up there about thirty deep.

I said, "if they're looking for me I'm a get them before I go to the service. I don't want motherfuckas to think I'm running or scared. I'll handle my business and get out of town. Y'all won't have to worry about them no more. I'll kill them myself." I sold my heat, but Folks in the hood had plenty of heat.

No sooner than I said that guess who is walking up to the park? Yahweh works in mysterious ways.

I look up and see these niggas and say, "there's Tracy and Ronald, what balls these niggas got."

It was a few Folks who turned Moes on 171st. Corey, Chip, Hubbard, Kevin Stroles and Big Brian all flip Stones. They were with Pookie and Norm. Pookie and Norm could ball their ass off too.

I played against them all the time in the park. I ain't got no smoke for these guys. All these guys I grew up with in the hood-playing ball. This was before either of us were plugged, so we were all cool.

I guess they came to plug with them at the wrong time. This was the wrong day to do that! It wasn't a Stone in sight. They come all the way in the park after they saw us.

Folks was like, "we going to smash em."

I said, "hold on, lets see what's up with my situation." Niggas will say anything to kick shit off. They'll have you wide open, using you as a tool. You can't get froggy, unless you know the whole hookup.

I jumped up off the bench after they got so far in the park. I walk and met them halfway. Folks put them in a 360 and I walked around to get in front of them and I say, "Tracy word on the street y'all looking to kill me."

He replied, "Were not trying to fuck with you, who said that? You think we would be walking in here like this and that's on the table."

I didn't believe him at first. Folks got them totally in a 360 and I'm talking to them in the middle of the circle. Folks are looking anxious to move. All they need is the word.

Ronald said, "if we wanted to get you. You would have been got already."

I said, "oh really!"

He replied, "We used to see you everyday at the L going to work on 187Th & State and coming home.

I did have a job for a while at Burger King. They knew where I worked. The Moes used to be on 187ᵀʰ ST. We're not looking for you, cause we could've got you plenty of times. They knew my moves and didn't move on me.

I told the Folks encircling us, "Tracy was right. I used to see the Moes up there and walk right by them. I had my heat though, but they didn't want no smoke."

I thought for a second and didn't access the demon. A few seconds earlier, I was thinking about smoking them. If I didn't see them that day, I'd have activated my killing demon on these niggas. That was the word. They were riding around with the heat looking for me. They got to go regardless, if I'm going to the service or not.

It's funny how the Yahweh works. I can put this behind me now and leave respectfully.

I agreed with them, "your right Tracey, Folks let them go."

Folks responds, "Folks these niggas lying, "Folk them….,

I calm everybody down by saying. "They told the truth on one part for sure Folks. They knew my M O. I saw at least two or three of them at the L every time I went to work." I told both of them to gone and get out of here. They walked out the park no smashing.

We up at the park about thirty deep. These niggas had to be shaking in their boots, but they didn't show it. I felt good letting them go. Right then, their lives were in my hand. It was the right thing to do, let them go. They let me go when they had the ups. Had it been Dave, they probably would be dead or severely fucked up.

I still wouldn't have moved. I wouldn't have activated in front of a park full of motherfuckas. I just didn't need any cases before I get out of here. My plan was different anyway on how I was going to handle it. It would have been, solo dipped by myself. Handle my function and leave town. You don't need a gang of motherfuckas to kill a couple of people.

Don't think for a minute, I believed Tracy and Ronald in the park. Obviously I was under surveillance, but they didn't move. I returned the favor. It will come out soon, if they are looking for me. All Tracy and Ronald can say about me now is I saved their asses.

Go back to the Moes and tell them that! Now the question is why is the police looking for me? Now I started to sweat, because if they're looking for me, my clearance is bold. I won't be going to the service, until I handle whatever needs to be handled.

People in the hood told me the police was looking for me too. I haven't any idea what they want me for, could be a lot of shit. I got to get out of here cause who knows. These nigga's on the street and the poe poes are looking for me. It must be Reico who is looking for me. I don't have any real beef with anybody else.

The Devil is Working

I had a couple of more days left. Back at the crib Scott and I was getting blasted. We were running through the little cheese I had, having fun. I was bubbly, but not drunk. We come out to kick it on the nine. Guess who we run into my old nemesis Big Ronald?

Ronald sees us and shouts from across the street. "What's up Scott, what you doing with this pussy?"

He just totally disrespected me. Scott, Ronald and John Lingo used to hang out couple of years earlier. I look at him and squint my eyes. I couldn't believe the words that were coming out of his mouth.

I hit him with, "you big pussy, you the pussy, hoe ass nigga." He could tell I was bubbling, because I slurred. He jumped on the opportunity.

He looked at me bubbled and then said, "shut the fuck up".

He knew he had me bubble, next he said, "shut the fuck up before I slap the shit out of you."

I look laughed and said, "you feel froggish, well slap the shit out of me and we got the slap boxing."

I was off, at a time when I needed to be on. I could get em, but I had to be on point. Now Ronald is 6'5" with an ugly reach. I could go at somebody else a little bubbly, but not Ronald. Ronald was too tall and too big at the time. We hadn't got into for about four years. Now he is really big. He was too big for me to be bubbling and slap boxing.

Even though I felt I lost our last encounter. I sent Ronald home with blows to the face. I struck him with my knuckles across the dome. He had some knots or something from the fight. He didn't dominate and I was winning at first. He won cause I couldn't continue. He was big when we were shorties, but now, he's really big.

I admit this day he did damage. Ronald is the only nigga who would've tried me. He didn't come on the nine all the time cause he off of 171st. That day he was talking mad shit. We square up and were slap boxing. Big Ronald damn near slap me to the ground from the force.

I tried to stick in there, but I couldn't get out the way. He was slapping the shit out of me. This is the reason why I never got too bubble. A motherfucka will take advantage of you.

Ronald talked bad once he knew he had the ups. "Get your hoe ass away from me for I fuck you up for real."

He was showing off for Scott. I couldn't fuck with him that day. He didn't get no real good slaps in, but I was bubbled. I couldn't keep my balance. He'd swing and I would roll with it and damn near fall down. I looked at Scott and gave him the eye. That means lets smashed this nigga!

Scott shook me off, "come on let's go Colo" then told Ronald, "you got him Ronald he's too bubbled today".

Ronald broke off talking shit. "Yeah get that pussy before I hurt him."

We walked away and Scott said, "naw Colo he just got you and he's Folks."

Look who is using morality Scott German. As we walked away I couldn't believe that Scott wasn't ready to move. He was right though! I just couldn't take all that shit talking Ronald was doing. He was real disrespectful to a nigga of my caliber. I still didn't forget he fucked my shoulder up and he doesn't even know it. I wished so so bad I wasn't bubbled at that moment. I was waiting for him to come at me for years. He did and I was too bubbly.

We had history Scott didn't know about. That day, if it wasn't for Scott. I would have been on some devious shit. I would've activated that demon in me. I was tired of Ronald and wanted to do him bad. I was just waiting on our next encounter. Ronald just didn't know it. I was waiting for him and he caught me bad.

I was glad Scott was there, because his missile wasn't far. I kept it in the basement of our burnt up house. I don't think I would've taken it that far. I did want to smash his ass. I sucked it up though! I lost. Before I ship off my record is 36 2- 1 in slap boxing.

Hubert Berry and I was about a tie, but that was before the lessons and high school. I really ain't counting anything, until I made it to high school. That was like amateur ranking at Rock Manor.

I do remember Hubert being formidable when we boxed head up in the alley. He called me out. I would say that was a tie he did surprise me with his skills. Ronald gave me my first loss in a fight. This is the first time I lost slap boxing. A lost is a lost even though I was bubbly. My last two losses come from this nigga four years apart!

I shouldn't have been boxing in that condition. I got called out bubbled that's why I was boxing. When you out here in these streets you got to be on your toes. Ronald caught me slipping and took advantage. I never back down from any challenges, especially Big Ronald. I got to focus on getting the fuck out of here. Big Ronald was trying to activate my demon. Scott was there to usher the love back in me. The treacherous feeling I had faded away.

Bossman

*I*t got around the hood quick, about what Ronald did to me slap boxing. At first I wasn't getting any challenges slap boxing. After Ronald got me Bossman wanted to go. At first he never wanted to go with me. He was a three-athlete guy. He played all three major sports like we did.

When we played Michigan he would play on Walter Readus team. Walter was the second string tailback for Metro. When we played against them in basketball it was always him, Reese and Steve Glover. It was he and Reese in baseball. The last time I played up at Brownell against Boss. I put Boss shit three stories up on top of Grime's building.

Boss was no joke he was a very aggressive guy. He stabbed a guy up at Meneen on the court for fucking with him. He told the dude to leave him a lone. The next day he came back with a knife. Dude started that same bullshit and Boss almost killed the dude.

Boss was Folks, but he was low-key back in the day. We were wide open and could be seen from a distant. You had to talk to Boss to know he was Folks. His head was too big to wear baseball hats so he didn't represent that way.

He hung out with Reese who was a descendant from Jeff Fort. That's right Reese who played second base and pitched for the Cardinals when we played. That's how Boss probably found out Ronald told Reese and Boss.

Anyway Boss catches me walking up 169th going toward Bennies on Indiana.

He finally said, "come on Colo let's slapbox."

I was surprised and said, "what you finally ready?" We square up and I was so anxious to get that loss out of my mind. I was going to take it out on Boss.

I was aggressive and fainted one time and swung with the right hand. He swung with the right hand. We smack each other hard as hell, Yaaak, Yaaak. I slapped him a little harder and was on him.

All of a sudden Boss said, "hold up Folks your nose is bleeding."

He started laughing while saying it. I then notice a couple of trickles of blood hitting the ground.

I looked and said, "it don't mean shit come on."

He was like, "naw Folks it's over you bleeding."

He didn't want to go anymore. I'm not used to getting touched this is humbling. Boss and I got to kicking it once I saw he didn't want to go anymore.

He asked me, "you heard what happen to Walter Readus?"

I was like what happen?

Boss said, "somebody killed him the other day."

I couldn't believe it. If you knew Walter Readus he didn't fuck with anybody. He was cool as hell. I asked Boss, "what they hit him for Boss?"

Boss said, "I think it was about some counterfeiting."

That's when the light bulb went off. Counterfeiting I told Boss. "Walter used to have a wad of money. Hundreds and fifties stacked up ugly."

"He would come to the store on King Drive buying little shit and busting hundreds. He'd bust a hundred just getting a bag of chips and some candy. He asked me to bust one for him outside the store and I did. I asked him, "why don't you just do it yourself?"

He played me off and I did it for him. I bought some chips and a pop and gave him the change. He didn't give me anything and had all that money. I didn't think anything of it. He was only seventeen years old. This is a dude who was a nice guy. He was nice guy up at Metro, didn't bother people.

What it was he got caught passing bills and had a court date. The Feds want to know where he got the bills. The guys he was messing with didn't let him make it to court. Walter was in a game too big for his britches. RIP

Gooch

Before I left, I kicked it with all the Folks who was major. All the Folks were glad I was getting out of here. The Folks in the hood that wasn't in our circle, didn't approve of my behavior on 169th. We were 100, but we did enter love before gangbanging at first. We weren't totally brainwashed into believing, because he wore red that's my enemy.

No I got roots with this guy and it should make a difference what he is riding. His mother fed me before at her table. Back off of dude he is family. I was respected throughout the land. All I had to do was put that respect with some money and I would have control shit. If you're not respected your money ain't no good. You got to work through someone who is respected.

Some of the Folks were so happy I was getting off the streets. That's one thing about it you can do things just for a moment in your life. Once it gets around, people tolerate you, but they don't approve. We were scandalous for a couple of years and the cocaine game was ripe for the taking.

When you try to change people are skeptical. When I made this move it was unexpected and they were proud of me. It also opened up or left a power vacuum that I didn't think about.

I had the power to squash beef in the street, because I knew everybody. I could go to table and speak up on someone behalf. I also could call upon an army. SteveO couldn't see that he was in a more of a 70's hustler. Things changed and the goons would be in control.

Gooch was one of the goons who took over! He and I got bubbled before I left. He was one of my nemesis back in the day too. He cooled out once I made it to goon status. When I was a neutron Gooch would try me at school, in the park, walking down the street. He would just try a motherfucka. Sometimes he was cool and sometimes he wasn't.

By the time we got to summer school we were cool. Gooch couldn't help it. He started shit with everybody. I stayed out of Gooch way, because I knew he was a major shit starter. When we were shorties, if Gooch saw me at the park he'd fuck with me. He'd just say some shit that challenged your heart. You had to play him, off because he was plugged in grammar school.

I am plugged now and not only that I was considered a tough guy. I can't walk away from shit anymore. I don't care who it is, it's niggas watching for any chink they can exploit.

People will say, "Oh that nigga is tough until wooo woo come around. When he's around dude is a big o pusssy."

Now that I'am plugged I can't back down to or in front of anybody. I couldn't do it when I wasn't plugged. My skills dictate that I don't have to take no shit. My heart has developed to a high level of confidence, against anybody.

Gooch and I had battles over the years. When we played basketball one on one and Gooch started losing. He'd start elbowing and playing dirty. I just started elbowing and playing dirty back. The game wasn't about basketball anymore. It was who could get off the quickest elbow. This is while you acting like you playing basketball.

After the game he knew I was no mark and I won the game. Gooch always hung out with the older BDs. He hung with first generation Folks and he was a shortie. He had a lot of respect and he'd move with the quickness.

He tested my resilience one more time. I was in the game room the one across the street from Mr. Reef's game room. The dude with the one leg from Nam opened that one up. I was playing Galga and I was a master at Galga. Emus was in there playing something else.

I had about twelve ships and was going hard. Gooch and Boya came in the game room.

He looked and said, "damn Folks you got a bunch of ships."

Gooch then kept bumping me and fucking up my ships talking about, "let me get a man Folks."

He's trying to beast my game cause he wanted to play.

He messed up about three ships and I said, "cool out Gooch." I can get those ships back, if he cools out. I tell him again, "cool out Gooch", with the grim look. He just laughed and turned it up. He started elbowing me on the game. I had a double ship on the bonus stage and both of them got hit. I look at the explosion like it was a real ship and got hot.

I stop playing the game and grabbed Gooch by his throat and walked him ten feet back and slammed him on the wall.

The dude with the one leg said, "take that shit outside."

I replied, "fuck yeah, lets go out side Gooch."

I run out the game room and jumped in my stance and shouts. "Let's go Gooch", right on 169th &King Drive. I was tired of Gooch years of testing me and was ready. We were sophomores at the time.

Boya walked out the game room and looked at us.

He got in the middles of us and said, "cool out Folks. Y'all shouldn't be fighting and y'all know it."

I said, "fuck that Gooch I'm tired of this nigga tripping."

Boya was like, "Folks it was just a game."

I replied, "it more than a game, it the principle." Gooch had a grin on his face, but wasn't aggressive.

Gooch was like, "cool out Folks it ain't shit."

Emus was like, "yeah come on Colo let's go."

I walked away with Emus. Ever since then Gooch and I were cool as a fan. That's one thing about Gooch. He was trying to see, if you were a mark.

If you were a mark you were going to get played like a mark. After the altercation Gooch had plenty much love for me. I stayed at his house too when I was on the street. The time when my house burnt down.

I'm real cool with Marge, that his mother. A lot of people mother's knew me, because I was their paperboy. They felt my pain when my house burnt down. They knew I had been working ever since I was a kid.

Gooch played football for the Robe so he was in a different crowd. He was cold on that corner for the Robe. I used to go to the football games and I was proud of him. The only reason I went was, because Bob was starting on the corner. He was off the Met and he was shining that game.

I kind of envied him cause I wanted to be out on that field for the Robe. That was the last game I went to my sophomore year. I couldn't take it, it hurt my soul, not to be on that field. He had an outstanding hit in the game that was a game changer. We won the game and you know fucking with the Robe, it's going to be a fight after the game.

Emus and John knows Robeson was the most scandalous school in the Chicago Pubic Schools.

Emus and John say in unisome, "yeah the Robe was rough."

On the way back home from the game Slept Rock and I was catching the bus back. It was like a riot. If you wasn't from the Robe, you was getting whoop. When you had on any of your school colors, it was nasty for you.

Literally, people were getting thrown out the window of the bus. They were getting smashed off the bus. The bus would be super crowded and driver kept moving. Student were getting smashed just trying to get on the bus.

Slept Rock and I didn't move. We just peeped and tripped on everything that happened. I was thirteen years old going through urban warfare. I ain't going to lie the shit was scary. I had my mask on though! I looked like a nigga you shouldn't fuck with.

Gooch and Myron were hommies, you remember Myron they used to hang all the time.

Myron was so cool it was a shame. He was so cool that his name should've been synonymous with cool. Gooch and Myron hung everyday. They used to wear those trench coats back in the day. Gooch did him bad in the park.

Word on the street Myron got on that Rachi dope real bad. I don't know if this true, but I do know this is true. Gooch thought Myron stole the VCR out his crib. He was telling me about it while we were just sitting in the swings at Iron Park.

He had been looking for Myron for a couple of days. We were in the park just cooling and here comes Myron strolling in from the 171st St. side. Gooch saw him and went unmerciful on him. Bang Bing Booom boom bang boom just dropping haymakers.

Myron didn't even really fight back. I know Myron could fight. It's only one or two reasons you don't fight. You scared or you were wrong, could be both.

He just kept saying, "Gooch you know I wouldn't steal Marge VCR."

Gooch didn't want to hear it. He ripped his clothes off and took his food and just did him bad. Yeah that dope is a bad motherfucka, if it makes you cross Gooch.

Marge knew I was a good kid gone terribly bad. The day when we picked Gooch up for graduation day, she was proud of me.

She was like, "Columbus you walking too."

His mother was a teacher and she could sense children. Everybody knew after my house burnt down I went down hill. I was a victim of my circumstance.

I only stayed a couple of days, because it was his brother, his sister Crystal, Lil Rich. I felt funny eating food that they would normally eat. Gooch broke bread with me in my time of need and that's love.

I had a ball kicking it with them though! Gooch was on his way to Marine Valley to play football. Both he and Slick Freddie were going to college to get down. It felt weird not even contemplating playing ball, but that's life.

I see Gooch walking down the nine though!

He was like, "Folks I heard you were going to the service."

I said, "yeah Gooch I'm going. I'm leaving in a couple of days."

He then says, "let get a session."

We go gets a gin and some weed and cool out. Creep was with Gooch at the time. We get back from the store and chill on my old porch on 169th drinking. Out of nowhere these two niggas walked up that we didn't know. The guy who got to us first asked a question and then quickly pulled the missile out.

His boy was standing behind him and he pulled one out too. The other dude was standing a few feet back with the unit so he could see everything.

They looked to me to be some dope feigns. Young dope feigns couldn't have been that much older than us. They had an ashy look on them. I still remember his face. This is a sign, that gives the dope feigns away the ashy look. We were caught in the middle of the girl and the boy.

That girl and that dog food were the main drugs of choice for attics. I still never considered weed drugs. The drugs the government hit us with in our era knocked us down. It was too much love in the eighties they had to do something.

After dropping that dope and those guns, the love deteriorated. The prerequisite to the heroine was syrup. A lot of teenagers were drinking syrup. You get a bean or pill with it. I guess it amplified the effect.

I couldn't do it because you'd be nodding wherever you were. When you're on the bus stop. You're on the bus stop nodding. You're outside kicking on the street, but you nodding.

Why come outside, if you're going to be sleep? This is no position for a stud who has people looking for him. The next level was that Karachi or the China white. Big and Lando were the only ones I knew on the Met who tooted dope besides Rodell.

It was a movie I seen when I was at Rock Manor in the fifth grade. They showed us a movie, about the end to a dope feign. The needle would be still hanging from the arm. A belt wrapped around the arm. Sores were all over the body and ankles swollen up. Track marks would be up and down the arm like a trail of ants. Once the dope enters the blood stream, is when their body goes limp. When they throw up it's good dope.

They'll erupt from the belly and say, "oh that some good dope."

They were scratching when they feel good. Most of the time was spent in the bathroom on the floor, if you were gone of the needle. What type of life is that?

This is what a dope feign look like to me. It's like their body is possessed. This got to be how your soul gets sucked out your body. Your extremity swells up and your skin turns dark in places. Under your eyes and your hands are dark and swollen. Your ankles look like their going to bust and looks full of dirty water.

The only way you get through your day is to wake up to the dope. When your gone bad and can't get up. Somebody got to feed you or you'll lay there hurting all day. Now just think, if you are a young goon and you get sick. This is a deadly concoction.

Anyway, "the dope feign say, "I got to have it all. Take y'all gold off and empty y'all pockets."

They must have peeped us, parked and walked up. Creep took his off immediately and gave it to dude. After he got Creep shit, Gooch acted like he was pulling his off.

When he raised his hand up to his neck reaching for the clasp to take the ropes off. He raised up with the gin of bottle, still in his hand. Dude with the heat looked at me for a second to see what I had. Gooch then swung with lightning speed and smashed the bottle and busted it across dude's face, splattTT.

When Gooch did that, he broke out down 169th St. toward King Drive. He figured like I figured the other dude was going to start blasting. The dude who got smacked with the bottle didn't bust immediately. He just backed up dazed with the missile out. He got hit across the forehead and the liquor burning the shit out of his eyes.

He was stunned and kept staggering backwards. I know his shit was gashed. He was still trying to get a bead on Gooch. He was looking to see where Gooch was while wiping the drank out of his eyes.

Creep and I broke to the alley when Bob got in the wind. I'm watching my back as I get in the wind. Dude was shaking his head left to right trying to get it together. We could've gotten on him, but his boy drew down, pointed, but didn't shoot.

Creep was hauling ass and said, "he was gone" and floated away. I haven't seen him since that day.

I was still in the alley peeking at my assailant's direction. I was peeking, but he couldn't see me. I was watching dude as soon as he started clear his vision he unloaded. His boy was standing next to him but didn't bust.

This whole thing happened in less than four seconds. He shook his head, cleared his eyes and then Pop pop pop pop pop. I heard the first pop then I tore ass up out of there and hit a gangway. That's what Gooch should've done and he would've been gone.

He headed down the nine and should've dipped. I didn't see what happened to Gooch, but he got hit. It was also a man sitting in a car that just missed getting hit. He was chilling and the bullet went through his headrest just missing his head.

Gooch was hit, but kept running and when he got to 169th & King Drive, collapsed. Just so happen his brother Rob was driving down King Drive saw Gooch fallout. Rob picked him up and took him to the hospital. This how quick it can happen in the Chi in broad day light. Dude is on our strip trying to rob us. Now that took balls. They had to be dope feigns.

Gooch really had balls to do that move, but it almost got him killed. This went down right before my eyes. Gooch is definitely no hoe. He got to the hospital and they took a .357 slug out of his back.

I was thinking to myself, "yeah its time to go. Shit goes down quick and it changes second to second. You got to pay attention to indicators. Your indicators will answer questions for you. You just don't know and your life changes for the rest of your life, in a split second."

I was eighteen at the time and was a straight goon. At this time you couldn't have bet me a million dollars. That a nigga would come down the nine and raise up on Gooch and I. It had to be random, because if they knew who we were. They wouldn't have done that!

That's one thing about dope feigns. That dope sick will make you activate your killer button. They gots to get that, sick off. You wouldn't have tried some guys like us in your regular mind. You would've aborted that mission by just looking at us.

Yeah it was time to go and you have to pay attention. This is an indicator to me that confirmed my decision. Gooch got hit and it could've been me on my own porch. It was burnt down but it was still my porch. It happened on my porch in broad daylight, it's really getting wild out here.

Gooch was already a legend, but this made him legendary.

He told me once I saw him again. "Folks I wasn't letting no marks rob us. I took one for the team. I had the ups on him so I split his shit. Gooch had the ups and they had the units on us.

My response, "I can see, if he was the only one with the unit, but his boy had a unit too. He just didn't pop thank God."

Had it been the other way around and I got hit with the bottle. It would've been scienara for all three of you. They didn't know what they were doing. Dude sticking us up was way too close to us with the gun. Not really though his boy was standing back. Gooch just wasn't having it. They got Creep's gold chain though.

The last few nights I hung at my sister's house.

That's so I could be close to some of my family. I kicked it with my nephew. I raised him from birth and baby sat him and saw his development. I feed him changed his diaper along with a lot of other things. He was about seven at the time. My sister used to baby him. I tried to make him tough. We would fall out constantly about my nephew. I'd check him for wimping out.

She'd be there saying, "leave him alone Columbus!"

Matthrew Loukas

*E*mus, John guess whom I saw at the Meps station? Our buddy Matthrew Loukas was going to the service too, but he chose the Navy. This is a coincidence that Matt and I are leaving on the same day. I could've gone to the navy. I just couldn't see being on the ocean in a ship. When you are at sea and your ship get hit by a torpedo and the ship is sinking.

I can't get out and run on water, like Jesus. I could swim pretty good, but in a ocean that's filled with sharks. I know I got to die, but not that way. Give me a gun or something to go out like a G.

Matt was the only who grew up with us who chose to be a Black P Stone. A lot of Folks flipped Stones, but most of them started out as Folks in my hood. In grammar school nobody liked Matt. Matt was running home from school, getting chase by the girls and the boys.

He transferred in the fifth grade from another city. He got fucked with bad, back in the day.

Emus agrees by shaking his head and says. "Matt had no idea about Chicago."

I agree and say, "In the seventh grade Charles Jennings was his boy. Charles stayed across the street from the Manor. We played strikeout after school all the time. Charles and I were competitive ever since the second grade. Charles was strong and had muscles, but I could get him at wrestling. We used to go at it.

Charles tried to get Matt to fight me for some reason. We were up at Rock Manor playing baseball, at the strike out box. It's after school and something happened and Charles and I had words. Matt jumped in and started talking shit to me.

Charles was instigating and Matt thought, because I was playing Charles off, I was scared. I knew Charles I didn't know him. Well I did, but he just got to the school. He couldn't say what Charles could say. Matt kept popping off and ended up pissing me off.

We quit playing ball and I was sitting on my put together Huffy bike. I got off the bike and caught myself on the vice scripts clamp to the seat pole. I hurt myself trying to get at him. I played it off and I swung on him a couple of times. He jumped in the wind.

That was one thing the boy could do was run for his life. I know why he turned, Stone. I didn't, but I did. All while we were in grammar school. They used to fuck with Matt. Matt was just like me, he didn't have any back up. He didn't know how to fight either though so he either ran or got beat up. This was normal for him every since he transferred to Rock Manor. Even his own hommies would punk him out.

Billy Raymond was supposed to be cool with Loukas. He'd be just standing there in the circle of guys. Billy would looked over at him, frowned, then hit him in his jaw, bammM. He was just showing off, because he knew Matt wasn't going to do anything.

While Matt is holding his jaw he'd ask, "why you hit me Billy", just like a white boy I thought!

After you get hit you don't care why. That's not a question a black guy going to ask after being hit. You just supposed to go to work.

Billy answer was, "shut the fuck up, before I hit you again".

Matt would hold his lips like he was mad, but didn't say shit. Not only that he'd still kicked it like nothing happened. Now that is a goofy mark.

Matt and I got cool trading comic books later. We got into that one fight, because of Charles. Other than that we were cool. He had some good comic books too. The one's he didn't traded me *I stole*, because he was sleep to the comic book game. He was trying to steal mine, but I caught him, so I stole his

His teacher Mr. Alexander used to book him. Book him meant he hit you upside the head with a book. He'll have everybody laughing at Matt. The teacher would throw a book across the room and hit Matt in the head. Matt used to sit there with his lips poked out and sucking it up. He was light complexion and had a good grade of hair and big red lips.

They talked about him relentless because of his big red lips and acne. I never bothered Matt and I kind of felt sorry for him.

I did not like Mr. Alexander for doing that to him. He knows everybody ganging up on Matt. He is a teacher and he'd join in on the action and the ridicule of Matt.

Matt ended up moving from off 170th & Eberhart down the street from Rock Manor, to our hood. When he moved on the 168Th Place I took him under my wing. Once he got around us.

When I was around I wouldn't let him get smashed by the Folks. He hung out with John Strong a lot too. Most people left him alone once they knew I spoke up for him. People got along well with him in our hood. He was cool, until he went to CZS and flipped Stone. Everybody in the hood was on him. They knew he was a mark.

When Matt was with me, he was relatively safe. I would talk to the Folks and sooner or later they just said fuck it. I felt that you were a man before anything. He couldn't stand nobody at the Manor and later from around the crib. They all fucked with him unmerciful so he flipped Black P Stone.

I didn't have anything against Stones, Vicelords or nobody from the black race. I didn't have anything against white people. Now how can I fight my own brothers on sight and I don't have anything against white people. To me it was something wrong with that picture. I made a conscious decision to honor a person's struggle no matter who you were.

I felt who's to say their organization doesn't have any good. I don't know anything about the five so why are we fighting. I never attacked anyone, because of what they represented. I attack, if you didn't respect my position.

When you seen a Stone or opposition, fight on sight or vice versa. I will fight when disrespected, until then I ain't got no beef. I was introducing logic to the Folks while with Matt.

You let the person determines his fate not the organization. The same man you are hitting in the head might've been a good friend. He also could be a cousin or an uncle. You just don't know.

We're all mixed up. Instead you rather put banging first. I said to myself, "just because Matt turned a Stone. It doesn't mean he's a different friend than yesterday." I was putting love for a person over the organization. This was unprecedented in the hood. Just like when Big D was getting mixed up and flipped. I still had love for him.

The reason why he turned Black P Stone, everybody who used to fuck with him was Folks. Tell me what organization would you join? Why would you join an organization where the members fucked with you all the time? No you'd join an organization that knows that respects you and gives you much Ps.

It was ironic Matt flipped Stone first. A little later a lot of those Folks who used to fuck with him. A lot of them crossed over to the Black P Stones or Vicelords from off 171st. A lot of them went to the Rock Manor.

The Moes from CZS didn't know Matt was a mark. They don't know about his past. They give him respect for holding the five down in our hood.

They'd ask him, "You stay over there with them Folks on 169th?"

They gave him much Ps for just that. He had a good thug look to himself. This had the mark in him, masked. He wore finger waves with the gold streak and bucks and looked like Folks, but he was a Stone.

Matt would fool you, if you didn't know him. He could hold a grim look good. He would talk a good game and look like you shouldn't fuck with him. When you came at him though! He'd fold up like a suitcase.

See Matt wasn't ready for Chicago. You have to be born in this shit. He missed the beginning of it. You just can't switch that late to the Chicago Public School system from another culture.

You're just like fresh meat in the joint. The only way you can gel quickly is to start knocking motherfuckas out. You have to know how to fight in Chicago we show no mercy.

Chicago has a scandalous heartless element to it from 1st grade on up. When you're coming from another place. You don't know anything about gangs. You have to go through making your bones, mentally and physically. You have to be prepared for what's going to come at you. I'm going to punk you, if you let me stage. That's what our neighborhood and schools were all about.

You got to show me that you are not a punk. When you can't show them that! You subject yourself to ridicule, first. Money checked in, second. Third, I am just going to smack you cause I know I can. Finally, the stage Billy had him. I am going to let everybody know you are a punk.

Now you are a goofy mark. Billy shot him through all the stages in front of the goons. That's what Matt was a mark and I hated it. I tried to help him out once he moved around our house.

Matt wasn't accustomed to standing his ground. If it's going down, it's going down, was my motto. When you meet evil eye to eye and show them you not scared. Show them you are not about to bow down. Usually, that man will respect you to the fullest. Dude pushes me in this corner I have no choice. You got to come out with everything you got.

Matt didn't establish that at first. He kept on taking punches. Subjected himself to be pass around to all the goons for quick easy check ins. This mean you could be walking down the street minding your own business.

Somebody you know sees you and he's with one of his hommies. His hommie doesn't know you and tells him you're a mark. Matt could smell it though as soon as he seen trouble. He'd jump in the wind quickly. All you could see was the back of his heels changing places.

Like Slept Rock did Charles when I was getting my transcripts from the Robe. I know he got some money lets get that. Take his hat. Do whatever, because he's a mark. You are free game to anybody. You like feeder fish in a piranha's tank.

I took him under my wing to get his confidence up. I tried to show him how to box, shoot ball, play baseball and talk to girls. I'd talk to girls I just wasn't getting no poonanny. I was getting numbers with my game. I can get the girls in my company, but I just couldn't seal the deal. When he got to Rock Manor he didn't know any of that. He had no athletic ability. I never saw a black guy without any skills in anything.

We had this spot on King Drive called the Missing Link. It was next to Mike store on King Drive. It had a pinball machine in it. Lil Will who was about four years younger than we were. He used to be in Mr. Reef's game room all the time with us playing games.

He used to always wine and cry when he lost on the games. We always used to give it to him, because he was such a baby. One day he invited us over to play pinball in the lounge. We go over there and Katherine the owner said it was okay, if we played.

Katherine was his grandmother. Once we knew Katherine we would go over there without Will and play.

She was cool and when she saw us peeking in to see if we can play.

She was like, "come on in boys you can play."

At first we filled the pinball machine up with quarters. After a while Emus, Matt and I had mastered that pinball machine. We could go in there with one quarter and be in there all day. We sometimes would have to spend a few dollars. We figured out exactly what to aim for to make the machine give us the free games.

Oh, the game made this sound that was music to my ears. The closer you got to getting a free the music would escalate. Once you did it enough it pop as many times as you could get it back in the hole. Sometimes we would have thirty games up on the machine. It was exciting getting to that point. You could fall off right before you could make it pop, that was the killer.

We knew how to hold the ball on the flipper or just let it hit the flipper and bounce to the other side. We were so sweet with keeping the ball in play off the sides. We knew how to bump and control that pinball without tilting the game.

We were experts. This is something Matt was good at! He was at his happiest playing pinball. He used to trip me out, because when it drained him he'd tilt the game. Everybody wasn't up on the spot. We were shorties and weren't supposed to be in a bar. My mother investigated and saw Katherine grandson was in there playing so it was cool.

We'd be in there so long that Katherine used to put us out. We'd keep telling her this was the last game, but kept on playing. After catching us bullshitting she'd crack our face. She would come over and aggressively unplug the game. All our games would disappear.

When we did what she said she'd keep the games up. We'd go back the next day and it would be free games waiting on us. We didn't let anybody fuck with Will. We talked about his little ass cause he used to cried so much, but you couldn't fuck with Will.

Matt slowly worked his way from being a mark. He started at least to make stands verbally. He wouldn't win, but at least he grimed back. We came up born gladiators off 169th. You are not going to just talk about it. You are not going to sell one wolf ticket, not in our hood.

Try to sell a wolf ticket, if you want. I bet you get banged the first one you try to sell. You have to be about it, Harold or you will be exploited. The only way Matt got a pass is when I was around. When Matt hung with me, Emus, John Strong or Rodell. When he was around us. You could fuck with him, but we wouldn't let you beat him up. I wanted to see him come out his shell so I worked with him.

Rodell used to look out for him. Rodell used him as a gofer, but didn't hurt him. He laughed at Matt all the time about how he got played, but that was cool. That's the most harm we did to Matt, was just laugh at him. We laughed at everybody, but when Matt was around the joke was on him. Matt could go with the signifying too, he didn't just sit there, he'd cracked back.

He was funny too. He used to get Emus just by saying his name a hundred times in different ways. This got up under Emus as good as he was he would get him with this every time.

He'd have me laughing saying, "Emus Emus em emm emmm emm Emus Emus em em Emus." He said it in so many different ways non-stop, it'll have Emus hot.

Yeah he used to get me with the shit, Emus comments.

Yeah Matt could just get under your skin. Matt was an atheist so we were at complete odds in that area. He'd asked you a thousand questions on, why do I believe in God? I'd answer a few, but after he pumped a few through. I used to just tell him, "Matt you have your beliefs and I have mine."

I don't want to talk about it and go to something else. You look at Matt and he just didn't add up. He listened to ACDC, Guns and Roses. I'd go over his house and he'd have a bunch of rock tapes. I shake my head, while he was trying to get me to really listen to it.

He just didn't have any nigga game at the time. I must say he didn't care what people thought of him. He had his own way. He had his own thoughts, but I believe they were misguided.

Dead Sleep

We had to be about fourteen when this incident happened to him. It snowed good the snow was up to our knees. Matt and I went out to hustle up on some chips when we were shorties. This is before I started hustling weed.

He came and got me and said, "let's go make some money, Columbus."

He knows I'm a hustler as soon as I see snow past my ankles. I would thank Jesus it's my time to get paid.

I layered my clothing so I could stay warm and grabbed the shovel. Matt and I went door to door with two shovels and got our money. We were out there for at least four to five hours shoveling snow. We'd go in the buildings hallways warm up and then hit the next house. We bang a pathway out quick in front of your house then around to your side door, working together.

Matt and I kept walking by this car just sitting there running. I noticed it a few times while shoveling out houses. We were trying to hunt down customers and they were watching.

We didn't think anything of it. They could be just getting high. The car was sitting on 170th place where I used to stay. It was about three older guys in the car. We paid them no attention. We just kept on working.

We were about done and I went over Larry house to warm up. I could come in, but Matt couldn't so he was waiting outside. I went in for a second, warmed up and came on back out. I really was just saying hi. I didn't stay long, because I knew Matt was out in the cold.

I come back out the house then walked in the alley. I see dude that was in the car had Matt cornered, in the alley. He had a bat in his hand and I see Matt face was disturbed.

The dude with the bat saw me and told me, "don't move, come on in the alley." He was telling Matt to give up his money and told me to get over by Matt. I walked over by Matt, but out of distance.

I had my money duffed anyway. Robbery back then was almost normal. You never kept money in your pockets. You put it in your shoes or socks draws or in your sleeve. You had your money somewhere other than your pockets, while your were in the streets.

I pulled my pockets out and told him. "I just dropped my money in the crib."

He then told Matt, "give me your money, before I hit you with this fucking bat".

Matt looked scared and said, "I don't have no money."

Dude acted like he was going to hit him with the bat by rearing back.

He raised it up, cocked it and said, "give me your fucking money nigga."

Matt came out of his pockets so fast it was a shame.

He was like a slot machine. "Here you go", ching ching.

I looked like, damn Matt that easy. He grabbed Matt's money. Backed up then ran and jumped in the car and they drove off.

They were definitely dope feigns. They robbed some kids thats hustling trying to make some money. We were in the snow in the cold hustling. They could've did the same thing, but chose to just rob us.

Dope feigns will do just about anything to get that sick off. They are in ways much more dangerous than a crackhead. These grown motherfuckas robbed a kid. Their bodies must hurt craving the variable to make the pain stop. Once it's in your system, dope gotch you!

Once the robbers drove off I looked at Matt face.

He was saying, "damn over and over again."

I chuckled and said, "Matt why didn't you run, you didn't even try?

He snapped a response, "Dude had a bat."

I shook my head and said, "Matt you're one of the fastest guys in the neighborhood. You should've ran and yelled something. He didn't have a gun it was a bat.

He then asked me, "What would you have done?"

I pulled my money out my duff spot. I showed him and said, "you see what I did." He looked at the money and then looked stupid as fuck. I busted up laughing and said, "Matt you just can't give it up that easy, we worked all day." We made about seventy dollars. We split the money in half so they got about $35 from him.

We started walking toward the nine. All the way to the game room I was laughing like a mothefucka cracking jokes. He is freezing cold and has this shovel in his hand, but no money.

I started doing the reenactment and saying, "give me the money."

Matt you said, "here you go ching ching. He had the money in his hand in a fraction of a second hee hee haw haw."

He replied, "fuck you Columbus."

Matt was mixed he was half white so you could see his emotions in his face. It was cold too. I couldn't help it dude face was blood red from the cold. You could see the red color moving in his face. It was like the red color was alive. The tops to his pimple's bumps were red as crayons on the top. Our feet and hands are cold and wet. All that work and Matt came up empty.

As we were walking down the alley I said, "let's go to the gameroom." I get to the game room and I put him on blast. Emus was already in the game room and that's all I needed. "Emus Emus

Matt got robbed for all his hustle money. I give him the lowdown. Emus I thought he was working for them he gave up the money so quick."

I tell Emus how it goes down and Emus went crazy with jokes. I'd join in too, I know y'all think were mean, but this was schooling Matt. I gave him a couple of dollars to play the games.

That's one thing about Matt it seems as, if he had bad luck. He got a social security check every month from his father passing. His Mom gave him the whole check. He never really sweated money.

He knew at the beginning of the month, he had money coming in to him. He kept nice clothes, but we still hustled quarters to play the games. Emus, Matt and I used to ask people for quarters to play the video games at Mr. Reefs. The bus stops was a good place to score quarters, right across the street from the game room.

This is what we do, if we didn't have money for the games. We would try to pick out who we thought would give up the quarters by the bus stop. We'd ask people getting on and off the bus for quarters. I got this one or naw this one's mine.

Matt asked this dude who was about thirty years old for a quarter. Dude looked at Matt grimed him. Next, he jumped in Matt space and face looking down on him.

He then said. "Hell naw I got no motherfuckin quarter. Get the fuck out of my face asking me for a motherfucking quarter. I should whoop your ass for asking me some shit like that."

He shouted loud than a motherfucka. Everybody in the vicinity stopped and looked. Emus and I looked astonished and surprise. This has never happened before. It was only a quarter. The answer was usually yes or no.

Matt looked like he jumped out of his skin and told dude, "I'm am sorry sir, I'm sorry sir."

Matt face looked crazy, because this was unexpected. Emus and I looked and cracked up. He was just unlucky that was the first and last time that every happened. We learned from his mistake. We stop asking people for money. We shelved the begging, because of what happen to Matt.

Matt could've stayed a neutron and he would've been cool. The Folks on the Met was cool with him being a neutron. It was just the people from grammar school he had problems. The niggas on 169th went to Meneen. They didn't know he was that much of a mark. He was with us so they assumed he was cool.

He didn't have any problems around the hood, until he flipped Stone. He knew what drama he was going to catch. He just flipped Stone to say fuck everybody who fucked with him.

He had protection, because him and Disco were boys. They both went to CZS so that's how they plug. Matt would come back with the stories of Disco exploits. That's how we knew what Disco was on!

Disco had him as a gofer though. This was Matt way of getting back at the Folks who fucked with him. I guess he said fuck it, Folks fucks with me anyway. What does it matter if I am a Stone? At least he got some help now, if I wanted it. He still couldn't bring the Stones in the hood. Matt still had to live over here.

Boya used to get into with Matt verbally all the time. Boya went to Dunbar school with Emus. One day Matt and I were standing up on 169th St. Matt got his hat bang to the left on 169th St. I got mine banged to the right. He could do that with me cause I could keep Folks off of him.

You couldn't stand on the nine at that time with a red hat on your head. It damn sure can't be banged to the left. He was trying to get his heart up. Who am I to tell him he can't do it? Let's see, if he can. He wanted to let all the Folks know he was a Stone now.

Boya gets off the King Drive bus coming from school. He sees Matt on the corner and his expression changed to seeing red. Once seeing him he makes a b line straight to his face. He was almost got nose to forehead, because Matt's looking down on him.

Boya snaps at him, "didn't I tell you don't be up here with your hat to the left?"

Matt was like, "fuck you I can stand where I want to stand."

I was like, "oh shit Matt has made a stand. He said it powerfully with the face to back it up. Just then one of Boya GD Folks from school jumped off the bus. It looked like from a distance Boya and I was about to whoop Matt ass.

He had his hat banged to the left. Boya and I hats are banged to the right looking at Matt. I was looking at him to see what Matt was going to do and smiling. I had showed him some moves and thought he would use them.

GD Folks, who jumped off the bus, looks, walks straight over, no words and gives Matt a three pieces. Boya tries to swing too, but Matt was in the wind already. I told Folks who jumped off the bus to stand down he's straight. By pulling him back.

Folks give Boya love after Boya comes back from chasing him a few feet.

Boya was like, "good looking out Folks you stole on that pussy."

Folks give him the shake. I give him the shake. He thought he was aid and assisting, so I give him love. I didn't feel good about it.

He told Boya, "I'll see you at school tomorrow."

Folks jumped on the next bus, which was one stop behind the last one. Folks looked seen what was happening with Boya. I watched him jumped off the bus, steal on Matt and jumped on the next bus coming.

This happened in less than forty seconds. That's how quick it happens. Andrea, you can't really help anybody who don't help themselves. Matt should've made a stand. I wouldn't have let him got rolled. I know Boya I would've just made them go head up.

After dude stole on Matt he just got back on the bus and left. You know how the King Drive bus runs during rush hour after school. They ride one behind the other full to the hilt.

I hated to be with Matt when he ran. It made me look like a hoe. No matter what everybody in the neighborhood sees us together all the time. He's my guy and he jumped in the wind. Now it looks like we set him up.

Boya got his back though, always fucking with niggas. He was trying to fuck with Chell, dude who used to hang with Kermit. Boya was a little evil nigga. When he laughed it sounded evil. He was short, but he was like Slept Rock, kept shit up. Chell was new to 169th street. Kermit brought him around. He was Folks who moved on 167th & Michigan.

I knew he was no hoe. Somebody was fucking with him on 169th & Calumet one day. He didn't say much he just went and got his back up. He came back with his older brother and they began whooping and stomping the shit out of dude. Chell beat the nigga with his belt like he was a kid.

Anyway Boya was trying to punk him and Chell started crying. I'm like damn this nigga is crying. I can't believe Folks is crying. All of a sudden he reached in inside his lapel of his coat and pulled his flask out.

He played like he was going to open it and drink it. In one motion swings and bangs Boya in the head, bamm. Boya was staggered. While he was still dizzy Chell lounged two steps at him and hit him again, bam, right across the head. This surprised the fuck out of us.

Chell start hollering, "I told you to leave me alone motherfucka."

He went from crying and into action. It was a very good deception. That was a good one. Boya never saw the swing coming. We stopped him after those couple upside the head and squashed it.

Boya took it sweet, "oh he got me. I thought he was a hoe."

I said to myself, "that was for what y'all did to Matt."

I could've stopped him after the first time he hit him. He was dizzy and didn't recover and he got him again.

Lil Todd didn't want Loukas standing on 169th street. I was with Matt and Todd caught him. Matt was on 169th street with the black hat with the rose on it, turned to the left.

I couldn't convince him to keep it straight at this point. After I see all he had were wolf tickets to sell. I used to be like, "Matt just keep your hat straight, niggas won't fuck with you."

Don't be representing, keep it low-key. He wasn't facing reality. He liked pissing the Folks off. I could see, if he could back it up, but when confronted he just ran. I said, "okay Matt." We were leaving the Missing Link lounge walking toward Calumet.

Todd already told me once. After he found out Matt flipped, Stone.

He said, "don't have the nigga on my porch no more. Don't bring him to the Met or he was fucking him up."

I told Matt I said, "Todd don't want you around anymore while we were in the Link playing pinball.

He responded, "fuck Todd, if it's on it's on! Fuck your cousin!"

He always talked tough when people weren't around. Todd happened to be standing on John's porch when we bent the corner. He was standing there talking to John.

John laughs and says, "Todd looked, frowned then walked up and got in Matt face. Up until then Matt was cool with Todd. Todd got Matt high all the time, while he was with me.

I guess he didn't think he was going to do anything. Todd grimed and reared back and slapped the shit out of him, WhaalloopP. Matt clutches his face and looks stunned after he slapped him. Todd told him to take his hat off and was trying to get at him.

Matt takes his hat off and says. "Get your cousin Colo Dog."

Todd was trying to get at him, but Matt was doing evasive moves.

I broke it up, because he wasn't fighting back as usual. I tell Todd to cool out.

Todd said, "you better get this nigga from over here cuz."

We walked away and Matt is holding his face. I am trying to keep myself from laughing.

I ask him, "Matt, if you don't fight back it's going to be like this every day. You got to fight one nigga real good so the word spread. He ain't no hoe no more. You already getting hit you might as well swing back."

He was hoping like I did with the Hawk. Hoping he would just stop on his own. I ask him, "why get into all this shit when you don't have too Matt?" Every time Spider G saw him. He would just jump in the wind. He knew it was trouble.

Matt and I were standing on the nine again. Spider would come down the street stacking them. I'd stack back at him. Spider was the coldest nigga in the hood with the stacking. I was right behind him.

The first time he found out Matt was a Stone he snapped. Spider hit him in the head with the top off of those metal garbage cans. Spider didn't want him on the nine either.

No matter what we were doing as soon as he saw Spider. He'd jumped in the wind. We could have twenty dollars worth of high and he'd leave and wouldn't come back. I had to keep an eye on Matt, because he wasn't street cut.

It's about that time to leave Sept 5th. Eddie gave me my last few bucks he owes me. I can make it till I leave. I wasn't worried about eating. My clearance came back and it was clear. Thank Yahweh this had me uneasy. My piss test came back clear. How, I don't know I was full of weed.

That's the only thing I was worried about. Now I am on my way. All I got to do is stay out of trouble. I had them pick me up at my sister's house. I gave Grimes the keys to the car a couple of day earlier. 'Kid make it', going to the army.

My Last day as a Civilian

The last night in Chicago I hung out all night. The recruiter was at my sister's house at eight am that morning. I had a few bags of clothes and that radio I took from Eric and I was off.

Matt said something about going, but I didn't know we were leaving at the same time. I caught him at the Meps station eating breakfast in the chow hall. I had a couple of joint so we slid off to smoke. I was going to smoke, until I couldn't smoke no more, literally.

We were downtown in the cut and smoked the last couple joints I had. I had planned it perfectly. I was just about out of money and weed. We cool out in the room they had us lounging in at the hotel. Matt and I talked about the nine and leaving it. Of course he was glad.

The only thing is Matt didn't know how to swim.

I'd ask him, "Matt how you going out in the middle of the ocean and you can't even swim."

Matt said, "they would teach him once he's in the navy."

I asked him the night right before we get ready to swear in and become soldiers. Matt is going to the navy and I'm going to the army. We are about to leave 169th into something more discipline than Matt or I ever thought. I don't think either one of us was prepared for what we were about to go through mentally.

I was eighteen years old and on the street, with power. You bet not say anything out of pocket to me. I controlled what happened to guys in a certain areas. The young Folks already considered me a legend.

That's on and off the court, with my hands I was one of the best, if not the best. I had respect from the older Folks. I had respect form the younger Folks so I was in on everything. I also was a voice of persuasion, if Folks were fucking up.

Going to the army I would have nothing as far as respect while in training. Now we were going to the ultimate form of discipline. Matt and I were tripping out that night about everything we've been through.

We can't believe we are on our way to the service. We said our goodbyes and he went off to his room to get ready. Emus and John was probably starting class right here in Austin. Jeff and I made it off the block too.

I shipped out September 9Th 1986, my mother's birthday. Colo Dog is in the army now headed to Fort Dix New Jersey. I made this move happen to better myself mentally, physically and financially.

This is the start of a new adventure for, "kid make it." I made it off 169th street in one piece. I left the police and the niggas looking for me, behind me. I left my life of crime behind me. I left my family behind me. I left snake alley behind me. I left that car that started it all behind me.

I didn't have a girl or kid to leave behind so I was free to go. I left Reico behind me or maybe we chased him off the strip. I didn't see him anymore after the incident. My first eighteen years on earth are behind me and this is a new start. Can you really leave your past behind you? I was going to try and see.

The only thing I'm taking with me is that demon that's developed in me. I couldn't leave that behind. How do you turn off all these years of evil doings and be a soldier? You just don't turn off eighteen years of habit. This is an adjustment I have to make, to better my position.

It was time to swear in and I was thinking about what Slick Freddie did. He left right before the swear in, and kept a civilian life. I can change my mind, if I wanted to right now. I was standing with about twelve other guys and we all swore in!

It wasn't no turning back for me. All I had was snake alley waiting on me. Hind site twenty twenty I should've stayed a nerd. I would be going to Illinois or Michigan State with a full ride. I was blessed with the will to seek knowledge and got side tracked. I did my will and that was to be like everybody else, due to circumstance. This changed my pathway to success, drastically.

I was gone though and I was glad to start a new adventure. My next three years I would be known as Private George. That's a long time as a Private in the army. Check it out, "I was known as Private I don't give a fuck, George, Chicago, Joe and "Double 0 Hood." I never got any rank over a Private. Y'all got to wait, until tomorrow though! I'm going to bed all this talking, drinking and eating and whooping Harold ass earlier got me tired.

Big dreams, out the gate!!!

I had to protect my mother and family and plugged with these guys!

This is the closest I got to going pro!

Gangsters graduate too, from high school to Berlin and back!

Check out, 'Private I don't give a f*** but I did......!' ColoDog went on a European experience by way of the United States Army! It was a struggle to commit to military life, but all he had was snake alley back in Chicago! Columbus battles his emotions and inner demons to get back on the righteous path! He is in a world wind of unknown and adventure!

ABOUT THE AUTHOR

*B*ryant Keith was born in Chicago, Illinois. He attended DeVry University and earned a bachelor's of science degree in business operation. He is an army veteran who did his tour in Nuremburg, Germany, during the Cold War.